CATHERINE DE' MEDICI

By Honore de Balzac

Translated by Katherine Prescott Wormeley

DEDICATION

To Monsieur le Marquis de Pastoret, Member of the Academie des Beaux-Arts.

When we think of the enormous number of volumes that have been published on the question as to where Hannibal crossed the Alps, without our being able to decide to-day whether it was (according to Whittaker and Rivaz) by Lyon, Geneva, the Great Saint-Bernard, and the valley of Aosta; or (according to Letronne, Follard, Saint-Simon and Fortia d'Urbano) by the Isere, Grenoble, Saint-Bonnet, Monte Genevra, Fenestrella, and the Susa passage; or (according to Larauza) by the Mont Cenis and the Susa; or (according to Strabo, Polybius and Lucanus) by the Rhone, Vienne, Yenne, and the Dent du Chat; or (according to some intelligent minds) by Genoa, La Bochetta, and La Scrivia,—an opinion which I share and which Napoleon adopted,—not to speak of the verjuice with which the Alpine rocks have been bespattered by other learned men,—is it surprising, Monsieur le marquis, to see modern history so bemuddled that many important points are still obscure, and the most odious calumnies still rest on names that ought to be respected?

And let me remark, in passing, that Hannibal's crossing has been made almost problematical by these very elucidations. For instance, Pere Menestrier thinks that the Scoras mentioned by Polybius is the Saona; Letronne, Larauza and Schweighauser think it is the Isere; Cochard, a learned Lyonnais, calls it the Drome, and for all who have eyes to see there are between Scoras and Scrivia great geographical and linguistical resemblances,—to say nothing of the probability, amounting almost to certainty, that the Carthaginian fleet was moored in the Gulf of Spezzia or the

1

roadstead of Genoa. I could understand these patient researches if there were any doubt as to the battle of Canna; but inasmuch as the results of that great battle are known, why blacken paper with all these suppositions (which are, as it were, the arabesques of hypothesis) while the history most important to the present day, that of the Reformation, is full of such obscurities that we are ignorant of the real name of the man who navigated a vessel by steam to Barcelona at the period when Luther and Calvin were inaugurating the insurrection of thought.[*]

You and I hold, I think, the same opinion, after having made, each in his own way, close researches as to the grand and splendid figure of Catherine de' Medici. Consequently, I have thought that my historical studies upon that queen might properly be dedicated to an author who has written so much on the history of the Reformation; while at the same time I offer to the character and fidelity of a monarchical writer a public homage which may, perhaps, be valuable on account of its rarity.

[*] The name of the man who tried this experiment at Barcelona should be given as Salomon de Caux, not Caus. That great man has always been unfortunate; even after his death his name is mangled. Salomon, whose portrait taken at the age of forty-six was discovered by the author of the "Comedy of Human Life" at Heidelberg, was born at Caux in Normandy. He was the author of a book entitled "The Causes of Moving Forces," in which he gave the theory of the expansion and condensation of steam. He died in 1635.

Contents
CATHERINE DE' MEDICI

INTRODUCTION

CATHERINE DE' MEDICI

INTRODUCTION

There is a general cry of paradox when scholars, struck by some historical error, attempt to correct it; but, for whoever studies modern history to its depths, it is plain that historians are privileged liars, who lend their pen to popular beliefs precisely as the newspapers of the day, or most of them, express the opinions of their readers.

Historical independence has shown itself much less among lay writers than among those of the Church. It is from the Benedictines, one of the glories of France, that the purest light has come to us in the matter of history,—so long, of course, as the interests of the order were not involved. About the middle of the eighteenth century great and learned controversialists, struck by the necessity of correcting popular errors endorsed by historians, made and published to the world very remarkable works. Thus Monsieur de Launoy, nicknamed the "Expeller of Saints," made cruel war upon the saints surreptitiously smuggled into the Church. Thus the emulators of the Benedictines, the members (too little recognized) of the Academie des Inscriptions et Belles-lettres, began on many obscure historical points a series of monographs, which are admirable for patience, erudition, and logical consistency. Thus Voltaire, for a mistaken purpose and with ill-judged passion, frequently cast the light of his mind on historical prejudices. Diderot undertook in this direction a book (much too long) on the era of imperial Rome. If it had not been for the French Revolution, *criticism* applied to history might then have prepared the elements of a good and true history of France, the proofs for which had long been gathered by the Benedictines. Louis XVI., a just mind, himself translated the English work in which Walpole endeavored to explain Richard III.,—a work much talked of in the last century.

Why do personages so celebrated as kings and queens, so important as the generals of armies, become objects of horror or derision? Half the world hesitates between the famous song on Marlborough and the history of England, and it also hesitates between history and popular tradition as to Charles IX. At all epochs when great struggles take place between the masses and authority, the populace creates for itself an *ogre-esque* personage—if it is allowable to coin a word to convey a just idea. Thus, to take an example in our own time, if it had not been for the "Memorial of Saint Helena," and the controversies between the Royalists

4

and the Bonapartists, there was every probability that the character of Napoleon would have been misunderstood. A few more Abbe de Pradits, a few more newspaper articles, and from being an emperor, Napoleon would have turned into an ogre.

How does error propagate itself? The mystery is accomplished under our very eyes without our perceiving it. No one suspects how much solidity the art of printing has given both to the envy which pursues greatness, and to the popular ridicule which fastens a contrary sense on a grand historical act. Thus, the name of the Prince de Polignac is given throughout the length and breadth of France to all bad horses that require whipping; and who knows how that will affect the opinion of the future as to the *coup d'Etat* of the Prince de Polignac himself? In consequence of a whim of Shakespeare—or perhaps it may have been a revenge, like that of Beaumarchais on Bergasse (Bergearss)—Falstaff is, in England, a type of the ridiculous; his very name provokes laughter; he is the king of clowns. Now, instead of being enormously pot-bellied, absurdly amorous, vain, drunken, old, and corrupted, Falstaff was one of the most distinguished men of his time, a Knight of the Garter, holding a high command in the army. At the accession of Henry V. Sir John Falstaff was only thirty-four years old. This general, who distinguished himself at the battle of Agincourt, and there took prisoner the Duc d'Alencon, captured, in 1420, the town of Montereau, which was vigorously defended. Moreover, under Henry VI. he defeated ten thousand French troops with fifteen hundred weary and famished men.

So much for war. Now let us pass to literature, and see our own Rabelais, a sober man who drank nothing but water, but is held to be, nevertheless, an extravagant lover of good cheer and a resolute drinker. A thousand ridiculous stories are told about the author of one of the finest books in French literature,—"Pantagruel." Aretino, the friend of Titian, and the Voltaire of his century, has, in our day, a reputation the exact opposite of his works and of his character; a reputation which he owes to a grossness of wit in keeping with the writings of his age, when broad farce was held in honor, and queens and cardinals wrote tales which would be called, in these days, licentious. One might go on multiplying such instances indefinitely.

In France, and that, too, during the most serious epoch of modern history, no woman, unless it be Brunehaut or Fredegonde, has suffered from popular error so much as Catherine de' Medici; whereas Marie de' Medici, all of whose actions were prejudicial to France, has escaped the shame which ought to cover her name. Marie de' Medici wasted the wealth amassed by Henri IV.; she never purged herself of the charge of having known of the king's assassination; her *intimate* was d'Epernon, who did not ward off Ravaillac's blow, and who was proved to have known the murderer personally for a long time. Marie's conduct was such that she forced her son to banish her from France, where she was encouraging her other son, Gaston, to rebel; and the victory Richelieu at last won over her (on the Day of the Dupes) was due solely to the discovery the cardinal made, and imparted to Louis XIII., of secret documents relating to the death of Henri IV.

Catherine de' Medici, on the contrary, saved the crown of France; she maintained the royal authority in the midst of circumstances under which more than one great prince would have succumbed. Having to make head against factions and ambitions like those of the Guises and the house of Bourbon, against men such as the two Cardinals of Lorraine, the two Balafres, and the two Condes, against the queen Jeanne d'Albret, Henri IV., the Connetable de Montmorency, Calvin, the three Colignys, Theodore de Beze, she needed to possess and to display the rare qualities and precious gifts of a statesman under the mocking fire of the Calvinist press.

Those facts are incontestable. Therefore, to whosoever burrows into the history of the sixteenth century in France, the figure of Catherine de' Medici will seem like that of a great king. When calumny is once dissipated by facts, recovered with difficulty from among the contradictions of pamphlets and false anecdotes, all explains itself to the fame of this extraordinary woman, who had none of the weaknesses of her sex, who lived chaste amid the license of the most dissolute court in Europe, and who, in spite of her lack of money, erected noble public buildings, as if to repair the loss caused by the iconoclasms of the Calvinists, who did as much harm to art as to the body politic. Hemmed in between the Guises who claimed to be the heirs of Charlemagne and the factious younger branch who sought to screen the treachery of the Connetable de Bourbon behind the throne, Catherine, forced to combat heresy which was seeking to annihilate the monarchy, without friends, aware of treachery among the leaders of the Catholic party, foreseeing a republic in the Calvinist party, Catherine employed the most dangerous but the surest weapon of public policy,—craft. She resolved to trick and so defeat, successively, the Guises who were seeking the ruin of the house of Valois, the Bourbons who sought the crown, and the Reformers (the Radicals of those days) who dreamed of an impossible republic— like those of our time; who have, however, nothing to reform. Consequently, so long as she lived, the Valois kept the throne of France. The great historian of that time, de Thou, knew well the value of this woman when, on hearing of her death, he exclaimed: "It is not a woman, it is monarchy itself that has died!"

Catherine had, in the highest degree, the sense of royalty, and she defended it with admirable courage and persistency. The reproaches which Calvinist writers have cast upon her are to her glory; she incurred them by reason only of her triumphs. Could she, placed as she was, triumph otherwise than by craft? The whole question lies there.

As for violence, that means is one of the most disputed questions of public policy; in our time it has been answered on the Place Louis XV., where they have now set up an Egyptian stone, as if to obliterate regicide and offer a symbol of the system of materialistic policy which governs us; it was answered at the Carmes and at the Abbaye; answered on the steps of Saint-Roch; answered once more by the people against the king before the Louvre in 1830, as it has since been answered by Lafayette's best of all possible republics against the republican insurrection at Saint-Merri and the rue Transnonnain. All power, legitimate or illegitimate, must defend itself when attacked; but the strange thing is that where the people are held heroic in their victory over the nobility, power is called murderous in its duel with the people. If it succumbs after its appeal to force, power is then called imbecile. The present government is attempting to save itself by two laws from the same evil Charles X. tried to escape by two ordinances; is it not a bitter derision? Is craft permissible in the hands of power against craft? may it kill those who seek to kill it? The massacres of the Revolution have replied to the massacres of Saint-Bartholomew. The people, become king, have done against the king and the nobility what the king and the nobility did against the insurgents of the sixteenth century. Therefore the popular historians, who know very well that in a like case the people will do the same thing over again, have no excuse for blaming Catherine de' Medici and Charles IX.

"All power," said Casimir Perier, on learning what power ought to be, "is a permanent conspiracy." We admire the anti-social maxims put forth by daring writers; why, then, this disapproval which, in France, attaches to all social truths when boldly proclaimed? This question will explain, in itself alone, historical errors. Apply the answer to the destructive doctrines which flatter popular passions, and to the conservative doctrines which repress the mad efforts of the people, and you will find the reason of the unpopularity and also the popularity of certain personages. Laubardemont and Laffemas were, like some men of to-day, devoted to the defence of power in which they believed. Soldiers or judges, they all obeyed royalty. In these days d'Orthez would be dismissed for having misunderstood the orders of the ministry, but Charles X. left him governor of a province. The power of the many is accountable to no one; the power of one is compelled to render account to its subjects, to the great as well as to the small.

Catherine, like Philip the Second and the Duke of Alba, like the Guises and Cardinal Granvelle, saw plainly the future that the Reformation was bringing upon Europe. She and they saw monarchies, religion, authority shaken. Catherine wrote, from the cabinet of the kings of France, a sentence of death to that spirit of inquiry which then began to threaten modern society; a sentence which Louis XIV. ended by executing. The revocation of the Edict of Nantes was an unfortunate measure only so far as it caused the irritation of all Europe against Louis XIV. At another period England, Holland, and the Holy Roman Empire would not have welcomed banished Frenchmen and encouraged revolt in France.

Why refuse, in these days, to the majestic adversary of the most barren of heresies the grandeur she derived from the struggle itself? Calvinists have written much against the "craftiness" of Charles IX.; but travel through France, see the ruins of noble churches, estimate the fearful wounds given by the religionists to the social body, learn what vengeance they inflicted, and you will ask yourself, as you deplore the evils of individualism (the disease of our present France, the germ of which was in the questions of liberty of conscience then agitated),—you will ask yourself, I say, on which side were the executioners. There are, unfortunately, as Catherine herself says in the third division of this Study of her career, "in all ages hypocritical writers always ready to weep over the fate of two hundred scoundrels killed necessarily." Caesar, who tried to move the senate to pity the attempt of Catiline, might perhaps have got the better of Cicero could he have had an Opposition and its newspapers at his command.

Another consideration explains the historical and popular disfavor in which Catherine is held. The Opposition in France has always been Protestant, because it has had no policy but that of *negation*; it inherits the theories of Lutherans, Calvinists, and Protestants on the terrible words "liberty," "tolerance," "progress," and "philosophy." Two centuries have been employed by the opponents of power in establishing the doubtful doctrine of the *libre arbitre*,—liberty of will. Two other centuries were employed in developing the first corollary of liberty of will, namely, liberty of conscience. Our century is endeavoring to establish the second, namely, political liberty.

Placed between the ground already lost and the ground still to be defended, Catherine and the Church proclaimed the salutary principle of modern societies, *una fides, unus dominus*, using their power of life and death upon the innovators. Though Catherine was vanquished, succeeding centuries have proved her justification. The product of liberty of will, religious liberty, and political liberty (not, observe this, to be

8

confounded with civil liberty) is the France of to-day. What is the France of 1840? A country occupied exclusively with material interests,—without patriotism, without conscience; where power has no vigor; where election, the fruit of liberty of will and political liberty, lifts to the surface none but commonplace men; where brute force has now become a necessity against popular violence; where discussion, spreading into everything, stifles the action of legislative bodies; where money rules all questions; where individualism—the dreadful product of the division of property *ad infinitum*—will suppress the family and devour all, even the nation, which egoism will some day deliver over to invasion. Men will say, "Why not the Czar?" just as they said, "Why not the Duc d'Orleans?" We don't cling to many things even now; but fifty years hence we shall cling to nothing.

Thus, according to Catherine de' Medici and according to all those who believe in a well-ordered society, in *social man*, the subject cannot have liberty of will, ought not to *teach* the dogma of liberty of conscience, or demand political liberty. But, as no society can exist without guarantees granted to the subject against the sovereign, there results for the subject *liberties* subject to restriction. Liberty, no; liberties, yes,—precise and well-defined liberties. That is in harmony with the nature of things.

It is, assuredly, beyond the reach of human power to prevent the liberty of thought; and no sovereign can interfere with money. The great statesmen who were vanquished in the long struggle (it lasted five centuries) recognized the right of subjects to great liberties; but they did not admit their right to publish anti-social thoughts, nor did they admit the indefinite liberty of the subject. To them the words "subject" and "liberty" were terms that contradicted each other; just as the theory of citizens being all equal constitutes an absurdity which nature contradicts at every moment. To recognize the necessity of a religion, the necessity of authority, and then to leave to subjects the right to deny religion, attack its worship, oppose the exercise of power by public expression communicable and communicated by thought, was an impossibility which the Catholics of the sixteenth century would not hear of.

Alas! the victory of Calvinism will cost France more in the future than it has yet cost her; for religious sects and humanitarian, equality-levelling politics are, to-day, the tail of Calvinism; and, judging by the mistakes of the present power, its contempt for intellect, its love for material interests, in which it seeks the basis of its support (though material interests are the most treacherous of all supports), we may predict that unless some providence intervenes, the genius of destruction will again carry the day over the genius of preservation. The assailants, who have nothing to lose and all to gain, understand each other thoroughly;

whereas their rich adversaries will not make any sacrifice either of money or self-love to draw to themselves supporters.

The art of printing came to the aid of the opposition begun by the Vaudois and the Albigenses. As soon as human thought, instead of condensing itself, as it was formerly forced to do to remain in communicable form, took on a multitude of garments and became, as it were, the people itself, instead of remaining a sort of axiomatic divinity, there were two multitudes to combat,—the multitude of ideas, and the multitude of men. The royal power succumbed in that warfare, and we are now assisting, in France, at its last combination with elements which render its existence difficult, not to say impossible. Power is action, and the elective principle is discussion. There is no policy, no statesmanship possible where discussion is permanent.

Therefore we ought to recognize the grandeur of the woman who had the eyes to see this future and fought it bravely. That the house of Bourbon was able to succeed to the house of Valois, that it found a crown preserved to it, was due solely to Catherine de' Medici. Suppose the second Balafre had lived? No matter how strong the Bearnais was, it is doubtful whether he could have seized the crown, seeing how dearly the Duc de Mayenne and the remains of the Guise party sold it to him. The means employed by Catherine, who certainly had to reproach herself with the deaths of Francois II. and Charles IX., whose lives might have been saved in time, were never, it is observable, made the subject of accusations by either the Calvinists or modern historians. Though there was no poisoning, as some grave writers have said, there was other conduct almost as criminal; there is no doubt she hindered Pare from saving one, and allowed the other to accomplish his own doom by moral assassination. But the sudden death of Francois II., and that of Charles IX., were no injury to the Calvinists, and therefore the causes of these two events remained in their secret sphere, and were never suspected either by the writers of the people of that day; they were not divined except by de Thou, l'Hopital, and minds of that calibre, or by the leaders of the two parties who were coveting or defending the throne, and believed such means necessary to their end.

Popular songs attacked, strangely enough, Catherine's morals. Every one knows the anecdote of the soldier who was roasting a goose in the courtyard of the chateau de Tours during the conference between Catherine and Henri IV., singing, as he did so, a song in which the queen was grossly insulted. Henri IV. drew his sword to go out and kill the man; but Catherine stopped him and contented herself with calling from the window to her insulter:—

"Eh! but it was Catherine who gave you the goose."

Though the executions at Amboise were attributed to Catherine, and though the Calvinists made her responsible for all the inevitable evils of that struggle, it was with her as it was, later, with Robespierre, who is still waiting to be justly judged. Catherine was, moreover, rightly punished for her preference for the Duc d'Anjou, to whose interests the two elder brothers were sacrificed. Henri III., like all spoilt children, ended in becoming absolutely indifferent to his mother, and he plunged voluntarily into the life of debauchery which made of him what his mother had made of Charles IX., a husband without sons, a king without heirs. Unhappily the Duc d'Alencon, Catherine's last male child, had already died, a natural death.

The last words of the great queen were like a summing up of her lifelong policy, which was, moreover, so plain in its common-sense that all cabinets are seen under similar circumstances to put it in practice.

"Enough cut off, my son," she said when Henri III. came to her death-bed to tell her that the great enemy of the crown was dead, "*now piece together.*"

By which she meant that the throne should at once reconcile itself with the house of Lorraine and make use of it, as the only means of preventing evil results from the hatred of the Guises,—by holding out to them the hope of surrounding the king. But the persistent craft and dissimulation of the woman and the Italian, which she had never failed to employ, was incompatible with the debauched life of her son. Catherine de' Medici once dead, the policy of the Valois died also.

Before undertaking to write the history of the manners and morals of this period in action, the author of this Study has patiently and minutely examined the principal reigns in the history of France, the quarrel of the Burgundians and the Armagnacs, that of the Guises and the Valois, each of which covers a century. His first intention was to write a picturesque history of France. Three women—Isabella of Bavaria, Catharine and Marie de' Medici—hold an enormous place in it, their sway reaching from the fourteenth to the seventeenth century, ending in Louis XIV. Of these three queens, Catherine is the finer and more interesting. Hers was virile power, dishonored neither by the terrible amours of Isabella nor by those, even more terrible, though less known, of Marie de' Medici. Isabella summoned the English into France against her son, and loved her brother-in-law, the Duc d'Orleans. The record of Marie de' Medici is heavier still. Neither had political genius.

It was in the course of these studies that the writer acquired the conviction of Catherine's greatness; as he became initiated into the constantly renewed difficulties of her position, he saw with what injustice historians—all influenced by Protestants—had treated this queen. Out of this conviction grew the three sketches which here follow; in which some erroneous opinions formed upon Catherine, also upon the persons who surrounded her, and on the events of her time, are refuted. If this book is placed among the Philosophical Studies, it is because it shows the Spirit of a Time, and because we may clearly see in it the influence of thought.

But before entering the political arena, where Catherine will be seen facing the two great difficulties of her career, it is necessary to give a succinct account of her preceding life, from the point of view of impartial criticism, in order to take in as much as possible of this vast and regal existence up to the moment when the first part of the present Study begins.

Never was there any period, in any land, in any sovereign family, a greater contempt for legitimacy than in the famous house of the Medici. On the subject of power they held the same doctrine now professed by Russia, namely: to whichever head the crown goes, he is the true, the legitimate sovereign. Mirabeau had reason to say: "There has been but one mesalliance in my family,—that of the Medici"; for in spite of the paid efforts of genealogists, it is certain that the Medici, before Everardo de' Medici, *gonfaloniero* of Florence in 1314, were simple Florentine merchants who became very rich. The first personage in this family who occupies an important place in the history of the famous Tuscan republic is Silvestro de' Medici, *gonfaloniero* in 1378. This Silvestro had two sons, Cosmo and Lorenzo de' Medici.

From Cosmo are descended Lorenzo the Magnificent, the Duc de Nemours, the Duc d'Urbino, father of Catherine, Pope Leo X., Pope Clement VII., and Alessandro, not Duke of Florence, as historians call him, but Duke *della citta di Penna*, a title given by Pope Clement VII., as a half-way station to that of Grand-duke of Tuscany.

From Lorenzo are descended the Florentine Brutus Lorenzino, who killed Alessandro, Cosmo, the first grand-duke, and all the sovereigns of Tuscany till 1737, at which period the house became extinct.

But neither of the two branches—the branch Cosmo and the branch Lorenzo—reigned through their direct and legitimate lines until the close of the sixteenth century, when the grand-dukes of Tuscany began to succeed each other peacefully. Alessandro de' Medici, he to whom the title of Duke *della citta di Penna* was given, was the son of the Duke d'Urbino, Catherine's father, by a Moorish slave. For this reason Lorenzino claimed a double right to kill Alessandro,—as a usurper in his house, as well as an oppressor of the city. Some historians believe that Alessandro was the son of Clement VII. The fact that led to the recognition of this bastard as chief of the republic and head of the house of the Medici was his marriage with Margaret of Austria, natural daughter of Charles V.

Francesco de' Medici, husband of Bianca Capello, accepted as his son a child of poor parents bought by the celebrated Venetian; and, strange to say, Ferdinando, on succeeding Francesco, maintained the substituted child in all his rights. That child, called Antonio de' Medici, was considered during four reigns as belonging to the family; he won the affection of everybody, rendered important services to the family, and died universally regretted.

Nearly all the first Medici had natural children, whose careers were invariably brilliant. For instance, the Cardinal Giulio de' Medici, afterwards Pope under the name of Clement VII., was the illegitimate son of Giuliano I. Cardinal Ippolito de' Medici was also a bastard, and came very near being Pope and the head of the family.

Lorenzo II., the father of Catherine, married in 1518, for his second wife, Madeleine de la Tour de Boulogne, in Auvergne, and died April 25, 1519, a few days after his wife, who died in giving birth to Catherine. Catherine was therefore orphaned of father and mother as soon as she drew breath. Hence the strange adventures of her childhood, mixed up as they were with the bloody efforts of the Florentines, then seeking to recover their liberty from the Medici. The latter, desirous of continuing to reign in Florence, behaved with such circumspection that Lorenzo, Catherine's father, had taken the name of Duke d'Urbino.

At Lorenzo's death, the head of the house of the Medici was Pope Leo X., who sent the illegitimate son of Giuliano, Giulio de' Medici, then cardinal, to govern Florence. Leo X. was great-uncle to Catherine, and this Cardinal Giulio, afterward Clement VII., was her uncle by the left hand.

It was during the siege of Florence, undertaken by the Medici to force their return there, that the Republican party, not content with having shut Catherine, then nine years old, into a convent, after robbing her of all her property, actually proposed, on the suggestion of one named Batista Cei, to expose her between two battlements on the walls to the artillery of the Medici. Bernardo Castiglione went further in a council held to determine how matters should be ended: he was of opinion that, so far from returning her to the Pope as the latter requested, she ought to be given to the soldiers for dishonor. This will show how all popular revolutions resemble each other. Catherine's subsequent policy, which upheld so firmly the royal power, may well have been instigated in part by such scenes, of which an Italian girl of nine years of age was assuredly not ignorant.

The rise of Alessandro de' Medici, to which the bastard Pope Clement

VII. powerfully contributed, was no doubt chiefly caused by the affection of Charles V. for his famous illegitimate daughter Margaret. Thus Pope and emperor were prompted by the same sentiment. At this epoch Venice had the commerce of the world; Rome had its moral government; Italy still reigned supreme through the poets, the generals, the statesmen born to her. At no period of the world's history, in any land, was there ever seen so remarkable, so abundant a collection of men of genius. There were so many, in fact, that even the lesser princes were superior men. Italy was crammed with talent, enterprise, knowledge, science, poesy, wealth, and gallantry, all the while torn by intestinal warfare and overrun with conquerors struggling for possession of her finest provinces. When men are so strong, they do not fear to admit their weaknesses. Hence, no doubt, this golden age for bastards. We must, moreover, do the illegitimate children of the house of the Medici the justice to say that they were ardently devoted to the glory, power, and increase of wealth of that famous family. Thus as soon as the *Duca della citta di Penna*, son of the Moorish woman, was installed as tyrant of Florence, he espoused the interest of Pope Clement VII., and gave a home to the daughter of Lorenzo II., then eleven years of age.

When we study the march of events and that of men in this curious sixteenth century, we ought never to forget that public policy had for its element a perpetual craftiness and a dissimulation which destroyed, in all characters, the straightforward, upright bearing our imaginations demand of eminent personages. In this, above all, is Catherine's absolution. It disposes of the vulgar and foolish accusations of treachery launched against her by the writers of the Reformation. This was the great age of that statesmanship the code of which was written by Macchiavelli as well as by Spinosa, by Hobbes as well as by Montesquieu,—for the dialogue between Sylla and Eucrates contains Montesquieu's true thought, which his connection with the Encyclopedists did not permit him to develop otherwise than as he did.

These principles are to-day the secret law of all cabinets in which plans for the conquest and maintenance of great power are laid. In France we blamed Napoleon when he made use of that Italian genius for craft which was bred in his bone,—though in his case it did not always succeed. But Charles V., Catherine, Philip II., and Pope Julius would not have acted otherwise than as he did in the affair of Spain. History, in the days when Catherine was born, if judged from the point of view of honesty, would seem an impossible tale. Charles V., obliged to sustain Catholicism against the attacks of Luther, who threatened the Throne in threatening the Tiara, allowed the siege of Rome and held Pope Clement VII. in prison! This same Clement, who had no bitterer enemy than

Charles V., courted him in order to make Alessandro de' Medici ruler of Florence, and obtained his favorite daughter for that bastard. No sooner was Alessandro established than he, conjointly with Clement VII., endeavored to injure Charles V. by allying himself with Francois I., king of France, by means of Catherine de' Medici; and both of them promised to assist Francois in reconquering Italy. Lorenzino de' Medici made himself the companion of Alessandro's debaucheries for the express purpose of finding an opportunity to kill him. Filippo Strozzi, one of the great minds of that day, held this murder in such respect that he swore that his sons should each marry a daughter of the murderer; and each son religiously fulfilled his father's oath when they might all have made, under Catherine's protection, brilliant marriages; for one was the rival of Doria, the other a marshal of France. Cosmo de' Medici, successor of Alessandro, with whom he had no relationship, avenged the death of that tyrant in the cruellest manner, with a persistency lasting twelve years; during which time his hatred continued keen against the persons who had, as a matter of fact, given him the power. He was eighteen years old when called to the sovereignty; his first act was to declare the rights of Alessandro's legitimate sons null and void,—all the while avenging their father's death! Charles V. confirmed the disinheriting of his grandsons, and recognized Cosmo instead of the son of Alessandro and his daughter Margaret. Cosmo, placed on the throne by Cardinal Cibo, instantly exiled the latter; and the cardinal revenged himself by accusing Cosmo (who was the first grand-duke) of murdering Alessandro's son. Cosmo, as jealous of his power as Charles V. was of his, abdicated in favor of his son Francesco, after causing the death of his other son, Garcia, to avenge the death of Cardinal Giovanni de' Medici, whom Garcia had assassinated. Cosmo the First and his son Francesco, who ought to have been devoted, body and soul, to the house of France, the only power on which they might really have relied, made themselves the lacqueys of Charles V. and Philip II., and were consequently the secret, base, and perfidious enemies of Catherine de' Medici, one of the glories of their house.

Such were the leading contradictory and illogical traits, the treachery, knavery, and black intrigues of a single house, that of the Medici. From this sketch, we may judge of the other princes of Italy and Europe. All the envoys of Cosmos I. to the court of France had, in their secret instructions, an order to poison Strozzi, Catherine's relation, when he arrived. Charles V. had already assassinated three of the ambassadors of Francois I.

It was early in the month of October, 1533, that the *Duca della citta di Penna* started from Florence for Livorno, accompanied by the sole heiress of Lorenzo II., namely, Catherine de' Medici. The duke and the Princess of Florence, for that was the title by which the young girl, then fourteen years of age, was known, left the city surrounded by a large retinue of servants, officers, and secretaries, preceded by armed men, and followed by an escort of cavalry. The young princess knew nothing as yet of what her fate was to be, except that the Pope was to have an interview at Livorno with the Duke Alessandro; but her uncle, Filippo Strozzi, very soon informed her of the future before her.

Filippo Strozzi had married Clarice de' Medici, half-sister on the father's side of Lorenzo de' Medici, Duke of Urbino, father of Catherine; but this marriage, which was brought about as much to convert one of the firmest supporters of the popular party to the cause of the Medici as to facilitate the recall of that family, then banished from Florence, never shook the stern champion from his course, though he was persecuted by his own party for making it. In spite of all apparent changes in his conduct (for this alliance naturally affected it somewhat) he remained faithful to the popular party, and declared himself openly against the Medici as soon as he foresaw their intention to enslave Florence. This great man even refused the offer of a principality made to him by Leo X.

At the time of which we are now writing Filippo Strozzi was a victim to the policy of the Medici, so vacillating in its means, so fixed and inflexible in its object. After sharing the misfortunes and the captivity of Clement VII. when the latter, surprised by the Colonna, took refuge in the Castle of Saint-Angelo, Strozzi was delivered up by Clement as a hostage and taken to Naples. As the Pope, when he got his liberty, turned savagely on his enemies, Strozzi came very near losing his life, and was forced to pay an enormous sum to be released from a prison where he was closely confined. When he found himself at liberty he had, with an instinct of kindness natural to an honest man, the simplicity to present himself before Clement VII., who had perhaps congratulated himself on being well rid of him. The Pope had such good cause to blush for his own conduct that he received Strozzi extremely ill.

Strozzi thus began, early in life, his apprenticeship in the misfortunes of an honest man in politics,—a man whose conscience cannot lend itself to the capriciousness of events; whose actions are acceptable only to the virtuous; and who is therefore persecuted by the world,—by the people, for opposing their blind passions; by power for opposing its usurpations. The life of such great citizens is a martyrdom, in which they are sustained only by the voice of their conscience and an heroic sense of social duty, which dictates their course in all things. There were many such men in the republic of Florence, all as great as Strozzi, and as able as their adversaries the Medici, though vanquished by the superior craft and wiliness of the latter. What could be more worthy of admiration than the conduct of the chief of the Pazzi at the time of the conspiracy of his house, when, his commerce being at that time enormous, he settled all his accounts with Asia, the Levant, and Europe before beginning that great attempt; so that, if it failed, his correspondents should lose nothing.

The history of the establishment of the house of the Medici in the fourteenth and fifteenth centuries is a magnificent tale which still remains to be written, though men of genius have already put their hands to it. It is not the history of a republic, nor of a society, nor of any special civilization; it is the history of *statesmen*, the eternal history of Politics,—that of usurpers, that of conquerors.

As soon as Filippo Strozzi returned to Florence he re-established the preceding form of government and ousted Ippolito de' Medici, another bastard, and the very Alessandro with whom, at the later period of which we are now writing, he was travelling to Livorno. Having completed this change of government, he became alarmed at the evident inconstancy of the people of Florence, and, fearing the vengeance of Clement VII., he went to Lyon to superintend a vast house of business he owned there, which corresponded with other banking-houses of his own in Venice, Rome, France, and Spain. Here we find a strange thing. These men who bore the weight of public affairs and of such a struggle as that with the Medici (not to speak of contentions with their own party) found time and strength to bear the burden of a vast business and all its speculations, also of banks and their complications, which the multiplicity of coinages and their falsification rendered even more difficult than it is in our day. The name "banker" comes from the *banc*(Anglice, *bench*) upon which the banker sat, and on which he rang the gold and silver pieces to try their quality. After a time Filippo found in the death of his wife, whom he adored, a pretext for renewing his relations with the Republican party, whose secret police becomes the more terrible in all republics, because every one makes himself a spy in the name of a liberty which justifies everything.

Filippo returned to Florence at the very moment when that city was compelled to adopt the yoke of Alessandro; but he had previously gone to Rome and seen Pope Clement VII., whose affairs were now so prosperous that his disposition toward Strozzi was much changed. In the hour of triumph the Medici were so much in need of a man like Filippo—were it only to smooth the return of Alessandro—that Clement urged him to take a seat at the Council of the bastard who was about to oppress the city; and Strozzi consented to accept the diploma of a senator. But, for the last two years and more, he had seen, like Seneca and Burrhus, the beginnings of tyranny in his Nero. He felt himself, at the moment of which we write, an object of so much distrust on the part of the people and so suspected by the Medici whom he was constantly resisting, that he was confident of some impending catastrophe. Consequently, as soon as he heard from Alessandro of the negotiation for Catherine's marriage with the son of Francois I., the final arrangements for which were to be made at Livorno, where the negotiators had appointed to meet, he formed the plan of going to France, and attaching himself to the fortunes of his niece, who needed a guardian. Alessandro, delighted to rid himself of a man so unaccommodating in the affairs of Florence, furthered a plan which relieved him of one murder at least, and advised Strozzi to put himself at the head of Catherine's household. In order to dazzle the eyes of France the Medici had selected a brilliant suite for her whom they styled, very unwarrantably, the Princess of Florence, and who also went by the name of the little Duchess d'Urbino. The cortege, at the head of which rode Alessandro, Catherine, and Strozzi, was composed of more than a thousand persons, not including the escort and servants. When the last of it issued from the gates of Florence the head had passed that first village beyond the city where they now braid the Tuscan straw hats. It was beginning to be rumored among the people that Catherine was to marry a son of Francois I.; but the rumor did not obtain much belief until the Tuscans beheld with their own eyes this triumphal procession from Florence to Livorno.

Catherine herself, judging by all the preparations she beheld, began to suspect that her marriage was in question, and her uncle then revealed to her the fact that the first ambitious project of his house had aborted, and that the hand of the dauphin had been refused to her. Alessandro still hoped that the Duke of Albany would succeed in changing this decision of the king of France who, willing as he was to buy the support of the Medici in Italy, would only grant them his second son, the Duc d'Orleans. This petty blunder lost Italy to France, and did not prevent Catherine from becoming queen.

The Duke of Albany, son of Alexander Stuart, brother of James III., king of Scotland, had married Anne de la Tour de Boulogne, sister of Madeleine de la Tour de Boulogne, Catherine's mother; he was therefore her maternal uncle. It was through her mother that Catherine was so rich and allied to so many great families; for, strangely enough, her rival, Diane de Poitiers, was also her cousin. Jean de Poitiers, father of Diane, was son of Jeanne de Boulogne, aunt of the Duchess d'Urbino. Catherine was also a cousin of Mary Stuart, her daughter-in-law.

Catherine now learned that her dowry in money was a hundred thousand ducats. A ducat was a gold piece of the size of an old French louis, though less thick. (The old louis was worth twenty-four francs—the present one is worth twenty). The Comtes of Auvergne and Lauraguais were also made a part of the dowry, and Pope Clement added one hundred thousand ducats in jewels, precious stones, and other wedding gifts; to which Alessandro likewise contributed his share.

On arriving at Livorno, Catherine, still so young, must have been flattered by the extreme magnificence displayed by Pope Clement ("her uncle in Notre-Dame," then head of the house of the Medici), in order to outdo the court of France. He had already arrived at Livorno in one of his galleys, which was lined with crimson satin fringed with gold, and covered with a tent-like awning in cloth of gold. This galley, the decoration of which cost twenty thousand ducats, contained several apartments destined for the bride of Henri of France, all of which were furnished with the richest treasures of art the Medici could collect. The rowers, magnificently apparelled, and the crew were under the command of a prior of the order of the Knights of Rhodes. The household of the Pope were in three other galleys. The galleys of the Duke of Albany, anchored near those of Clement VII., added to the size and dignity of the flotilla.

Duke Alessandro presented the officers of Catherine's household to the Pope, with whom he had a secret conference, in which, it would appear, he presented to his Holiness Count Sebastiano Montecuculi, who had just left, somewhat abruptly, the service of Charles V. and that of his two generals, Antonio di Leyva and Ferdinando di Gonzago. Was there between the two bastards, Giulio and Alessandro, a premeditated intention of making the Duc d'Orleans dauphin? What reward was promised to Sebastiano Montecuculi, who, before entering the service of Charles V. had studied medicine? History is silent on that point. We shall see presently what clouds hang round that fact. The obscurity is so great that, quite recently, grave and conscientious historians have admitted Montecuculi's innocence.

Catherine then heard officially from the Pope's own lips of the alliance reserved for her. The Duke of Albany had been able to do no more than hold the king of France, and that with difficulty, to his promise of giving Catherine the hand of his second son, the Duc d'Orleans. The Pope's impatience was so great, and he was so afraid that his plans would be thwarted either by some intrigue of the emperor, or by the refusal of France, or by the grandees of the kingdom looking with evil eye upon the marriage, that he gave orders to embark at once, and sailed for Marseille, where he arrived toward the end of October, 1533.

Notwithstanding its wealth, the house of the Medici was eclipsed on this occasion by the court of France. To show the lengths to which the

Medici pushed their magnificence, it is enough to say that the "dozen" put into the bride's purse by the Pope were twelve gold medals of priceless historical value, which were then unique. But Francois I., who loved the display of festivals, distinguished himself on this occasion. The wedding festivities of Henri de Valois and Catherine de' Medici lasted thirty-four days.

It is useless to repeat the details, which have been given in all the histories of Provence and Marseille, as to this celebrated interview between the Pope and the king of France, which was opened by a jest of the Duke of Albany as to the duty of keeping fasts,—a jest mentioned by Brantome and much enjoyed by the court, which shows the tone of the manners of that day.

Many conjectures have been made as to Catherine's barrenness, which lasted ten years. Strange calumnies still rest upon this queen, all of whose actions were fated to be misjudged. It is sufficient to say that the cause was solely in Henri II. After the difficulty was removed, Catherine had ten children. The delay was, in one respect, fortunate for France. If Henri II. had had children by Diane de Poitiers the politics of the kingdom would have been dangerously complicated. When the difficulty was removed the Duchesse de Valentinois had reached the period of a woman's second youth. This matter alone will show that the true life of Catherine de' Medici is still to be written, and also—as Napoleon said with profound wisdom—that the history of France should be either in one volume only, or one thousand.

Here is a contemporaneous and succinct account of the meeting of Clement VII. and the king of France:

"His Holiness the Pope, having been conducted to the palace, which was, as I have said, prepared beyond the port, every one retired to their own quarters till the morrow, when his Holiness was to make his entry; the which was made with great sumptuousness and magnificence, he being seated in a chair carried on the shoulders of two men and wearing his pontifical robes, but not the tiara. Pacing before him was a white hackney, bearing the sacrament of the altar,—the said hackney being led by reins of white silk held by two footmen finely equipped. Next came all the cardinals in their robes, on pontifical mules, and Madame la Duchesse d'Urbino in great magnificence, accompanied by a vast number of ladies and gentlemen, both French and Italian.

"The Holy Father having arrived in the midst of this company at the place appointed for his lodging, every one retired; and all this, being well-ordered, took place without disorder or tumult.

While the Pope was thus making his entry, the king crossed the water in a frigate and went to the lodging the Pope had just quitted, in order to go the next day and make obeisance to the Holy Father as a Most Christian king.

"The next day the king being prepared set forth for the palace where was the Pope, accompanied by the princes of the blood, such as Monseigneur le Duc de Vendomois (father of the Vidame de Chartres), the Comte de Sainct-Pol, Messieurs de Montpensier and la Roche-sur-Yon, the Duc de Nemours (brother of the Duc de Savoie) who died in this said place, the Duke of Albany, and many others, whether counts, barons, or seigneurs; nearest to the king was the Seigneur de Montmorency, his Grand-master.

"The king, being arrived at the palace, was received by the Pope and all the college of cardinals, assembled in consistory, most civilly. This done, each retired to the place ordained for him, the king taking with him several cardinals to feast them,—among them Cardinal de' Medici, nephew of the Pope, a very splendid man with a fine retinue.

"On the morrow those persons chosen by his Holiness and by the king began to assemble to discuss the matters for which the meeting was made. First, the matter of the Faith was treated of, and a bull was put forth repressing heresy and preventing that things come to greater combustion than they now are.

"After this was concluded the marriage of the Duc d'Orleans, second son of the king, with Catherine de' Medici, Duchesse d'Urbino, niece of his Holiness, under the conditions such, or like to those, as were proposed formerly by the Duke of Albany. The said espousals were celebrated with great magnificence, and our Holy Father himself wedded the pair. The marriage thus consummated, the Holy Father held a consistory at which he created four cardinals and devoted them to the king,—to wit: Cardinal Le Veneur, formerly bishop of Lisieux and grand almoner; the Cardinal de Boulogne of the family of la Chambre, brother on the mother's side of the Duke of Albany; the Cardinal de Chatillon of the house of Coligny, nephew of the Sire de Montmorency, and the Cardinal de Givry."

When Strozzi delivered the dowry in presence of the court he noticed some surprise on the part of the French seigneurs; they even said aloud that it was little enough for such a mesalliance (what would they have said in these days?). Cardinal Ippolito replied, saying:—

"You must be ill-informed as to the secrets of your king. His Holiness has bound himself to give to France three pearls of inestimable value, namely: Genoa, Milan, and Naples."

The Pope left Sebastiano Montecuculi to present himself to the court of France, to which the count offered his services, complaining of his treatment by Antonio di Leyva and Ferdinando di Gonzago, for which reason his services were accepted. Montecuculi was not made a part of Catherine's household, which was wholly composed of French men and women, for, by a law of the monarchy, the execution of which the Pope saw with great satisfaction, Catherine was naturalized by letters-patent as a Frenchwoman before the marriage. Montecuculi was appointed in the first instance to the household of the queen, the sister of Charles V. After a while he passed into the service of the dauphin as cup-bearer.

The new Duchesse d'Orleans soon found herself a nullity at the court of Francois I. Her young husband was in love with Diane de Poitiers, who certainly, in the matter of birth, could rival Catherine, and was far more of a great lady than the little Florentine. The daughter of the Medici was also outdone by Queen Eleonore, sister of Charles V., and by Madame d'Etampes, whose marriage with the head of the house of Brosse made her one of the most powerful and best titled women in France. Catherine's aunt the Duchess of Albany, the Queen of Navarre, the Duchesse de Guise, the Duchesse de Vendome, Madame la Connetable de Montmorency, and other women of like importance, eclipsed by birth and by their rights, as well as by their power at the most sumptuous court of France (not excepting that of Louis XIV.), the daughter of the Florentine grocers, who was richer and more illustrious through the house of the Tour de Boulogne than by her own family of Medici.

The position of his niece was so bad and difficult that the republican Filippo Strozzi, wholly incapable of guiding her in the midst of such conflicting interests, left her after the first year, being recalled to Italy by the death of Clement VII. Catherine's conduct, when we remember that she was scarcely fifteen years old, was a model of prudence. She attached herself closely to the king, her father-in-law; she left him as little as she could, following him on horseback both in hunting and in war. Her idolatry for Francois I. saved the house of the Medici from all suspicion when the dauphin was poisoned. Catherine was then, and so was her husband, at the headquarters of the king in Provence; for Charles V. had speedily invaded France and the late scene of the marriage festivities had become the theatre of a cruel war.

At the moment when Charles V. was put to flight, leaving the bones of his army in Provence, the dauphin was returning to Lyon by the Rhone. He stopped to sleep at Tournon, and, by way of pastime, practised some violent physical exercises,—which were nearly all the education his brother and he, in consequence of their detention as hostages, had ever received. The prince had the imprudence—it being the month of August, and the weather very hot—to ask for a glass of water, which Montecuculi, as his cup-bearer, gave to him, with ice in it. The dauphin died almost immediately. Francois I. adored his son. The dauphin was, according to all accounts, a charming young man. His father, in despair, gave the utmost publicity to the proceedings against Montecuculi, which he placed in the hands of the most able magistrates of that day. The count, after heroically enduring the first tortures without confessing anything, finally made admissions by which he implicated Charles V. and his two generals, Antonio di Leyva and Ferdinando di Gonzago. No affair was ever more solemnly debated. Here is what the king did, in the words of an ocular witness:—

"The king called an assembly at Lyon of all the princes of his blood, all the knights of his order, and other great personages of the kingdom; also the legal and papal nuncio, the cardinals who were at his court, together with the ambassadors of England, Scotland, Portugal, Venice, Ferrara, and others; also all the princes and noble strangers, both Italian and German, who were then residing at his court in great numbers. These all being assembled, he caused to be read to them, in presence of each other, from beginning to end, the trial of the unhappy man who poisoned Monseigneur the late dauphin,—with all the interrogatories, confessions, confrontings, and other ceremonies usual in criminal trials; he, the king, not being willing that the sentence should be executed until all present had given their opinion on this heinous and miserable case."

The fidelity, devotion, and cautious skill of the Comte de Montecuculi may seem extraordinary in our time, when all the world, even ministers of State, tell everything about the least little event with which they have to do; but in those days princes could find devoted servants, or knew how to choose them. Monarchical Moreys existed because in those days there was *faith*. Never ask devotion of *self-interest*, because such interest may change; but expect all from sentiments, religious faith, monarchical faith, patriotic faith. Those three beliefs produced such men as the Berthereaus of Geneva, the Sydneys and Straffords of England, the murderers of Thomas a Becket, the Jacques Coeurs, the Jeanne d'Arcs, the Richelieus, Dantons, Bonchamps, Talmonts, and also the Clements, Chabots, and others.

The dauphin was poisoned in the same manner, and possibly by the same drug which afterwards served MADAME under Louis XIV. Pope Clement VII. had been dead two years; Duke Alessandro, plunged in debauchery, seemed to have no interest in the elevation of the Duc d'Orleans; Catherine, then seventeen, and full of admiration for her father-in-law, was with him at the time; Charles V. alone appeared to have an interest in his death, for Francois I. was negotiating for his son an alliance which would assuredly have aggrandized France. The count's confession was therefore very skilfully based on the passions and politics of the moment; Charles V. was then flying from France, leaving his armies buried in Provence with his happiness, his reputation, and his hopes of dominion. It is to be remarked that if torture had forced admissions from an innocent man, Francois I. gave Montecuculi full liberty to speak in presence of an imposing assembly, and before persons in whose eyes innocence had some chance to triumph. The king, who wanted the truth, sought it in good faith.

In spite of her now brilliant future, Catherine's situation at court was not changed by the death of the dauphin. Her barrenness gave reason to fear a divorce in case her husband should ascend the throne. The dauphin was under the spell of Diane de Poitiers, who assumed to rival Madame d'Etampes, the king's mistress. Catherine redoubled in care and cajolery of her father-in-law, being well aware that her sole support was in him. The first ten years of Catherine's married life were years of ever-renewed grief, caused by the failure, one by one, of her hopes of pregnancy, and the vexations of her rivalry with Diane. Imagine what must have been the life of a young princess, watched by a jealous mistress who was supported by a powerful party,—the Catholic party,—and by the two powerful alliances Diane had made in marrying one daughter to Robert de la Mark, Duc de Bouillon, Prince of Sedan, and the other to Claude de Lorraine, Duc d'Aumale.

Catherine, helpless between the party of Madame d'Etampes and the party of the Senechale (such was Diane's title during the reign of Francois I.), which divided the court and politics into factions for these mortal enemies, endeavored to make herself the friend of both Diane de Poitiers and Madame d'Etampes. She, who was destined to become so great a queen, played the part of a servant. Thus she served her apprenticeship in that double-faced policy which was ever the secret motor of her life. Later, the *queen* was to stand between Catholics and Calvinists, just as the *woman* had stood for ten years between Madame d'Etampes and Madame de Poitiers. She studied the contradictions of

French politics; she saw Francois I. sustaining Calvin and the Lutherans in order to embarrass Charles V., and then, after secretly and patiently protecting the Reformation in Germany, and tolerating the residence of Calvin at the court of Navarre, he suddenly turned against it with excessive rigor. Catherine beheld on the one hand the court, and the women of the court, playing with the fire of heresy, and on the other, Diane at the head of the Catholic party with the Guises, solely because the Duchesse d'Etampes supported Calvin and the Protestants.

Such was the political education of this queen, who saw in the cabinet of the king of France the same errors committed as in the house of the Medici. The dauphin opposed his father in everything; he was a bad son. He forgot the cruel but most vital maxim of royalty, namely, that thrones need solidarity; and that a son who creates opposition during the lifetime of his father must follow that father's policy when he mounts the throne. Spinosa, who was as great a statesman as he was a philosopher, said—in the case of one king succeeding another by insurrection or crime,—

"If the new king desires to secure the safety of his throne and of his own life he must show such ardor in avenging the death of his predecessor that no one shall feel a desire to commit the same crime. But to avenge it worthily it is not enough to shed the blood of his subjects, he must approve the axioms of the king he replaces, and take the same course in governing."

It was the application of this maxim which gave Florence to the Medici. Cosmo I. caused to be assassinated at Venice, after eleven years' sway, the Florentine Brutus, and, as we have already said, persecuted the Strozzi. It was forgetfulness of this maxim which ruined Louis XVI. That king was false to every principle of royal government when he re-established the parliaments suppressed by his grandfather. Louis XV. saw the matter clearly. The parliaments, and notably that of Paris, counted for fully half in the troubles which necessitated the convocation of the States-general. The fault of Louis XV. was, that in breaking down that barrier which separated the throne from the people he did not erect a stronger; in other words, that he did not substitute for parliament a strong constitution of the provinces. There lay the remedy for the evils of the monarchy; thence should have come the voting on taxes, the regulation of them, and a slow approval of reforms that were necessary to the system of monarchy.

The first act of Henri II. was to give his confidence to the Connetable de Montmorency, whom his father had enjoined him to leave in disgrace. The Connetable de Montmorency was, with Diane de Poitiers, to whom he was closely bound, the master of the State. Catherine was therefore less happy and less powerful after she became queen of France than while she was dauphiness. From 1543 she had a child every year for ten years, and was occupied with maternal cares during the period covered by the last three years of the reign of Francois I. and nearly the whole of the reign of Henri II. We may see in this recurring fecundity the influence of a rival, who was able thus to rid herself of the legitimate wife,—a barbarity of feminine policy which must have been one of Catherine's grievances against Diane.

Thus set aside from public life, this superior woman passed her time in observing the self-interests of the court people and of the various parties which were formed about her. All the Italians who had followed her were objects of violent suspicion. After the execution of Montecuculi the Connetable de Montmorency, Diane, and many of the keenest politicians of the court were filled with suspicion of the Medici; though Francois I. always repelled it. Consequently, the Gondi, Strozzi, Ruggieri, Sardini, etc.,—in short, all those who were called distinctively "the Italians,"—were compelled to employ greater resources of mind, shrewd policy, and courage, to maintain themselves at court against the weight of disfavor which pressed upon them.

During her husband's reign Catherine's amiability to Diane de Poitiers went to such great lengths that intelligent persons must regard it as proof of that profound dissimulation which men, events, and the conduct of Henri II. compelled Catherine de' Medici to employ. But they go too far when they declare that she never claimed her rights as wife and queen. In the first place, the sense of dignity which Catherine possessed in the highest degree forbade her claiming what historians call her rights as a wife. The ten children of the marriage explain Henri's conduct; and his wife's maternal occupations left him free to pass his time with Diane de Poitiers. But the king was never lacking in anything that was due to himself; and he gave Catherine an "entry" into Paris, to be crowned as queen, which was worthy of all such pageants that had ever taken place. The archives of the Parliament, and those of the Cour des Comptes, show that those two great bodies went to meet her outside of Paris as far as Saint Lazare. Here is an extract from du Tillet's account of it:—

"A platform had been erected at Saint-Lazare, on which was a throne (du Tillet calls it a chair de parement). Catherine took her seat upon it, wearing a surcoat, or species of ermine short-cloak covered with precious stones, a bodice beneath it with the royal mantle, and on her head a crown enriched with pearls and diamonds, and held in place by the Marechale de la Mark, her lady of honor. Around her stood the princes of the blood, and other princes and seigneurs, richly apparelled, also the chancellor of

France in a robe of gold damask on a background of crimson-red. Before the queen, and on the same platform, were seated, in two rows, twelve duchesses or countesses, wearing ermine surcoats, bodices, robes, and circlets,—that is to say, the coronets of duchesses and countesses. These were the Duchesses d'Estouteville, Montpensier (elder and younger); the Princesses de la Roche-sur-Yon; the Duchesses de Guise, de Nivernois, d'Aumale, de Valentinois (Diane de Poitiers), Mademoiselle la batarde legitimee de France (the title of the king's daughter, Diane, who was Duchesse de Castro-Farnese and afterwards Duchesse de Montmorency-Damville), Madame la Connetable, and Mademoiselle de Nemours; without mentioning other demoiselles who were not seated. The four presidents of the courts of justice, wearing their caps, several other members of the court, and the clerk du Tillet, mounted the platform, made reverent bows, and the chief judge, Lizet, kneeling down, harangued the queen. The chancellor then knelt down and answered. The queen made her entry at half-past three o'clock in an open litter, having Madame Marguerite de France sitting opposite to her, and on either side of the litter the Cardinals of Amboise, Chatillon, Boulogne, and de Lenoncourt in their episcopal robes. She left her litter at the church of Notre-Dame, where she was received by the clergy. After offering her prayer, she was conducted by the rue de la Calandre to the palace, where the royal supper was served in the great hall. She there appeared, seated at the middle of the marble table, beneath a velvet dais strewn with golden fleur-de-lis."

We may here put an end to one of those popular beliefs which are repeated in many writers from Sauval down. It has been said that Henri II. pushed his neglect of the proprieties so far as to put the initials of his mistress on the buildings which Catherine advised him to continue or to begin with so much magnificence. But the double monogram which can be seen at the Louvre offers a daily denial to those who are so little clear-sighted as to believe in silly nonsense which gratuitously insults our kings and queens. The H or Henri and the two C's of Catherine which back it, appear to represent the two D's of Diane. The coincidence may have pleased Henri II., but it is none the less true that the royal monogram contained officially the initial of the king and that of the queen. This is so true that the monogram can still be seen on the column of the Halle au Ble, which was built by Catherine alone. It can also be seen in the crypt of Saint-Denis, on the tomb which Catherine erected for herself in her lifetime beside that of Henri II., where her figure is

27

modelled from nature by the sculptor to whom she sat for it.

On a solemn occasion, when he was starting, March 25, 1552, for his expedition into Germany, Henri II. declared Catherine regent during his absence, and also in case of his death. Catherine's most cruel enemy, the author of "Marvellous Discourses on Catherine the Second's Behavior" admits that she carried on the government with universal approval and that the king was satisfied with her administration. Henri received both money and men at the time he wanted them; and finally, after the fatal day of Saint-Quentin, Catherine obtained considerable sums of money from the people of Paris, which she sent to Compiegne, where the king then was.

In politics, Catherine made immense efforts to obtain a little influence. She was clever enough to bring the Connetable de Montmorency, all-powerful under Henri II., to her interests. We all know the terrible answer that the king made, on being harassed by Montmorency in her favor. This answer was the result of an attempt by Catherine to give the king good advice, in the few moments she was ever alone with him, when she explained the Florentine policy of pitting the grandees of the kingdom one against another and establishing the royal authority on their ruins. But Henri II., who saw things only through the eyes of Diane and the Connetable, was a truly feudal king and the friend of all the great families of his kingdom.

After the futile attempt of the Connetable in her favor, which must have been made in the year 1556, Catherine began to cajole the Guises for the purpose of detaching them from Diane and opposing them to the Connetable. Unfortunately, Diane and Montmorency were as vehement against the Protestants as the Guises. There was therefore not the same animosity in their struggle as there might have been had the religious question entered it. Moreover, Diane boldly entered the lists against the queen's project by coquetting with the Guises and giving her daughter to the Duc d'Aumale. She even went so far that certain authors declared she gave more than mere good-will to the gallant Cardinal de Lorraine; and the lampooners of the time made the following quatrain on Henri II:

"Sire, if you're weak and let your will relax
Till Diane and Lorraine do govern you,
Pound, knead and mould, re-melt and model you,
Sire, you are nothing—nothing else than wax."

It is impossible to regard as sincere the signs of grief and the ostentation of mourning which Catherine showed on the death of Henri II. The fact that the king was attached by an unalterable passion to Diane de Poitiers naturally made Catherine play the part of a neglected wife who adores her husband; but, like all women who act by their head, she persisted in this dissimulation and never ceased to speak tenderly of Henri II. In like manner Diane, as we know, wore mourning all her life for her husband the Senechal de Breze. Her colors were black and white, and the king was wearing them at the tournament when he was killed. Catherine, no doubt in imitation of her rival, wore mourning for Henri II. for the rest of her life. She showed a consummate perfidy toward Diane de Poitiers, to which historians have not given due attention. At the king's death the Duchesse de Valentinois was completely disgraced and shamefully abandoned by the Connetable, a man who was always below his reputation. Diane offered her estate and chateau of Chenonceaux to the queen. Catherine then said, in presence of witnesses:—

"I can never forget that she made the happiness of my dear Henri. I am ashamed to accept her gift; I wish to give her a domain in place of it, and I shall offer her that of Chaumont-sur-Loire."

Accordingly, the deed of exchange was signed at Blois in 1559. Diane, whose sons-in-law were the Duc d'Aumale and the Duc de Bouillon (then a sovereign prince), kept her wealth, and died in 1566 aged sixty-six. She was therefore nineteen years older than Henri II. These dates, taken from her epitaph which was copied from her tomb by the historian who concerned himself so much about her at the close of the last century, clear up quite a number of historical difficulties. Some historians have declared she was forty, others that she was sixteen at the time of her father's condemnation in 1523; in point of fact she was then twenty-four. After reading everything for and against her conduct towards Francois I. we are unable to affirm or to deny anything. This is one of the passages of history that will ever remain obscure. We may see by what happens in our own day how history is falsified at the very moment when events happen.

Catherine, who had founded great hopes on the age of her rival, tried more than once to overthrow her. It was a dumb, underhand, terrible struggle. The day came when Catherine believed herself for a moment on the verge of success. In 1554, Diane, who was ill, begged the king to go to Saint-Germain and leave her for a short time until she recovered. This stately coquette did not choose to be seen in the midst of medical appliances and without the splendors of apparel. Catherine arranged, as a welcome to her husband, a magnificent ballet, in which six beautiful young girls were to recite a poem in his honor. She chose for this function Miss Fleming, a relation of her uncle the Duke of Albany, the handsomest young woman, some say, that was ever seen, white and very fair; also one of her own relations, Clarice Strozzi, a magnificent Italian with superb black hair, and hands that were of rare beauty; Miss

Lewiston, maid of honor to Mary Stuart; Mary Stuart herself; Madame Elizabeth of France (who was afterwards that unfortunate Queen of Spain); and Madame Claude. Elizabeth and Claude were eight and nine years old, Mary Stuart twelve; evidently the queen intended to bring forward Miss Fleming and Clarice Strozzi and present them without rivals to the king. The king fell in love with Miss Fleming, by whom he had a natural son, Henri de Valois, Comte d'Angouleme, grand-prior of France. But the power and influence of Diane were not shaken. Like Madame de Pompadour with Louis XV., the Duchesse de Valentinois forgave all. But what sort of love did this attempt show in Catherine? Was it love to her husband or love of power? Women may decide.

A great deal is said in these days of the license of the press; but it is difficult to imagine the lengths to which it went when printing was first invented. We know that Aretino, the Voltaire of his time, made kings and emperors tremble, more especially Charles V.; but the world does not know so well the audacity and license of pamphlets. The chateau de Chenonceaux, which we have just mentioned, was given to Diane, or rather not given, she was implored to accept it to make her forget one of the most horrible publications ever levelled against a woman, and which shows the violence of the warfare between herself and Madame d'Etampes. In 1537, when she was thirty-eight years of age, a rhymester of Champagne named Jean Voute, published a collection of Latin verses in which were three epigrams upon her. It is to be supposed that the poet was sure of protection in high places, for the pamphlet has a preface in praise of itself, signed by Salmon Macrin, first valet-de-chambre to the king. Only one passage is quotable from these epigrams, which are entitled: IN PICTAVIAM, ANAM AULIGAM.

"A painted trap catches no game," says the poet, after telling Diane that she painted her face and bought her teeth and hair. "You may buy all that superficially makes a woman, but you can't buy that your lover wants; for he wants life, and you are dead."

This collection, printed by Simon de Colines, is dedicated to a bishop!—to Francois Bohier, the brother of the man who, to save his credit at court and redeem his offence, offered to Diane, on the accession of Henri II., the chateau de Chenonceaux, built by his father, Thomas Bohier, a councillor of state under four kings: Louis XI., Charles VIII., Louis XII., and Francois I. What were the pamphlets published against Madame de Pompadour and against Marie-Antoinette compared to these verses, which might have been written by Martial? Voute must have made a bad end. The estate and chateau cost Diane nothing more than the forgiveness enjoined by the gospel. After all, the penalties inflicted on the press, though not decreed by juries, were somewhat more severe than those of to-day.

The queens of France, on becoming widows, were required to remain in the king's chamber forty days without other light than that of wax tapers; they did not leave the room until after the burial of the king. This inviolable custom was a great annoyance to Catherine, who feared cabals; and, by chance, she found a means to evade it, thus: Cardinal de Lorraine, leaving, very early in the morning, the house of the *belle Romaine*, a celebrated courtesan of the period, who lived in the rue Culture-Sainte-Catherine, was set upon and maltreated by a party of libertines. "On which his holiness, being much astonished" (says Henri Estienne), "gave out that the heretics were preparing ambushes against him." The court at once removed from Paris to Saint-Germain, and the queen-mother, declaring that she would not abandon the king her son, went with him.

The accession of Francois II., the period at which Catherine confidently believed she could get possession of the regal power, was a moment of cruel disappointment, after the twenty-six years of misery she had lived through at the court of France. The Guises laid hands on power with incredible audacity. The Duc de Guise was placed in command of the army; the Connetable was dismissed; the cardinal took charge of the treasury and the clergy.

Catherine now began her political career by a drama which, though it did not have the dreadful fame of those of later years, was, nevertheless, most horrible; and it must, undoubtedly, have accustomed her to the terrible after emotions of her life. While appearing to be in harmony with the Guises, she endeavored to pave the way for her ultimate triumph by seeking a support in the house of Bourbon, and the means she took were as follows: Whether it was that (before the death of Henri II.), and after fruitlessly attempting violent measures, she wished to awaken jealousy in order to bring the king back to her; or whether as she approached middle-age it seemed to her cruel that she had never known love, certain it is that she showed a strong interest in a seigneur of the royal blood, Francois de Vendome, son of Louis de Vendome (the house from which that of the Bourbons sprang), and Vidame de Chartres, the name under which he is known in history. The secret hatred which Catherine bore to Diane was revealed in many ways, to which historians, preoccupied by political interests, have paid no attention. Catherine's attachment to the vidame proceeded from the fact that the young man had offered an insult to the favorite. Diane's greatest ambition was for the honor of an alliance with the royal family of France. The hand of her second daughter (afterwards Duchesse d'Aumale) was offered on her behalf to the Vidame de Chartres, who was kept poor by the far-sighted policy of Francois I. In fact, when the Vidame de Chartres and the Prince de

Conde first came to court, Francois I. gave them—what? The office of chamberlain, with a paltry salary of twelve hundred crowns a year, the same that he gave to the simplest gentlemen. Though Diane de Poitiers offered an immense dowry, a fine office under the crown, and the favor of the king, the vidame refused. After which, this Bourbon, already factious, married Jeanne, daughter of the Baron d'Estissac, by whom he had no children. This act of pride naturally commended him to Catherine, who greeted him after that with marked favor and made a devoted friend of him.

Historians have compared the last Duc de Montmorency, beheaded at Toulouse, to the Vidame de Chartres, in the art of pleasing, in attainments, accomplishments, and talent. Henri II. showed no jealousy; he seemed not even to suppose that a queen of France could fail in her duty, or a Medici forget the honor done to her by a Valois. But during this time when the queen was, it is said, coquetting with the Vidame de Chartres, the king, after the birth of her last child, had virtually abandoned her. This attempt at making him jealous was to no purpose, for Henri died wearing the colors of Diane de Poitiers.

At the time of the king's death Catherine was, therefore, on terms of gallantry with the vidame,—a situation which was quite in conformity with the manners and morals of a time when love was both so chivalrous and so licentious that the noblest actions were as natural as the most blamable; although historians, as usual, have committed the mistake in this case of taking the exception for the rule.

The four sons of Henri II. of course rendered null the position of the Bourbons, who were all extremely poor and were now crushed down by the contempt which the Connetable de Montmorency's treachery brought upon them, in spite of the fact that the latter had thought best to fly the kingdom.

The Vidame de Chartres—who was to the first Prince de Conde what Richelieu was to Mazarin, his father in policy, his model, and, above all, his master in gallantry—concealed the excessive ambition of his house beneath an external appearance of light-hearted gaiety. Unable during the reign of Henri II. to make head against the Guises, the Montmorencys, the Scottish princes, the cardinals, and the Bouillons, he distinguished himself by his graceful bearing, his manners, his wit, which won him the favor of many charming women and the heart of some for whom he cared nothing. He was one of those privileged beings whose seductions are irresistible, and who owe to love the power of maintaining themselves according to their rank. The Bourbons would not have resented, as did Jarnac, the slander of la Chataigneraie; they were willing enough to accept the lands and castles of their mistresses,—

witness the Prince de Conde, who accepted the estate of Saint-Valery from Madame la Marechale de Saint-Andre.

During the first twenty days of mourning after the death of Henri II. the situation of the vidame suddenly changed. As the object of the queen mother's regard, and permitted to pay his court to her as court is paid to a queen, very secretly, he seemed destined to play an important role, and Catherine did, in fact, resolve to use him. The vidame received letters from her for the Prince de Conde, in which she pointed out to the latter the necessity of an alliance against the Guises. Informed of this intrigue, the Guises entered the queen's chamber for the purpose of compelling her to issue an order consigning the vidame to the Bastille, and Catherine, to save herself, was under the hard necessity of obeying them. After a captivity of some months, the vidame died on the very day he left prison, which was shortly before the conspiracy of Amboise. Such was the conclusion of the first and only amour of Catherine de' Medici. Protestant historians have said that the queen caused the vidame to be poisoned, to lay the secret of her gallantries in a tomb!

We have now shown what was the apprenticeship of this woman for the exercise of her royal power.

PART I. THE CALVINIST MARTYR

I. A HOUSE WHICH NO LONGER EXISTS

AT THE CORNER OF A STREET WHICH NO LONGER EXISTS IN A PARIS WHICH NO LONGER EXISTS

Few persons in the present day know how plain and unpretentious were the dwellings of the burghers of Paris in the sixteenth century, and how simple their lives. Perhaps this simplicity of habits and of thought was the cause of the grandeur of that old bourgeoisie which was certainly grand, free, and noble,—more so, perhaps, than the bourgeoisie of the present day. Its history is still to be written; it requires and it awaits a man of genius. This reflection will doubtless rise to the lips of every one after reading the almost unknown incident which forms the basis of this Study and is one of the most remarkable facts in the history of that bourgeoisie. It will not be the first time in history that conclusion has preceded facts.

In 1560, the houses of the rue de la Vieille-Pelleterie skirted the left bank of the Seine, between the pont Notre-Dame and the pont au Change. A public footpath and the houses then occupied the space covered by the present roadway. Each house, standing almost in the river, allowed its dwellers to get down to the water by stone or wooden stairways, closed and protected by strong iron railings or wooden gates, clamped with iron. The houses, like those in Venice, had an entrance on *terra firma* and a water entrance. At the moment when the present sketch is published, only one of these houses remains to recall the old Paris of which we speak, and that is soon to disappear; it stands at the corner of the Petit-Pont, directly opposite to the guard-house of the Hotel-Dieu.

Formerly each dwelling presented on the river-side the fantastic appearance given either by the trade of its occupant and his habits, or by the originality of the exterior constructions invented by the proprietors to use or abuse the Seine. The bridges being encumbered with more mills than the necessities of navigation could allow, the Seine formed as many enclosed basins as there were bridges. Some of these basins in the heart of old Paris would have offered precious scenes and tones of color to painters. What a forest of crossbeams supported the mills with their huge sails and their wheels! What strange effects were produced by the piles or props driven into the water to project the upper floors of the houses above the stream! Unfortunately, the art of genre painting did not exist in those days, and that of engraving was in its infancy. We have therefore lost that curious spectacle, still offered, though in miniature, by certain provincial towns, where the rivers are overhung with wooden houses, and where, as at Vendome, the basins, full of water grasses, are enclosed by immense iron railings, to isolate each proprietor's share of the stream, which extends from bank to bank.

The name of this street, which has now disappeared from the map, sufficiently indicates the trade that was carried on in it. In those days the merchants of each class of commerce, instead of dispersing themselves about the city, kept together in the same neighborhood and protected themselves mutually. Associated in corporations which limited their number, they were still further united into guilds by the Church. In this way prices were maintained. Also, the masters were not at the mercy of their workmen, and did not obey their whims as they do to-day; on the contrary, they made them their children, their apprentices, took care of them, and taught them the intricacies of the trade. In order to become a master, a workman had to produce a masterpiece, which was always dedicated to the saint of his guild. Will any one dare to say that the absence of competition destroyed the desire for perfection, or lessened the beauty of products? What say you, you whose admiration for the masterpieces of past ages has created the modern trade of the sellers of bric-a-brac?

In the fifteenth and sixteenth centuries the trade of the furrier was one of the most flourishing industries. The difficulty of obtaining furs, which, being all brought from the north, required long and perilous journeys, gave a very high price and value to those products. Then, as now, high prices led to consumption; for vanity likes to override obstacles. In France, as in other kingdoms, not only did royal ordinances restrict the use of furs to the nobility (proved by the part which ermine plays in the old blazons), but also certain rare furs, such as *vair* (which was undoubtedly Siberian sable), could not be worn by any but kings, dukes, and certain lords clothed with official powers. A distinction was made between the greater and lesser *vair*. The very name has been so long disused, that in a vast number of editions of Perrault's famous tale, Cinderella's slipper, which was no doubt of *vair* (the fur), is said to have been made of *verre* (glass). Lately one of our most distinguished poets was obliged to establish the true orthography of the word for the instruction of his brother-feuilletonists in giving an account of the opera of the "Cenerentola," where the symbolic slipper has been replaced by a ring, which symbolizes nothing at all.

Naturally the sumptuary laws about the wearing of fur were perpetually infringed upon, to the great satisfaction of the furriers. The costliness of stuffs and furs made a garment in those days a durable thing,—as lasting as the furniture, the armor, and other items of that strong life of the fifteenth century. A woman of rank, a seigneur, all rich men, also all the burghers, possessed at the most two garments for each season, which lasted their lifetime and beyond it. These garments were bequeathed to their children. Consequently the clause in the marriage-contract relating to arms and clothes, which in these days is almost a dead letter because of the small value of wardrobes that need constant renewing, was then of much importance. Great costs brought with them solidity. The toilet of a woman constituted a large capital; it was reckoned among the family possessions, and was kept in those enormous chests which threaten to break through the floors of our modern houses. The jewels of a woman of 1840 would have been the *undress* ornaments of a great lady in 1540.

To-day, the discovery of America, the facilities of transportation, the ruin of social distinctions which has paved the way for the ruin of apparent distinctions, has reduced the trade of the furrier to what it now is,—next to nothing. The article which a furrier sells to-day, as in former days, for twenty *livres* has followed the depreciation of money: formerly the *livre*, which is now worth one franc and is usually so called, was worth twenty francs. To-day, the lesser bourgeoisie and the courtesans who edge their capes with sable, are ignorant than in 1440 an ill-disposed police-officer would have incontinently arrested them and marched them before the justice at the Chatelet. Englishwomen, who are so fond of ermine, do not know that in former times none but queens, duchesses, and chancellors were allowed to wear that royal fur. There are to-day in France several ennobled families whose true name is Pelletier or Lepelletier, the origin of which is evidently derived from some rich furrier's counter, for most of our burgher's names began in some such way.

This digression will explain, not only the long feud as to precedence which the guild of drapers maintained for two centuries against the guild of furriers and also of mercers (each claiming the right to walk first, as being the most important guild in Paris), but it will also serve to explain the importance of the Sieur Lecamus, a furrier honored with the custom of two queens, Catherine de' Medici and Mary Stuart, also the custom of the parliament,—a man who for twenty years was the syndic of his corporation, and who lived in the street we have just described.

The house of Lecamus was one of three which formed the three angles of the open space at the end of the pont au Change, where nothing now remains but the tower of the Palais de Justice, which made the fourth angle. On the corner of this house, which stood at the angle of the pont au Change and the quai now called the quai aux Fleurs, the architect had constructed a little shrine for a Madonna, which was always lighted by wax-tapers and decked with real flowers in summer and artificial ones in winter. On the side of the house toward the rue du Pont, as on the side toward the rue de la Vieille-Pelleterie, the upper story of the house was supported by wooden pillars. All the houses in this mercantile quarter had an arcade behind these pillars, where the passers in the street walked under cover on a ground of trodden mud which kept the place always dirty. In all French towns these arcades or galleries are called *les piliers*, a general term to which was added the name of the business transacted under them,—as "piliers des Halles" (markets), "piliers de la Boucherie" (butchers).

These galleries, a necessity in the Parisian climate, which is so changeable and so rainy, gave this part of the city a peculiar character of its own; but they have now disappeared. Not a single house in the river bank remains, and not more than about a hundred feet of the old "piliers des Halles," the last that have resisted the action of time, are left; and before long even that relic of the sombre labyrinth of old Paris will be demolished. Certainly, the existence of such old ruins of the middle-ages is incompatible with the grandeurs of modern Paris. These observations are meant not so much to regret the destruction of the old town, as to preserve in words, and by the history of those who lived there, the memory of a place now turned to dust, and to excuse the following description, which may be precious to a future age now treading on the heels of our own.

The walls of this house were of wood covered with slate. The spaces between the uprights had been filled in, as we may still see in some provincial towns, with brick, so placed, by reversing their thickness, as to make a pattern called "Hungarian point." The window-casings and lintels, also in wood, were richly carved, and so was the corner pillar where it rose above the shrine of the Madonna, and all the other pillars in front of the house. Each window, and each main beam which separated the different storeys, was covered with arabesques of fantastic personages and animals wreathed with conventional foliage. On the street side, as on the river side, the house was capped with a roof looking as if two cards were set up one against the other,—thus presenting a gable to the street and a gable to the water. This roof, like the roof of a Swiss chalet, overhung the building so far that on the second floor there was an outside gallery with a balustrade, on which the owners of the house could walk under cover and survey the street, also the river basin between the bridges and the two lines of houses.

These houses on the river bank were very valuable. In those days a system of drains and fountains was still to be invented; nothing of the kind as yet existed except the circuit sewer, constructed by Aubriot, provost of Paris under Charles the Wise, who also built the Bastille, the pont Saint-Michel and other bridges, and was the first man of genius who ever thought of the sanitary improvement of Paris. The houses situated like that of Lecamus took from the river the water necessary for the purposes of life, and also made the river serve as a natural drain for rain-water and household refuse. The great works that the "merchants' provosts" did in this direction are fast disappearing. Middle-aged persons alone can remember to have seen the great holes in the rue Montmartre, rue du Temple, etc., down which the waters poured. Those terrible open jaws were in the olden time of immense benefit to Paris. Their place will probably be forever marked by the sudden rise of the paved roadways at the spots where they opened,—another archaeological detail which will be quite inexplicable to the historian two centuries hence. One day, about 1816, a little girl who was carrying a case of diamonds to an actress at the Ambigu, for her part as queen, was overtaken by a shower and so nearly washed down the great drainhole in the rue du Temple that she would have disappeared had it not been for a passer who heard her cries. Unluckily, she had let go the diamonds, which were, however, recovered later at a man-hole. This event made a great noise, and gave rise to many petitions against these engulfers of water and little girls. They were singular constructions about five feet high, furnished with iron railings, more or less movable, which often caused the inundation of the neighboring cellars, whenever the artificial river produced by sudden rains was arrested in its course by the filth and refuse collected about these railings, which the owners of the abutting houses sometimes forgot to open.

The front of this shop of the Sieur Lecamus was all window, formed of sashes of leaded panes, which made the interior very dark. The furs were taken for selection to the houses of rich customers. As for those who came to the shop to buy, the goods were shown to them outside, between the pillars,—the arcade being, let us remark, encumbered during the day-time with tables, and clerks sitting on stools, such as we all remember seeing some fifteen years ago under the "piliers des Halles." From these outposts, the clerks and apprentices talked, questioned, answered each other, and called to the passers,—customs which the great Walter Scott has made use of in his "Fortunes of Nigel."

The sign, which represented an ermine, hung outside, as we still see in some village hostelries, from a rich bracket of gilded iron filagree. Above the ermine, on one side of the sign, were the words:—

LECAMVS

FURRIER

TO MADAME LA ROYNE ET DU ROY NOSTRE SIRE.
On the other side of the sign were the words:—

TO MADAME LA ROYNE-MERE

AND MESSIEURS DV PARLEMENT.

The words "Madame la Royne-mere" had been lately added. The gilding was fresh. This addition showed the recent changes produced by the sudden and violent death of Henri II., which overturned many fortunes at court and began that of the Guises.

The back-shop opened on the river. In this room usually sat the respectable proprietor himself and Mademoiselle Lecamus. In those days the wife of a man who was not noble had no right to the title of dame, "madame"; but the wives of the burghers of Paris were allowed to use that of "mademoiselle," in virtue of privileges granted and confirmed to their husbands by the several kings to whom they had done service. Between this back-shop and the main shop was the well of a corkscrew-staircase which gave access to the upper story, where were the great ware-room and the dwelling-rooms of the old couple, and the garrets lighted by skylights, where slept the children, the servant-woman, the apprentices, and the clerks.

This crowding of families, servants, and apprentices, the little space which each took up in the building where the apprentices all slept in one large chamber under the roof, explains the enormous population of Paris then agglomerated on one-tenth of the surface of the present city; also the queer details of private life in the middle ages; also, the contrivances of love which, with all due deference to historians, are found only in the pages of the romance-writers, without whom they would be lost to the world. At this period very great *seigneurs*, such, for instance, as Admiral de Coligny, occupied three rooms, and their suites lived at some neighboring inn. There were not, in those days, more than fifty private mansions in Paris, and those were fifty palaces belonging to sovereign princes, or to great vassals, whose way of living was superior to that of the greatest German rulers, such as the Duke of Bavaria and the Elector of Saxony.

The kitchen of the Lecamus family was beneath the back-shop and looked out upon the river. It had a glass door opening upon a sort of iron balcony, from which the cook drew up water in a bucket, and where the household washing was done. The back-shop was made the dining-room, office, and salon of the merchant. In this important room (in all such houses richly panelled and adorned with some special work of art, and also a carved chest) the life of the merchant was passed; there the joyous suppers after the work of the day was over, there the secret conferences on the political interests of the burghers and of royalty took place. The formidable corporations of Paris were at that time able to arm a hundred thousand men. Therefore the opinions of the merchants were backed by their servants, their clerks, their apprentices, their workmen. The burghers had a chief in the "provost of the merchants" who commanded them, and in the Hotel de Ville, a palace where they possessed the right to assemble. In the famous "burghers' parlor" their solemn deliberations took place. Had it not been for the continual sacrifices which by that time made war intolerable to the corporations, who were weary of their losses and of the famine, Henri IV., that factionist who became king, might never perhaps have entered Paris.

Every one can now picture to himself the appearance of this corner of old Paris, where the bridge and quai still are, where the trees of the quai aux Fleurs now stand, but where no trace remains of the period of which we write except the tall and famous tower of the Palais de Justice, from which the signal was given for the Saint Bartholomew. Strange circumstance! one of the houses standing at the foot of that tower then surrounded by wooden shops, that, namely, of Lecamus, was about to witness the birth of facts which were destined to prepare for that night of massacre, which was, unhappily, more favorable than fatal to Calvinism.

At the moment when our history begins, the audacity of the new religious doctrines was putting all Paris in a ferment. A Scotchman named Stuart had just assassinated President Minard, the member of the Parliament to whom public opinion attributed the largest share in the execution of Councillor Anne du Bourg; who was burned on the place de Greve after the king's tailor—to whom Henri II. and Diane de Poitiers had caused the torture of the "question" to be applied in their very presence. Paris was so closely watched that the archers compelled all passers along the street to pray before the shrines of the Madonna so as to discover heretics by their unwillingness or even refusal to do an act contrary to their beliefs.

The two archers who were stationed at the corner of the Lecamus house had departed, and Cristophe, son of the furrier, vehemently suspected of deserting Catholicism, was able to leave the shop without fear of being made to adore the Virgin. By seven in the evening, in April, 1560, darkness was already falling, and the apprentices, seeing no signs of customers on either side of the arcade, were beginning to take in the merchandise exposed as samples beneath the pillars, in order to close the shop. Christophe Lecamus, an ardent young man about twenty-two years old, was standing on the sill of the shop-door, apparently watching the apprentices.

"Monsieur," said one of them, addressing Christophe and pointing to a man who was walking to and fro under the gallery with an air of indecision, "perhaps that's a thief or a spy; anyhow, the shabby wretch can't be an honest man; if he wanted to speak to us he would come over frankly, instead of sidling along as he does—and what a face!" continued the apprentice, mimicking the man, "with his nose in his cloak, his yellow eyes, and that famished look!"

When the stranger thus described caught sight of Christophe alone on the door-sill, he suddenly left the opposite gallery where he was then walking, crossed the street rapidly, and came under the arcade in front of the Lecamus house. There he passed slowly along in front of the shop, and before the apprentices returned to close the outer shutters he said to Christophe in a low voice:—

"I am Chaudieu."

Hearing the name of one of the most illustrious ministers and devoted actors in the terrible drama called "The Reformation," Christophe quivered as a faithful peasant might have quivered on recognizing his disguised king.

"Perhaps you would like to see some furs? Though it is almost dark I will show you some myself," said Christophe, wishing to throw the apprentices, whom he heard behind him, off the scent.

With a wave of his hand he invited the minister to enter the shop, but the latter replied that he preferred to converse outside. Christophe then fetched his cap and followed the disciple of Calvin.

Though banished by an edict, Chaudieu, the secret envoy of Theodore de Beze and Calvin (who were directing the French Reformation from Geneva), went and came, risking the cruel punishment to which the Parliament, in unison with the Church and Royalty, had condemned one of their number, the celebrated Anne du Bourg, in order to make a terrible example. Chaudieu, whose brother was a captain and one of Admiral Coligny's best soldiers, was a powerful auxiliary by whose arm Calvin shook France at the beginning of the twenty two years of religious warfare now on the point of breaking out. This minister was one of the hidden wheels whose movements can best exhibit the wide-spread action of the Reform.

Chaudieu led Christophe to the water's edge through an underground passage, which was like that of the Marion tunnel filled up by the authorities about ten years ago. This passage, which was situated between the Lecamus house and the one adjoining it, ran under the rue de la Vieille-Pelleterie, and was called the Pont-aux-Fourreurs. It was used by the dyers of the City to go to the river and wash their flax and silks, and other stuffs. A little boat was at the entrance of it, rowed by a single sailor. In the bow was a man unknown to Christophe, a man of low stature and very simply dressed. Chaudieu and Christophe entered the boat, which in a moment was in the middle of the Seine; the sailor then directed its course beneath one of the wooden arches of the pont au Change, where he tied up quickly to an iron ring. As yet, no one had said a word.

"Here we can speak without fear; there are no traitors or spies here," said Chaudieu, looking at the two as yet unnamed men. Then, turning an ardent face to Christophe, "Are you," he said, "full of that devotion that should animate a martyr? Are you ready to endure all for our sacred cause? Do you fear the tortures applied to the Councillor du Bourg, to the king's tailor,—tortures which await the majority of us?"

"I shall confess the gospel," replied Lecamus, simply, looking at the windows of his father's back-shop.

The family lamp, standing on the table where his father was making up his books for the day, spoke to him, no doubt, of the joys of family and the peaceful existence which he now renounced. The vision was rapid, but complete. His mind took in, at a glance, the burgher quarter full of its own harmonies, where his happy childhood had been spent, where lived his promised bride, Babette Lallier, where all things promised him a sweet and full existence; he saw the past; he saw the future, and he sacrificed it, or, at any rate, he staked it all. Such were the men of that day.

"We need ask no more," said the impetuous sailor; "we know him for one of our *saints*. If the Scotchman had not done the deed he would kill us that infamous Minard."

"Yes," said Lecamus, "my life belongs to the church; I shall give it with joy for the triumph of the Reformation, on which I have seriously reflected. I know that what we do is for the happiness of the peoples. In two words: Popery drives to celibacy, the Reformation establishes the family. It is time to rid France of her monks, to restore their lands to the Crown, who will, sooner or later, sell them to the burghers. Let us learn to die for our children, and make our families some day free and prosperous."

The face of the young enthusiast, that of Chaudieu, that of the sailor, that of the stranger seated in the bow, lighted by the last gleams of the twilight, formed a picture which ought the more to be described because the description contains in itself the whole history of the times—if it is, indeed, true that to certain men it is given to sum up in their own persons the spirit of their age.

The religious reform undertaken by Luther in Germany, John Knox in Scotland, Calvin in France, took hold especially of those minds in the lower classes into which thought had penetrated. The great lords sustained the movement only to serve interests that were foreign to the religious cause. To these two classes were added adventurers, ruined noblemen, younger sons, to whom all troubles were equally acceptable. But among the artisan and merchant classes the new faith was sincere and based on calculation. The masses of the poorer people adhered at once to a religion which gave the ecclesiastical property to the State, and deprived the dignitaries of the Church of their enormous revenues. Commerce everywhere reckoned up the profits of this religious operation, and devoted itself body, soul, and purse, to the cause.

But among the young men of the French bourgeoisie the Protestant movement found that noble inclination to sacrifices of all kinds which inspires youth, to which selfishness is, as yet, unknown. Eminent men, sagacious minds, discerned the Republic in the Reformation; they desired to establish throughout Europe the government of the United Provinces, which ended by triumphing over the greatest Power of those times,—Spain, under Philip the Second, represented in the Low

Countries by the Duke of Alba. Jean Hotoman was then meditating his famous book, in which this project is put forth,—a book which spread throughout France the leaven of these ideas, which were stirred up anew by the Ligue, repressed by Richelieu, then by Louis XIV., always protected by the younger branches, by the house of Orleans in 1789, as by the house of Bourbon in 1589. Whoso says "Investigate" says "Revolt." All revolt is either the cloak that hides a prince, or the swaddling-clothes of a new mastery. The house of Bourbon, the younger sons of the Valois, were at work beneath the surface of the Reformation.

At the moment when the little boat floated beneath the arch of the pont au Change the question was strangely complicated by the ambitions of the Guises, who were rivalling the Bourbons. Thus the Crown, represented by Catherine de' Medici, was able to sustain the struggle for thirty years by pitting the one house against the other house; whereas later, the Crown, instead of standing between various jealous ambitions, found itself without a barrier, face to face with the people: Richelieu and Louis XIV. had broken down the barrier of the Nobility; Louis XV. had broken down that of the Parliaments. Alone before the people, as Louis XVI. was, a king must inevitably succumb.

Christophe Lecamus was a fine representative of the ardent and devoted portion of the people. His wan face had the sharp hectic tones which distinguish certain fair complexions; his hair was yellow, of a coppery shade; his gray-blue eyes were sparkling. In them alone was his fine soul visible; for his ill-proportioned face did not atone for its triangular shape by the noble mien of an elevated mind, and his low forehead indicated only extreme energy. Life seemed to centre in his chest, which was rather hollow. More nervous than sanguine, Cristophe's bodily appearance was thin and threadlike, but wiry. His pointed noise expressed the shrewdness of the people, and his countenance revealed an intelligence capable of conducting itself well on a single point of the circumference, without having the faculty of seeing all around it. His eyes, the arching brows of which, scarcely covered with a whitish down, projected like an awning, were strongly circled by a pale-blue band, the skin being white and shining at the spring of the nose,—a sign which almost always denotes excessive enthusiasm. Christophe was of the people,—the people who devote themselves, who fight for their devotions, who let themselves be inveigled and betrayed; intelligent enough to comprehend and serve an idea, too upright to turn it to his own account, too noble to sell himself.

Contrasting with this son of Lecamus, Chaudieu, the ardent minister, with brown hair thinned by vigils, a yellow skin, an eloquent mouth, a militant brow, with flaming brown eyes, and a short and prominent chin, embodied well the Christian faith which brought to the Reformation so many sincere and fanatical pastors, whose courage and spirit aroused the populations. The aide-de-camp of Calvin and Theodore de Beze contrasted admirably with the son of the furrier. He represented the fiery cause of which the effect was seen in Christophe.

The sailor, an impetuous being, tanned by the open air, accustomed to dewy nights and burning days, with closed lips, hasty gestures, orange eyes, ravenous as those of a vulture, and black, frizzled hair, was the embodiment of an adventurer who risks all in a venture, as a gambler stakes all on a card. His whole appearance revealed terrific passions, and an audacity that flinched at nothing. His vigorous muscles were made to be quiescent as well as to act. His manner was more audacious than noble. His nose, though thin, turned up and snuffed battle. He seemed agile and capable. You would have known him in all ages for the leader of a party. If he were not of the Reformation, he might have been Pizarro, Fernando Cortez, or Morgan the Exterminator,—a man of violent action of some kind.

The fourth man, sitting on a thwart wrapped in his cloak, belonged, evidently, to the highest portion of society. The fineness of his linen, its cut, the material and scent of his clothing, the style and skin of his gloves, showed him to be a man of courts, just as his bearing, his haughtiness, his composure and his all-embracing glance proved him to be a man of war. The aspect of this personage made a spectator uneasy in the first place, and then inclined him to respect. We respect a man who respects himself. Though short and deformed, his manners instantly redeemed the disadvantages of his figure. The ice once broken, he showed a lively rapidity of decision, with an indefinable dash and fire which made him seem affable and winning. He had the blue eyes and the curved nose of the house of Navarre, and the Spanish cut of the marked features which were in after days the type of the Bourbon kings.

In a word, the scene now assumed a startling interest.

"Well," said Chaudieu, as young Lecamus ended his speech, "this boatman is La Renaudie. And here is Monsiegneur the Prince de Conde," he added, motioning to the deformed little man.

Thus these four men represented the faith of the people, the spirit of the Scriptures, the mailed hand of the soldier, and royalty itself hidden in that dark shadow of the bridge.

"You shall now know what we expect of you," resumed the minister, after allowing a short pause for Christophe's astonishment. "In order that you may make no mistake, we feel obliged to initiate you into the most important secrets of the Reformation."

The prince and La Renaudie emphasized the minister's speech by a gesture, the latter having paused to allow the prince to speak, if he so wished. Like all great men engaged in plotting, whose system it is to conceal their hand until the decisive moment, the prince kept silence— but not from cowardice. In these crises he was always the soul of the conspiracy; recoiling from no danger and ready to risk his own head; but from a sort of royal dignity he left the explanation of the enterprise to his minister, and contented himself with studying the new instrument he was about to use.

"My child," said Chaudieu, in the Huguenot style of address, "we are about to do battle for the first time with the Roman prostitute. In a few days either our legions will be dying on the scaffold, or the Guises will be dead. This is the first call to arms on behalf of our religion in France, and France will not lay down those arms till they have conquered. The question, mark you this, concerns the nation, not the kingdom. The majority of the nobles of the kingdom see plainly what the Cardinal de Lorraine and his brother are seeking. Under pretext of defending the Catholic religion, the house of Lorraine means to claim the crown of France as its patrimony. Relying on the Church, it has made the Church a formidable ally; the monks are its support, its acolytes, its spies. It has assumed the post of guardian to the throne it is seeking to usurp; it protects the house of Valois which it means to destroy. We have decided to take up arms because the liberties of the people and the interests of the nobles are equally threatened. Let us smother at its birth a faction as odious as that of the Burgundians who formerly put Paris and all France to fire and sword. It required a Louis XI. to put a stop to the quarrel between the Burgundians and the Crown; and to-day a prince de Conde is needed to prevent the house of Lorraine from re-attempting that struggle. This is not a civil war; it is a duel between the Guises and the Reformation,—a duel to the death! We will make their heads fall, or they shall have ours."

"Well said!" cried the prince.

"In this crisis, Christophe," said La Renaudie, "we mean to neglect nothing which shall strengthen our party,—for there is a party in the Reformation, the party of thwarted interests, of nobles sacrificed to the Lorrains, of old captains shamefully treated at Fontainebleau, from which the cardinal has banished them by setting up gibbets on which to hang those who ask the king for the cost of their equipment and their back-pay."

"This, my child," resumed Chaudieu, observing a sort of terror in Christophe, "this it is which compels us to conquer by arms instead of conquering by conviction and by martyrdom. The queen-mother is on the point of entering into our views. Not that she means to abjure; she has not reached that decision as yet; but she may be forced to it by our triumph. However that may be, Queen Catherine, humiliated and in despair at seeing the power she expected to wield on the death of the king passing into the hands of the Guises, alarmed at the empire of the young queen, Mary, niece of the Lorrains and their auxiliary, Queen Catherine is doubtless inclined to lend her support to the princes and lords who are now about to make an attempt which will deliver her from the Guises. At this moment, devoted as she may seem to them, she hates them; she desires their overthrow, and will try to make use of us against them; but Monseigneur the Prince de Conde intends to make use of her against all. The queen-mother will, undoubtedly, consent to all our plans. We shall have the Connetable on our side; Monseigneur has just been to see him at Chantilly; but he does not wish to move without an order from his masters. Being the uncle of Monseigneur, he will not leave him in the lurch; and this generous prince does not hesitate to fling himself into danger to force Anne de Montmorency to a decision. All is prepared, and we have cast our eyes on you as the means of communicating to Queen Catherine our treaty of alliance, the drafts of edicts, and the bases of the new government. The court is at Blois. Many of our friends are with it; but they are to be our future chiefs, and, like Monseigneur," he added, motioning to the prince, "they must not be suspected. The queen-mother and our friends are so closely watched that it is impossible to employ as intermediary any known person of importance; they would instantly be suspected and kept from communicating with Madame Catherine. God sends us at this crisis the shepherd David and his sling to do battle with Goliath of Guise. Your father, unfortunately for him a good Catholic, is furrier to the two queens. He is constantly supplying them with garments. Get him to send you on some errand to the court. You will excite no suspicion, and you cannot compromise Queen Catherine in any way. All our leaders would lose their heads if a single imprudent act allowed their connivance with the queen-mother to be seen. Where a great lord, if discovered, would give the alarm and destroy our chances, an insignificant man like you will pass unnoticed. See! The Guises keep the town so full of spies that we have only the river where we can talk without fear. You are now, my son, like a sentinel who must die at his post. Remember this: if you are discovered, we shall all abandon you; we shall even cast, if necessary, opprobrium and infamy upon you. We shall say that you are a creature of the Guises, made to play this part to ruin us. You see therefore that we ask of you a total sacrifice."

"If you perish," said the Prince de Conde, "I pledge my honor as a noble that your family shall be sacred for the house of Navarre; I will bear it on my heart and serve it in all things."

"Those words, my prince, suffice," replied Christophe, without reflecting that the conspirator was a Gascon. "We live in times when each man, prince or burgher, must do his duty."

"There speaks the true Huguenot. If all our men were like that," said La Renaudie, laying his hand on Christophe's shoulder, "we should be conquerors to-morrow."

"Young man," resumed the prince, "I desire to show you that if Chaudieu preaches, if the nobleman goes armed, the prince fights. Therefore, in this hot game all stakes are played."

"Now listen to me," said La Renaudie. "I will not give you the papers until you reach Beaugency; for they must not be risked during the whole of your journey. You will find me waiting for you there on the wharf; my face, voice, and clothes will be so changed you cannot recognize me, but I shall say to you, 'Are you a *guepin*?' and you will answer, 'Ready to serve.' As to the performance of your mission, these are the means: You will find a horse at the 'Pinte Fleurie,' close to Saint-Germain l'Auxerrois. You will there ask for Jean le Breton, who will take you to the stable and give you one of my ponies which is known to do thirty leagues in eight hours. Leave by the gate of Bussy. Breton has a pass for me; use it yourself, and make your way by skirting the towns. You can thus reach Orleans by daybreak."

"But the horse?" said young Lecamus.

"He will not give out till you reach Orleans," replied La Renaudie. "Leave him at the entrance of the faubourg Bannier; for the gates are well guarded, and you must not excite suspicion. It is for you, friend, to play your part intelligently. You must invent whatever fable seems to you best to reach the third house to the left on entering Orleans; it belongs to a certain Tourillon, glove-maker. Strike three blows on the door, and call out: 'On service from Messieurs de Guise!' The man will appear to be a rabid Guisist; no one knows but our four selves that he is one of us. He will give you a faithful boatman,—another Guisist of his own cut. Go down at once to the wharf, and embark in a boat painted green and edged with white. You will doubtless land at Beaugency to-morrow about mid-day. There I will arrange to find you a boat which will take you to Blois without running any risk. Our enemies the Guises do not watch the rivers, only the landings. Thus you will be able to see the queen-mother to-morrow or the day after."

"Your words are written there," said Christophe, touching his forehead.

Chaudieu embraced his child with singular religious effusion; he was proud of him.

"God keep thee!" he said, pointing to the ruddy light of the sinking sun, which was touching the old roofs covered with shingles and sending its gleams slantwise through the forest of piles among which the water was rippling.

"You belong to the race of the Jacques Bonhomme," said La Renaudie, pressing Christophe's hand.

"We shall meet again, *monsieur*," said the prince, with a gesture of infinite grace, in which there was something that seemed almost friendship.

With a stroke of his oars La Renaudie put the boat at the lower step of the stairway which led to the house. Christophe landed, and the boat disappeared instantly beneath the arches of the pont au Change.

II. THE BURGHERS

Christophe shook the iron railing which closed the stairway on the river, and called. His mother heard him, opened one of the windows of the back shop, and asked what he was doing there. Christophe answered that he was cold and wanted to get in.

"Ha! my master," said the Burgundian maid, "you went out by the street-door, and you return by the water-gate. Your father will be fine and angry."

Christophe, bewildered by a confidence which had just brought him into communication with the Prince de Conde, La Renaudie, and Chaudieu, and still more moved at the prospect of impending civil war, made no answer; he ran hastily up from the kitchen to the back shop; but his mother, a rabid Catholic, could not control her anger.

"I'll wager those three men I saw you talking with are Ref—"

"Hold your tongue, wife!" said the cautious old man with white hair who was turning over a thick ledger. "You dawdling fellows," he went on, addressing three journeymen, who had long finished their suppers, "why don't you go to bed? It is eight o'clock, and you have to be up at five; besides, you must carry home to-night President de Thou's cap and mantle. All three of you had better go, and take your sticks and rapiers; and then, if you meet scamps like yourselves, at least you'll be in force."

"Are we going to take the ermine surcoat the young queen has ordered to be sent to the hotel des Soissons? there's an express going from there to Blois for the queen-mother," said one of the clerks.

"No," said his master, "the queen-mother's bill amounts to three thousand crowns; it is time to get the money, and I am going to Blois myself very soon."

"Father, I do not think it right at your age and in these dangerous times to expose yourself on the high-roads. I am twenty-two years old, and you ought to employ me on such errands," said Christophe, eyeing the box which he supposed contained the surcoat.

"Are you glued to your seats?" cried the old man to his apprentices, who at once jumped up and seized their rapiers, cloaks, and Monsieur de Thou's furs.

The next day the Parliament was to receive in state, as its president, this illustrious judge, who, after signing the death warrant of Councillor du Bourg, was destined before the close of the year to sit in judgment on the Prince de Conde!

"Here!" said the old man, calling to the maid, "go and ask friend Lallier if he will come and sup with us and bring the wine; we'll furnish the victuals. Tell him, above all, to bring his daughter."

Lecamus, the syndic of the guild of furriers, was a handsome old man of sixty, with white hair, and a broad, open brow. As court furrier for the last forty years, he had witnessed all the revolutions of the reign of Francois I. He had seen the arrival at the French court of the young girl Catherine de' Medici, then scarcely fifteen years of age. He had observed her giving way before the Duchesse d'Etampes, her father-in-law's mistress; giving way before the Duchesse de Valentinois, the mistress of her husband the late king. But the furrier had brought himself safely through all the chances and changes by which court merchants were often involved in the disgrace and overthrow of mistresses. His caution led to his good luck. He maintained an attitude of extreme humility. Pride had never caught him in its toils. He made himself so small, so gentle, so compliant, of so little account at court and before the queens and princesses and favorites, that this modesty, combined with good-humor, had kept the royal sign above his door.

Such a policy was, of course, indicative of a shrewd and perspicacious mind. Humble as Lecamus seemed to the outer world, he was despotic in his own home; there he was an autocrat. Most respected and honored by his brother craftsmen, he owed to his long possession of the first place in the trade much of the consideration that was shown to him. He was, besides, very willing to do kindnesses to others, and among the many services he had rendered, none was more striking than the assistance he had long given to the greatest surgeon of the sixteenth century, Ambroise Pare, who owed to him the possibility of studying for his profession. In all the difficulties which came up among the merchants Lecamus was always conciliating. Thus a general good opinion of him consolidated his position among his equals; while his borrowed characteristics kept him steadily in favor with the court.

Not only this, but having intrigued for the honor of being on the vestry of his parish church, he did what was necessary to bring him into the odor of sanctity with the rector of Saint-Pierre aux Boeufs, who looked upon him as one of the men most devoted to the Catholic religion in Paris. Consequently, at the time of the convocation of the States-General he was unanimously elected to represent the *tiers etat* through the influence of the clergy of Paris,—an influence which at that period was immense. This old man was, in short, one of those secretly ambitious souls who will bend for fifty years before all the world, gliding from office to office, no one exactly knowing how it came about that he was found securely and peacefully seated at last where no man, even the boldest, would have had the ambition at the beginning of life to fancy himself; so great was the distance, so many the gulfs and the precipices to cross! Lecamus, who had immense concealed wealth, would not run any risks, and was silently preparing a brilliant future for his son. Instead of having the personal ambition which sacrifices the future to the present, he had family ambition,—a lost sentiment in our time, a sentiment suppressed by the folly of our laws of inheritance. Lecamus saw himself first president of the Parliament of Paris in the person of his grandson.

Christophe, godson of the famous historian de Thou, was given a most solid education; but it had led him to doubt and to the spirit of examination which was then affecting both the Faculties and the students of the universities. Christophe was, at the period of which we are now writing, pursuing his studies for the bar, that first step toward the magistracy. The old furrier was pretending to some hesitation as to his son. Sometimes he seemed to wish to make Christophe his successor; then again he spoke of him as a lawyer; but in his heart he was ambitious of a place for this son as Councillor of the Parliament. He wanted to put the Lecamus family on a level with those old and celebrated burgher families from which came the Pasquiers, the Moles, the Mirons, the Seguiers, Lamoignon, du Tillet, Lecoigneux, Lescalopier, Goix, Arnauld, those famous sheriffs and grand-provosts of the merchants, among whom the throne found such strong defenders.

Therefore, in order that Christophe might in due course of time maintain his rank, he wished to marry him to the daughter of the richest jeweller in the city, his friend Lallier, whose nephew was destined to present to Henri IV. the keys of Paris. The strongest desire rooted in the heart of the worthy burgher was to use half of his fortune and half of that of the jeweller in the purchase of a large and beautiful seignorial estate, which, in those days, was a long and very difficult affair. But his shrewd mind knew the age in which he lived too well to be ignorant of the great movements which were now in preparation. He saw clearly, and he saw justly, and knew that the kingdom was about to be divided into two camps. The useless executions in the Place de l'Estrapade, that of the king's tailor and the more recent one of the Councillor Anne du Bourg, the actual connivance of the great lords, and that of the favorite of Francois I. with the Reformers, were terrible indications. The furrier resolved to remain, whatever happened, Catholic, royalist, and parliamentarian; but it suited him, privately, that Christophe should belong to the Reformation. He knew he was rich enough to ransom his son if Christophe was too much compromised; and on the other hand if France became Calvinist his son could save the family in the event of one of those furious Parisian riots, the memory of which was ever-living with the bourgeoisie,—riots they were destined to see renewed through four reigns.

But these thoughts the old furrier, like Louis XI., did not even say to himself; his wariness went so far as to deceive his wife and son. This grave personage had long been the chief man of the richest and most populous quarter of Paris, that of the centre, under the title of *quartenier*,—the title and office which became so celebrated some fifteen months later. Clothed in cloth like all the prudent burghers who obeyed the sumptuary laws, Sieur Lecamus (he was tenacious of that title which Charles V. granted to the burghers of Paris, permitting them also to buy baronial estates and call their wives by the fine name of *demoiselle*, but not by that of madame) wore neither gold chains nor silk, but always a good doublet with large tarnished silver buttons, cloth gaiters mounting to the knee, and leather shoes with clasps. His shirt, of fine linen, showed, according to the fashion of the time, in great puffs between his half-opened jacket and his breeches. Though his large and handsome face received the full light of the lamp standing on the table, Christophe had no conception of the thoughts which lay buried beneath the rich and florid Dutch skin of the old man; but he understood well enough the advantage he himself had expected to obtain from his affection for pretty Babette Lallier. So Christophe, with the air of a man who had come to a decision, smiled bitterly as he heard of the invitation to his promised bride.

When the Burgundian cook and the apprentices had departed on their several errands, old Lecamus looked at his wife with a glance which showed the firmness and resolution of his character.

"You will not be satisfied till you have got that boy hanged with your damned tongue," he said, in a stern voice.

"I would rather see him hanged and saved than living and a Huguenot," she answered, gloomily. "To think that a child whom I carried nine months in my womb should be a bad Catholic, and be doomed to hell for all eternity!"

She began to weep.

"Old silly," said the furrier; "let him live, if only to convert him. You said, before the apprentices, a word which may set fire to our house, and roast us all, like fleas in a straw bed."

The mother crossed herself, and sat down silently.

"Now, then, you," said the old man, with a judicial glance at his son, "explain to me what you were doing on the river with—come closer, that I may speak to you," he added, grasping his son by the arm, and drawing him to him—"with the Prince de Conde," he whispered. Christophe trembled. "Do you suppose the court furrier does not know every face that frequents the palace? Think you I am ignorant of what is going on? Monseigneur the Grand Master has been giving orders to send troops to Amboise. Withdrawing troops from Paris to send them to Amboise when the king is at Blois, and making them march through Chartres and Vendome, instead of going by Orleans—isn't the meaning of that clear enough? There'll be troubles. If the queens want their surcoats, they must send for them. The Prince de Conde has perhaps made up his mind to kill Messieurs de Guise; who, on their side, expect to rid themselves of him. The prince will use the Huguenots to protect himself. Why should the son of a furrier get himself into that fray? When you are married, and when you are councillor to the Parliament, you will be as prudent as your father. Before belonging to the new religion, the son of a furrier ought to wait until the rest of the world belongs to it. I don't condemn the Reformers; it is not my business to do so; but the court is Catholic, the two queens are Catholic, the Parliament is Catholic; we must supply them with furs, and therefore we must be Catholic ourselves. You shall not go out from here, Christophe; if you do, I will send you to your godfather, President de Thou, who will keep you night and day blackening paper, instead of blackening your soul in company with those damned Genevese."

"Father," said Christophe, leaning upon the back of the old man's chair, "send me to Blois to carry that surcoat to Queen Mary and get our money from the queen-mother. If you do not, I am lost; and you care for your son."

"Lost?" repeated the old man, without showing the least surprise. "If you stay here you can't be lost; I shall have my eye on you all the time."

"They will kill me here."

"Why?"

"The most powerful among the Huguenots have cast their eyes on me to serve them in a certain matter; if I fail to do what I have just promised to do, they will kill me in open day, here in the street, as they killed Minard. But if you send me to court on your affairs, perhaps I can justify myself equally well to both sides. Either I shall succeed without having run any danger at all, and shall then win a fine position in the party; or, if the danger turns out very great, I shall be there simply on your business."

The father rose as if his chair was of red-hot iron.

"Wife," he said, "leave us; and watch that we are left quite alone, Christophe and I."

When Mademoiselle Lecamus had left them the furrier took his son by a button and led him to the corner of the room which made the angle of the bridge.

"Christophe," he said, whispering in his ear as he had done when he mentioned the name of the Prince of Conde, "be a Huguenot, if you have that vice; but be so cautiously, in the depths of your soul, and not in a way to be pointed at as a heretic throughout the quarter. What you have just confessed to me shows that the leaders have confidence in you. What are you going to do for them at court?"

"I cannot tell you that," replied Christophe; "for I do not know myself."

"Hum! hum!" muttered the old man, looking at his son, "the scamp means to hoodwink his father; he'll go far. You are not going to court," he went on in a low tone, "to carry remittances to Messieurs de Guise or to the little king our master, or to the little Queen Marie. All those hearts are Catholic; but I would take my oath the Italian woman has some spite against the Scotch girl and against the Lorrains. I know her. She has a desperate desire to put her hand into the dough. The late king was so afraid of her that he did as the jewellers do, he cut diamond by diamond, he pitted one woman against another. That caused Queen Catherine's hatred to the poor Duchesse de Valentinois, from whom she took the beautiful chateau of Chenonceaux. If it hadn't been for the Connetable, the duchess might have been strangled. Back, back, my son; don't put yourself in the hands of that Italian, who has no passion except in her brain; and that's a bad kind of woman! Yes, what they are sending you to do at court may give you a very bad headache," cried the father, seeing that Christophe was about to reply. "My son, I have plans for your future which you will not upset by making yourself useful to Queen Catherine; but, heavens and earth! don't risk your head. Messieurs de Guise would cut it off as easily as the Burgundian cuts a turnip, and then those persons who are now employing you will disown you utterly."

"I know that, father," said Christophe.

"What! are you really so strong, my son? You know it, and are willing to risk all?"

"Yes, father."

"By the powers above us!" cried the father, pressing his son in his arms, "we can understand each other; you are worthy of your father. My child, you'll be the honor of the family, and I see that your old father can speak plainly with you. But do not be more Huguenot than Messieurs de Coligny. Never draw your sword; be a pen man; keep to your future role of lawyer. Now, then, tell me nothing until after you have succeeded. If I do not hear from you by the fourth day after you reach Blois, that silence will tell me that you are in some danger. The old man will go to save the young one. I have not sold furs for thirty-two years without a good knowledge of the wrong side of court robes. I have the means of making my way through many doors."

Christophe opened his eyes very wide as he heard his father talking thus; but he thought there might be some parental trap in it, and he made no reply further than to say:—

"Well, make out the bill, and write a letter to the queen; I must start at once, or the greatest misfortunes may happen."

"Start? How?"

"I shall buy a horse. Write at once, in God's name."

"Hey! mother! give your son some money," cried the furrier to his wife.

The mother returned, went to her chest, took out a purse of gold, and gave it to Christophe, who kissed her with emotion.

"The bill was all ready," said his father; "here it is. I will write the letter at once."

Christophe took the bill and put it in his pocket.

"But you will sup with us, at any rate," said the old man. "In such a crisis you ought to exchange rings with Lallier's daughter."

"Very well, I will go and fetch her," said Christophe.

The young man was distrustful of his father's stability in the matter. The old man's character was not yet fully known to him. He ran up to his room, dressed himself, took a valise, came downstairs softly and laid it on a counter in the shop, together with his rapier and cloak.

"What the devil are you doing?" asked his father, hearing him.

Christophe came up to the old man and kissed him on both cheeks.

"I don't want any one to see my preparations for departure, and I have put them on a counter in the shop," he whispered.

"Here is the letter," said his father.

Christophe took the paper and went out as if to fetch his young neighbor.

A few moments after his departure the goodman Lallier and his daughter arrived, preceded by a servant-woman, bearing three bottles of old wine.

"Well, where is Christophe?" said old Lecamus.

"Christophe!" exclaimed Babette. "We have not seen him."

"Ha! ha! my son is a bold scamp! He tricks me as if I had no beard. My dear crony, what think you he will turn out to be? We live in days when the children have more sense than their fathers."

"Why, the quarter has long been saying he is in some mischief," said Lallier.

"Excuse him on that point, crony," said the furrier. "Youth is foolish; it runs after new things; but Babette will keep him quiet; she is newer than Calvin."

Babette smiled; she loved Christophe, and was angry when anything was said against him. She was one of those daughters of the old bourgeoisie brought up under the eyes of a mother who never left her. Her bearing was gentle and correct as her face; she always wore woollen stuffs of gray, harmonious in tone; her chemisette, simply pleated, contrasted its whiteness against the gown. Her cap of brown velvet was like an infant's coif, but it was trimmed with a ruche and lappets of tanned gauze, that is, of a tan color, which came down on each side of her face. Though fair and white as a true blonde, she seemed to be shrewd and roguish, all the while trying to hide her roguishness under the air and manner of a well-trained girl. While the two servant-women went and came, laying the cloth and placing the jugs, the great pewter dishes, and the knives and forks, the jeweller and his daughter, the furrier and his wife, sat before the tall chimney-piece draped with lambrequins of red serge and black fringes, and were talking of trifles. Babette asked once or twice where Christophe could be, and the father and mother of the young Huguenot gave evasive answers; but when the two families were seated at table, and the two servants had retired to the kitchen, Lecamus said to his future daughter-in-law:—

"Christophe has gone to court."

"To Blois! Such a journey as that without bidding me good-bye!" she said.

"The matter was pressing," said the old mother.

"Crony," said the furrier, resuming a suspended conversation. "We are going to have troublous times in France. The Reformers are bestirring themselves."

"If they triumph, it will only be after a long war, during which business will be at a standstill," said Lallier, incapable of rising higher than the commercial sphere.

"My father, who saw the wars between the Burgundians and the Armagnacs told me that our family would never have come out safely if one of his grandfathers—his mother's father—had not been a Goix, one of those famous butchers in the Market who stood by the Burgundians; whereas the other, the Lecamus, was for the Armagnacs; they seemed ready to flay each other alive before the world, but they were excellent friends in the family. So, let us both try to save Christophe; perhaps the time may come when he will save us."

"You are a shrewd one," said the jeweller.

"No," replied Lecamus. "The burghers ought to think of themselves; the populace and the nobility are both against them. The Parisian bourgeoisie alarms everybody except the king, who knows it is his friend."

"You who are so wise and have seen so many things," said Babette, timidly, "explain to me what the Reformers really want."

"Yes, tell us that, crony," cried the jeweller. "I knew the late king's tailor, and I held him to be a man of simple life, without great talent; he was something like you; a man to whom they'd give the sacrament without confession; and behold! he plunged to the depths of this new religion,— he! a man whose two ears were worth all of a hundred thousand crowns apiece. He must have had secrets to reveal to induce the king and the Duchesse de Valentinois to be present at his torture."

"And terrible secrets, too!" said the furrier. "The Reformation, my friends," he continued in a low voice, "will give back to the bourgeoisie the estates of the Church. When the ecclesiastical privileges are suppressed the Reformers intend to ask that the *vilain* shall be imposed on nobles as well as on burghers, and they mean to insist that the king alone shall be above others—if indeed, they allow the State to have a king."

"Suppress the Throne!" ejaculated Lallier.

"Hey! crony," said Lecamus, "in the Low Countries the burghers govern themselves with burgomasters of their own, who elect their own temporary head."

"God bless me, crony; we ought to do these fine things and yet stay Catholics," cried the jeweller.

"We are too old, you and I, to see the triumph of the Parisian bourgeoisie, but it will triumph, I tell you, in times to come as it did of yore. Ha! the king must rest upon it in order to resist, and we have always sold him our help dear. The last time, all the burghers were ennobled, and he gave them permission to buy seignorial estates and take titles from the land without special letters from the king. You and I, grandsons of the Goix through our mothers, are not we as good as any lord?"

These words were so alarming to the jeweller and the two women that they were followed by a dead silence. The ferments of 1789 were already tingling in the veins of Lecamus, who was not yet so old but what he could live to see the bold burghers of the Ligue.

"Are you selling well in spite of these troubles?" said Lallier to Mademoiselle Lecamus.

"Troubles always do harm," she replied.

"That's one reason why I am so set on making my son a lawyer," said

Lecamus; "for squabbles and law go on forever."

The conversation then turned to commonplace topics, to the great satisfaction of the jeweller, who was not fond of either political troubles or audacity of thought.

III. THE CHATEAU DE BLOIS

The banks of the Loire, from Blois to Angers, were the favorite resort of the last two branches of the royal race which occupied the throne before the house of Bourbon. That beautiful valley plain so well deserves the honor bestowed upon it by kings that we must here repeat what was said of it by one of our most eloquent writers:—

*"There is one province in France which is never sufficiently
admired. Fragrant as Italy, flowery as the banks of the
Guadalquivir, beautiful especially in its own characteristics,
wholly French, having always been French,—unlike in that respect
to our northern provinces, which have degenerated by contact with
Germany, and to our southern provinces, which have lived in
concubinage with Moors, Spaniards, and all other nationalities
that adjoined them. This pure, chaste, brave, and loyal province
is Touraine. Historic France is there! Auvergne is Auvergne,
Languedoc is only Languedoc; but Touraine is France; the most
national river for Frenchmen is the Loire, which waters Touraine.
For this reason we ought not to be surprised at the great number
of historically noble buildings possessed by those departments
which have taken the name, or derivations of the name, of the
Loire. At every step we take in this land of enchantment we
discover a new picture, bordered, it may be, by a river, or a
tranquil lake reflecting in its liquid depths a castle with
towers, and woods and sparkling waterfalls. It is quite natural
that in a region chosen by Royalty for its sojourn, where the
court was long established, great families and fortunes and
distinguished men should have settled and built palaces as grand
as themselves."*

But is it not incomprehensible that Royalty did not follow the advice indirectly given by Louis XI. to place the capital of the kingdom at Tours? There, without great expense, the Loire might have been made accessible for the merchant service, and also for vessels-of-war of light draught. There, too, the seat of government would have been safe from the dangers of invasion. Had this been done, the northern cities would not have required such vast sums of money spent to fortify them,—sums as vast as were those expended on the sumptuous glories of Versailles. If Louis XIV. had listened to Vauban, who wished to build his great palace at Mont Louis, between the Loire and the Cher, perhaps the revolution of 1789 might never have taken place.

These beautiful shores still bear the marks of royal tenderness. The chateaus of Chambord, Amboise, Blois, Chenonceaux, Chaumont, Plessis-les-Tours, all those which the mistresses of kings, financiers, and nobles built at Veretz, Azay-le-Rideau, Usse, Villandri, Valencay, Chanteloup, Duretal, some of which have disappeared, though most of them still remain, are admirable relics which remind us of the marvels of a period that is little understood by the literary sect of the Middle-agists.

Among all these chateaus, that of Blois, where the court was then staying, is one on which the magnificence of the houses of Orleans and of Valois has placed its brilliant sign-manual,—making it the most interesting of all for historians, archaeologists, and Catholics. It was at the time of which we write completely isolated. The town, enclosed by massive walls supported by towers, lay below the fortress,—for the chateau served, in fact, as fort and pleasure-house. Above the town, with its blue-tiled, crowded roofs extending then, as now, from the river to the crest of the hill which commands the right bank, lies a triangular plateau, bounded to the west by a streamlet, which in these days is of no importance, for it flows beneath the town; but in the fifteenth century, so say historians, it formed quite a deep ravine, of which there still remains a sunken road, almost an abyss, between the suburbs of the town and the chateau.

It was on this plateau, with a double exposure to the north and south, that the counts of Blois built, in the architecture of the twelfth century, a castle where the famous Thibault de Tircheur, Thibault le Vieux, and others held a celebrated court. In those days of pure fuedality, in which the king was merely *primus inter pares* (to use the fine expression of a king of Poland), the counts of Champagne, the counts of Blois, those of Anjou, the simple barons of Normandie, the dukes of Bretagne, lived with the splendor of sovereign princes and gave kings to the proudest kingdoms. The Plantagenets of Anjou, the Lusignans of Poitou, the Roberts of Normandie, maintained with a bold hand the royal races, and sometimes simple knights like du Glaicquin refused the purple, preferring the sword of a connetable.

When the Crown annexed the county of Blois to its domain, Louis XII., who had a liking for this residence (perhaps to escape Plessis of sinister memory), built at the back of the first building another building, facing east and west, which connected the chateau of the counts of Blois with the rest of the old structures, of which nothing now remains but the vast hall in which the States-general were held under Henri III.

Before he became enamoured of Chambord, Francois I. wished to complete the chateau of Blois by adding two other wings, which would have made the structure a perfect square. But Chambord weaned him from Blois, where he built only one wing, which in his time and that of his grandchildren was the only inhabited part of the chateau. This third building erected by Francois I. is more vast and far more decorated than the Louvre, the chateau of Henri II. It is in the style of architecture now called Renaissance, and presents the most fantastic features of that style. Therefore, at a period when a strict and jealous architecture ruled construction, when the Middle Ages were not even considered, at a time when literature was not as clearly welded to art as it is now, La Fontaine said of the chateau de Blois, in his hearty, good-humored way: "The part that Francois I. built, if looked at from the outside, pleased me better than all the rest; there I saw numbers of little galleries, little windows, little balconies, little ornamentations without order or regularity, and they make up a grand whole which I like."

The chateau of Blois had, therefore, the merit of representing three orders of architecture, three epochs, three systems, three dominions. Perhaps there is no other royal residence that can compare with it in that respect. This immense structure presents to the eye in one enclosure, round one courtyard, a complete and perfect image of that grand presentation of the manners and customs and life of nations which is called Architecture. At the moment when Christophe was to visit the court, that part of the adjacent land which in our day is covered by a fourth palace, built seventy years later (by Gaston, the rebellious brother of Louis XIII., then exiled to Blois), was an open space containing pleasure-grounds and hanging gardens, picturesquely placed among the battlements and unfinished turrets of Francois I.'s chateau.

These gardens communicated, by a bridge of a fine, bold construction (which the old men of Blois may still remember to have seen demolished) with a pleasure-ground on the other side of the chateau, which, by the lay of the land, was on the same level. The nobles attached to the Court of Anne de Bretagne, or those of that province who came to solicit favors, or to confer with the queen as to the fate and condition of Brittany, awaited in this pleasure-ground the opportunity for an audience, either at the queen's rising, or at her coming out to walk. Consequently, history has given the name of "Perchoir aux Bretons" to this piece of ground, which, in our day, is the fruit-garden of a worthy bourgeois, and forms a projection into the place des Jesuites. The latter place was included in the gardens of this beautiful royal residence, which had, as we have said, its upper and its lower gardens. Not far from the place des Jesuites may still be seen a pavilion built by Catherine de' Medici, where, according to the historians of Blois, warm mineral baths were placed for her to use. This detail enables us to trace the very irregular disposition of the gardens, which went up or down according to the undulations of the ground, becoming extremely intricate around the chateau,—a fact which helped to give it strength, and caused, as we shall see, the discomfiture of the Duc de Guise.

The gardens were reached from the chateau through external and internal galleries, the most important of which was called the "Galerie des Cerfs" on account of its decoration. This gallery led to the magnificent staircase which, no doubt, inspired the famous double staircase of Chambord. It led, from floor to floor, to all the apartments of the castle.

Though La Fontaine preferred the chateau of Francois I. to that of Louis XII., perhaps the naivete of that of the good king will give true artists more pleasure, while at the same time they admire the magnificent structure of the knightly king. The elegance of the two staircases which are placed at each end of the chateau of Louis XII., the delicate carving and sculpture, so original in design, which abound everywhere, the remains of which, though time has done its worst, still charm the antiquary, all, even to the semi-cloistral distribution of the apartments, reveals a great simplicity of manners. Evidently, the *court* did not yet exist; it had not developed, as it did under Francois I. and Catherine de' Medici, to the great detriment of feudal customs. As we admire the galleries, or most of them, the capitals of the columns, and certain figurines of exquisite delicacy, it is impossible not to imagine that Michel Columb, that great sculptor, the Michel-Angelo of Brittany, passed that way for the pleasure of Queen Anne, whom he afterwards immortalized on the tomb of her father, the last duke of Brittany.

Whatever La Fontaine may choose to say about the "little galleries" and the "little ornamentations," nothing can be more grandiose than the dwelling of the splendid Francois. Thanks to I know not what indifference, to forgetfulness perhaps, the apartments occupied by Catherine de' Medici and her son Francois II. present to us to-day the leading features of that time. The historian can there restore the tragic scenes of the drama of the Reformation,—a drama in which the dual struggle of the Guises and of the Bourbons against the Valois was a series of most complicated acts, the plot of which was here unravelled.

The chateau of Francois I. completely crushes the artless habitation of Louis XII. by its imposing masses. On the side of the gardens, that is, toward the modern place des Jesuites, the castle presents an elevation nearly double that which it shows on the side of the courtyard. The ground-floor on this side forms the second floor on the side of the gardens, where are placed the celebrated galleries. Thus the first floor above the ground-floor toward the courtyard (where Queen Catherine was lodged) is the third floor on the garden side, and the king's apartments were four storeys above the garden, which at the time of which we write was separated from the base of the castle by a deep moat. The chateau, already colossal as viewed from the courtyard, appears gigantic when seen from below, as La Fontaine saw it. He mentions particularly that he did not enter either the courtyard or the apartments, and it is to be remarked that from the place des Jesuites all the details seem small. The balconies on which the courtiers promenaded; the galleries, marvellously executed; the sculptured windows, whose embrasures are so deep as to form boudoirs—for which indeed they served—resemble at that great height the fantastic decorations which scene-painters give to a fairy palace at the opera.

But in the courtyard, although the three storeys above the ground-floor rise as high as the clock-tower of the Tuileries, the infinite delicacy of the architecture reveals itself to the rapture of our astonished eyes. This wing of the great building, in which the two queens, Catherine de' Medici and Mary Stuart, held their sumptuous court, is divided in the centre by a hexagon tower, in the empty well of which winds up a spiral staircase,—a Moorish caprice, designed by giants, made by dwarfs, which gives to this wonderful facade the effect of a dream. The baluster of this staircase forms a spiral connecting itself by a square landing to five of the six sides of the tower, requiring at each landing transversal corbels which are decorated with arabesque carvings without and within. This bewildering creation of ingenious and delicate details, of marvels which give speech to stones, can be compared only to the deeply worked and crowded carving of the Chinese ivories. Stone is made to look like lace-work. The flowers, the figures of men and animals clinging to the structure of the stairway, are multiplied, step by step, until they crown the tower with a key-stone on which the chisels of the art of the sixteenth century have contended against the naive cutters of images who fifty years earlier had carved the key-stones of Louis XII.'s two stairways.

However dazzled we may be by these recurring forms of indefatigable labor, we cannot fail to see that money was lacking to Francois I. for Blois, as it was to Louis XIV. for Versailles. More than one figurine lifts its delicate head from a block of rough stone behind it; more than one fantastic flower is merely indicated by chiselled touches on the abandoned stone, though dampness has since laid its blossoms of mouldy greenery upon it. On the facade, side by side with the tracery of one window, another window presents its masses of jagged stone carved only by the hand of time. Here, to the least artistic and the least trained eye, is a ravishing contrast between this frontage, where marvels throng, and the interior frontage of the chateau of Louis XII., which is composed of a ground-floor of arcades of fairy lightness supported by tiny columns resting at their base on a graceful platform, and of two storeys above it, the windows of which are carved with delightful sobriety. Beneath the arcade is a gallery, the walls of which are painted in fresco, the ceiling also being painted; traces can still be found of this magnificence, derived from Italy, and testifying to the expeditions of our kings, to which the principality of Milan then belonged.

Opposite to Francois I.'s wing was the chapel of the counts of Blois, the facade of which is almost in harmony with the architecture of the later dwelling of Louis XII. No words can picture the majestic solidity of these three distinct masses of building. In spite of their nonconformity of style, Royalty, powerful and firm, demonstrating its dangers by the greatness of its precautions, was a bond, uniting these three edifices, so different in character, two of which rested against the vast hall of the States-general, towering high like a church.

Certainly, neither the simplicity nor the strength of the burgher existence (which were depicted at the beginning of this history) in which Art was always represented, were lacking to this royal habitation. Blois was the fruitful and brilliant example to which the Bourgeoisie and Feudality, Wealth and Nobility, gave such splendid replies in the towns and in the rural regions. Imagination could not desire any other sort of dwelling for the prince who reigned over France in the sixteenth century. The richness of seignorial garments, the luxury of female adornment, must have harmonized delightfully with the lace-work of these stones so wonderfully manipulated. From floor to floor, as the king of France went up the marvellous staircase of his chateau of Blois, he could see the broad expanse of the beautiful Loire, which brought him news of all his kingdom as it lay on either side of the great river, two halves of a State facing each other, and semi-rivals. If, instead of building Chambord in a barren, gloomy plain two leagues away, Francois I. had placed it where, seventy years later, Gaston built his palace, Versailles would never have existed, and Blois would have become, necessarily, the capital of France.

Four Valois and Catherine de' Medici lavished their wealth on the wing built by Francois I. at Blois. Who can look at those massive partition-walls, the spinal column of the castle, in which are sunken deep alcoves, secret staircases, cabinets, while they themselves enclose halls as vast as that great council-room, the guardroom, and the royal chambers, in which, in our day, a regiment of infantry is comfortably lodged—who can look at all this and not be aware of the prodigalities of Crown and court? Even if a visitor does not at once understand how the splendor within must have corresponded with the splendor without, the remaining vestiges of Catherine de' Medici's cabinet, where Christophe was about to be introduced, would bear sufficient testimony to the elegances of Art which peopled these apartments with animated designs in which salamanders sparkled among the wreaths, and the palette of the sixteenth century illumined the darkest corners with its brilliant coloring. In this cabinet an observer will still find traces of that taste for gilding which Catherine brought with her from Italy; for the princesses of her house loved, in the words of the author already quoted, to veneer the castles of France with the gold earned by their ancestors in commerce, and to hang out their wealth on the walls of their apartments.

The queen-mother occupied on the first upper floor of the apartments of Queen Claude of France, wife of Francois I., in which may still be seen, delicately carved, the double C accompanied by figures, purely white, of swans and lilies, signifying *candidior candidis*—more white than the whitest—the motto of the queen whose name began, like that of Catherine, with a C, and which applied as well to the daughter of Louis XII. as to the mother of the last Valois; for no suspicion, in spite of the violence of Calvinist calumny, has tarnished the fidelity of Catherine de' Medici to Henri II.

The queen-mother, still charged with the care of two young children (him who was afterward Duc d'Alencon, and Marguerite, the wife of Henri IV., the sister whom Charles IX. called Margot), had need of the whole of the first upper floor.

The king, Francois II., and the queen, Mary Stuart, occupied, on the second floor, the royal apartments which had formerly been those of Francois I. and were, subsequently, those of Henri III. This floor, like that taken by the queen-mother, is divided in two parts throughout its whole length by the famous partition-wall, which is more than four feet thick, against which rests the enormous walls which separate the rooms from each other. Thus, on both floors, the apartments are in two distinct halves. One half, to the south, looking to the courtyard, served for public receptions and for the transaction of business; whereas the private apartments were placed, partly to escape the heat, to the north, overlooking the gardens, on which side is the splendid facade with its balconies and galleries looking out upon the open country of the Vendomois, and down upon the "Perchoir des Bretons" and the moat, the only side of which La Fontaine speaks.

The chateau of Francois I. was, in those days, terminated by an enormous unfinished tower which was intended to mark the colossal angle of the building when the succeeding wing was built. Later, Gaston took down one side of it, in order to build his palace on to it; but he never finished the work, and the tower remained in ruins. This royal stronghold served as a prison or dungeon, according to popular tradition.

As we wander to-day through the halls of this matchless chateau, so precious to art and to history, what poet would not be haunted by regrets, and grieved for France, at seeing the arabesques of Catherine's boudoir *whitewashed* and almost obliterated, by order of the quartermaster of the barracks (this royal residence is now a barrack) at the time of an outbreak of cholera. The panels of Catherine's boudoir, a room of which we are about to speak, is the last remaining relic of the rich decorations accumulated by five artistic kings. Making our way through the labyrinth of chambers, halls, stairways, towers, we may say to ourselves with solemn certitude: "Here Mary Stuart cajoled her husband on behalf of the Guises." "There, the Guises insulted Catherine." "Later, at that very spot the second Balafre fell beneath the daggers of the avengers of the Crown." "A century earlier, from this very window, Louis XII. made signs to his friend Cardinal d'Amboise to come to him." "Here, on this balcony, d'Epernon, the accomplice of Ravaillac, met Marie de' Medici, who knew, it was said, of the proposed regicide, and allowed it to be committed."

In the chapel, where the marriage of Henri IV. and Marguerite de Valois took place, the sole remaining fragment of the chateau of the counts of Blois, a regiment now makes it shoes. This wonderful structure, in which so many styles may still be seen, so many great deeds have been performed, is in a state of dilapidation which disgraces France. What grief for those who love the great historic monuments of our country to know that soon those eloquent stones will be lost to sight and knowledge, like others at the corner of the rue de la Vieille-Pelleterie; possibly, they will exist nowhere but in these pages.

It is necessary to remark that, in order to watch the royal court more closely, the Guises, although they had a house of their own in the town, which still exists, had obtained permission to occupy the upper floor above the apartments of Louis XII., the same lodgings afterwards occupied by the Duchesse de Nemours under the roof.

The young king, Francois II., and his bride Mary Stuart, in love with each other like the girl and boy of sixteen which they were, had been abruptly transferred, in the depth of winter, from the chateau de Saint-Germain, which the Duc de Guise thought liable to attack, to the fortress which the chateau of Blois then was, being isolated and protected on three sides by precipices, and admirably defended as to its entrance. The Guises, uncles of Mary Stuart, had powerful reasons for not residing in

64

Paris and for keeping the king and court in a castle the whole exterior surroundings of which could easily be watched and defended. A struggle was now beginning around the throne, between the house of Lorraine and the house of Valois, which was destined to end in this very chateau, twenty-eight years later, namely in 1588, when Henri III., under the very eyes of his mother, at that moment deeply humiliated by the Lorrains, heard fall upon the floor of his own cabinet, the head of the boldest of all the Guises, the second Balafre, son of that first Balafre by whom Catherine de' Medici was now being tricked, watched, threatened, and virtually imprisoned.

IV. THE QUEEN-MOTHER

This noble chateau of Blois was to Catherine de' Medici the narrowest of prisons. On the death of her husband, who had always held her in subjection, she expected to reign; but, on the contrary, she found herself crushed under the thraldom of strangers, whose polished manners were really far more brutal than those of jailers. No action of hers could be done secretly. The women who attended her either had lovers among the Guises or were watched by Argus eyes. These were times when passions notably exhibited the strange effects produced in all ages by the strong antagonism of two powerful conflicting interests in the State. Gallantry, which served Catherine so well, was also an auxiliary of the Guises. The Prince de Conde, the first leader of the Reformation, was a lover of the Marechale de Saint-Andre, whose husband was the tool of the Grand Master. The cardinal, convinced by the affair of the Vidame de Chartres, that Catherine was more unconquered than invulnerable as to love, was paying court to her. The play of all these passions strangely complicated those of politics,—making, as it were, a double game of chess, in which both parties had to watch the head and heart of their opponent, in order to know, when a crisis came, whether the one would betray the other.

Though she was constantly in presence of the Cardinal de Lorraine or of Duc Francois de Guise, who both distrusted her, the closest and ablest enemy of Catherine de' Medici was her daughter-in-law, Queen Mary, a fair little creature, malicious as a waiting-maid, proud as a Stuart wearing three crowns, learned as an old pedant, giddy as a school-girl, as much in love with her husband as a courtesan is with her lover, devoted to her uncles whom she admired, and delighted to see the king share (at her instigation) the regard she had for them. A mother-in-law is always a person whom the daughter-in-law is inclined not to like; especially when she wears the crown and wishes to retain it, which Catherine had imprudently made but too well known. Her former position, when Diane de Poitiers had ruled Henri II., was more tolerable than this; then at least she received the external honors that were due to a queen, and the homage of the court. But now the duke and the cardinal, who had none but their own minions about them, seemed to take pleasure in abasing her. Catherine, hemmed in on all sides by their courtiers, received, not only day by day but from hour to hour, terrible blows to her pride and her self-love; for the Guises were determined to treat her on the same system of repression which the late king, her husband, had so long pursued.

The thirty-six years of anguish which were now about to desolate France may, perhaps, be said to have begun by the scene in which the son of the furrier of the two queens was sent on the perilous errand which makes him the chief figure of our present Study. The danger into which this zealous Reformer was about to fall became imminent the very morning on which he started from the port of Beaugency for the chateau de Blois, bearing precious documents which compromised the highest heads of the nobility, placed in his hands by that wily partisan, the indefatigable La Renaudie, who met him, as agreed upon, at Beaugency, having reached that port before him.

While the tow-boat, in which Christophe now embarked floated, impelled by a light east wind, down the river Loire the famous Cardinal de Lorraine, and his brother the second Duc de Guise, one of the greatest warriors of those days, were contemplating, like eagles perched on a rocky summit, their present situation, and looking prudently about them before striking the great blow by which they intended to kill the Reform in France at Amboise,—an attempt renewed twelve years later in Paris, August 24, 1572, on the feast of Saint-Bartholomew.

During the night three *seigneurs*, who each played a great part in the twelve years' drama which followed this double plot now laid by the Guises and also by the Reformers, had arrived at Blois from different directions, each riding at full speed, and leaving their horses half-dead at the postern-gate of the chateau, which was guarded by captains and soldiers absolutely devoted to the Duc de Guise, the idol of all warriors.

One word about that great man,—a word that must tell, in the first instance, whence his fortunes took their rise.

His mother was Antoinette de Bourbon, great-aunt of Henri IV. Of what avail is consanguinity? He was, at this moment, aiming at the head of his cousin the Prince de Conde. His niece was Mary Stuart. His wife was Anne, daughter of the Duke of Ferrara. The Grand Connetable de Montmorency called the Duc de Guise "Monseigneur" as he would the king,—ending his letter with "Your very humble servant." Guise, Grand Master of the king's household, replied "Monsieur le connetable," and signed, as he did for the Parliament, "Your very good friend."

As for the cardinal, called the transalpine pope, and his Holiness, by Estienne, he had the whole monastic Church of France on his side, and treated the Holy Father as an equal. Vain of his eloquence, and one of the greatest theologians of his time, he kept incessant watch over France and Italy by means of three religious orders who were absolutely devoted to him, toiling day and night in his service and serving him as spies and counsellors.

These few words will explain to what heights of power the duke and the cardinal had attained. In spite of their wealth and the enormous revenues of their several offices, they were so personally disinterested, so eagerly carried away on the current of their statesmanship, and so generous at heart, that they were always in debt, doubtless after the manner of Caesar. When Henri III. caused the death of the second Balafre, whose life was a menace to him, the house of Guise was necessarily ruined. The costs of endeavoring to seize the crown during a whole century will explain the lowered position of this great house during the reigns of Louis XIII. and Louis XIV., when the sudden death of MADAME told all Europe the infamous part which a Chevalier de Lorraine had debased himself to play.

Calling themselves the heirs of the dispossessed Carolovingians, the duke and cardinal acted with the utmost insolence towards Catherine de' Medici, the mother-in-law of their niece. The Duchesse de Guise spared her no mortification. This duchesse was a d'Este, and Catherine was a Medici, the daughter of upstart Florentine merchants, whom the sovereigns of Europe had never yet admitted into their royal fraternity. Francois I. himself has always considered his son's marriage with a Medici as a mesalliance, and only consented to it under the expectation that his second son would never be dauphin. Hence his fury when his eldest son was poisoned by the Florentine Montecuculi. The d'Estes refused to recognize the Medici as Italian princes. Those former merchants were in fact trying to solve the impossible problem of maintaining a throne in the midst of republican institutions. The title of grand-duke was only granted very tardily by Philip the Second, king of Spain, to reward those Medici who bought it by betraying France their benefactress, and servilely attaching themselves to the court of Spain, which was at the very time covertly counteracting them in Italy.

"Flatter none but your enemies," the famous saying of Catherine de' Medici, seems to have been the political rule of life with that family of merchant princes, in which great men were never lacking until their destinies became great, when they fell, before their time, into that degeneracy in which royal races and noble families are wont to end.

For three generations there had been a great Lorrain warrior and a great Lorrain churchman; and, what is more singular, the churchmen all bore a strong resemblance in the face to Ximenes, as did Cardinal Richelieu in after days. These five great cardinals all had sly, mean, and yet terrible faces; while the warriors, on the other hand, were of that type of Basque mountaineer which we see in Henri IV. The two Balafres, father and son, wounded and scarred in the same manner, lost something of this type, but not the grace and affability by which, as much as by their bravery, they won the hearts of the soldiery.

It is not useless to relate how the present Grand Master received his wound; for it was healed by the heroic measures of a personage of our drama,—by Ambroise Pare, the man we have already mentioned as under obligations to Lecamus, syndic of the guild of furriers. At the siege of Calais the duke had his face pierced through and through by a lance, the point of which, after entering the cheek just below the right eye, went through to the neck, below the left eye, and remained, broken off, in the face. The duke lay dying in his tent in the midst of universal distress, and he would have died had it not been for the devotion and prompt courage of Ambroise Pare. "The duke is not dead, gentlemen," he said to the weeping attendants, "but he soon will die if I dare not treat him as I would a dead man; and I shall risk doing so, no matter what it may cost me in the end. See!" And with that he put his left foot on the duke's breast, took the broken wooden end of the lance in his fingers, shook and loosened it by degrees in the wound, and finally succeeded in drawing out the iron head, as if he were handling a thing and not a man. Though he saved the prince by this heroic treatment, he could not prevent the horrible scar which gave the great soldier his nickname,—Le Balafre, the Scarred. This name descended to the son, and for a similar reason.

Absolutely masters of Francois II., whom his wife ruled through their mutual and excessive passion, these two great Lorrain princes, the duke and the cardinal, were masters of France, and had no other enemy at court than Catherine de' Medici. No great statesmen ever played a closer or more watchful game.

The mutual position of the ambitious widow of Henri II. and the ambitious house of Lorraine was pictured, as it were, to the eye by a scene which took place on the terrace of the chateau de Blois very early in the morning of the day on which Christophe Lecamus was destined to arrive there. The queen-mother, who feigned an extreme attachment to the Guises, had asked to be informed of the news brought by the three *seigneurs* coming from three different parts of the kingdom; but she had the mortification of being courteously dismissed by the cardinal. She then walked to the parterres which overhung the Loire, where she was building, under the superintendence of her astrologer, Ruggieri, an observatory, which is still standing, and from which the eye may range over the whole landscape of that delightful valley. The two Lorrain princes were at the other end of the terrace, facing the Vendomois, which overlooks the upper part of the town, the perch of the Bretons, and the postern gate of the chateau.

Catherine had deceived the two brothers by pretending to a slight displeasure; for she was in reality very well pleased to have an opportunity to speak to one of the three young men who had arrived in such haste. This was a young nobleman named Chiverni, apparently a tool of the cardinal, in reality a devoted servant of Catherine. Catherine also counted among her devoted servants two Florentine nobles, the Gondi; but they were so suspected by the Guises that she dared not send them on any errand away from the court, where she kept them, watched, it is true, in all their words and actions, but where at least they were able to watch and study the Guises and counsel Catherine. These two Florentines maintained in the interests of the queen-mother another Italian, Birago,—a clever Piedmontese, who pretended, with Chiverni, to have abandoned their mistress, and gone over to the Guises, who encouraged their enterprises and employed them to watch Catherine.

Chiverni had come from Paris and Ecouen. The last to arrive was Saint-Andre, who was marshal of France and became so important that the Guises, whose creature he was, made him the third person in the triumvirate they formed the following year against Catherine. The other *seigneur* who had arrived during the night was Vieilleville, also a creature of the Guises and a marshal of France, who was returning from a secret mission known only to the Grand Master, who had entrusted it to him. As for Saint-Andre, he was in charge of military measures taken with the object of driving all Reformers under arms into Amboise; a scheme which now formed the subject of a council held by the duke and cardinal, Birago, Chiverni, Vieilleville, and Saint-Andre. As the two Lorrains employed Birago, it is to be supposed that they relied upon their own powers; for they knew of his attachment to the queen-mother. At this singular epoch the double part played by many of the political men of the day was well known to both parties; they were like cards in the hands of gamblers,—the cleverest player won the game. During this council the two brothers maintained the most impenetrable reserve. A conversation which now took place between Catherine and certain of her friends will explain the object of this council, held by the Guises in the open air, in the hanging gardens, at break of day, as if they feared to speak within the walls of the chateau de Blois.

The queen-mother, under pretence of examining the observatory then in process of construction, walked in that direction accompanied by the two Gondis, glancing with a suspicious and inquisitive eye at the group of enemies who were still standing at the farther end of the terrace, and from whom Chiverni now detached himself to join the queen-mother. She was then at the corner of the terrace which looks down upon the Church of Saint-Nicholas; there, at least, there could be no danger of the slightest overhearing. The wall of the terrace is on a level with the towers of the church, and the Guises invariably held their council at the farther corner of the same terrace at the base of the great unfinished keep or dungeon,—going and returning between the Perchoir des Bretons and the gallery by the bridge which joined them to the gardens. No one was within sight. Chiverni raised the hand of the queen-mother to kiss it, and as he did so he slipped a little note from his hand to hers, without being observed by the two Italians. Catherine turned to the angle of the parapet and read as follows:—

You are powerful enough to hold the balance between the leaders and to force them into a struggle as to who shall serve you; your house is full of kings, and you have nothing to fear from the Lorrains or the Bourbons provided you pit them one against the other, for both are striving to snatch the crown from your children. Be the mistress and not the servant of your counsellors; support them, in turn, one against the other, or the kingdom will go from bad to worse, and mighty wars may come of it.

L'Hopital.

The queen put the letter in the hollow of her corset, resolving to burn it as soon as she was alone.

"When did you see him?" she asked Chiverni.

"On my way back from visiting the Connetable, at Melun, where I met him with the Duchesse de Berry, whom he was most impatient to convey to Savoie, that he might return here and open the eyes of the chancellor Olivier, who is now completely duped by the Lorrains. As soon as Monsieur l'Hopital saw the true object of the Guises he determined to support your interests. That is why he is so anxious to get here and give you his vote at the councils."

"Is he sincere?" asked Catherine. "You know very well that if the Lorrains have put him in the council it is that he may help them to reign."

"L'Hopital is a Frenchman who comes of too good a stock not to be honest and sincere," said Chiverni; "Besides, his note is a sufficiently strong pledge."

"What answer did the Connetable send to the Guises?"

"He replied that he was the servant of the king and would await his orders. On receiving that answer the cardinal, to suppress all resistance, determined to propose the appointment of his brother as lieutenant-general of the kingdom."

"Have they got as far as that?" exclaimed Catherine, alarmed. "Well, did Monsieur l'Hopital send me no other message?"

"He told me to say to you, madame, that you alone could stand between the Crown and the Guises."

"Does he think that I ought to use the Huguenots as a weapon?"

"Ah! madame," cried Chiverni, surprised at such astuteness, "we never dreamed of casting you into such difficulties."

"Does he know the position I am in?" asked the queen, calmly.

"Very nearly. He thinks you were duped after the death of the king into accepting that castle on Madame Diane's overthrow. The Guises consider themselves released toward the queen by having satisfied the woman."

"Yes," said the queen, looking at the two Gondi, "I made a blunder."

"A blunder of the gods," replied Charles de Gondi.

"Gentlemen," said Catherine, "if I go over openly to the Reformers I shall become the slave of a party."

"Madame," said Chiverni, eagerly, "I approve entirely of your meaning. You must use them, but not serve them."

"Though your support does, undoubtedly, for the time being lie there," said Charles de Gondi, "we must not conceal from ourselves that success and defeat are both equally perilous."

"I know it," said the queen; "a single false step would be a pretext on which the Guises would seize at once to get rid of me."

"The niece of a Pope, the mother of four Valois, a queen of France, the widow of the most ardent persecutor of the Huguenots, an Italian Catholic, the aunt of Leo X.,—can *she* ally herself with the Reformation?" asked Charles de Gondi.

"But," said his brother Albert, "if she seconds the Guises does she not play into the hands of a usurpation? We have to do with men who see a crown to seize in the coming struggle between Catholicism and Reform. It is possible to support the Reformers without abjuring."

"Reflect, madame, that your family, which ought to have been wholly devoted to the king of France, is at this moment the servant of the king of Spain; and to-morrow it will be that of the Reformation if the Reformation could make a king of the Duke of Florence."

"I am certainly disposed to lend a hand, for a time, to the Huguenots," said Catherine, "if only to revenge myself on that soldier and that priest and that woman!" As she spoke, she called attention with her subtile Italian glance to the duke and cardinal, and then to the second floor of the chateau on which were the apartments of her son and Mary Stuart. "That trio has taken from my hands the reins of State, for which I waited long while the old woman filled my place," she said gloomily, glancing toward Chenonceaux, the chateau she had lately exchanged with Diane de Poitiers against that of Chaumont. "*Ma*," she added in Italian, "it seems that these reforming gentry in Geneva have not the wit to address themselves to me; and, on my conscience, I cannot go to them. Not one of you would dare to risk carrying them a message!" She stamped her foot. "I did hope you would have met the cripple at Ecouen—*he* has sense," she said to Chiverni.

"The Prince de Conde was there, madame," said Chiverni, "but he could not persuade the Connetable to join him. Monsieur de Montmorency wants to overthrow the Guises, who have sent him into exile, but he will not encourage heresy."

"What will ever break these individual wills which are forever thwarting royalty? God's truth!" exclaimed the queen, "the great nobles must be made to destroy each other, as Louis XI., the greatest of your kings, did with those of his time. There are four or five parties now in this kingdom, and the weakest of them is that of my children."

"The Reformation is an *idea*," said Charles de Gondi; "the parties that Louis XI. crushed were moved by self-interests only."

"Ideas are behind selfish interests," replied Chiverni. "Under Louis XI. the idea was the great Fiefs—"

"Make heresy an axe," said Albert de Gondi, "and you will escape the odium of executions."

"Ah!" cried the queen, "but I am ignorant of the strength and also of the plans of the Reformers; and I have no safe way of communicating with them. If I were detected in any manoeuvre of that kind, either by the queen, who watches me like an infant in a cradle, or by those two jailers over there, I should be banished from France and sent back to Florence with a terrible escort, commanded by Guise minions. Thank you, no, my daughter-in-law!—but I wish *you* the fate of being a prisoner in your own home, that you may know what you have made me suffer."

"Their plans!" exclaimed Chiverni; "the duke and the cardinal know what they are, but those two foxes will not divulge them. If you could induce them to do so, madame, I would sacrifice myself for your sake and come to an understanding with the Prince de Conde."

"How much of the Guises' own plans have they been forced to reveal to you?" asked the queen, with a glance at the two brothers.

"Monsieur de Vieilleville and Monsieur de Saint-Andre have just received fresh orders, the nature of which is concealed from us; but I think the duke is intending to concentrate his best troops on the left bank. Within a few days you will all be moved to Amboise. The duke has been studying the position from this terrace and decides that Blois is not a propitious spot for his secret schemes. What can he want better?" added Chiverni, pointing to the precipices which surrounded the chateau. "There is no place in the world where the court is more secure from attack than it is here."

"Abdicate or reign," said Albert in a low voice to the queen, who stood motionless and thoughtful.

A terrible expression of inward rage passed over the fine ivory face of Catherine de' Medici, who was not yet forty years old, though she had lived for twenty-six years at the court of France,—without power, she, who from the moment of her arrival intended to play a leading part! Then, in her native language, the language of Dante, these terrible words came slowly from her lips:—

"Nothing so long as that son lives!—His little wife bewitches him," she added after a pause.

Catherine's exclamation was inspired by a prophecy which had been made to her a few days earlier at the chateau de Chaumont on the opposite bank of the river; where she had been taken by Ruggieri, her astrologer, to obtain information as to the lives of her four children from a celebrated female seer, secretly brought there by Nostradamus (chief among the physicians of that great sixteenth century) who practised, like the Ruggieri, the Cardans, Paracelsus, and others, the occult sciences. This woman, whose name and life have eluded history, foretold one year as the length of Francois's reign.

"Give me your opinion on all this," said Catherine to Chiverni.

"We shall have a battle," replied the prudent courtier. "The king of Navarre—"

"Oh! say the queen," interrupted Catherine.

"True, the queen," said Chiverni, smiling, "the queen has given the Prince de Conde as leader to the Reformers, and he, in his position of younger son, can venture all; consequently the cardinal talks of ordering him here."

"If he comes," cried the queen, "I am saved!"

Thus the leaders of the great movement of the Reformation in France were justified in hoping for an ally in Catherine de' Medici.

"There is one thing to be considered," said the queen. "The Bourbons may fool the Huguenots and the Sieurs Calvin and de Beze may fool the

Bourbons, but are we strong enough to fool Huguenots, Bourbons, and Guises? In presence of three such enemies it is allowable to feel one's pulse."

"But they have not the king," said Albert de Gondi. "You will always triumph, having the king on your side."

"*Maladetta Maria*!" muttered Catherine between her teeth.

"The Lorrains are, even now, endeavoring to turn the burghers against you," remarked Birago.

V. THE COURT

The hope of gaining the crown was not the result of a premeditated plan in the minds of the restless Guises. Nothing warranted such a hope or such a plan. Circumstances alone inspired their audacity. The two cardinals and the two Balafres were four ambitious minds, superior in talents to all the other politicians who surrounded them. This family was never really brought low except by Henri IV.; a factionist himself, trained in the great school of which Catherine and the Guises were masters,—by whose lessons he had profited but too well.

At this moment the two brothers, the duke and cardinal, were the arbiters of the greatest revolution attempted in Europe since that of Henry VIII. in England, which was the direct consequence of the invention of printing. Adversaries to the Reformation, they meant to stifle it, power being in their hands. But their opponent, Calvin, though less famous than Luther, was far the stronger of the two. Calvin saw government where Luther saw dogma only. While the stout beer-drinker and amorous German fought with the devil and flung an inkbottle at his head, the man from Picardy, a sickly celibate, made plans of campaign, directed battles, armed princes, and roused whole peoples by sowing republican doctrines in the hearts of the burghers—recouping his continual defeats in the field by fresh progress in the mind of the nations.

The Cardinal de Lorraine and the Duc de Guise, like Philip the Second and the Duke of Alba, knew where and when the monarchy was threatened, and how close the alliance ought to be between Catholicism and Royalty. Charles the Fifth, drunk with the wine of Charlemagne's cup, believing too blindly in the strength of his monarchy, and confident of sharing the world with Suleiman, did not at first feel the blow at his head; but no sooner had Cardinal Granvelle made him aware of the extent of the wound than he abdicated. The Guises had but one scheme,—that of annihilating heresy at a single blow. This blow they were now to attempt, for the first time, to strike at Amboise; failing there they tried it again, twelve years later, at the Saint-Bartholomew,—on the latter occasion in conjunction with Catherine de' Medici, enlightened by that time by the flames of a twelve years' war, enlightened above all by the significant word "republic," uttered later and printed by the writers of the Reformation, but already foreseen (as we have said before) by Lecamus, that type of the Parisian bourgeoisie.

The two Guises, now on the point of striking a murderous blow at the heart of the French nobility, in order to separate it once for all from a religious party whose triumph would be its ruin, still stood together on the terrace, concerting as to the best means of revealing their coup-d'Etat to the king, while Catherine was talking with her counsellors.

"Jeanne d'Albret knew what she was about when she declared herself protectress of the Huguenots! She has a battering-ram in the Reformation, and she knows how to use it," said the duke, who fathomed the deep designs of the Queen of Navarre, one of the great minds of the century.

"Theodore de Beze is now at Nerac," remarked the cardinal, "after first going to Geneva to take Calvin's orders."

"What men these burghers know how to find!" exclaimed the duke.

"Ah! we have none on our side of the quality of La Renaudie!" cried the cardinal. "He is a true Catiline."

"Such men always act for their own interests," replied the duke. "Didn't I fathom La Renaudie? I loaded him with favors; I helped him to escape when he was condemned by the parliament of Bourgogne; I brought him back from exile by obtaining a revision of his sentence; I intended to do far more for him; and all the while he was plotting a diabolical conspiracy against us! That rascal has united the Protestants of Germany with the heretics of France by reconciling the differences that grew up between the dogmas of Luther and those of Calvin. He has brought the discontented great seigneurs into the party of the Reformation without obliging them to abjure Catholicism openly. For the last year he has had thirty captains under him! He is everywhere at once,—at Lyon, in Languedoc, at Nantes! It was he who drew up those minutes of a consultation which were hawked about all Germany, in which the theologians declared that force might be resorted to in order to withdraw the king from our rule and tutelage; the paper is now being circulated from town to town. Wherever we look for him we never find him! And yet I have never done him anything but good! It comes to this, that we must now either thrash him like a dog, or try to throw him a golden bridge by which he will cross into our camp."

"Bretagne, Languedoc, in fact the whole kingdom is in league to deal us a mortal blow," said the cardinal. "After the fete was over yesterday I spent the rest of the night in reading the reports sent me by the monks; in which I found that the only persons who have compromised themselves are poor gentlemen, artisans, as to whom it doesn't signify whether you hang them or let them live. The Colignys and Condes do not show their hand as yet, though they hold the threads of the whole conspiracy."

"Yes," replied the duke, "and, therefore, as soon as that lawyer Avenelles sold the secret of the plot, I told Braguelonne to let the conspirators carry it out. They have no suspicion that we know it; they are so sure of surprising us that the leaders may possibly show themselves then. My advice is to allow ourselves to be beaten for forty-eight hours."

"Half an hour would be too much," cried the cardinal, alarmed.

"So this is your courage, is it?" retorted the Balafre.

The cardinal, quite unmoved, replied: "Whether the Prince de Conde is compromised or not, if we are certain that he is the leader, we should strike him down at once and secure tranquillity. We need judges rather than soldiers for this business—and judges are never lacking. Victory is always more certain in the parliament than on the field, and it costs less."

"I consent, willingly," said the duke; "but do you think the Prince de Conde is powerful enough to inspire, himself alone, the audacity of those who are making this first attack upon us? Isn't there, behind him—"

"The king of Navarre," said the cardinal.

"Pooh! a fool who speaks to me cap in hand!" replied the duke. "The coquetries of that Florentine woman seem to blind your eyes—"

"Oh! as for that," exclaimed the priest, "if I do play the gallant with her it is only that I may read to the bottom of her heart."

"She has no heart," said the duke, sharply; "she is even more ambitious than you and I."

"You are a brave soldier," said the cardinal; "but, believe me, I distance you in this matter. I have had Catherine watched by Mary Stuart long before you even suspected her. She has no more religion than my shoe; if she is not the soul of this plot it is not for want of will. But we shall now be able to test her on the scene itself, and find out then how she stands by us. Up to this time, however, I am certain she has held no communication whatever with the heretics."

"Well, it is time now to reveal the whole plot to the king, and to the queen-mother, who, you say, knows nothing of it,—that is the sole proof of her innocence; perhaps the conspirators have waited till the last moment, expecting to dazzle her with the probabilities of success. La Renaudie must soon discover by my arrangements that we are warned. Last night Nemours was to follow detachments of the Reformers who are pouring in along the cross-roads, and the conspirators will be forced to attack us at Amboise, which place I intend to let them enter. Here," added the duke, pointing to three sides of the rock on which the chateau de Blois is built; "we should have an assault without any result; the Huguenots could come and go at will. Blois is an open hall with four entrances; whereas Amboise is a sack with a single mouth."

"I shall not leave Catherine's side," said the cardinal.

"We have made a blunder," remarked the duke, who was playing with his dagger, tossing it into the air and catching it by the hilt. "We ought to have treated her as we did the Reformers,—given her complete freedom of action and caught her in the act."

The cardinal looked at his brother for an instant and shook his head.

"What does Pardaillan want?" said the duke, observing the approach of the young nobleman who was later to become celebrated by his encounter with La Renaudie, in which they both lost their lives.

"Monseigneur, a man sent by the queen's furrier is at the gate, and says he has an ermine suit to convey to her. Am I to let him enter?"

"Ah! yes,—the ermine coat she spoke of yesterday," returned the cardinal; "let the shop-fellow pass; she will want the garment for the voyage down the Loire."

"How did he get here without being stopped until he reached the gate?" asked the duke.

"I do not know," replied Pardaillan.

"I'll ask to see him when he is with the queen," thought the Balafre. "Let him wait in the *salle des gardes*," he said aloud. "Is he young, Pardaillan?"

"Yes, monseigneur; he says he is a son of Lecamus the furrier."

"Lecamus is a good Catholic," remarked the cardinal, who, like his brother the duke, was endowed with Caesar's memory. "The rector of Saint-Pierre-aux-Boeufs relies upon him; he is the provost of that quarter."

"Nevertheless," said the duke, "make the son talk with the captain of the Scotch guard," laying an emphasis on the verb which was readily understood. "Ambroise is in the chateau; he can tell us whether the fellow is really the son of Lecamus, for the old man did him good service in times past. Send for Ambroise Pare."

It was at this moment that Queen Catherine went, unattended, toward the two brothers, who hastened to meet her with their accustomed show of respect, in which the Italian princess detected constant irony.

"Messieurs," she said, "will you deign to inform me of what is about to take place? Is the widow of your former master of less importance in your esteem than the Sieurs Vieilleville, Birago, and Chiverni?"

"Madame," replied the cardinal, in a tone of gallantry, "our duty as men, taking precedence of that of statecraft, forbids us to alarm the fair sex by false reports. But this morning there is indeed good reason to confer with you on the affairs of the country. You must excuse my brother for having already given orders to the gentlemen you mention,—orders which were purely military, and therefore did not concern you; the matters of real importance are still to be decided. If you are willing, we will now go the *lever* of the king and queen; it is nearly time."

"But what is all this, Monsieur le duc?" cried Catherine, pretending alarm. "Is anything the matter?"

"The Reformation, madame, is no longer a mere heresy; it is a party, which has taken arms and is coming here to snatch the king away from you."

Catherine, the cardinal, the duke, and the three gentlemen made their way to the staircase through the gallery, which was crowded with courtiers who, being off duty, no longer had the right of entrance to the royal apartments, and stood in two hedges on either side. Gondi, who watched them while the queen-mother talked with the Lorraine princes, whispered in her ear, in good Tuscan, two words which afterwards became proverbs,—words which are the keynote to one aspect of her regal character: "Odiate e aspettate"—"Hate and wait."

Pardaillan, who had gone to order the officer of the guard at the gate of the chateau to let the clerk of the queen's furrier enter, found Christophe open-mouthed before the portal, staring at the facade built by the good king Louis XII., on which there was at that time a much greater number of grotesque carvings than we see there to-day,—grotesque, that is to say, if we may judge by those that remain to us. For instance, persons curious in such matters may remark the figurine of a woman carved on the capital of one of the portal columns, with her robe caught up to show to a stout monk crouching in the capital of the corresponding column "that which Brunelle showed to Marphise"; while above this portal stood, at the time of which we write, the statue of Louis XII. Several of the window-casings of this facade, carved in the same style, and now, unfortunately, destroyed, amused, or seemed to amuse Christophe, on whom the arquebusiers of the guard were raining jests.

"He would like to live there," said the sub-corporal, playing with the cartridges of his weapon, which were prepared for use in the shape of little sugar-loaves, and slung to the baldricks of the men.

"Hey, Parisian!" said another; "you never saw the like of that, did you?"

"He recognizes the good King Louis XII.," said a third.

Christophe pretended not to hear, and tried to exaggerate his amazement, the result being that his silly attitude and his behavior before the guard proved an excellent passport to the eyes of Pardaillan.

"The queen has not yet risen," said the young captain; "come and wait for her in the *salle des gardes*."

Christophe followed Pardaillan rather slowly. On the way he stopped to admire the pretty gallery in the form of an arcade, where the courtiers of Louis XII. awaited the reception-hour when it rained, and where, at the present moment, were several seigneurs attached to the Guises; for the staircase (so well preserved to the present day) which led to their apartments is at the end of this gallery in a tower, the architecture of which commends itself to the admiration of intelligent beholders.

"Well, well! did you come here to study the carving of images?" cried Pardaillan, as Christophe stopped before the charming sculptures of the balustrade which unites, or, if you prefer it, separates the columns of each arcade.

Christophe followed the young officer to the grand staircase, not without a glance of ecstasy at the semi-Moorish tower. The weather was fine, and the court was crowded with staff-officers and seigneurs, talking together in little groups,—their dazzling uniforms and court-dresses brightening a spot which the marvels of architecture, then fresh and new, had already made so brilliant.

"Come in here," said Pardaillan, making Lecamus a sign to follow him through a carved wooden door leading to the second floor, which the door-keeper opened on recognizing the young officer.

It is easy to imagine Christophe's amazement as he entered the great *salle des gardes*, then so vast that military necessity has since divided it by a partition into two chambers. It occupied on the second floor (that of the king), as did the corresponding hall on the first floor (that of the queen-mother), one third of the whole front of the chateau facing the courtyard; and it was lighted by two windows to right and two to left of the tower in which the famous staircase winds up. The young captain went to the door of the royal chamber, which opened upon this vast hall, and told one of the two pages on duty to inform Madame Dayelles, the queen's bedchamber woman, that the furrier was in the hall with her surcoat.

On a sign from Pardaillan Christophe placed himself near an officer, who was seated on a stool at the corner of a fireplace as large as his father's whole shop, which was at the end of the great hall, opposite to a precisely similar fireplace at the other end. While talking to this officer, a lieutenant, he contrived to interest him with an account of the stagnation of trade. Christophe seemed so thoroughly a shopkeeper that the officer imparted that conviction to the captain of the Scotch guard, who came in from the courtyard to question Lecamus, all the while watching him covertly and narrowly.

However much Christophe Lecamus had been warned, it was impossible for him to really apprehend the cold ferocity of the interests between which Chaudieu had slipped him. To an observer of this scene, who had known the secrets of it as the historian understands it in the light of to-day, there was indeed cause to tremble for this young man,—the hope of two families,—thrust between those powerful and pitiless machines, Catherine and the Guises. But do courageous beings, as a rule, measure the full extent of their dangers? By the way in which the port of Blois, the chateau, and the town were guarded, Christophe was prepared to find spies and traps everywhere; and he therefore resolved to conceal the importance of his mission and the tension of his mind under the empty-headed and shopkeeping appearance with which he presented himself to the eyes of young Pardaillan, the officer of the guard, and the Scottish captain.

The agitation which, in a royal castle, always attends the hour of the king's rising, was beginning to show itself. The great lords, whose horses, pages, or grooms remained in the outer courtyard,—for no one, except the king and the queens, had the right to enter the inner courtyard on horseback,—were mounting by groups the magnificent staircase, and filling by degrees the vast hall, the beams of which are now stripped of the decorations that then adorned them. Miserable little red tiles have replaced the ingenious mosaics of the floors; and the thick walls, then draped with the crown tapestries and glowing with all the arts of that unique period of the splendors of humanity, are now denuded and whitewashed! Reformers and Catholics were pressing in to hear the news and to watch faces, quite as much as to pay their duty to the king. Francois II.'s excessive love for Mary Stuart, to which neither the queen-mother nor the Guises made any opposition, and the politic compliance of Mary Stuart herself, deprived the king of all regal power. At seventeen years of age he knew nothing of royalty but its pleasures, or of marriage beyond the indulgence of first passion. As a matter of fact, all present paid their court to Queen Mary and to her uncles, the Cardinal de Lorraine and the Duc de Guise, rather than to the king.

This stir took place before Christophe, who watched the arrival of each new personage with natural eagerness. A magnificent portiere, on either side of which stood two pages and two soldiers of the Scotch guard, then on duty, showed him the entrance to the royal chamber,—the chamber so fatal to the son of the present Duc de Guise, the second Balafre, who fell at the foot of the bed now occupied by Mary Stuart and Francois II. The queen's maids of honor surrounded the fireplace opposite to that where Christophe was being "talked with" by the captain of the guard. This second fireplace was considered the *chimney of honor*. It was built in the thick wall of the Salle de Conseil, between the door of the royal chamber and that of the council-hall, so that the maids of honor and the lords in waiting who had the right to be there were on the direct passage of the king and queen. The courtiers were certain on this occasion of seeing Catherine, for her maids of honor, dressed like the rest of the court ladies, in black, came up the staircase from the queen-mother's apartment, and took their places, marshalled by the Comtesse de Fiesque, on the side toward the council-hall and opposite to the maids of honor of the young queen, led by the Duchesse de Guise, who occupied the other side of the fireplace on the side of the royal bedroom. The courtiers left an open space between the ranks of these young ladies (who all belonged to the first families of the kingdom), which none but the greatest lords had the right to enter. The Comtesse de Fiesque and the Duchesse de Guise were, in virtue of their office, seated in the midst of these noble maids, who were all standing.

The first gentleman who approached the dangerous ranks was the Duc d'Orleans, the king's brother, who had come down from his apartment on the third floor, accompanied by Monsieur de Cypierre, his governor. This young prince, destined before the end of the year to reign under the title of Charles IX., was only ten years old and extremely timid. The Duc d'Anjou and the Duc d'Alencon, his younger brothers, also the Princesse Marguerite, afterwards the wife of Henri IV. (la Reine Margot), were too young to come to court, and were therefore kept by their mother in her own apartments. The Duc d'Orleans, richly dressed after the fashion of the times, in silken trunk-hose, a close-fitting jacket of cloth of gold embroidered with black flowers, and a little mantle of embroidered velvet, all black, for he still wore mourning for his father, bowed to the two ladies of honor and took his place beside his mother's maids. Already full of antipathy for the adherents of the house of Guise, he replied coldly to the remarks of the duchess and leaned his arm on the back of the chair of the Comtesse de Fiesque. His governor, Monsieur de Cypierre, one of the noblest characters of that day, stood beside him like a shield. Amyot (afterwards Bishop of Auxerre and translator of Plutarch), in the simple soutane of an abbe, also accompanied the young prince, being his tutor, as he was of the two other princes, whose affection became so profitable to him.

Between the "chimney of honor" and the other chimney at the end of the hall, around which were grouped the guards, their captain, a few courtiers, and Christophe carrying his box of furs, the Chancellor Olivier, protector and predecessor of l'Hopital, in the robes which the chancellors of France have always worn, was walking up and down with the Cardinal de Tournon, who had recently returned from Rome. The pair were exchanging a few whispered sentences in the midst of great attention from the lords of the court, massed against the wall which separated the *salle des gardes* from the royal bedroom, like a living tapestry backed by the rich tapestry of art crowded by a thousand personages. In spite of the present grave events, the court presented the appearance of all courts in all lands, at all epochs, and in the midst of the greatest dangers. The courtiers talked of trivial matters, thinking of serious ones; they jested as they studied faces, and apparently concerned themselves about love and the marriage of rich heiresses amid the bloodiest catastrophes.

"What did you think of yesterday's fete?" asked Bourdeilles, seigneur of Brantome, approaching Mademoiselle de Piennes, one of the queen-mother's maids of honor.

"Messieurs du Baif et du Bellay were inspired with delightful ideas," she replied, indicating the organizers of the fete, who were standing near. "I thought it all in the worst taste," she added in a low voice.

"You had no part to play in it, I think?" remarked Mademoiselle de Lewiston from the opposite ranks of Queen Mary's maids.

"What are you reading there, madame?" asked Amyot of the Comtesse de Fiesque.

"'Amadis de Gaule,' by the Seigneur des Essarts, commissary in ordinary to the king's artillery," she replied.

"A charming work," remarked the beautiful girl who was afterwards so celebrated under the name of Fosseuse when she was lady of honor to Queen Marguerite of Navarre.

"The style is a novelty in form," said Amyot. "Do you accept such barbarisms?" he added, addressing Brantome.

"They please the ladies, you know," said Brantome, crossing over to the Duchesse de Guise, who held the "Decamerone" in her hand. "Some of the women of your house must appear in the book, madame," he said. "It is a pity that the Sieur Boccaccio did not live in our day; he would have known plenty of ladies to swell his volume—"

"How shrewd that Monsieur de Brantome is," said the beautiful Mademoiselle de Limueil to the Comtesse de Fiesque; "he came to us first, but he means to remain in the Guise quarters."

"Hush!" said Madame de Fiesque glancing at the beautiful Limueil. "Attend to what concerns yourself."

The young girl turned her eyes to the door. She was expecting Sardini, a noble Italian, with whom the queen-mother, her relative, married her after an "accident" which happened in the dressing-room of Catherine de' Medici herself; but which the young lady won the honor of having a queen as midwife.

"By the holy Alipantin! Mademoiselle Davila seems to me prettier and prettier every morning," said Monsieur de Robertet, secretary of State, bowing to the ladies of the queen-mother.

The arrival of the secretary of State made no commotion whatever, though his office was precisely what that of a minister is in these days.

"If you really think so, monsieur," said the beauty, "lend me the squib which was written against the Messieurs de Guise; I know it was lent to you."

"It is no longer in my possession," replied the secretary, turning round to bow to the Duchesse de Guise.

"I have it," said the Comte de Grammont to Mademoiselle Davila, "but I will give it you on one condition only."

"Condition! fie!" exclaimed Madame de Fiesque.

"You don't know what it is," replied Grammont.

"Oh! it is easy to guess," remarked la Limueil.

The Italian custom of calling ladies, as peasants call their wives, "*la* Such-a-one" was then the fashion at the court of France.

"You are mistaken," said the count, hastily, "the matter is simply to give a letter from my cousin de Jarnac to one of the maids on the other side, Mademoiselle de Matha."

"You must not compromise my young ladies," said the Comtesse de Fiesque. "I will deliver the letter myself.—Do you know what is happening in Flanders?" she continued, turning to the Cardinal de Tournon. "It seems that Monsieur d'Egmont is given to surprises."

"He and the Prince of Orange," remarked Cypierre, with a significant shrug of his shoulders.

"The Duke of Alba and Cardinal Granvelle are going there, are they not, monsieur?" said Amyot to the Cardinal de Tournon, who remained standing, gloomy and anxious between the opposing groups after his conversation with the chancellor.

"Happily we are at peace; we need only conquer heresy on the stage," remarked the young Duc d'Orleans, alluding to a part he had played the night before,—that of a knight subduing a hydra which bore upon its foreheads the word "Reformation."

Catherine de' Medici, agreeing in this with her daughter-in-law, had allowed a theatre to be made of the great hall (afterwards arranged for the Parliament of Blois), which, as we have already said, connected the chateau of Francois I. with that of Louis XII.

The cardinal made no answer to Amyot's question, but resumed his walk through the centre of the hall, talking in low tones with Monsieur de Robertet and the chancellor. Many persons are ignorant of the difficulties which secretaries of State (subsequently called ministers) met with at the first establishment of their office, and how much trouble the kings of France had in creating it. At this epoch a secretary of State like Robertet was purely and simply a writer; he counted for almost nothing among the princes and grandees who decided the affairs of State. His functions were little more than those of the superintendent of finances, the chancellor, and the keeper of the seals. The kings granted seats at the council by letters-patent to those of their subjects whose advice seemed to them useful in the management of public affairs. Entrance to the council was given in this way to a president of the Chamber of Parliament, to a bishop, or to an untitled favorite. Once admitted to the council, the subject strengthened his position there by obtaining various crown offices on which devolved such prerogatives as the sword of a Constable, the government of provinces, the grand-mastership of artillery, the baton of a marshal, a leading rank in the army, or the admiralty, or a captaincy of the galleys, often some office at court, like that of grand-master of the household, now held, as we have already said, by the Duc de Guise.

"Do you think that the Duc de Nemours will marry Francoise?" said Madame de Guise to the tutor of the Duc d'Orleans.

"Ah, madame," he replied, "I know nothing but Latin."

This answer made all who were within hearing of it smile. The seduction of Francoise de Rohan by the Duc de Nemours was the topic of all conversations; but, as the duke was cousin to Francois II., and doubly allied to the house of Valois through his mother, the Guises regarded him more as the seduced than the seducer. Nevertheless, the power of the house of Rohan was such that the Duc de Nemours was obliged, after the death of Francois II., to leave France on consequence of suits brought against him by the Rohans; which suits the Guises settled. The duke's marriage with the Duchesse de Guise after Poltrot's assassination of her husband in 1563, may explain the question which she put to Amyot, by revealing the rivalry which must have existed between Mademoiselle de Rohan and the duchess.

"Do see that group of the discontented over there?" said the Comte de Grammont, motioning toward the Messieurs de Coligny, the Cardinal de Chatillon, Danville, Thore, Moret, and several other seigneurs suspected of tampering with the Reformation, who were standing between two windows on the other side of the fireplace.

"The Huguenots are bestirring themselves," said Cypierre. "We know that Theodore de Beze has gone to Nerac to induce the Queen of Navarre to declare for the Reformers—by abjuring publicly," he added, looking at the *bailli* of Orleans, who held the office of chancellor to the Queen of Navarre, and was watching the court attentively.

"She will do it!" said the *bailli*, dryly.

This personage, the Orleans Jacques Coeur, one of the richest burghers of the day, was named Groslot, and had charge of Jeanne d'Albret's business with the court of France.

"Do you really think so?" said the chancellor of France, appreciating the full importance of Groslot's declaration.

"Are you not aware," said the burgher, "that the Queen of Navarre has nothing of the woman in her except sex? She is wholly for things virile; her powerful mind turns to the great affairs of State; her heart is invincible under adversity."

"Monsieur le cardinal," whispered the Chancellor Olivier to Monsieur de Tournon, who had overheard Groslot, "what do you think of that audacity?"

"The Queen of Navarre did well in choosing for her chancellor a man from whom the house of Lorraine borrows money, and who offers his house to the king, if his Majesty visits Orleans," replied the cardinal.

The chancellor and the cardinal looked at each other, without venturing to further communicate their thoughts; but Robertet expressed them, for he thought it necessary to show more devotion to the Guises than these great personages, inasmuch as he was smaller than they.

"It is a great misfortune that the house of Navarre, instead of abjuring the religion of its fathers, does not abjure the spirit of vengeance and rebellion which the Connetable de Bourbon breathed into it," he said aloud. "We shall see the quarrels of the Armagnacs and the Bourguignons revive in our day."

"No," said Groslot, "there's another Louis XI. in the Cardinal de Lorraine."

"And also in Queen Catherine," replied Robertet.

At this moment Madame Dayelle, the favorite bedchamber woman of Queen Mary Stuart, crossed the hall, and went toward the royal chamber. Her passage caused a general commotion.

"We shall soon enter," said Madame de Fisque.

"I don't think so," replied the Duchesse de Guise. "Their Majesties will come out; a grand council is to be held."

VI. THE LITTLE LEVER OF FRANCOIS II.

Madame Dayelle glided into the royal chamber after scratching on the door,—a respectful custom, invented by Catherine de' Medici and adopted by the court of France.

"How is the weather, my dear Dayelle?" said Queen Mary, showing her fresh young face out of the bed, and shaking the curtains.

"Ah! madame—"

"What's the matter, my Dayelle? You look as if the archers of the guard were after you."

"Oh! madame, is the king still asleep?"

"Yes."

"We are to leave the chateau; Monsieur le cardinal requests me to tell you so, and to ask you to make the king agree to it.

"Do you know why, my good Dayelle?"

"The Reformers want to seize you and carry you off."

"Ah! that new religion does not leave me a minute's peace! I dreamed last night that I was in prison,—I, who will some day unite the crowns of the three noblest kingdoms in the world!"

"Therefore it could only be a dream, madame."

"Carry me off! well, 'twould be rather pleasant; but on account of religion, and by heretics—oh, that would be horrid."

The queen sprang from the bed and placed herself in a large arm-chair of red velvet before the fireplace, after Dayelle had given her a dressing-gown of black velvet, which she fastened loosely round her waist by a silken cord. Dayelle lit the fire, for the mornings are cool on the banks of the Loire in the month of May.

"My uncles must have received some news during the night?" said the queen, inquiringly to Dayelle, whom she treated with great familiarity.

"Messieurs de Guise have been walking together from early morning on the terrace, so as not to be overheard by any one; and there they received messengers, who came in hot haste from all the different points of the kingdom where the Reformers are stirring. Madame la reine mere was there too, with her Italians, hoping she would be consulted; but no, she was not admitted to the council."

"She must have been furious."

"All the more because she was so angry yesterday," replied Dayelle. "They say that when she saw your Majesty appear in that beautiful dress of woven gold, with the charming veil of tan-colored crape, she was none too pleased—"

"Leave us, my good Dayelle, the king is waking up. Let no one, even those who have the little *entrees*, disturb us; an affair of State is in hand, and my uncles will not disturb us."

"Why! my dear Mary, already out of bed? Is it daylight?" said the young king, waking up.

"My dear darling, while we were asleep the wicked waked, and now they are forcing us to leave this delightful place."

"What makes you think of wicked people, my treasure? I am sure we enjoyed the prettiest fete in the world last night—if it were not for the Latin words those gentlemen will put into our French."

"Ah!" said Mary, "your language is really in very good taste, and Rabelais exhibits it finely."

"You are such a learned woman! I am so vexed that I can't sing your praises in verse. If I were not the king, I would take my brother's tutor, Amyot, and let him make me as accomplished as Charles."

"You need not envy your brother, who writes verses and shows them to me, asking for mine in return. You are the best of the four, and will make as good a king as you are the dearest of lovers. Perhaps that is why your mother does not like you! But never mind! I, dear heart, will love you for all the world."

"I have no great merit in loving such a perfect queen," said the little king. "I don't know what prevented me from kissing you before the whole court when you danced the *branle* with the torches last night! I saw plainly that all the other women were mere servants compared to you, my beautiful Mary."

"It may be only prose you speak, but it is ravishing speech, dear darling, for it is love that says those words. And you—you know well, my beloved, that were you only a poor little page, I should love you as much as I do now. And yet, there is nothing so sweet as to whisper to one's self: 'My lover is king!'"

"Oh! the pretty arm! Why must we dress ourselves? I love to pass my fingers through your silky hair and tangle its blond curls. Ah ca! sweet one, don't let your women kiss that pretty throat and those white shoulders any more; don't allow it, I say. It is too much that the fogs of Scotland ever touched them!"

"Won't you come with me to see my dear country? The Scotch love you; there are no rebellions *there*!"

"Who rebels in this our kingdom?" said Francois, crossing his dressing-gown and taking Mary Stuart on his knee.

"Oh! 'tis all very charming, I know that," she said, withdrawing her cheek from the king; "but it is your business to reign, if you please, my sweet sire."

"Why talk of reigning? This morning I wish—"

"Why say *wish* when you have only to will all? That's not the speech of a king, nor that of a lover.—But no more of love just now; let us drop it! We have business more important to speak of."

"Oh!" cried the king, "it is long since we have had any business. Is it amusing?"

"No," said Mary, "not at all; we are to move from Blois."

"I'll wager, darling, you have seen your uncles, who manage so well that

I, at seventeen years of age, am no better than a *roi faineant*. In fact, I don't know why I have attended any of the councils since the first. They could manage matters just as well by putting the crown in my chair; I see only through their eyes, and am forced to consent to things blindly."

"Oh! monsieur," said the queen, rising from the king's knee with a little air of indignation, "you said you would never worry me again on this subject, and that my uncles used the royal power only for the good of your people. Your people!—they are so nice! They would gobble you up like a strawberry if you tried to rule them yourself. You want a warrior, a rough master with mailed hands; whereas you—you are a darling whom I love as you are; whom I should never love otherwise,—do you hear me, monsieur?" she added, kissing the forehead of the lad, who seemed inclined to rebel at her speech, but softened at her kisses.

"Oh! how I wish they were not your uncles!" cried Francois II. "I particularly dislike the cardinal; and when he puts on his wheedling air and his submissive manner and says to me, bowing: 'Sire, the honor of the crown and the faith of your fathers forbid your Majesty to—this and that,' I am sure he is working only for his cursed house of Lorraine."

"Oh, how well you mimicked him!" cried the queen. "But why don't you make the Guises inform you of what is going on, so that when you attain your grand majority you may know how to reign yourself? I am your wife, and your honor is mine. Trust me! we will reign together, my darling; but it won't be a bed of roses for us until the day comes when we have our own wills. There is nothing so difficult for a king as to reign. Am I a queen, for example? Don't you know that your mother returns me evil for all the good my uncles do to raise the splendor of your throne? Hey! what difference between them! My uncles are great princes, nephews of Charlemagne, filled with ardor and ready to die for you; whereas this daughter of a doctor or a shopkeeper, queen of France by accident, scolds like a burgher-woman who can't manage her own household. She is discontented because she can't set every one by the ears; and then she looks at me with a sour, pale face, and says from her pinched lips: 'My daughter, you are a queen; I am only the second woman in the kingdom' (she is really furious, you know, my darling), 'but if I were in your place I should not wear crimson velvet while all the court is in mourning; neither should I appear in public with my own hair and no jewels, because what is not becoming in a simple lady is still less becoming in a queen. Also I should not dance myself, I should content myself with seeing others dance.'—that is what she says to me—"

"Heavens!" cried the king, "I think I hear her coming. If she were to know—"

"Oh, how you tremble before her. She worries you. Only say so, and we will send her away. Faith, she's Florentine and we can't help her tricking you, but when it comes to worrying—"

"For Heaven's sake, Mary, hold your tongue!" said Francois, frightened and also pleased; "I don't want you to lose her good-will."

"Don't be afraid that she will ever break with *me*, who will some day wear the three noblest crowns in the world, my dearest little king," cried Mary Stuart. "Though she hates me for a thousand reasons she is always caressing me in the hope of turning me against my uncles."

"Hates you!"

"Yes, my angel; and if I had not proofs of that feeling such as women only understand, for they alone know its malignity, I would forgive her perpetual opposition to our dear love, my darling. Is it my fault that your father could not endure Mademoiselle Medici or that his son loves me? The truth is, she hates me so much that if you had not put yourself into a rage, we should each have had our separate chamber at Saint-Germain, and also here. She pretended it was the custom of the kings and queens of France. Custom, indeed! it was your father's custom, and that is easily understood. As for your grandfather, Francois, the good man set up the custom for the convenience of his loves. Therefore, I say, take care. And if we have to leave this place, be sure that we are not separated."

"Leave Blois! Mary, what do you mean? I don't wish to leave this beautiful chateau, where we can see the Loire and the country all round us, with a town at our feet and all these pretty gardens. If I go away it will be to Italy with you, to see St. Peter's, and Raffaelle's pictures."

"And the orange-trees? Oh! my darling king, if you knew the longing your Mary has to ramble among the orange-groves in fruit and flower!"

"Let us go, then!" cried the king.

"Go!" exclaimed the grand-master as he entered the room. "Yes, sire, you must leave Blois. Pardon my boldness in entering your chamber; but circumstances are stronger than etiquette, and I come to entreat you to hold a council."

Finding themselves thus surprised, Mary and Francois hastily separated, and on their faces was the same expression of offended royal majesty.

"You are too much of a grand-master, Monsieur de Guise," said the king, though controlling his anger.

"The devil take lovers," murmured the cardinal in Catherine's ear.

"My son," said the queen-mother, appearing behind the cardinal; "it is a matter concerning your safety and that of your kingdom."

"Heresy wakes while you have slept, sire," said the cardinal.

"Withdraw into the hall," cried the little king, "and then we will hold a council."

"Madame," said the grand-master to the young queen; "the son of your furrier has brought some furs, which was just in time for the journey, for it is probable we shall sail down the Loire. But," he added, turning to the queen-mother, "he also wishes to speak to you, madame. While the king dresses, you and Madame la reine had better see and dismiss him, so that we may not be delayed and harassed by this trifle."

"Certainly," said Catherine, thinking to herself, "If he expects to get rid of me by any such trick he little knows me."

The cardinal and the duke withdrew, leaving the two queens and the king alone together. As they crossed the *salle des gardes* to enter the council-chamber, the grand-master told the usher to bring the queen's furrier to him. When Christophe saw the usher approaching from the farther end of the great hall, he took him, on account of his uniform, for some great personage, and his heart sank within him. But that sensation, natural as it was at the approach of the critical moment, grew terrible when the usher, whose movement had attracted the eyes of all that brilliant assembly upon Christophe, his homely face and his bundles, said to him:—

"Messeigneurs the Cardinal de Lorraine and the Grand-master wish to speak to you in the council chamber."

"Can I have been betrayed?" thought the helpless ambassador of the Reformers.

Christophe followed the usher with lowered eyes, which he did not raise till he stood in the great council-chamber, the size of which is almost equal to that of the *salle des gardes*. The two Lorrain princes were there alone, standing before the magnificent fireplace, which backs against that in the *salle des gardes* around which the ladies of the two queens were grouped.

"You have come from Paris; which route did you take?" said the cardinal.

"I came by water, monseigneur," replied the reformer.

"How did you enter Blois?" asked the grand-master.

"By the docks, monseigneur."

"Did no one question you?" exclaimed the duke, who was watching the young man closely.

"No, monseigneur. To the first soldier who looked as if he meant to stop me I said I came on duty to the two queens, to whom my father was furrier."

"What is happening in Paris?" asked the cardinal.

"They are still looking for the murderer of the President Minard."

"Are you not the son of my surgeon's greatest friend?" said the Duc de Guise, misled by the candor of Christophe's expression after his first alarm had passed away.

"Yes, monseigneur."

The Grand-master turned aside, abruptly raised the portiere which concealed the double door of the council-chamber, and showed his face to the whole assembly, among whom he was searching for the king's surgeon. Ambroise Pare, standing in a corner, caught a glance which the duke cast upon him, and immediately advanced. Ambroise, who at this time was inclined to the reformed religion, eventually adopted it; but the friendship of the Guises and that of the kings of France guaranteed him against the evils which overtook his co-religionists. The duke, who considered himself under obligations for life to Ambroise Pare, had lately caused him to be appointed chief-surgeon to the king.

"What is it, monseigneur?" said Ambroise. "Is the king ill? I think it likely."

"Likely? Why?"

"The queen is too pretty," replied the surgeon.

"Ah!" exclaimed the duke in astonishment. "However, that is not the matter now," he added after a pause. "Ambroise, I want you to see a friend of yours." So saying he drew him to the door of the council-room, and showed him Christophe.

"Ha! true, monseigneur," cried the surgeon, extending his hand to the young furrier. "How is your father, my lad?"

"Very well, Maitre Ambroise," replied Christophe.

"What are you doing at court?" asked the surgeon. "It is not your business to carry parcels; your father intends you for the law. Do you want the protection of these two great princes to make you a solicitor?"

"Indeed I do!" said Christophe; "but I am here only in the interests of my father; and if you could intercede for us, please do so," he added in a piteous tone; "and ask the Grand Master for an order to pay certain sums that are due to my father, for he is at his wit's end just now for money."

The cardinal and the duke glanced at each other and seemed satisfied.

"Now leave us," said the duke to the surgeon, making him a sign. "And you my friend," turning to Christophe; "do your errand quickly and return to Paris. My secretary will give you a pass, for it is not safe, *mordieu*, to be travelling on the high-roads!"

Neither of the brothers formed the slightest suspicion of the grave importance of Christophe's errand, convinced, as they now were, that he was really the son of the good Catholic Lecamus, the court furrier, sent to collect payment for their wares.

"Take him close to the door of the queen's chamber; she will probably ask for him soon," said the cardinal to the surgeon, motioning to Christophe.

While the son of the furrier was undergoing this brief examination in the council-chamber, the king, leaving the queen in company with her mother-in-law, had passed into his dressing-room, which was entered through another small room next to the chamber.

Standing in the wide recess of an immense window, Catherine looked at the gardens, her mind a prey to painful thoughts. She saw that in all probability one of the greatest captains of the age would be foisted that very day into the place and power of her son, the king of France, under the formidable title of lieutenant-general of the kingdom. Before this peril she stood alone, without power of action, without defence. She might have been likened to a phantom, as she stood there in her mourning garments (which she had not quitted since the death of Henri II.) so motionless was her pallid face in the grasp of her bitter reflections. Her black eyes floated in that species of indecision for which great statesmen are so often blamed, though it comes from the vast extent of the glance with which they embrace all difficulties,—setting one against the other, and adding up, as it were, all chances before deciding on a course. Her ears rang, her blood tingled, and yet she stood there calm and dignified, all the while measuring in her soul the depths of the political abyss which lay before her, like the natural depths which rolled away at her feet. This day was the second of those terrible days (that of the arrest of the Vidame of Chartres being the first) which she was destined to meet in so great numbers throughout her regal life; it also witnessed her last blunder in the school of power. Though the sceptre seemed escaping from her hands, she wished to seize it; and she did seize it by a flash of that power of will which was never relaxed by either the disdain of her father-in-law, Francois I., and his court,—where, in spite of her rank of dauphiness, she had been of no account,—or the constant repulses of her husband, Henri II., and the terrible opposition of her rival, Diane de Poitiers. A man would never have fathomed this thwarted queen; but the fair-haired Mary—so subtle, so clever, so girlish, and already so well-trained—examined her out of the corners of her eyes as she hummed an Italian air and assumed a careless countenance. Without being able to guess the storms of repressed ambition which sent the dew of a cold sweat to the forehead of the Florentine, the pretty Scotch girl, with her wilful, piquant face, knew very well that the advancement of her uncle the Duc de Guise to the lieutenant-generalship of the kingdom was filling the queen-mother with inward rage. Nothing amused her more than to watch her mother-in-law, in whom she saw only an intriguing woman of low birth, always ready to avenge herself. The face of the one was grave and gloomy, and somewhat terrible, by reason of the livid tones which transform the skin of Italian women to yellow ivory by daylight, though it recovers its dazzling brilliancy under candlelight; the face of the other was fair and fresh and gay. At sixteen, Mary Stuart's skin had that exquisite blond whiteness which made her beauty so celebrated. Her fresh and piquant face, with its pure lines, shone with the roguish mischief of childhood, expressed in the regular eyebrows, the vivacious eyes, and the archness of the pretty mouth. Already she displayed those feline graces which nothing, not even captivity nor the sight of her dreadful scaffold, could lessen. The two queens—one at the dawn, the other in the midsummer of life—presented at this moment the utmost contrast. Catherine was an imposing queen, an impenetrable widow, without other passion than that of power. Mary was a light-hearted, careless bride, making playthings of her triple crowns. One foreboded great evils,—foreseeing the assassination of the Guises as the only means of suppressing enemies who were resolved to rise above the Throne and the Parliament; foreseeing also the bloodshed of a long and bitter struggle; while the other little anticipated her own judicial murder. A sudden and strange reflection calmed the mind of the Italian.

"That sorceress and Ruggiero both declare this reign is coming to an end; my difficulties will not last long," she thought.

And so, strangely enough, an occult science forgotten in our day—that of astrology—supported Catherine at this moment, as it did, in fact, throughout her life; for, as she witnessed the minute fulfilment of the prophecies of those who practised the art, her belief in it steadily increased.

"You are very gloomy, madame," said Mary Stuart, taking from the hands of her waiting-woman, Dayelle, a little cap and placing the point of it on the parting of her hair, while two wings of rich lace surrounded the tufts of blond curls which clustered on her temples.

The pencil of many painters have so frequently represented this head-dress that it is thought to have belonged exclusively to Mary Queen of Scots; whereas it was really invented by Catherine de' Medici, when she put on mourning for Henri II. But she never knew how to wear it with the grace of her daughter-in-law, to whom it was becoming. This annoyance was not the least among the many which the queen-mother cherished against the young queen.

"Is the queen reproving me?" said Catherine, turning to Mary.

"I owe you all respect, and should not dare to do so," said the Scottish queen, maliciously, glancing at Dayelle.

Placed between the rival queens, the favorite waiting-woman stood rigid as an andiron; a smile of comprehension might have cost her her life.

"Can I be as gay as you, after losing the late king, and now beholding my son's kingdom about to burst into flames?"

"Public affairs do not concern women," said Mary Stuart. "Besides, my uncles are there."

These words were, under the circumstances, like so many poisoned arrows.

"Let us look at our furs, madame," replied the Italian, sarcastically; "that will employ us on our legitimate female affairs while your uncles decide those of the kingdom."

"Oh! but we will go the Council, madame; we shall be more useful than you think."

"We!" said Catherine, with an air of astonishment. "But I do not understand Latin, myself."

"You think me very learned," cried Mary Stuart, laughing, "but I assure you, madame, I study only to reach the level of the Medici, and learn how to *cure* the wounds of the kingdom."

Catherine was silenced by this sharp thrust, which referred to the origin of the Medici, who were descended, some said, from a doctor of medicine, others from a rich druggist. She made no direct answer. Dayelle colored as her mistress looked at her, asking for the applause that even queens demand from their inferiors if there are no other spectators.

"Your charming speeches, madame, will unfortunately cure the wounds of neither Church nor State," said Catherine at last, with her calm and cold dignity. "The science of my fathers in that direction gave them thrones; whereas if you continue to trifle in the midst of danger you are liable to lose yours."

It was at this moment that Ambroise Pare, the chief surgeon, scratched softly on the door, and Madame Dayelle, opening it, admitted Christophe.

VII. A DRAMA IN A SURCOAT

The young reformer intended to study Catherine's face, all the while affecting a natural embarrassment at finding himself in such a place; but his proceedings were much hastened by the eagerness with which the younger queen darted to the cartons to see her surcoat.

"Madame," said Christophe, addressing Catherine.

He turned his back on the other queen and on Dayelle, instantly profiting by the attention the two women were eager to bestow upon the furs to play a bold stroke.

"What do you want of me?" said Catherine giving him a searching look.

Christophe had put the treaty proposed by the Prince de Conde, the plan of the Reformers, and the detail of their forces in his bosom between his shirt and his cloth jacket, folding them, however, within the bill which Catherine owed to the furrier.

"Madame," he said, "my father is in horrible need of money, and if you will deign to cast your eyes over your bill," here he unfolded the paper and put the treaty on the top of it, "you will see that your Majesty owes him six thousand crowns. Have the goodness to take pity on us. See, madame!" and he held the treaty out to her. "Read it; the account dates from the time the late king came to the throne."

Catherine was bewildered by the preamble of the treaty which met her eye, but she did not lose her head. She folded the paper quickly, admiring the audacity and presence of mind of the youth, and feeling sure that after performing such a masterly stroke he would not fail to understand her. She therefore tapped him on the head with the folded paper, saying:—

"It is very clumsy of you, my little friend, to present your bill before the furs. Learn to know women. You must never ask us to pay until the moment when we are satisfied."

"Is that traditional?" said the young queen, turning to her mother-in-law, who made no reply.

"Ah, mesdames, pray excuse my father," said Christophe. "If he had not had such need of money you would not have had your furs at all. The country is in arms, and there are so many dangers to run in getting here that nothing but our great distress would have brought me. No one but me was willing to risk them."

"The lad is new to his business," said Mary Stuart, smiling.

It may not be useless, for the understanding of this trifling, but very important scene, to remark that a surcoat was, as the name implies (*sur cotte*), a species of close-fitting spencer which women wore over their bodies and down to their thighs, defining the figure. This garment protected the back, chest, and throat from cold. These surcoats were lined with fur, a band of which, wide or narrow as the case might be, bordered the outer material. Mary Stuart, as she tried the garment on, looked at herself in a large Venetian mirror to see the effect behind, thus leaving her mother-in-law an opportunity to examine the papers, the bulk of which might have excited the young queen's suspicions had she noticed it.

"Never tell women of the dangers you have run when you have come out of them safe and sound," she said, turning to show herself to Christophe.

"Ah! madame, I have your bill, too," he said, looking at her with well-played simplicity.

The young queen eyed him, but did not take the paper; and she noticed, though without at the moment drawing any conclusions, that he had taken her bill from his pocket, whereas he had carried Queen Catherine's in his bosom. Neither did she find in the lad's eyes that glance of admiration which her presence invariably excited in all beholders. But she was so engrossed by her surcoat that, for the moment, she did not ask herself the meaning of such indifference.

"Take the bill, Dayelle," she said to her waiting-woman; "give it to Monsieur de Versailles (Lomenie) and tell him from me to pay it."

"Oh! madame," said Christophe, "if you do not ask the king or monseigneur the grand-master to sign me an order your gracious word will have no effect."

"You are rather more eager than becomes a subject, my friend," said Mary Stuart. "Do you not believe my royal word?"

The king now appeared, in silk stockings and trunk-hose (the breeches of that period), but without his doublet and mantle; he had, however, a rich loose coat of velvet edged with minever.

"Who is the wretch who dares to doubt your word?" he said, overhearing, in spite of his distance, his wife's last words.

The door of the dressing-room was hidden by the royal bed. This room was afterwards called "the old cabinet," to distinguish it from the fine cabinet of pictures which Henri III. constructed at the farther end of the same suite of rooms, next to the hall of the States-general. It was in the old cabinet that Henri III. hid the murderers when he sent for the Duc de Guise, while he himself remained hidden in the new cabinet during the murder, only emerging in time to see the overbearing subject for whom there were no longer prisons, tribunals, judges, nor even laws, draw his last breath. Were it not for these terrible circumstances the historian of to-day could hardly trace the former occupation of these cabinets, now filled with soldiers. A quartermaster writes to his mistress on the very spot where the pensive Catherine once decided on her course between the parties.

"Come with me, my friend," said the queen-mother, "and I will see that you are paid. Commerce must live, and money is its backbone."

"Go, my lad," cried the young queen, laughing; "my august mother knows more than I do about commerce."

Catherine was about to leave the room without replying to this last taunt; but she remembered that her indifference to it might provoke suspicion, and she answered hastily:—

"But you, my dear, understand the business of love."

Then she descended to her own apartments.

"Put away these furs, Dayelle, and let us go to the Council, monsieur," said Mary to the young king, enchanted with the opportunity of deciding in the absence of the queen-mother so important a question as the lieutenant-generalship of the kingdom.

Mary Stuart took the king's arm. Dayelle went out before them, whispering to the pages; one of whom (it was young Teligny, who afterwards perished so miserably during the Saint-Bartholomew) cried out:—

"The king!"

Hearing the words, the two soldiers of the guard presented arms, and the two pages went forward to the door of the Council-room through the lane of courtiers and that of the maids of honor of the two queens. All the members of the Council then grouped themselves about the door of their chamber, which was not very far from the door to the staircase. The grand-master, the cardinal, and the chancellor advanced to meet the young sovereign, who smiled to several of the maids of honor and replied to the remarks of a few courtiers more privileged than the rest. But the queen, evidently impatient, drew Francois II. as quickly as possible toward the Council-chamber. When the sound of arquebuses, dropping heavily on the floor, had announced the entrance of the couple, the pages replaced their caps upon their heads, and the private talk among the courtiers on the gravity of the matters now about to be discussed began again.

"They sent Chiverni to fetch the Connetable, but he has not come," said one.

"There is not a single prince of the blood present," said another.

"The chancellor and Monsieur de Tournon looked anxious," remarked a third.

"The grand-master sent word to the keeper of the seals to be sure not to miss this Council; therefore you may be certain they will issue letters-patent."

"Why does the queen-mother stay in her own apartments at such a time?"

"They'll cut out plenty of work for us," remarked Groslot to Cardinal de Chatillon.

In short, everybody had a word to say. Some went and came, in and out of the great hall; others hovered about the maids of honor of both queens, as if it might be possible to catch a few words through a wall three feet thick or through the double doors draped on each side with heavy curtains.

Seated at the upper end of a long table covered with blue velvet, which stood in the middle of the room, the king, near to whom the young queen was seated in an arm-chair, waited for his mother. Robertet, the secretary, was mending pens. The two cardinals, the grand-master, the chancellor, the keeper of the seals, and all the rest of the council looked at the little king, wondering why he did not give them the usual order to sit down.

The two Lorrain princes attributed the queen-mother's absence to some trick of their niece. Incited presently by a significant glance, the audacious cardinal said to his Majesty:—

"Is it the king's good pleasure to begin the council without waiting for Madame la reine-mere?"

Francois II., without daring to answer directly, said: "Messieurs, be seated."

The cardinal then explained succinctly the dangers of the situation. This great political character, who showed extraordinary ability under these pressing circumstances, led up to the question of the lieutenancy of the kingdom in the midst of the deepest silence. The young king doubtless felt the tyranny that was being exercised over him; he knew that his mother had a deep sense of the rights of the Crown and was fully aware of the danger that threatened his power; he therefore replied to a positive question addressed to him by the cardinal by saying:—

"We will wait for the queen, my mother."

Suddenly enlightened by the queen-mother's delay, Mary Stuart recalled, in a flash of thought, three circumstances which now struck her vividly; first, the bulk of the papers presented to her mother-in-law, which she had noticed, absorbed as she was,—for a woman who seems to see nothing is often a lynx; next, the place where Christophe had carried them to keep them separate from hers: "Why so?" she thought to herself; and thirdly, she remembered the cold, indifferent glance of the young man, which she suddenly attributed to the hatred of the Reformers to a niece of the Guises. A voice cried to her, "He may have been an emissary of the Huguenots!" Obeying, like all excitable natures, her first impulse, she exclaimed:—

"I will go and fetch my mother myself!"

Then she left the room hurriedly, ran down the staircase, to the amazement of the courtiers and the ladies of honor, entered her mother-in-law's apartments, crossed the guard-room, opened the door of the chamber with the caution of a thief, glided like a shadow over the carpet, saw no one, and bethought her that she should surely surprise the queen-mother in that magnificent dressing-room which comes between the bedroom and the oratory. The arrangement of this oratory, to which the manners of that period gave a role in private life like that of the boudoirs of our day, can still be traced.

By an almost inexplicable chance, when we consider the state of dilapidation into which the Crown has allowed the chateau of Blois to fall, the admirable woodwork of Catherine's cabinet still exists; and in those delicately carved panels, persons interested in such things may still see traces of Italian splendor, and discover the secret hiding-places employed by the queen-mother. An exact description of these curious arrangements is necessary in order to give a clear understanding of what was now to happen. The woodwork of the oratory then consisted of about a hundred and eighty oblong panels, one hundred of which still exist, all presenting arabesques of different designs, evidently suggested by the most beautiful arabesques of Italy. The wood is live-oak. The red tones, seen through the layer of whitewash put on to avert cholera (useless precaution!), shows very plainly that the ground of the panels was formerly gilt. Certain portions of the design, visible where the wash has fallen away, seem to show that they once detached themselves from the gilded ground in colors, either blue, or red, or green. The multitude of these panels shows an evident intention to foil a search; but even if this could be doubted, the concierge of the chateau, while devoting the memory of Catherine to the execration of the humanity of our day, shows at the base of these panels and close to the floor a rather heavy foot-board, which can be lifted, and beneath which still remain the ingenious springs which move the panels. By pressing a knob thus hidden, the queen was able to open certain panels known to her alone, behind which, sunk in the wall, were hiding-places, oblong like the panels, and more or less deep. It is difficult, even in these days of dilapidation, for the best-trained eye to detect which of those panels is thus hinged; but when the eye was distracted by colors and gilding, cleverly used to conceal the joints, we can readily conceive that to find one or two such panels among two hundred was almost an impossible thing.

At the moment when Mary Stuart laid her hand on the somewhat complicated lock of the door of this oratory, the queen-mother, who had just become convinced of the greatness of the Prince de Conde's plans, had touched the spring hidden beneath the foot-board, and one of the mysterious panels had turned over on its hinges. Catherine was in the act of lifting the papers from the table to hide them, intending after that to secure the safety of the devoted messenger who had brought them to her, when, hearing the sudden opening of the door, she at once knew that none but Queen Mary herself would dare thus to enter without announcement.

"You are lost!" she said to Christophe, perceiving that she could no longer put away the papers, nor close with sufficient rapidity the open panel, the secret of which was now betrayed.

Christophe answered her with a glance that was sublime.

"*Povero mio!*" said Catherine, before she looked at her daughter-in-law.

"Treason, madame! I hold the traitors at last," she cried. "Send for the duke and the cardinal; and see that that man," pointing to Christophe, "does not escape."

In an instant the able woman had seen the necessity of sacrificing the poor youth. She could not hide him; it was impossible to save him. Eight days earlier it might have been done; but the Guises now knew of the plot; they must already possess the lists she held in her hand, and were evidently drawing the Reformers into a trap. Thus, rejoiced to find in these adversaries the very spirit she desired them to have, her policy now led her to make a merit of the discovery of their plot. These horrible calculations were made during the rapid moment while the young queen was opening the door. Mary Stuart stood dumb for an instant; the gay look left her eyes, which took on the acuteness that suspicion gives to the eyes of all, and which, in hers, became terrible from the suddenness of the change. She glanced from Christophe to the queen-mother and from the queen-mother back to Christophe,—her face expressing malignant doubt. Then she seized a bell, at the sound of which one of the queen-mother's maids of honor came running in.

"Mademoiselle du Rouet, send for the captain of the guard," said Mary Stuart to the maid of honor, contrary to all etiquette, which was necessarily violated under the circumstances.

While the young queen gave this order, Catherine looked intently at Christophe, as if saying to him, "Courage!"

The Reformer understood, and replied by another glance, which seemed to say, "Sacrifice me, as *they* have sacrificed me!"

"Rely on me," said Catherine by a gesture. Then she absorbed herself in the documents as her daughter-in-law turned to him.

"You belong to the Reformed religion?" inquired Mary Stuart of Christophe.

"Yes, madame," he answered.

"I was not mistaken," she murmured as she again noticed in the eyes of the young Reformer the same cold glance in which dislike was hidden beneath an expression of humility.

Pardaillan suddenly appeared, sent by the two Lorrain princes and by the king to escort the queens. The captain of the guard called for by Mary Stuart followed the young officer, who was devoted to the Guises.

"Go and tell the king and the grand-master and the cardinal, from me, to come here at once, and say that I should not take the liberty of sending for them if something of the utmost importance had not occurred. Go, Pardaillan.—As for you, Lewiston, keep guard over that traitor of a Reformer," she said to the Scotchman in his mother-tongue, pointing to Christophe.

The young queen and queen-mother maintained a total silence until the arrival of the king and princes. The moments that elapsed were terrible. Mary Stuart had betrayed to her mother-in-law, in its fullest extent, the part her uncles were inducing her to play; her constant and habitual distrust and espionage were now revealed, and her young conscience told her how dishonoring to a great queen was the work that she was doing. Catherine, on the other hand, had yielded out of fear; she was still afraid of being rightly understood, and she trembled for her future. Both women, one ashamed and angry, the other filled with hatred and yet calm, went to the embrasure of the window and leaned against the casing, one to right, the other to left, silent; but their feelings were expressed in such speaking glances that they averted their eyes and, with mutual artfulness, gazed through the window at the sky. These two great and superior women had, at this crisis, no greater art of behavior than the vulgarest of their sex. Perhaps it is always thus when circumstances arise which overwhelm the human being. There is, inevitably, a moment when genius itself feels its littleness in presence of great catastrophes.

As for Christophe, he was like a man in the act of rolling down a precipice. Lewiston, the Scotch captain, listened to this silence, watching the son of the furrier and the two queens with soldierly curiosity. The entrance of the king and Mary Stuart's two uncles put an end to the painful situation.

VIII. MARTYRDOM

The cardinal went straight to the queen-mother.

"I hold the threads of the conspiracy of the heretics," said Catherine. "They have sent me this treaty and these documents by the hands of that child," she added.

During the time that Catherine was explaining matters to the cardinal, Queen Mary whispered a few words to the grand-master.

"What is all this about?" asked the young king, who was left alone in the midst of the violent clash of interests.

"The proofs of what I was telling to your Majesty have not been long in reaching us," said the cardinal, who had grasped the papers.

The Duc de Guise drew his brother aside without caring that he interrupted him, and said in his ear, "This makes me lieutenant-general without opposition."

A shrewd glance was the cardinal's only answer; showing his brother that he fully understood the advantages to be gained from Catherine's false position.

"Who sent you here?" said the duke to Christophe.

"Chaudieu, the minister," he replied.

"Young man, you lie!" said the soldier, sharply; "it was the Prince de Conde."

"The Prince de Conde, monseigneur!" replied Christophe, with a puzzled look. "I never met him. I am studying law with Monsieur de Thou; I am his secretary, and he does not know that I belong to the Reformed religion. I yielded only to the entreaties of the minister."

"Enough!" exclaimed the cardinal. "Call Monsieur de Robertet," he said to Lewiston, "for this young scamp is slyer than an old statesman; he has managed to deceive my brother, and me too; an hour ago I would have given him the sacrament without confession."

"You are not a child, *morbleu*!" cried the duke, "and we'll treat you as a man."

"The heretics have attempted to beguile your august mother," said the cardinal, addressing the king, and trying to draw him apart to win him over to their ends.

"Alas!" said the queen-mother to her son, assuming a reproachful look and stopping the king at the moment when the cardinal was leading him into the oratory to subject him to his dangerous eloquence, "you see the result of the situation in which I am; they think me irritated by the little influence that I have in public affairs,—I, the mother of four princes of the house of Valois!"

The young king listened attentively. Mary Stuart, seeing the frown upon his brow, took his arm and led him away into the recess of the window, where she cajoled him with sweet speeches in a low voice, no doubt like those she had used that morning in their chamber. The two Guises read the documents given up to them by Catherine. Finding that they contained information which their spies, and Monsieur Braguelonne, the lieutenant of the Chatelet, had not obtained, they were inclined to believe in the sincerity of Catherine de' Medici. Robertet came and received certain secret orders relative to Christophe. The youthful instrument of the leaders of the Reformation was then led away by four soldiers of the Scottish guard, who took him down the stairs and delivered him to Monsieur de Montresor, provost of the chateau. That terrible personage himself, accompanied by six of his men, conducted Christophe to the prison in the vaulted cellar of the tower, now in ruins, which the concierge of the chateau de Blois shows you with the information that these were the dungeons.

After such an event the Council could be only a formality. The king, the young queen, the Grand-master, and the cardinal returned to it, taking with them the vanquished Catherine, who said no word except to approve the measures proposed by the Guises. In spite of a slight opposition from the Chancelier Olivier (the only person present who said one word that expressed the independence to which his office bound him), the Duc de Guise was appointed lieutenant-general of the kingdom. Robertet brought the required documents, showing a devotion which might be called collusion. The king, giving his arm to his mother, recrossed the *salle des gardes*, announcing to the court as he passed along that on the following day he should leave Blois for the chateau of Amboise. The latter residence had been abandoned since the time when Charles VIII. accidentally killed himself by striking his head against the casing of a door on which he had ordered carvings, supposing that he could enter without stooping below the scaffolding. Catherine, to mask the plans of the Guises, remarked aloud that they intended to complete the chateau of Amboise for the Crown at the same time that her own chateau of Chemonceaux was finished. But no one was the dupe of that pretext, and all present awaited great events.

After spending about two hours endeavoring to see where he was in the obscurity of the dungeon, Christophe ended by discovering that the place was sheathed in rough woodwork, thick enough to make the square hole into which he was put both healthy and habitable. The door, like that of a pig-pen, was so low that he stooped almost double on entering it. Beside this door was a heavy iron grating, opening upon a sort of corridor, which gave a little light and a little air. This arrangement, in all respects like that of the dungeons of Venice, showed plainly that the architecture of the chateau of Blois belonged to the Venetian school, which during the Middle Ages, sent so many builders into all parts of Europe. By tapping this species of pit above the woodwork Christophe discovered that the walls which separated his cell to right and left from the adjoining ones were made of brick. Striking one of them to get an idea of its thickness, he was somewhat surprised to hear return blows given on the other side.

"Who are you?" said his neighbor, speaking to him through the corridor.

"I am Christophe Lecamus."

"I," replied the voice, "am Captain Chaudieu, brother of the minister. I was taken prisoner to-night at Beaugency; but, luckily, there is nothing against me."

"All is discovered," said Christophe; "you are fortunate to be saved from the fray."

"We have three thousand men at this moment in the forests of the Vendomois, all determined men, who mean to abduct the king and the queen-mother during their journey. Happily La Renaudie was cleverer than I; he managed to escape. You had only just left us when the Guise men surprised us—"

"But I don't know La Renaudie."

"Pooh! my brother has told me all about it," said the captain.

Hearing that, Christophe sat down upon his bench and made no further answer to the pretended captain, for he knew enough of the police to be aware how necessary it was to act with prudence in a prison. In the middle of the night he saw the pale light of a lantern in the corridor, after hearing the ponderous locks of the iron door which closed the cellar groan as they were turned. The provost himself had come to fetch Christophe. This attention to a prisoner who had been left in his dark dungeon for hours without food, struck the poor lad as singular. One of the provost's men bound his hands with a rope and held him by the end of it until they reached one of the lower halls of the chateau of Louis XII., which was evidently the antechamber to the apartments of some important personage. The provost and his men bade him sit upon a bench, and the man then bound his feet as he had before bound his hands. On a sign from Monsieur de Montresor the man left the room.

"Now listen to me, my friend," said the provost-marshal, toying with the collar of the Order; for, late as the hour was, he was in full uniform.

This little circumstance gave the young man several thoughts; he saw that all was not over; on the contrary, it was evidently neither to hang nor yet to condemn him that he was brought here.

"My friend, you may spare yourself cruel torture by telling me all you know of the understanding between Monsieur le Prince de Conde and Queen Catherine. Not only will no harm be done to you, but you shall enter the service of Monseigneur the lieutenant-general of the kingdom, who likes intelligent men and on whom your honest face has produced a good impression. The queen-mother is about to be sent back to Florence, and Monsieur de Conde will no doubt be brought to trial. Therefore, believe me, humble folks ought to attach themselves to the great men who are in power. Tell me all; and you will find your profit in it."

"Alas, monsieur," replied Christophe; "I have nothing to tell. I told all I know to Messieurs de Guise in the queen's chamber. Chaudieu persuaded me to put those papers under the eyes of the queen-mother; assuring me that they concerned the peace of the kingdom."

"You have never seen the Prince de Conde?"

"Never."

Thereupon Monsieur de Montresor left Christophe and went into the adjoining room; but the youth was not left long alone. The door through which he had been brought opened and gave entrance to several men, who did not close it. Sounds that were far from reassuring were heard from the courtyard; men were bringing wood and machinery, evidently intended for the punishment of the Reformer's messenger. Christophe's anxiety soon had matter for reflection in the preparations which were made in the hall before his eyes.

Two coarse and ill-dressed serving-men obeyed the orders of a stout, squat, vigorous man, who cast upon Christophe, as he entered, the glance of a cannibal upon his victim; he looked him over and *estimated* him,— measuring, like a connoisseur, the strength of his nerves, their power and their endurance. The man was the executioner of Blois. Coming and going, his assistants brought in a mattress, several mallets and wooden wedges, also planks and other articles, the use of which was not plain, nor their look comforting to the poor boy concerned in these preparations, whose blood now curdled in his veins from a vague but most terrible apprehension. Two personages entered the hall at the moment when Monsieur de Montresor reappeared.

"Hey, nothing ready!" cried the provost-marshal, to whom the new-comers bowed with great respect. "Don't you know," he said, addressing the stout man and his two assistants, "that Monseigneur the cardinal thinks you already at work? Doctor," added the provost, turning to one of the new-comers, "this is the man"; and he pointed to Christophe.

The doctor went straight to the prisoner, unbound his hands, and struck him on the breast and back. Science now continued, in a serious manner, the truculent examination of the executioner's eye. During this time a servant in the livery of the house of Guise brought in several arm-chairs, a table, and writing-materials.

"Begin the *proces verbal*," said Monsieur de Montresor, motioning to the table the second personage, who was dressed in black, and was evidently a clerk. Then the provost went up to Christophe, and said to him in a very gentle way: "My friend, the chancellor, having learned that you refuse to answer me in a satisfactory manner, decrees that you be put to the question, ordinary and extraordinary."

"Is he in good health, and can he bear it?" said the clerk to the doctor.

"Yes," replied the latter, who was one of the physicians of the house of Lorraine.

"In that case, retire to the next room; we will send for you whenever we require your advice."

The physician left the hall.

His first terror having passed, Christophe rallied his courage; the hour of his martyrdom had come. Thenceforth he looked with cold curiosity at the arrangements that were made by the executioner and his men. After hastily preparing a bed, the two assistants got ready certain appliances called *boots*; which consisted of several planks, between which each leg of the victim was placed. The legs thus placed were brought close together. The apparatus used by binders to press their volumes between two boards, which they fasten by cords, will give an exact idea of the manner in which each leg of the prisoner was bound. We can imagine the effect produced by the insertion of wooden wedges, driven in by hammers between the planks of the two bound legs,—the two sets of planks of course not yielding, being themselves bound together by ropes. These wedges were driven in on a line with the knees and the ankles. The choice of these places where there is little flesh, and where, consequently, the wedge could only be forced in by crushing the bones, made this form of torture, called the "question," horribly painful. In the "ordinary question" four wedges were driven in,—two at the knees, two at the ankles; but in the "extraordinary question" the number was increased to eight, provided the doctor certified that the prisoner's vitality was not exhausted. At the time of which we write the "boots" were also applied in the same manner to the hands and wrists; but, being pressed for time, the cardinal, the lieutenant-general, and the chancellor spared Christophe that additional suffering.

The *proces verbal* was begun; the provost dictated a few sentences as he walked up and down with a meditative air, asking Christophe his name, baptismal name, age, and profession; then he inquired the name of the person from whom he had received the papers he had given to the queen.

"From the minister Chaudieu," answered Christophe.

"Where did he give them to you?"

"In Paris."

"In giving them to you he must have told you whether the queen-mother would receive you with pleasure?"

"He told me nothing of that kind," said Christophe. "He merely asked me to give them to Queen Catherine secretly."

"You must have seen Chaudieu frequently, or he would not have known that you were going to Blois."

"The minister did not know from me that in carrying furs to the queen I was also to ask on my father's behalf for the money the queen-mother owes him; and I did not have time to ask the minister who had told him of it."

"But these papers, which were given to you without being sealed or enveloped, contained a treaty between the rebels and Queen Catherine. You must have seen that they exposed you to the punishment of all those who assist in a rebellion."

"Yes."

"The persons who persuaded you to this act of high treason must have promised you rewards and the protection of the queen-mother."

"I did it out of attachment to Chaudieu, the only person whom I saw in the matter."

"Do you persist in saying you did not see the Prince de Conde?"

"Yes."

"The Prince de Conde did not tell you that the queen-mother was inclined to enter into his views against the Messieurs de Guise?"

"I did not see him."

"Take care! one of your accomplices, La Renaudie, has been arrested. Strong as he is, he was not able to bear the 'question,' which will now be put to you; he confessed at last that both he and the Prince de Conde had an interview with you. If you wish to escape the torture of the question, I exhort you to tell me the simple truth. Perhaps you will thus obtain your full pardon."

Christophe answered that he could not state a thing of which he had no knowledge, or give himself accomplices when he had none. Hearing these words, the provost-marshal signed to the executioner and retired himself to the inner room. At that fatal sign Christophe's brows contracted, his forehead worked with nervous convulsion, as he prepared himself to suffer. His hands closed with such violence that the nails entered the flesh without his feeling them. Three men seized him, took him to the camp bed and laid him there, letting his legs hang down. While the executioner fastened him to the rough bedstead with strong cords, the assistants bound his legs into the "boots." Presently the cords were tightened, by means of a wrench, without the pressure causing much pain to the young Reformer. When each leg was thus held as it were in a vice, the executioner grasped his hammer and picked up the wedges, looking alternately at the victim and at the clerk.

"Do you persist in your denial?" asked the clerk.

"I have told the truth," replied Christophe.

"Very well. Go on," said the clerk, closing his eyes.

The cords were tightened with great force. This was perhaps the most painful moment of the torture; the flesh being suddenly compressed, the blood rushed violently toward the breast. The poor boy could not restrain a dreadful cry and seemed about to faint. The doctor was called in. After feeling Christophe's pulse, he told the executioner to wait a quarter of an hour before driving the first wedge in, to let the action of the blood subside and allow the victim to recover his full sensitiveness. The clerk suggested, kindly, that if he could not bear this beginning of sufferings which he could not escape, it would be better to reveal all at once; but Christophe made no reply except to say, "The king's tailor! the king's tailor!"

"What do you mean by those words?" asked the clerk.

"Seeing what torture I must bear," said Christophe, slowly, hoping to gain time to rest, "I call up all my strength, and try to increase it by thinking of the martyrdom borne by the king's tailor for the holy cause of the Reformation, when the question was applied to him in presence of Madame la Duchesse de Valentinois and the king. I shall try to be worthy of him."

While the physician exhorted the unfortunate lad not to force them to have recourse to more violent measures, the cardinal and the duke, impatient to know the result of the interrogations, entered the hall and themselves asked Christophe to speak the truth, immediately. The young man repeated the only confession he had allowed himself to make, which implicated no one but Chaudieu. The princes made a sign, on which the executioner and his assistant seized their hammers, taking each a wedge, which then they drove in between the joints, standing one to right, the other to left of their victim; the executioner's wedge was driven in at the knees, his assistant's at the ankles.

The eyes of all present fastened on those of Christophe, and he, no doubt excited by the presence of those great personages, shot forth such burning glances that they appeared to have all the brilliancy of flame. As the third and fourth wedges were driven in, a dreadful groan escaped him. When he saw the executioner take up the wedges for the "extraordinary question" he said no word and made no sound, but his eyes took on so terrible a fixity, and he cast upon the two great princes who were watching him a glance so penetrating, that the duke and cardinal were forced to drop their eyes. Philippe le Bel met with the same resistance when the torture of the pendulum was applied in his presence to the Templars. That punishment consisted in striking the victim on the breast with one arm of the balance pole with which money is coined, its end being covered with a pad of leather. One of the knights thus tortured, looked so intently at the king that Philippe could not detach his eyes from him. At the third blow the king left the chamber on hearing the knight summon him to appear within a year before the judgment-seat of God,—as, in fact, he did. At the fifth blow, the first of the "extraordinary question," Christophe said to the cardinal: "Monseigneur, put an end to my torture; it is useless."

The cardinal and the duke re-entered the adjoining hall, and Christophe distinctly heard the following words said by Queen Catherine: "Go on; after all, he is only a heretic."

She judged it prudent to be more stern to her accomplice than the executioners themselves.

The sixth and seventh wedges were driven in without a word of complaint from Christophe. His face shone with extraordinary brilliancy, due, no doubt, to the excess of strength which his fanatic devotion gave him. Where else but in the feelings of the soul can we find the power necessary to bear such sufferings? Finally, he smiled when he saw the executioner lifting the eighth and last wedge. This horrible torture had lasted by this time over an hour.

The clerk now went to call the physician that he might decide whether the eighth wedge could be driven in without endangering the life of the victim. During this delay the duke returned to look at Christophe.

"*Ventre-de-biche*! you are a fine fellow," he said to him, bending down to whisper the words. "I love brave men. Enter my service, and you shall be rich and happy; my favors shall heal those wounded limbs. I do not propose to you any baseness; I will not ask you to return to your party and betray its plans,—there are always traitors enough for that, and the proof is in the prisons of Blois; tell me only on what terms are the queen-mother and the Prince de Conde?"

"I know nothing about it, monseigneur," replied Christophe Lecamus.

The physician came, examined the victim, and said that he could bear the eighth wedge.

"Then insert it," said the cardinal. "After all, as the queen says, he is only a heretic," he added, looking at Christophe with a dreadful smile.

At this moment Catherine came with slow steps from the adjoining apartment and stood before Christophe, coldly observing him. Instantly she was the object of the closest attention on the part of the two brothers, who watched alternately the queen and her accomplice. On this solemn test the whole future of that ambitious woman depended; she felt the keenest admiration for Christophe, yet she gazed sternly at him; she hated the Guises, and she smiled upon them!

"Young man," said the queen, "confess that you have seen the Prince de Conde, and you will be richly rewarded."

"Ah! what a business this is for you, madame!" cried Christophe, pitying her.

The queen quivered.

"He insults me!" she exclaimed. "Why do you not hang him?" she cried, turning to the two brothers, who stood thoughtful.

"What a woman!" said the duke in a glance at his brother, consulting him by his eye, and leading him to the window.

"I shall stay in France and be revenged upon them," thought the queen. "Come, make him confess, or let him die!" she said aloud, addressing Montresor.

The provost-marshal turned away his eyes, the executioners were busy with the wedges; Catherine was free to cast one glance upon the martyr, unseen by others, which fell on Christophe like the dew. The eyes of the great queen seemed to him moist; two tears were in them, but they did not fall. The wedges were driven; a plank was broken by the blow. Christophe gave one dreadful cry, after which he was silent; his face shone,—he believed he was dying.

"Let him die?" said the cardinal, echoing the queen's last words with a sort of irony; "no, no! don't break that thread," he said to the provost.

The duke and the cardinal consulted together in a low voice.

"What is to be done with him?" asked the executioner.

"Send him to the prison at Orleans," said the duke, addressing Monsieur de Montresor; "and don't hang him without my order."

The extreme sensitiveness to which Christophe's internal organism had been brought, increased by a resistance which called into play every power of the human body, existed to the same degree, in his senses. He alone heard the following words whispered by the Duc de Guise in the ear of his brother the cardinal:

"I don't give up all hope of getting the truth out of that little fellow yet."

When the princes had left the hall the executioners unbound the legs of their victim roughly and without compassion.

"Did any one ever see a criminal with such strength?" said the chief executioner to his aids. "The rascal bore that last wedge when he ought to have died; I've lost the price of his body."

"Unbind me gently; don't make me suffer, friends," said poor Christophe. "Some day I will reward you—"

"Come, come, show some humanity," said the physician. "Monseigneur esteems the young man, and told me to look after him."

"I am going to Amboise with my assistants,—take care of him yourself," said the executioner, brutally. "Besides, here comes the jailer."

The executioner departed, leaving Christophe in the hands of the soft-spoken doctor, who by the aid of Christophe's future jailer, carried the poor boy to a bed, brought him some broth, helped him to swallow it, sat down beside him, felt his pulse, and tried to comfort him.

"You won't die of this," he said. "You ought to feel great inward comfort, knowing that you have done your duty.—The queen-mother bids me take care of you," he added in a whisper.

"The queen is very good," said Christophe, whose terrible sufferings had developed an extraordinary lucidity in his mind, and who, after enduring such unspeakable sufferings, was determined not to compromise the results of his devotion. "But she might have spared me much agony be telling my persecutors herself the secrets that I know nothing about, instead of urging them on."

Hearing that reply, the doctor took his cap and cloak and left Christophe, rightly judging that he could worm nothing out of a man of that stamp. The jailer of Blois now ordered the poor lad to be carried away on a stretcher by four men, who took him to the prison in the town, where Christophe immediately fell into the deep sleep which, they say, comes to most mothers after the terrible pangs of childbirth.

IX. THE TUMULT AT AMBOISE

By moving the court to the chateau of Amboise, the two Lorrain princes intended to set a trap for the leader of the party of the Reformation, the Prince de Conde, whom they had made the king summon to his presence. As vassal of the Crown and prince of the blood, Conde was bound to obey the summons of his sovereign. Not to come to Amboise would constitute the crime of treason; but if he came, he put himself in the power of the Crown. Now, at this moment, as we have seen, the Crown, the council, the court, and all their powers were solely in the hands of the Duc de Guise and the Cardinal de Lorraine. The Prince de Conde showed, at this delicate crisis, a presence of mind and a decision and willingness which made him the worthy exponent of Jeanne d'Albret and the valorous general of the Reformers. He travelled at the rear of the conspirators as far as Vendome, intending to support them in case of their success. When the first uprising ended by a brief skirmish, in which the flower of the nobility beguiled by Calvin perished, the prince arrived, with fifty noblemen, at the chateau of Amboise on the very day after that fight, which the politic Guises termed "the Tumult of Amboise." As soon as the duke and cardinal heard of his coming they sent the Marechal de Saint-Andre with an escort of a hundred men to meet him. When the prince and his own escort reached the gates of the chateau the marechal refused entrance to the latter.

"You must enter alone, monseigneur," said the Chancellor Olivier, the Cardinal de Tournon, and Birago, who were stationed outside of the portcullis.

"And why?"

"You are suspected of treason," replied the chancellor.

The prince, who saw that his suite were already surrounded by the troop of the Duc de Nemours, replied tranquilly: "If that is so, I will go alone to my cousin, and prove to him my innocence."

He dismounted, talked with perfect freedom of mind to Birago, the Cardinal de Tournon, the chancellor, and the Duc de Nemours, from whom he asked for particulars of the "tumult."

"Monseigneur," replied the duke, "the rebels had confederates in Amboise. A captain, named Lanoue, had introduced armed men, who opened the gate to them, through which they entered and made themselves masters of the town—"

"That is to say, you opened the mouth of a sack, and they ran into it," replied the prince, looking at Birago.

"If they had been supported by the attack which Captain Chaudieu, the preacher's brother, was expected to make before the gate of the Bon-Hommes, they would have been completely successful," replied the Duc de Nemours. "But in consequence of the position which the Duc de Guise ordered me to take up, Captain Chaudieu was obliged to turn my flank to avoid a fight. So instead of arriving by night, like the rest, this rebel and his men got there at daybreak, by which time the king's troops had crushed the invaders of the town."

"And you had a reserve force to recover the gate which had been opened to them?" said the prince.

"Monsieur le Marechal de Saint-Andre was there with five hundred men-at-arms."

The prince gave the highest praise to these military arrangements.

"The lieutenant-general must have been fully aware of the plans of the Reformers, to have acted as he did," he said in conclusion. "They were no doubt betrayed."

The prince was treated with increasing harshness. After separating him from his escort at the gates, the cardinal and the chancellor barred his way when he reached the staircase which led to the apartments of the king.

"We are directed by his Majesty, monseigneur, to take you to your own apartments," they said.

"Am I, then, a prisoner?"

"If that were the king's intention you would not be accompanied by a prince of the Church, nor by me," replied the chancellor.

These two personages escorted the prince to an apartment, where guards of honor—so-called—were given him. There he remained, without seeing any one, for some hours. From his window he looked down upon the Loire and the meadows of the beautiful valley stretching from Amboise to Tours. He was reflecting on the situation, and asking himself whether the Guises would really dare anything against his person, when the door of his chamber opened and Chicot, the king's fool, formerly a dependent of his own, entered the room.

"They told me you were in disgrace," said the prince.

"You'd never believe how virtuous the court has become since the death of Henri II."

"But the king loves a laugh."

"Which king,—Francois II., or Francois de Lorraine?"

"You are not afraid of the duke, if you talk in that way!"

"He wouldn't punish me for it, monseigneur," replied Chicot, laughing.

"To what do I owe the honor of this visit?"

"Hey! Isn't it due to you on your return? I bring you my cap and bells."

"Can I go out?"

"Try."

"Suppose I do go out, what then?"

"I should say that you had won the game by playing against the rules."

"Chicot, you alarm me. Are you sent here by some one who takes an interest in me?"

"Yes," said Chicot, nodding. He came nearer to the prince, and made him understand that they were being watched and overheard.

"What have you to say to me?" asked the Prince de Conde, in a low voice.

"Boldness alone can pull you out of this scrape; the message comes from the queen-mother," replied the fool, slipping his words into the ear of the prince.

"Tell those who sent you," replied Conde, "that I should not have entered this chateau if I had anything to reproach myself with, or to fear."

"I rush to report that lofty answer!" cried the fool.

Two hours later, that is, about one o'clock in the afternoon, before the king's dinner, the chancellor and Cardinal de Tournon came to fetch the prince and present him to Francois II. in the great gallery of the chateau of Amboise, where the councils were held. There, before the whole court, Conde pretended surprise at the coldness with which the little king received him, and asked the reason of it.

"You are accused, cousin," said the queen-mother, sternly, "of taking part in the conspiracy of the Reformers; and you must prove yourself a faithful subject and a good Catholic, if you do not desire to draw down upon your house the anger of the king."

Hearing these words said, in the midst of the most profound silence, by Catherine de' Medici, on whose right arm the king was leaning, the Duc d'Orleans being on her left side, the Prince de Conde recoiled three steps, laid his hand on his sword with a proud motion, and looked at all the persons who surrounded him.

"Those who said that, madame," he cried in an angry voice, "lied in their throats!"

Then he flung his glove at the king's feet, saying: "Let him who believes that calumny come forward!"

The whole court trembled as the Duc de Guise was seen to leave his place; but instead of picking up the glove, he advanced to the intrepid hunchback.

"If you desire a second in that duel, monseigneur, do me the honor to accept my services," he said. "I will answer for you; I know that you will

113

show the Reformers how mistaken they are if they think to have you for their leader."

The prince was forced to take the hand of the lieutenant-general of the kingdom. Chicot picked up the glove and returned it to Monsieur de Conde.

"Cousin," said the little king, "you must draw your sword only for the defence of the kingdom. Come and dine."

The Cardinal de Lorraine, surprised at his brother's action, drew him away to his own apartments. The Prince de Conde, having escaped his apparent danger, offered his hand to Mary Stuart to lead her to the dining hall; but all the while that he made her flattering speeches he pondered in his mind what trap the astute Balafre was setting for him. In vain he worked his brains, for it was not until Queen Mary herself betrayed it that he guessed the intention of the Guises.

"'Twould have been a great pity," she said laughing, "if so clever a head had fallen; you must admit that my uncle has been generous."

"Yes, madame; for my head is only useful on my shoulders, though one of them is notoriously higher than the other. But is this really your uncle's generosity? Is he not getting the credit of it rather cheaply? Do you think it would be so easy to take off the head of a prince of the blood?"

"All is not over yet," she said. "We shall see what your conduct will be at the execution of the noblemen, your friends, at which the Council has decided to make a great public display of severity."

"I shall do," said the prince, "whatever the king does."

"The king, the queen-mother, and myself will be present at the execution, together with the whole court and the ambassadors—"

"A fete!" said the prince, sarcastically.

"Better than that," said the young queen, "an *act of faith*, an act of the highest policy. 'Tis a question of forcing the noblemen of France to submit themselves to the Crown, and compelling them to give up their tastes for plots and factions—"

"You will not break their belligerent tempers by the show of danger, madame; you will risk the Crown itself in the attempt," replied the prince. At the end of the dinner, which was gloomy enough, Queen Mary had the cruel boldness to turn the conversation openly upon the trial of the noblemen on the charge of being seized with arms in their hands, and to speak of the necessity of making a great public show of their execution.

"Madame," said Francois II., "is it not enough for the king of France to know that so much brave blood is to flow? Must he make a triumph of it?"

"No, sire; but an example," replied Catherine.

114

"It was the custom of your father and your grandfather to be present at the burning of heretics," said Mary Stuart.

"The kings who reigned before me did as they thought best, and I choose to do as I please," said the little king.

"Philip the Second," remarked Catherine, "who is certainly a great king, lately postponed an *auto da fe* until he could return from the Low Countries to Valladolid."

"What do you think, cousin?" said the king to Prince de Conde.

"Sire, you cannot avoid it, and the papal nuncio and all the ambassadors should be present. I shall go willingly, as these ladies take part in the fete."

Thus the Prince de Conde, at a glance from Catherine de' Medici, bravely chose his course.

At the moment when the Prince de Conde was entering the chateau d'Amboise, Lecamus, the furrier of the two queens, was also arriving from Paris, brought to Amboise by the anxiety into which the news of the tumult had thrown both his family and that of Lallier. When the old man presented himself at the gate of the chateau, the captain of the guard, on hearing that he was the queens' furrier, said:—

"My good man, if you want to be hanged you have only to set foot in this courtyard."

Hearing these words, the father, in despair, sat down on a stone at a little distance and waited until some retainer of the two queens or some servant-woman might pass who would give him news of his son. But he sat there all day without seeing any one whom he knew, and was forced at last to go down into the town, where he found, not without some difficulty, a lodging in a hostelry on the public square where the executions took place. He was obliged to pay a pound a day to obtain a room with a window looking on the square. The next day he had the courage to watch, from his window, the execution of all the abettors of the rebellion who were condemned to be broken on the wheel or hanged, as persons of little importance. He was happy indeed not to see his own son among the victims.

When the execution was over he went into the square and put himself in the way of the clerk of the court. After giving his name, and slipping a purse full of crowns into the man's hand, he begged him to look on the records and see if the name of Christophe Lecamus appeared in either of the three preceding executions. The clerk, touched by the manner and the tones of the despairing father, took him to his own house. After a careful search he was able to give the old man an absolute assurance that Christophe was not among the persons thus far executed, nor among those who were to be put to death within a few days.

"My dear man," said the clerk, "Parliament has taken charge of the trial of the great lords implicated in the affair, and also that of the principal leaders. Perhaps your son is detained in the prisons of the chateau, and he may be brought forth for the magnificent execution which their Excellencies the Duc de Guise and the Cardinal de Lorraine are now preparing. The heads of twenty-seven barons, eleven counts, and seven marquises,—in all, fifty noblemen or leaders of the Reformers,—are to be cut off. As the justiciary of the county of Tourine is quite distinct from that of the parliament of Paris, if you are determined to know about your son, I advise you to go and see the Chancelier Olivier, who has the management of this great trial under orders from the lieutenant-general of the kingdom."

The poor old man, acting on this advice, went three times to see the chancellor, standing in a long queue of persons waiting to ask mercy for their friends. But as the titled men were made to pass before the burghers, he was obliged to give up the hope of speaking to the chancellor, though he saw him several times leave the house to go either to the chateau or to the committee appointed by the Parliament,—passing each time between a double hedge of petitioners who were kept back by the guards to allow him free passage. It was a horrible scene of anguish and desolation; for among these petitioners were many women, wives, mothers, daughters, whole families in distress. Old Lecamus gave much gold to the footmen of the chateau, entreating them to put certain letters which he wrote into the hand either of Dayelle, Queen Mary's woman, or into that of the queen-mother; but the footmen took the poor man's money and carried the letters, according to the general order of the cardinal, to the provost-marshal. By displaying such unheard-of cruelty the Guises knew that they incurred great dangers from revenge, and never did they take such precautions for their safety as they did while the court was at Amboise; consequently, neither the greatest of all corrupters, gold, nor the incessant and active search which the old furrier instituted gave him the slightest gleam of light on the fate of his son. He went about the little town with a mournful air, watching the great preparations made by order of the cardinal for the dreadful show at which the Prince de Conde had agreed to be present.

Public curiosity was stimulated from Paris to Nantes by the means adopted on this occasion. The execution was announced from all pulpits by the rectors of the churches, while at the same time they gave thanks for the victory of the king over the heretics. Three handsome balconies, the middle one more sumptuous than the other two, were built against the terrace of the chateau of Amboise, at the foot of which the executions were appointed to take place. Around the open square, stagings were erected, and these were filled with an immense crowd of people attracted by the wide-spread notoriety given to this "act of faith." Ten thousand persons camped in the adjoining fields the night before the day on which the horrible spectacle was appointed to take place. The roofs on the houses were crowded with spectators, and windows were let at ten pounds apiece,—an enormous sum in those days. The poor old father had engaged, as we may well believe, one of the best places from which the eye could take in the whole of the terrible scene, where so many men of noble blood were to perish on a vast scaffold covered with black cloth, erected in the middle of the open square. Thither, on the morning of the fatal day, they brought the *chouquet*,—a name given to the block on which the condemned man laid his head as he knelt before it. After this they brought an arm-chair draped with black, for the clerk of the Parliament, whose business it was to call up the condemned noblemen to their death and read their sentences. The whole square was guarded from early morning by the Scottish guard and the gendarmes of the king's household, in order to keep back the crowd which threatened to fill it before the hour of the execution.

After a solemn mass said at the chateau and in the churches of the town, the condemned lords, the last of the conspirators who were left alive, were led out. These gentlemen, some of whom had been put to the torture, were grouped at the foot of the scaffold and surrounded by monks, who endeavored to make them abjure the doctrines of Calvin. But not a single man listened to the words of the priests who had been appointed for this duty by the Cardinal of Lorraine; among whom the gentlemen no doubt feared to find spies of the Guises. In order to avoid the importunity of these antagonists they chanted a psalm, put into French verse by Clement Marot. Calvin, as we all know, had ordained that prayers to God should be in the language of each country, as much from a principle of common sense as in opposition to the Roman worship. To those in the crowd who pitied these unfortunate gentlemen it was a moving incident to hear them chant the following verse at the very moment when the king and court arrived and took their places:—

"God be merciful unto us,
  And bless us!
And show us the light of his countenance,
  And be merciful unto us."

The eyes of all the Reformers turned to their leader, the Prince de Conde, who was placed intentionally between Queen Mary and the young Duc d'Orleans. Catherine de' Medici was beside the king, and the rest of the court were on her left. The papal nuncio stood behind Queen Mary; the lieutenant-general of the kingdom, the Duc de Guise, was on horseback below the balcony, with two of the marshals of France and his staff captains. When the Prince de Conde appeared all the condemned noblemen who knew him bowed to him, and the brave hunchback returned their salutation.

"It would be hard," he remarked to the Duc d'Orleans, "not to be civil to those about to die."

The two other balconies were filled by invited guests, courtiers, and persons on duty about the court. In short, the whole company of the chateau de Blois had come to Amboise to assist at this festival of death, precisely as it passed, a little later, from the pleasures of a court to the perils of war, with an easy facility, which will always seem to foreigners one of the main supports of their policy toward France.

The poor syndic of the furriers of Paris was filled with the keenest joy at not seeing his son among the fifty-seven gentlemen who were condemned to die.

At a sign from the Duc de Guise, the clerk seated on the scaffold cried in a loud voice:—

"Jean-Louis-Alberic, Baron de Raunay, guilty of heresy, of the crime of *lese-majeste*, and assault with armed hand against the person of the king."

A tall handsome man mounted the scaffold with a firm step, bowed to the people and the court, and said:

"That sentence lies. I took arms to deliver the king from his enemies, the Guises."

He placed his head on the block, and it fell. The Reformers chanted:—

"Thou, O God! hast proved us;
Thou hast tried us;
As silver is tried in the fire,
So hast thou purified us."

"Robert-Jean-Rene Briquemart, Comte de Villemongis, guilty of the crime of *lese-majeste*, and of attempts against the person of the king!" called the clerk.

The count dipped his hands in the blood of the Baron de Raunay, and said:—

"May this blood recoil upon those who are really guilty of those crimes."

The Reformers chanted:—

"Thou broughtest us into the snare;
Thou laidest afflictions upon our loins;
Thou hast suffered our enemies

To ride over us."

"You must admit, monseigneur," said the Prince de Conde to the papal nuncio, "that if these French gentlemen know how to conspire, they also know how to die."

"What hatreds, brother!" whispered the Duchesse de Guise to the Cardinal de Lorraine, "you are drawing down upon the heads of our children!"

"The sight makes me sick," said the young king, turning pale at the flow of blood.

"Pooh! only rebels!" replied Catherine de' Medici.

The chants went on; the axe still fell. The sublime spectacle of men singing as they died, and, above all, the impression produced upon the crowd by the progressive diminution of the chanting voices, superseded the fear inspired by the Guises.

"Mercy!" cried the people with one voice, when they heard the solitary chant of the last and most important of the great lords, who was saved to be the final victim. He alone remained at the foot of the steps by which the others had mounted the scaffold, and he chanted:—

"Thou, O God, be merciful unto us,
And bless us,
And cause thy face to shine upon us.
Amen!"

"Come, Duc de Nemours," said the Prince de Conde, weary of the part he was playing; "you who have the credit of the skirmish, and who helped to make these men prisoners, do you not feel under an obligation to ask mercy for this one? It is Castelnau, who, they say, received your word of honor that he should be courteously treated if he surrendered."

"Do you think I waited till he was here before trying to save him?" said the Duc de Nemours, stung by the stern reproach.

The clerk called slowly—no doubt he was intentionally slow:—

"Michel-Jean-Louis, Baron de Castelnau-Chalosse, accused and convicted of the crime of *lese-majeste*, and of attempts against the person of the king."

"No," said Castelnau, proudly, "it cannot be a crime to oppose the tyranny and the projected usurpation of the Guises."

The executioner, sick of his task, saw a movement in the king's gallery, and fumbled with his axe.

"Monsieur le baron," he said, "I do not want to execute you; a moment's delay may save you."

All the people again cried, "Mercy!"

"Come!" said the king, "mercy for that poor Castelnau, who saved the life of the Duc d'Orleans."

The cardinal intentionally misunderstood the king's speech.

"Go on," he motioned to the executioner, and the head of Castelnau fell at the very moment when the king had pronounced his pardon.

"That head, cardinal, goes to your account," said Catherine de' Medici.

The day after this dreadful execution the Prince de Conde returned to Navarre.

The affair produced a great sensation in France and at all the foreign courts. The torrents of noble blood then shed caused such anguish to the chancellor Olivier that his honorable mind, perceiving at last the real end and aim of the Guises disguised under a pretext of defending religion and the monarchy, felt itself no longer able to make head against them. Though he was their creature, he was not willing to sacrifice his duty and the Throne to their ambition; and he withdrew from his post, suggesting l'Hopital as his rightful successor. Catherine, hearing of Olivier's suggestion, immediately proposed Birago, and put much warmth into her request. The cardinal, knowing nothing of the letter written by l'Hopital to the queen-mother, and supposing him faithful to the house of Lorraine, pressed his appointment in opposition to that of Birago, and Catherine allowed herself to seem vanquished. From the moment that l'Hopital entered upon his duties he took measures against the Inquisition, which the Cardinal de Lorraine was desirous of introducing into France; and he thwarted so successfully all the anti-gallican policy of the Guises, and proved himself so true a Frenchmen, that in order to subdue him he was exiled, within three months of his appointment, to his country-seat of Vignay, near Etampes.

The worthy old Lecamus waited impatiently till the court left Amboise, being unable to find an opportunity to speak to either of the queens, and hoping to put himself in their way as the court advanced along the river-bank on its return to Blois. He disguised himself as a pauper, at the risk of being taken for a spy, and by means of this travesty, he mingled with the crowd of beggars which lined the roadway. After the departure of the Prince de Conde, and the execution of the leaders, the duke and cardinal thought they had sufficiently silenced the Reformers to allow the queen-mother a little more freedom. Lecamus knew that, instead of travelling in a litter, Catherine intended to go on horseback, *a la planchette*,—such was the name given to a sort of stirrup invented for or by the queen-mother, who, having hurt her leg on some occasion, ordered a velvet-covered saddle with a plank on which she could place both feet by sitting sideways on the horse and passing one leg through a depression in the saddle. As the queen-mother had very handsome legs, she was accused of inventing this method of riding, in order to show them. The old furrier fortunately found a moment when he could present himself to her sight; but the instant that the queen recognized him she gave signs of displeasure.

"Go away, my good man, and let no one see you speak to me," she said with anxiety. "Get yourself elected deputy to the States-general, by the guild of your trade, and act for me when the Assembly convenes at Orleans; you shall know whom to trust in the matter of your son."

"Is he living?" asked the old man.

"Alas!" said the queen, "I hope so."

Lecamus was obliged to return to Paris with nothing better than those doubtful words and the secret of the approaching convocation of the States-general, thus confided to him by the queen-mother.

X. COSMO RUGGIERO

The Cardinal de Lorraine obtained, within a few days of the events just related, certain revelations as to the culpability of the court of Navarre. At Lyon, and at Mouvans in Dauphine, a body of Reformers, under command of the most enterprising prince of the house of Bourbon had endeavored to incite the populace to rise. Such audacity, after the bloody executions at Amboise, astonished the Guises, who (no doubt to put an end to heresy by means known only to themselves) proposed the convocation of the States-general at Orleans. Catherine de' Medici, seeing a chance of support to her policy in a national representation, joyfully agreed to it. The cardinal, bent on recovering his prey and degrading the house of Bourbon, convoked the States for the sole purpose of bringing the Prince de Conde and the king of Navarre (Antoine de Bourbon, father of Henri IV.) to Orleans,—intending to make use of Christophe to convict the prince of high treason if he succeeded in again getting him within the power of the Crown.

After two months had passed in the prison at Blois, Christophe was removed on a litter to a tow-boat, which sailed up the Loire to Orleans, helped by a westerly wind. He arrived there in the evening and was taken at once to the celebrated tower of Saint-Aignan. The poor lad, who did not know what to think of his removal, had plenty of time to reflect on his conduct and on his future. He remained there two months, lying on his pallet, unable to move his legs. The bones of his joints were broken. When he asked for the help of a surgeon of the town, the jailer replied that the orders were so strict about him that he dared not allow any one but himself even to bring him food. This severity, which placed him virtually in solitary confinement, amazed Christophe. To his mind, he ought either to be hanged or released; for he was, of course, entirely ignorant of the events at Amboise.

In spite of certain secret advice sent to them by Catherine de' Medici, the two chiefs of the house of Bourbon resolved to be present at the States-general, so completely did the autograph letters they received from the king reassure them; and no sooner had the court established itself at Orleans than it learned, not without amazement, from Groslot, chancellor of Navarre, that the Bourbon princes had arrived.

Francois II. established himself in the house of the chancellor of Navarre, who was also *bailli*, in other words, chief justice of the law courts, at Orleans. This Groslot, whose dual position was one of the singularities of this period—when Reformers themselves owned abbeys—Groslot, the Jacques Coeur of Orleans, one of the richest burghers of the day, did not bequeath his name to the house, for in after years it was called Le Bailliage, having been, undoubtedly, purchased either by the heirs of the Crown or by the provinces as the proper place in which to hold the legal courts. This charming structure, built by the bourgeoisie of the sixteenth century, which completes so admirably the history of a period in which king, nobles, and burghers rivalled each other in the grace, elegance, and richness of their dwellings (witness Varangeville, the splendid manor-house of Ango, and the mansion, called that of Hercules, in Paris), exists to this day, though in a state to fill archaeologists and lovers of the Middle Ages with despair. It would be difficult, however, to go to Orleans and not take notice of the Hotel-de-Ville which stands on the place de l'Estape. This hotel-de-ville, or town-hall, is the former Bailliage, the mansion of Groslot, the most illustrious house in Orleans, and the most neglected.

The remains of this old building will still show, to the eyes of an archaeologist, how magnificent it was at a period when the houses of the burghers were commonly built of wood rather than stone, a period when noblemen alone had the right to build *manors*,—a significant word. Having served as the dwelling of the king at a period when the court displayed much pomp and luxury, the hotel Groslot must have been the most splendid house in Orleans. It was here, on the place de l'Estape, that the Guises and the king reviewed the burgher guard, of which Monsieur de Cypierre was made the commander during the sojourn of the king. At this period the cathedral of Sainte-Croix, afterward completed by Henri IV.,—who chose to give that proof of the sincerity of his conversion,—was in process of erection, and its neighborhood, heaped with stones and cumbered with piles of wood, was occupied by the Guises and their retainers, who were quartered in the bishop's palace, now destroyed.

The town was under military discipline, and the measures taken by the Guises proved how little liberty they intended to leave to the States-general, the members of which flocked into the town, raising the rents of the poorest lodgings. The court, the burgher militia, the nobility, and the burghers themselves were all in a state of expectation, awaiting some *coup-d'Etat*; and they found themselves not mistaken when the princes of the blood arrived. As the Bourbon princes entered the king's chamber, the court saw with terror the insolent bearing of Cardinal de Lorraine. Determined to show his intentions openly, he remained covered, while the king of Navarre stood before him bare-headed. Catherine de' Medici lowered her eyes, not to show the indignation that she felt. Then followed a solemn explanation between the young king and the two chiefs of the younger branch. It was short, for that the first words of the Prince de Conde Francois II. interrupted him, with threatening looks:

"Messieurs, my cousins, I had supposed the affair of Amboise over; I find it is not so, and you are compelling us to regret the indulgence which we showed."

"It is not the king so much as the Messieurs de Guise who now address us," replied the Prince de Conde.

"Adieu, monsieur," cried the little king, crimson with anger. When he left the king's presence the prince found his way barred in the great hall by two officers of the Scottish guard. As the captain of the French guard advanced, the prince drew a letter from his doublet, and said to him in presence of the whole court:—

"Can you read that paper aloud to me, Monsieur de Maille-Breze?"

"Willingly," said the French captain:—

*"'My cousin, come in all security; I give you my royal word that
you can do so. If you have need of a safe conduct, this letter
will serve as one.'"*

"Signed?" said the shrewd and courageous hunchback.

"Signed 'Francois,'" said Maille.

"No, no!" exclaimed the prince, "it is signed: 'Your good cousin and friend, Francois,'—Messieurs," he said to the Scotch guard, "I follow you to the prison to which you are ordered, on behalf of the king, to conduct me. There is enough nobility in this hall to understand the matter!"

The profound silence which followed these words ought to have enlightened the Guises, but silence is that to which all princes listen least.

"Monseigneur," said the Cardinal de Tournon, who was following the prince, "you know well that since the affair at Amboise you have made certain attempts both at Lyon and at Mouvans in Dauphine against the royal authority, of which the king had no knowledge when he wrote to you in those terms."

"Tricksters!" cried the prince, laughing.

"You have made a public declaration against the Mass and in favor of heresy."

"We are masters in Navarre," said the prince.

"You mean to say in Bearn. But you owe homage to the Crown," replied President de Thou.

"Ha! you here, president?" cried the prince, sarcastically. "Is the whole Parliament with you?"

So saying, he cast a look of contempt upon the cardinal and left the hall. He saw plainly enough that they meant to have his head. The next day, when Messieurs de Thou, de Viole, d'Espesse, the procureur-general Bourdin, and the chief clerk of the court du Tillet, entered his presence, he kept them standing, and expressed his regrets to see them charged with a duty which did not belong to them. Then he said to the clerk, "Write down what I say," and dictated as follows:—

"I, Louis de Bourbon, Prince de Conde, peer of the kingdom, Marquis de Conti, Comte de Soissons, prince of the blood of France, do declare that I formally refuse to recognize any commission appointed to try me, because, in my quality and in virtue of the privilege appertaining to all members of the royal house, I can only be accused, tried, and judged by the Parliament of peers, both Chambers assembled, the king being seated on his bed of justice."

"You ought to know that, gentlemen, better than others," he added; "and this reply is all that you will get from me. For the rest, I trust in God and my right."

The magistrates continued to address him notwithstanding his obstinate silence. The king of Navarre was left at liberty, but closely watched; his prison was larger than that of the prince, and this was the only real difference in the position of the two brothers,—the intention being that their heads should fall together.

Christophe was therefore kept in the strictest solitary confinement by order of the cardinal and the lieutenant-general of the kingdom, for no other purpose than to give the judges proof of the culpability of the Prince de Conde. The letters seized on Lasagne, the prince's secretary, though intelligible to statesmen, where not sufficiently plain proof for judges. The cardinal intended to confront the prince and Christophe by accident; and it was not without intention that the young Reformer was placed in one of the lower rooms in the tower of Saint-Aignan, with a window looking on the prison yard. Each time that Christophe was brought before the magistrates, and subjected to a close examination, he sheltered himself behind a total and complete denial, which prolonged his trial until after the opening of the States-general.

Old Lecamus, who by that time had got himself elected deputy of the *tiers-etat* by the burghers of Paris, arrived at Orleans a few days after the arrest of the Prince de Conde. This news, which reached him at Etampes, redoubled his anxiety; for he fully understood—he, who alone knew of Christophe's interview with the prince under the bridge near his own house—that his son's fate was closely bound up with that of the leader of the Reformed party. He therefore determined to study the dark tangle of interests which were struggling together at court in order to discover some means of rescuing his son. It was useless to think of Queen Catherine, who refused to see her furrier. No one about the court whom he was able to address could give him any satisfactory information about Christophe; and he fell at last into a state of such utter despair that he was on the verge of appealing to the cardinal himself, when he learned that Monsieur de Thou (and this was the great stain upon that good man's life) had consented to be one of the judges of the Prince de Conde. The old furrier went at once to see him, and learned at last that Christophe was still living, though a prisoner.

Tourillon, the glover (to whom La Renaudie sent Christophe on his way to Blois), had offered a room in his house to the Sieur Lecamus for the whole time of his stay in Orleans during the sittings of the States-general. The glover believed the furrier to be, like himself, secretly attached to the Reformed religion; but he soon saw that a father who fears for the life of his child pays no heed to shades of religious opinion, but flings himself prone upon the bosom of God without caring what insignia men give to Him. The poor old man, repulsed in all his efforts, wandered like one bewildered through the streets. Contrary to his expectations, his money availed him nothing; Monsieur de Thou had warned him that if he bribed any servant of the house of Guise he would merely lose his money, for the duke and cardinal allowed nothing that related to Christophe to transpire. De Thou, whose fame is somewhat tarnished by the part he played at this crisis, endeavored to give some hope to the poor father; but he trembled so much himself for the fate of his godson that his attempts at consolation only alarmed the old man still more. Lecamus roamed the streets; in three months he had shrunk visibly. His only hope now lay in the warm friendship which for so many years had bound him to the Hippocrates of the sixteenth century. Ambroise Pare tried to say a word to Queen Mary on leaving the chamber of the king, who was then indisposed; but no sooner had he named Christophe than the daughter of the Stuarts, nervous at the prospect of her fate should any evil happen to the king, and believing that the Reformers were attempting to poison him, cried out:—

"If my uncles had only listened to me, that fanatic would have been hanged already."

The evening on which this fatal answer was repeated to old Lecamus, by his friend Pare on the place de l'Estape, he returned home half dead to his own chamber, refusing to eat any supper. Tourillon, uneasy about him, went up to his room and found him in tears; the aged eyes showed the inflamed red lining of their lids, so that the glover fancied for a moment that he was weeping tears of blood.

"Comfort yourself, father," said the Reformer; "the burghers of Orleans are furious to see their city treated as though it were taken by assault, and guarded by the soldiers of Monsieur de Cypierre. If the life of the Prince de Conde is in any real danger we will soon demolish the tower of Saint-Aignan; the whole town is on the side of the Reformers, and it will rise in rebellion; you may be sure of that!"

"But, even if they hang the Guises, it will not give me back my son," said the wretched father.

At that instant some one rapped cautiously on Tourillon's outer door, and the glover went downstairs to open it himself. The night was dark. In these troublous times the masters of all households took minute precautions. Tourillon looked through the peep-holes cut in the door, and saw a stranger, whose accent indicated an Italian. The man, who was dressed in black, asked to speak with Lecamus on matters of business, and Tourillon admitted him. When the furrier caught sight of his visitor he shuddered violently; but the stranger managed, unseen by Tourillon, to lay his fingers on his lips. Lecamus, understanding the gesture, said immediately:—

"You have come, I suppose, to offer furs?"

"*Si*," said the Italian, discreetly.

This personage was no other than the famous Ruggiero, astrologer to the queen-mother. Tourillon went below to his own apartment, feeling convinced that he was one too many in that of his guest.

"Where can we talk without danger of being overheard?" said the cautious Florentine.

"We ought to be in the open fields for that," replied Lecamus. "But we are not allowed to leave the town; you know the severity with which the gates are guarded. No one can leave Orleans without a pass from Monsieur de Cypierre," he added,—"not even I, who am a member of

126

the States-general. Complaint is to be made at to-morrow's session of this restriction of liberty."

"Work like a mole, but don't let your paws be seen in anything, no matter what," said the wary Italian. "To-morrow will, no doubt, prove a decisive day. Judging by my observations, you may, perhaps, recover your son to-morrow, or the day after."

"May God hear you—you who are thought to traffic with the devil!"

"Come to my place," said the astrologer, smiling. "I live in the tower of Sieur Touchet de Beauvais, the lieutenant of the Bailliage, whose daughter the little Duc d'Orleans has taken such a fancy to; it is there that I observe the planets. I have drawn the girl's horoscope, and it says that she will become a great lady and be beloved by a king. The lieutenant, her father, is a clever man; he loves science, and the queen sent me to lodge with him. He has had the sense to be a rabid Guisist while awaiting the reign of Charles IX."

The furrier and the astrologer reached the house of the Sieur de Beauvais without being met or even seen; but, in case Lecamus' visit should be discovered, the Florentine intended to give a pretext of an astrological consultation on his son's fate. When they were safely at the top of the tower, where the astrologer did his work, Lecamus said to him:—

"Is my son really living?"

"Yes, he still lives," replied Ruggiero; "and the question now is how to save him. Remember this, seller of skins, I would not give two farthings for yours if ever in all your life a single syllable should escape you of what I am about to say."

"That is a useless caution, my friend; I have been furrier to the court since the time of the late Louis XII.; this is the fourth reign that I have seen."

"And you may soon see the fifth," remarked Ruggiero.

"What do you know about my son?"

"He has been put to the question."

"Poor boy!" said the old man, raising his eyes to heaven.

"His knees and ankles were a bit injured, but he has won a royal protection which will extend over his whole life," said the Florentine hastily, seeing the terror of the poor father. "Your little Christophe has done a service to our great queen, Catherine. If we manage to pull him out of the claws of the Guises you will see him some day councillor to the Parliament. Any man would gladly have his bones cracked three times over to stand so high in the good graces of this dear sovereign,—a grand and noble genius, who will triumph in the end over all obstacles. I have drawn the horoscope of the Duc de Guise; he will be killed within a year. Well, so Christophe saw the Prince de Conde—"

"You who read the future ought to know the past," said the furrier.

"My good man, I am not questioning you, I am telling you a fact. Now, if your son, who will to-morrow be placed in the prince's way as he passes, should recognize him, or if the prince should recognize your son, the head of Monsieur de Conde will fall. God knows what will become of his accomplice! However, don't be alarmed. Neither your son nor the prince will die; I have drawn their horoscope,—they will live; but I do not know in what way they will get out of this affair. Without distrusting the certainty of my calculations, we must do something to bring about results. To-morrow the prince will receive, from sure hands, a prayer-book in which we convey the information to him. God grant that your son be cautious, for him we cannot warn. A single glance of recognition will cost the prince's life. Therefore, although the queen-mother has every reason to trust in Christophe's faithfulness—"

"They've put it to a cruel test!" cried the furrier.

"Don't speak so! Do you think the queen-mother is on a bed of roses? She is taking measures as if the Guises had already decided on the death of the prince, and right she is, the wise and prudent queen! Now listen to me; she counts on you to help her in all things. You have some influence with the *tiers-etat*, where you represent the body of the guilds of Paris, and though the Guisards may promise you to set your son at liberty, try to fool them and maintain the independence of the guilds. Demand the queen-mother as regent; the king of Navarre will publicly accept the proposal at the session of the States-general."

"But the king?"

"The king will die," replied Ruggiero; "I have read his horoscope. What the queen-mother requires you to do for her at the States-general is a very simple thing; but there is a far greater service which she asks of you. You helped Ambroise Pare in his studies, you are his friend—"

"Ambroise now loves the Duc de Guise more than he loves me; and he is right, for he owes his place to him. Besides, he is faithful to the king. Though he inclines to the Reformed religion, he will never do anything against his duty."

"Curse these honest men!" cried the Florentine. "Ambroise boasted this evening that he could bring the little king safely through his present illness (for he is really ill). If the king recovers his health, the Guises triumph, the princes die, the house of Bourbon becomes extinct, we shall return to Florence, your son will be hanged, and the Lorrains will easily get the better of the other sons of France—"

"Great God!" exclaimed Lecamus.

"Don't cry out in that way,—it is like a burgher who knows nothing of the court,—but go at once to Ambroise and find out from him what he intends to do to save the king's life. If there is anything decided on, come back to me at once, and tell me the treatment in which he has such faith."

"But—" said Lecamus.

"Obey blindly, my dear friend; otherwise you will get your mind bewildered."

"He is right," thought the furrier. "I had better not know more"; and he went at once in search of the king's surgeon, who lived at a hostelry in the place du Martroi.

Catherine de' Medici was at this moment in a political extremity very much like that in which poor Christophe had seen her at Blois. Though she had been in a way trained by the struggle, though she had exercised her lofty intellect by the lessons of that first defeat, her present situation, while nearly the same, had become more critical, more perilous than it was at Amboise. Events, like the woman herself, had magnified. Though she seemed to be in full accordance with the Guises, Catherine held in her hand the threads of a wisely planned conspiracy against her terrible associates, and was only awaiting a propitious moment to throw off the mask. The cardinal had just obtained the positive certainty that Catherine was deceiving him. Her subtle Italian spirit felt that the Younger branch was the best hindrance she could offer to the ambition of the duke and the cardinal; and (in spite of the advice of the two Gondis, who urged her to let the Guises wreak their vengeance on the Bourbons) she defeated the scheme concocted by them with Spain to seize the province of Bearn, by warning Jeanne d'Albret, queen of Navarre, of that threatened danger. As this state secret was known only to them and to the queen-mother, the Guises knew of course who had betrayed it, and resolved to send her back to Florence. But in order to make themselves perfectly sure of what they called her treason against the State (the State being the house of Lorraine), the duke and cardinal confided to her their intention of getting rid of the king of Navarre. The precautions instantly taken by Antoine proved conclusively to the two brothers that the secrets known only to them and the queen-mother had been divulged by the latter. The cardinal instantly taxed her with treachery, in presence of Francois II.,— threatening her with an edict of banishment in case of future indiscretion, which might, as they said, put the kingdom in danger.

Catherine, who then felt herself in the utmost peril, acted in the spirit of a great king, giving proof of her high capacity. It must be added, however, that she was ably seconded by her friends. L'Hopital managed to send her a note, written in the following terms:—

"Do not allow a prince of the blood to be put to death by a committee; or you will yourself be carried off in some way."

Catherine sent Birago to Vignay to tell the chancellor (l'Hopital) to come to Orleans at once, in spite of his being in disgrace. Birago returned the very night of which we are writing, and was now a few miles from Orleans with l'Hopital, who heartily avowed himself for the queen-mother. Chiverni, whose fidelity was very justly suspected by the Guises, had escaped from Orleans and reached Ecouen in ten hours, by a forced march which almost cost him his life. There he told the Connetable de Montmorency of the peril of his nephew, the Prince de Conde, and the audacious hopes of the Guises. The Connetable, furious at the thought that the prince's life hung upon that of Francois II., started for Orleans at once with a hundred noblemen and fifteen hundred cavalry. In order to take the Messieurs de Guise by surprise he avoided Paris, and came direct from Ecouen to Corbeil, and from Corbeil to Pithiviers by the valley of the Essonne.

"Soldier against soldier, we must leave no chances," he said on the occasion of this bold march.

Anne de Montmorency, who had saved France at the time of the invasion of Provence by Charles V., and the Duc de Guise, who had stopped the second invasion by the emperor at Metz, were, in truth, the two great warriors of France at this period. Catherine had awaited this precise moment to rouse the inextinguishable hatred of the Connetable, whose disgrace and banishment were the work of the Guises. The Marquis de Simeuse, however, who commanded at Gien, being made aware of the large force approaching under command of the Connetable, jumped on his horse hoping to reach Orleans in time to warn the duke and cardinal.

Sure that the Connetable would come to the rescue of his nephew, and full of confidence in the Chancelier l'Hopital's devotion to the royal cause, the queen-mother revived the hopes and the boldness of the Reformed party. The Colignys and the friends of the house of Bourbon, aware of their danger, now made common cause with the adherents of the queen-mother. A coalition between these opposing interests, attacked by a common enemy, formed itself silently in the States-general, where it soon became a question of appointing Catherine as regent in case the king should die. Catherine, whose faith in astrology was much greater than her faith in the Church, now dared all against her oppressors, seeing that her son was ill and apparently dying at the expiration of the time assigned to his life by the famous sorceress, whom Nostradamus had brought to her at the chateau of Chaumont.

XI. AMBROISE PARE

Some days before the terrible end of the reign of Francois II., the king insisted on sailing down the Loire, wishing not to be in the town of Orleans on the day when the Prince de Conde was executed. Having yielded the head of the prince to the Cardinal de Lorraine, he was equally in dread of a rebellion among the townspeople and of the prayers and supplications of the Princesse de Conde. At the moment of embarkation, one of the cold winds which sweep along the Loire at the beginning of winter gave him so sharp an ear-ache that he was obliged to return to his apartments; there he took to his bed, not leaving it again until he died. In contradiction of the doctors, who, with the exception of Chapelain, were his enemies, Ambroise Pare insisted that an abscess was formed in the king's head, and that unless an issue were given to it, the danger of death would increase daily. Notwithstanding the lateness of the hour, and the curfew law, which was sternly enforced in Orleans, at this time practically in a state of siege, Pare's lamp shone from his window, and he was deep in study, when Lecamus called to him from below. Recognizing the voice of his old friend, Pare ordered that he should be admitted.

"You take no rest, Ambroise; while saving the lives of others you are wasting your own," said the furrier as he entered, looking at the surgeon, who sat, with opened books and scattered instruments, before the head of a dead man, lately buried and now disinterred, in which he had cut an opening.

"It is a matter of saving the king's life."

"Are you sure of doing it, Ambroise?" cried the old man, trembling.

"As sure as I am of my own existence. The king, my old friend, has a morbid ulcer pressing on his brain, which will presently suffice it if no vent is given to it, and the danger is imminent. But by boring the skull I expect to release the pus and clear the head. I have already performed this operation three times. It was invented by a Piedmontese; but I have had the honor to perfect it. The first operation I performed was at the siege of Metz, on Monsieur de Pienne, whom I cured, who was afterwards all the more intelligent in consequence. His was an abscess caused by the blow of an arquebuse. The second was on the head of a pauper, on whom I wanted to prove the value of the audacious operation Monsieur de Pienne had allowed me to perform. The third I did in Paris on a gentleman who is now entirely recovered. Trepanning—that is the name given to the operation—is very little known. Patients refuse it, partly because of the imperfection of the instruments; but I have at last improved them. I am practising now on this skull, that I may be sure of

131

not failing to-morrow, when I operate on the head of the king."

"You ought indeed to be very sure you are right, for your own head would be in danger in case—"

"I'd wager my life I can cure him," replied Ambroise, with the conviction of a man of genius. "Ah! my old friend, where's the danger of boring into a skull with proper precautions? That is what soldiers do in battle every day of their lives, without taking any precautions."

"My son," said the burgher, boldly, "do you know that to save the king is to ruin France? Do you know that this instrument of yours will place the crown of the Valois on the head of the Lorrain who calls himself the heir of Charlemagne? Do you know that surgery and policy are at this moment sternly opposed to each other? Yes, the triumph of your genius will be the death of your religion. If the Guises gain the regency, the blood of the Reformers will flow like water. Be a greater citizen than you are a surgeon; oversleep yourself to-morrow morning and leave a free field to the other doctors who if they cannot cure the king will cure France."

"I!" exclaimed Pare. "I leave a man to die when I can cure him? No, no! were I to hang as an abettor of Calvin I shall go early to court. Do you not feel that the first and only reward I shall ask will be the life of your Christophe? Surely at such a moment Queen Mary can deny me nothing."

"Alas! my friend," returned Lecamus, "the little king has refused the pardon of the Prince de Conde to the princess. Do not kill your religion by saving the life of a man who ought to die."

"Do not you meddle with God's ordering of the future!" cried Pare. "Honest men can have but one motto: *Fais ce que dois, advienne que pourra!*—do thy duty, come what will. That is what I did at the siege of Calais when I put my foot on the face of the Duc de Guise,—I ran the risk of being strangled by his friends and his servants; but to-day I am surgeon to the king; moreover I am of the Reformed religion; and yet the Guises are my friends. I shall save the king," cried the surgeon, with the sacred enthusiasm of a conviction bestowed by genius, "and God will save France!"

A knock was heard on the street door and presently one of Pare's servants gave a paper to Lecamus, who read aloud these terrifying words:—

"A scaffold is being erected at the convent of the Recollets: the Prince de Conde will be beheaded there to-morrow."

Ambroise and Lecamus looked at each other with an expression of the deepest horror.

"I will go and see it for myself," said the furrier.

No sooner was he in the open street than Ruggiero took his arm and asked by what means Ambroise Pare proposed to save the king. Fearing some trickery, the old man, instead of answering, replied that he wished to go and see the scaffold. The astrologer accompanied him to the place des Recollets, and there, truly enough, they found the carpenters putting up the horrible framework by torchlight.

"Hey, my friend," said Lecamus to one of the men, "what are you doing here at this time of night?"

"We are preparing for the hanging of heretics, as the blood-letting at Amboise didn't cure them," said a young Recollet who was superintending the work.

"Monseigneur the cardinal is very right," said Ruggiero, prudently; "but in my country we do better."

"What do you do?" said the young priest.

"We burn them."

Lecamus was forced to lean on the astrologer's arm, for his legs gave way beneath him; he thought it probable that on the morrow his son would hang from one of those gibbets. The poor old man was thrust between two sciences, astrology and surgery, both of which promised him the life of his son, for whom in all probability that scaffold was now erecting. In the trouble and distress of his mind, the Florentine was able to knead him like dough.

"Well, my worthy dealer in minever, what do you say now to the Lorraine jokes?" whispered Ruggiero.

"Alas! you know I would give my skin if that of my son were safe and sound."

"That is talking like your trade," said the Italian; "but explain to me the operation which Ambroise means to perform upon the king, and in return I will promise you the life of your son."

"Faithfully?" exclaimed the old furrier.

"Shall I swear it to you?" said Ruggiero.

Thereupon the poor old man repeated his conversation with Ambroise Pare to the astrologer, who, the moment that the secret of the great surgeon was divulged to him, left the poor father abruptly in the street in utter despair.

"What the devil does he mean, that miscreant?" cried Lecamus, as he watched Ruggiero hurrying with rapid steps to the place de l'Estape.

Lecamus was ignorant of the terrible scene that was taking place around the royal bed, where the imminent danger of the king's death and the consequent loss of power to the Guises had caused the hasty erection of the scaffold for the Prince de Conde, whose sentence had been pronounced, as it were by default,—the execution of it being delayed by the king's illness.

Absolutely no one but the persons on duty were in the halls, staircases, and courtyard of the royal residence, Le Bailliage. The crowd of courtiers were flocking to the house of the king of Navarre, on whom the regency would devolve on the death of the king, according to the laws of the kingdom. The French nobility, alarmed by the audacity of the Guises, felt the need of rallying around the chief of the younger branch, when, ignorant of the queen-mother's Italian policy, they saw her the apparent slave of the duke and cardinal. Antoine de Bourbon, faithful to his secret agreement with Catherine, was bound not to renounce the regency in her favor until the States-general had declared for it.

The solitude in which the king's house was left had a powerful effect on the mind of the Duc de Guise when, on his return from an inspection, made by way of precaution through the city, he found no one there but the friends who were attached exclusively to his own fortunes. The chamber in which was the king's bed adjoined the great hall of the Bailliage. It was at that period panelled in oak. The ceiling, composed of long, narrow boards carefully joined and painted, was covered with blue arabesques on a gold ground, a part of which being torn down about fifty years ago was instantly purchased by a lover of antiquities. This room, hung with tapestry, the floor being covered with a carpet, was so dark and gloomy that the torches threw scarcely any light. The vast four-post bedstead with its silken curtains was like a tomb. Beside her husband, close to his pillow, sat Mary Stuart, and near her the Cardinal de Lorraine. Catherine was seated in a chair at a little distance. The famous Jean Chapelain, the physician on duty (who was afterwards chief physician to Charles IX.) was standing before the fireplace. The deepest silence reigned. The young king, pale and shrunken, lay as if buried in his sheets, his pinched little face scarcely showing on the pillow. The Duchesse de Guise, sitting on a stool, attended Queen Mary, while on the other side, near Catherine, in the recess of a window, Madame de Fiesque stood watching the gestures and looks of the queen-mother; for she knew the dangers of her position.

In the hall, notwithstanding the lateness of the hour, Monsieur de Cypierre, governor of the Duc d'Orleans and now appointed governor of the town, occupied one corner of the fireplace with the two Gondis. Cardinal de Tournon, who in this crisis espoused the interests of the queen-mother on finding himself treated as an inferior by the Cardinal de Lorraine, of whom he was certainly the ecclesiastical equal, talked in a low voice to the Gondis. The marshals de Vieilleville and Saint-Andre and the keeper of the seals, who presided at the States-general, were talking together in a whisper of the dangers to which the Guises were exposed.

The lieutenant-general of the kingdom crossed the room on his entrance, casting a rapid glance about him, and bowed to the Duc d'Orleans whom he saw there.

"Monseigneur," he said, "this will teach you to know men. The Catholic nobility of the kingdom have gone to pay court to a heretic prince, believing that the States-general will give the regency to the heirs of a traitor who long detained in prison your illustrious grandfather."

Then having said these words, which were destined to plough a furrow in the heart of the young prince, he passed into the bedroom, where the king was not so much asleep as plunged in a heavy torpor. The Duc de Guise was usually able to correct the sinister aspect of his scarred face by an affable and pleasing manner, but on this occasion, when he saw the instrument of his power breaking in his very hands, he was unable to force a smile. The cardinal, whose civil courage was equal to his brother's military daring, advanced a few steps to meet him.

"Robertet thinks that little Pinard is sold to the queen-mother," he whispered, leading the duke into the hall; "they are using him to work upon the members of the States-general."

"Well, what does it signify if we are betrayed by a secretary when all else betrays us?" cried the lieutenant-general. "The town is for the Reformation, and we are on the eve of a revolt. Yes! the *Wasps* are discontented"; he continued, giving the Orleans people their nickname; "and if Pare does not save the king we shall have a terrible uprising. Before long we shall be forced to besiege Orleans, which is nothing but a bog of Huguenots."

"I have been watching that Italian woman," said the cardinal, "as she sits there with absolute insensibility. She is watching and waiting, God forgive her! for the death of her son; and I ask myself whether we should not do a wise thing to arrest her at once, and also the king of Navarre."

"It is already more than we want upon our hands to have the Prince de Conde in prison," replied the duke.

The sound of a horseman riding in haste to the gate of the Bailliage echoed through the hall. The duke and cardinal went to the window, and by the light of the torches which were in the portico the duke recognized on the rider's hat the famous Lorraine cross, which the cardinal had lately ordered his partisans to wear. He sent an officer of the guard, who was stationed in the antechamber, to give entrance to the new-comer; and went himself, followed by his brother, to meet him on the landing.

"What is it, my dear Simeuse?" asked the duke, with that charm of manner which he always displayed to military men, as soon as he recognized the governor of Gien.

"The Connetable has reached Pithiviers; he left Ecouen with two thousand cavalry and one hundred nobles."

"With their suites?"

"Yes, monseigneur," replied Simeuse; "in all, two thousand six hundred men. Some say that Thore is behind them with a body of infantry. If the Connetable delays awhile, expecting his son, you still have time to repulse him."

"Is that all you know? Are the reasons of this sudden call to arms made known?"

"Montmorency talks as little as he writes; go you and meet him, brother, while I prepare to welcome him with the head of his nephew," said the cardinal, giving orders that Robertet be sent to him at once.

"Vieilleville!" cried the duke to the marechal, who came immediately. "The Connetable has the audacity to come here under arms; if I go to meet him will you be responsible to hold the town?"

"As soon as you leave it the burghers will fly to arms; and who can answer for the result of an affair between cavalry and citizens in these narrow streets?" replied the marechal.

"Monseigneur," said Robertet, rushing hastily up the stairs, "the Chancelier de l'Hopital is at the gate and asks to enter; are we to let him in?"

"Yes, open the gate," answered the cardinal. "Connetable and chancelier together would be dangerous; we must separate them. We have been boldly tricked by the queen-mother into choosing l'Hopital as chancellor."

Robertet nodded to a captain of the guard, who awaited an answer at the foot of the staircase; then he turned round quickly to receive the orders of the cardinal.

"Monseigneur, I take the liberty," he said, making one last effort, "to point out that the sentence should be approved by *the king in council*. If you violate the law on a prince of the blood, it will not be respected for either a cardinal or a Duc de Guise."

"Pinard has upset your mind, Robertet," said the cardinal, sternly. "Do you not know that the king signed the order of execution the day he was about to leave Orleans, in order that the sentence might be carried out in his absence?"

The lieutenant-general listened to this discussion without a word, but he took his brother by the arm and led him into a corner of the hall.

"Undoubtedly," he said, "the heirs of Charlemagne have the right to recover the crown which was usurped from their house by Hugh Capet; but can they do it? The pear is not yet ripe. Our nephew is dying, and the

136

whole court has gone over to the king of Navarre."

"The king's heart failed him, or the Bearnais would have been stabbed before now," said the cardinal; "and we could easily have disposed of the Valois children."

"We are very ill-placed here," said the duke; "the rebellion of the town will be supported by the States-general. L'Hopital, whom we protected while the queen-mother opposed his appointment, is to-day against us, and yet it is all-important that we should have the justiciary with us. Catherine has too many supporters at the present time; we cannot send her back to Italy. Besides, there are still three Valois princes—"

"She is no longer a mother, she is all queen," said the cardinal. "In my opinion, this is the moment to make an end of her. Vigor, and more and more vigor! that's my prescription!" he cried.

So saying, the cardinal returned to the king's chamber, followed by the duke. The priest went straight to the queen-mother.

"The papers of Lasagne, the secretary of the Prince de Conde, have been communicated to you, and you now know that the Bourbons are endeavoring to dethrone your son."

"I know all that," said Catherine.

"Well, then, will you give orders to arrest the king of Navarre?"

"There is," she said with dignity, "a lieutenant-general of the kingdom."

At this instant Francois II. groaned piteously, complaining aloud of the terrible pains in his ear. The physician left the fireplace where he was warming himself, and went to the bedside to examine the king's head.

"Well, monsieur?" said the Duc de Guise, interrogatively.

"I dare not take upon myself to apply a blister to draw the abscess. Maitre Ambroise has promised to save the king's life by an operation, and I might thwart it."

"Let us postpone the treatment till to-morrow morning," said Catherine, coldly, "and order all the physicians to be present; for we all know the calumnies to which the death of kings gives rise."

She went to her son and kissed his hand; then she withdrew to her own apartments.

"With what composure that audacious daughter of a shop-keeper alluded to the death of the dauphin, poisoned by Montecuculi, one of her own Italian followers!" said Mary Stuart.

"Mary!" cried the little king, "my grandfather never doubted her innocence."

"Can we prevent that woman from coming here to-morrow?" said the queen to her uncles in a low voice.

"What will become of us if the king dies?" returned the cardinal, in a whisper. "Catherine will shovel us all into his grave."

Thus the question was plainly put between Catherine de' Medici and the house of Lorraine during that fatal night. The arrival of the Connetable de Montmorency and the Chancelier de l'Hopital were distinct indications of rebellion; the morning of the next day would therefore be decisive.

XII. DEATH OF FRANCOIS II

On the morrow the queen-mother was the first to enter the king's chamber. She found no one there but Mary Stuart, pale and weary, who had passed the night in prayer beside the bed. The Duchesse de Guise had kept her mistress company, and the maids of honor had taken turns in relieving one another. The young king slept. Neither the duke nor the cardinal had yet appeared. The priest, who was bolder than the soldier, had, it was afterward said, put forth his utmost energy during the night to induce his brother to make himself king. But, in face of the assembled States-general, and threatened by a battle with Montmorency, the Balafre declared the circumstances unfavorable; he refused, against his brother's utmost urgency, to arrest the king of Navarre, the queen-mother, l'Hopital, the Cardinal de Tournon, the Gondis, Ruggiero, and Birago, objecting that such violent measures would bring on a general rebellion. He postponed the cardinal's scheme until the fate of Francois II. should be determined.

The deepest silence reigned in the king's chamber. Catherine, accompanied by Madame de Fiesque, went to the bedside and gazed at her son with a semblance of grief that was admirably simulated. She put her handkerchief to her eyes and walked to the window where Madame de Fiesque brought her a seat. Thence she could see into the courtyard.

It had been agreed between Catherine and the Cardinal de Tournon that if the Connetable should successfully enter the town the cardinal would come to the king's house with the two Gondis; if otherwise, he would come alone. At nine in the morning the duke and cardinal, followed by their gentlemen, who remained in the hall, entered the king's bedroom,— the captain on duty having informed them that Ambroise Pare had arrived, together with Chapelain and three other physicians, who hated Pare and were all in the queen-mother's interests.

A few moments later and the great hall of the Bailliage presented much the same aspect as that of the Salle des gardes at Blois on the day when Christophe was put to the torture and the Duc de Guise was proclaimed lieutenant-governor of the kingdom,—with the single exception that whereas love and joy overflowed the royal chamber and the Guises triumphed, death and mourning now reigned within that darkened room, and the Guises felt that power was slipping through their fingers. The maids of honor of the two queens were again in their separate camps on either side of the fireplace, in which glowed a monstrous fire. The hall was filled with courtiers. The news—spread about, no one knew how—of some daring operation contemplated by Ambroise Pare to save the king's life, had brought back the lords and gentlemen who had deserted the house the day before. The outer staircase and courtyard were filled by an anxious crowd. The scaffold erected during the night for the Prince de Conde opposite to the convent of the Recollets, had amazed and startled the whole nobility. All present spoke in a low voice and the talk was the same mixture as at Blois, of frivolous and serious, light and earnest matters. The habit of expecting troubles, sudden revolutions, calls to arms, rebellions, and great events, which marked the long period during which the house of Valois was slowly being extinguished in spite of Catherine de' Medici's great efforts to preserve it, took its rise at this time.

A deep silence prevailed for a certain distance beyond the door of the king's chamber, which was guarded by two halberdiers, two pages, and by the captain of the Scotch guard. Antoine de Bourbon, king of Navarre, held a prisoner in his own house, learned by his present desertion the hopes of the courtiers who had flocked to him the day before, and was horrified by the news of the preparations made during the night for the execution of his brother.

Standing before the fireplace in the great hall of the Bailliage was one of the greatest and noblest figures of that day,—the Chancelier de l'Hopital, wearing his crimson robe lined and edged with ermine, and his cap on his head according to the privilege of his office. This courageous man, seeing that his benefactors were traitorous and self-seeking, held firmly to the cause of the kings, represented by the queen-mother; at the risk of losing his head, he had gone to Rouen to consult with the Connetable de Montmorency. No one ventured to draw him from the reverie in which he was plunged. Robertet, the secretary of State, two marshals of France, Vieilleville, and Saint-Andre, and the keeper of the seals, were collected in a group before the chancellor. The courtiers present were not precisely jesting; but their talk was malicious, especially among those who were not for the Guises.

Presently voices were heard to rise in the king's chamber. The two marshals, Robertet, and the chancellor went nearer to the door; for not only was the life of the king in question, but, as the whole court knew well, the chancellor, the queen-mother, and her adherents were in the utmost danger. A deep silence fell on the whole assembly.

Ambroise Pare had by this time examined the king's head; he thought the moment propitious for his operation; if it was not performed suffusion would take place, and Francois II. might die at any moment. As soon as the duke and cardinal entered the chamber he explained to all present that in so urgent a case it was necessary to trepan the head, and he now waited till the king's physician ordered him to perform the operation.

"Cut the head of my son as though it were a plank!—with that horrible instrument!" cried Catherine de' Medici. "Maitre Ambroise, I will not permit it."

The physicians were consulting together; but Catherine spoke in so loud a voice that her words reached, as she intended they should, beyond the door.

"But, madame, if there is no other way to save him?" said Mary Stuart, weeping.

"Ambroise," cried Catherine; "remember that your head will answer for the king's life."

"We are opposed to the treatment suggested by Maitre Ambroise," said the three physicians. "The king can be saved by injecting through the ear a remedy which will draw the contents of the abscess through that passage."

The Duc de Guise, who was watching Catherine's face, suddenly went up to her and drew her into the recess of the window.

"Madame," he said, "you wish the death of your son; you are in league with our enemies, and have been since Blois. This morning the Counsellor Viole told the son of your furrier that the Prince de Conde's head was about to be cut off. That young man, who, when the question was applied, persisted in denying all relations with the prince, made a sign of farewell to him as he passed before the window of his dungeon. You saw your unhappy accomplice tortured with royal insensibility. You are now endeavoring to prevent the recovery of your eldest son. Your conduct forces us to believe that the death of the dauphin, which placed the crown on your husband's head was not a natural one, and that Montecuculi was your—"

"Monsieur le chancilier!" cried Catherine, at a sign from whom Madame de Fiesque opened both sides of the bedroom door.

The company in the hall then saw the scene that was taking place in the royal chamber: the livid little king, his face half dead, his eyes sightless, his lips stammering the word "Mary," as he held the hand of the weeping queen; the Duchesse de Guise motionless, frightened by Catherine's daring act; the duke and cardinal, also alarmed, keeping close to the queen-mother and resolving to have her arrested on the spot by Maille-

Breze; lastly, the tall Ambroise Pare, assisted by the king's physician, holding his instrument in his hand but not daring to begin the operation, for which composure and total silence were as necessary as the consent of the other surgeons.

"Monsieur le chancelier," said Catherine, "the Messieurs de Guise wish to authorize a strange operation upon the person of the king; Ambroise Pare is preparing to cut open his head. I, as the king's mother and a member of the council of the regency,—I protest against what appears to me a crime of *lese-majeste*. The king's physicians advise an injection through the ear, which seems to me as efficacious and less dangerous than the brutal operation proposed by Pare."

When the company in the hall heard these words a smothered murmur rose from their midst; the cardinal allowed the chancellor to enter the bedroom and then he closed the door.

"I am lieutenant-general of the kingdom," said the Duc de Guise; "and I would have you know, Monsieur le chancelier, that Ambroise, the king's surgeon, answers for his life."

"Ah! if this be the turn that things are taking!" exclaimed Ambroise Pare. "I know my rights and how I should proceed." He stretched his arm over the bed. "This bed and the king are mine. I claim to be sole master of this case and solely responsible. I know the duties of my office; I shall operate upon the king without the sanction of the physicians."

"Save him!" said the cardinal, "and you shall be the richest man in France."

"Go on!" cried Mary Stuart, pressing the surgeon's hand.

"I cannot prevent it," said the chancellor; "but I shall record the protest of the queen-mother."

"Robertet!" called the Duc de Guise.

When Robertet entered, the lieutenant-general pointed to the chancellor.

"I appoint you chancellor of France in the place of that traitor," he said. "Monsieur de Maille, take Monsieur de l'Hopital and put him in the prison of the Prince de Conde. As for you, madame," he added, turning to Catherine; "your protest will not be received; you ought to be aware that any such protest must be supported by sufficient force. I act as the faithful subject and loyal servant of king Francois II., my master. Go on, Antoine," he added, looking at the surgeon.

"Monsieur de Guise," said l'Hopital; "if you employ violence either upon the king or upon the chancellor of France, remember that enough of the nobility of France are in that hall to rise and arrest you as a traitor."

"Oh! my lords," cried the great surgeon; "if you continue these arguments you will soon proclaim Charles IX!—for king Francois is about to die."

Catherine de' Medici, absolutely impassive, gazed from the window.

"Well, then, we shall employ force to make ourselves masters of this room," said the cardinal, advancing to the door.

But when he opened it even he was terrified; the whole house was deserted! The courtiers, certain now of the death of the king, had gone in a body to the king of Navarre.

"Well, go on, perform your duty," cried Mary Stuart, vehemently, to Ambroise. "I—and you, duchess," she said to Madame de Guise,—"will protect you."

"Madame," said Ambroise; "my zeal was carrying me away. The doctors, with the exception of my friend Chapelain, prefer an injection, and it is my duty to submit to their wishes. If I had been chief surgeon and chief physician, which I am not, the king's life would probably have been saved. Give that to me, gentlemen," he said, stretching out his hand for the syringe, which he proceeded to fill.

"Good God!" cried Mary Start, "but I order you to—"

"Alas! madame," said Ambroise, "I am under the direction of these gentlemen."

The young queen placed herself between the surgeon, the doctors, and the other persons present. The chief physician held the king's head, and Ambroise made the injection into the ear. The duke and the cardinal watched the proceeding attentively. Robertet and Monsieur de Maille stood motionless. Madame de Fiesque, at a sign from Catherine, glided unperceived from the room. A moment later l'Hopital boldly opened the door of the king's chamber.

"I arrive in good time," said the voice of a man whose hasty steps echoed through the great hall, and who stood the next moment on the threshold of the open door. "Ah, messieurs, so you meant to take off the head of my good nephew, the Prince de Conde? Instead of that, you have forced the lion from his lair and—here I am!" added the Connetable de Montmorency. "Ambroise, you shall not plunge your knife into the head of my king. The first prince of the blood, Antoine de Bourbon, the Prince de Conde, the queen-mother, the Connetable, and the chancellor forbid the operation."

To Catherine's great satisfaction, the king of Navarre and the Prince de Conde now entered the room.

"What does this mean?" said the Duc de Guise, laying his hand on his dagger.

"It means that in my capacity as Connetable, I have dismissed the sentinels of all your posts. *Tete Dieu*! you are not in an enemy's country, methinks. The king, our master, is in the midst of his loyal subjects, and the States-general must be suffered to deliberate at liberty. I come, messieurs, from the States-general. I carried the protest of my nephew de Conde before that assembly, and three hundred of those gentlemen have released him. You wish to shed royal blood and to decimate the nobility of the kingdom, do you? Ha! in future, I defy you, and all your schemes, Messieurs de Lorraine. If you order the king's head opened, by this sword which saved France from Charles V., I say it shall not be done—"

"All the more," said Ambroise Pare; "because it is now too late; the suffusion has begun."

"Your reign is over, messieurs," said Catherine to the Guises, seeing from Pare's face that there was no longer any hope.

"Ah! madame, you have killed your own son," cried Mary Stuart as she bounded like a lioness from the bed to the window and seized the queen-mother by the arm, gripping it violently.

"My dear," replied Catherine, giving her daughter-in-law a cold, keen glance in which she allowed her hatred, repressed for the last six months, to overflow; "you, to whose inordinate love we owe this death, you will now go to reign in your Scotland, and you will start to-morrow. I am regent *de facto*." The three physicians having made her a sign, "Messieurs," she added, addressing the Guises, "it is agreed between Monsieur de Bourbon, appointed lieutenant-general of the kingdom by the States-general, and me that the conduct of the affairs of the State is our business solely. Come, monsieur le chancelier."

"The king is dead!" said the Duc de Guise, compelled to perform his duties as Grand-master.

"Long live King Charles IX.!" cried all the noblemen who had come with the king of Navarre, the Prince de Conde, and the Connetable.

The ceremonies which follow the death of a king of France were performed in almost total solitude. When the king-at-arms proclaimed aloud three times in the hall, "The king is dead!" there were very few persons present to reply, "Vive le roi!"

The queen-mother, to whom the Comtesse de Fiesque had brought the Duc d'Orleans, now Charles IX., left the chamber, leading her son by the hand, and all the remaining courtiers followed her. No one was left in the house where Francois II. had drawn his last breath, but the duke and the cardinal, the Duchesse de Guise, Mary Stuart, and Dayelle, together with the sentries at the door, the pages of the Grand-master, those of the cardinal, and their private secretaries.

"Vive la France!" cried several Reformers in the street, sounding the first cry of the opposition.

Robertet, who owed all he was to the duke and cardinal, terrified by their scheme and its present failure, went over secretly to the queen-mother, whom the ambassadors of Spain, England, the Empire, and Poland, hastened to meet on the staircase, brought thither by Cardinal de Tournon, who had gone to notify them as soon as he had made Queen Catherine a sign from the courtyard at the moment when she protested against the operation of Ambroise Pare.

"Well!" said the cardinal to the duke, "so the sons of Louis d'Outre-mer, the heirs of Charles de Lorraine flinched and lacked courage."

"We should have been exiled to Lorraine," replied the duke. "I declare to you, Charles, that if the crown lay there before me I would not stretch out my hand to pick it up. That's for my son to do."

"Will he have, as you have had, the army and Church on his side?"

"He will have something better."

"What?"

"The people!"

"Ah!" exclaimed Mary Stuart, clasping the stiffened hand of her first husband, now dead, "there is none but me to weep for this poor boy who loved me so!"

"How can we patch up matters with the queen-mother?" said the cardinal.

"Wait till she quarrels with the Huguenots," replied the duchess.

The conflicting interests of the house of Bourbon, of Catherine, of the Guises, and of the Reformed party produced such confusion in the town of Orleans that, three days after the king's death, his body, completely forgotten in the Bailliage and put into a coffin by the menials of the house, was taken to Saint-Denis in a covered waggon, accompanied only by the Bishop of Senlis and two gentlemen. When the pitiable procession reached the little town of Etampes, a servant of the Chancelier l'Hopital fastened to the waggon this severe inscription, which history has preserved: "Tanneguy de Chastel, where art thou? and yet thou wert a Frenchman!"—a stern reproach, which fell with equal force on Catherine de' Medici, Mary Stuart, and the Guises. What Frenchman does not know that Tanneguy de Chastel spent thirty thousand crowns of the coinage of that day (one million of our francs) at the funeral of Charles VII., the benefactor of his house?

No sooner did the tolling of the bells announce to the town of Orleans that Francois II. was dead, and the rumor spread that the Connetable de Montmorency had ordered the flinging open of the gates of the town, than Tourillon, the glover, rushed up into the garret of his house and went to a secret hiding-place.

"Good heavens! can he be dead?" he cried.

Hearing the words, a man rose to his feet and answered, "Ready to serve!"—the password of the Reformers who belonged to Calvin.

This man was Chaudieu, to whom Tourillon now related the events of the last eight days, during which time he had prudently left the minister alone in his hiding-place with a twelve-pound loaf of bread for his sole nourishment.

"Go instantly to the Prince de Conde, brother: ask him to give me a safe-conduct; and find me a horse," cried the minister. "I must start at once."

"Write me a line, or he will not receive me."

"Here," said Chaudieu, after writing a few words, "ask for a pass from the king of Navarre, for I must go to Geneva without a moment's loss of time."

XIII. CALVIN

Two hours later all was ready, and the ardent minister was on his way to Switzerland, accompanied by a nobleman in the service of the king of Navarre (of whom Chaudieu pretended to be the secretary), carrying with him despatches from the Reformers in the Dauphine. This sudden departure was chiefly in the interests of Catherine de' Medici, who, in order to gain time to establish her power, had made a bold proposition to the Reformers which was kept a profound secret. This strange proceeding explains the understanding so suddenly apparent between herself and the leaders of the Reform. The wily woman gave, as a pledge of her good faith, an intimation of her desire to heal all differences between the two churches by calling an assembly, which should be neither a council, nor a conclave, nor a synod, but should be known by some new and distinctive name, if Calvin consented to the project. When this secret was afterwards divulged (be it remarked in passing) it led to an alliance between the Duc de Guise and the Connetable de Montmorency against Catherine and the king of Navarre,—a strange alliance! known in history as the Triumvirate, the Marechal de Saint-Andre being the third personage in the purely Catholic coalition to which this singular proposition for a "colloquy" gave rise. The secret of Catherine's wily policy was rightly understood by the Guises; they felt certain that the queen cared nothing for this mysterious assembly, and was only temporizing with her new allies in order to secure a period of peace until the majority of Charles IX.; but none the less did they deceive the Connetable into fearing a collusion of real interests between the queen and the Bourbons,—whereas, in reality, Catherine was playing them all one against another.

The queen had become, as the reader will perceive, extremely powerful in a very short time. The spirit of discussion and controversy which now sprang up was singularly favorable to her position. The Catholics and the

Reformers were equally pleased to exhibit their brilliancy one after another in this tournament of words; for that is what it actually was, and no more. It is extraordinary that historians have mistaken one of the wiliest schemes of the great queen for uncertainty and hesitation! Catherine never went more directly to her own ends than in just such schemes which appeared to thwart them. The king of Navarre, quite incapable of understanding her motives, fell into her plan in all sincerity, and despatched Chaudieu to Calvin, as we have seen. The minister had risked his life to be secretly in Orleans and watch events; for he was, while there, in hourly peril of being discovered and hung as a man under sentence of banishment.

According to the then fashion of travelling, Chaudieu could not reach Geneva before the month of February, and the negotiations were not likely to be concluded before the end of March; consequently the assembly could certainly not take place before the month of May, 1561. Catherine, meantime, intended to amuse the court and the various conflicting interests by the coronation of the king, and the ceremonies of his first "lit de justice," at which l'Hopital and de Thou recorded the letters-patent by which Charles IX. confided the administration to his mother in common with the present lieutenant-general of the kingdom, Antoine de Navarre, the weakest prince of those days.

Is it not a strange spectacle this of the great kingdom of France waiting in suspense for the "yes" or "no" of a French burgher, hitherto an obscure man, living for many years past in Geneva? The transalpine pope held in check by the pontiff of Geneva! The two Lorrain princes, lately all-powerful, now paralyzed by the momentary coalition of the queen-mother and the first prince of the blood with Calvin! Is not this, I say, one of the most instructive lessons ever given to kings by history,— a lesson which should teach them to study men, to seek out genius, and employ it, as did Louis XIV., wherever God has placed it?

Calvin, whose name was not Calvin but Cauvin, was the son of a cooper at Noyon in Picardy. The region of his birth explains in some degree the obstinacy combined with capricious eagerness which distinguished this arbiter of the destinies of France in the sixteenth century. Nothing is less known than the nature of this man, who gave birth to Geneva and to the spirit that emanated from that city. Jean-Jacques Rousseau, who had very little historical knowledge, has completely ignored the influence of Calvin on his republic. At first the embryo Reformer, who lived in one of the humblest houses in the upper town, near the church of Saint-Pierre, over a carpenter's shop (first resemblance between him and Robespierre), had no great authority in Geneva. In fact for a long time his power was malevolently checked by the Genevese. The town was the residence in those days of a citizen whose fame, like that of several others, remained unknown to the world at large and for a time to Geneva itself. This man, Farel, about the year 1537, detained Calvin in Geneva, pointing out to him that the place could be made the safe centre of a reformation more active and thorough than that of Luther. Farel and Calvin regarded Lutheranism as an incomplete work,—insufficient in itself and without any real grip upon France. Geneva, midway between France and Italy, and speaking the French language, was admirably situated for ready communication with Germany, France, and Italy. Calvin thereupon adopted Geneva as the site of his moral fortunes; he made it thenceforth the citadel of his ideas.

The Council of Geneva, at Farel's entreaty, authorized Calvin in September, 1538, to give lectures on theology. Calvin left the duties of the ministry to Farel, his first disciple, and gave himself up patiently to the work of teaching his doctrine. His authority, which became so absolute in the last years of his life, was obtained with difficulty and very slowly. The great agitator met with such serious obstacles that he was banished for a time from Geneva on account of the severity of his reform. A party of honest citizens still clung to their old luxury and their old customs. But, as usually happens, these good people, fearing ridicule, would not admit the real object of their efforts, and kept up their warfare against the new doctrines on points altogether foreign to the real question. Calvin insisted that *leavened bread* should be used for the communion, and that all feasts should be abolished except Sundays. These innovations were disapproved of at Berne and at Lausanne. Notice was served on the Genevese to conform to the ritual of Switzerland. Calvin and Farel resisted; their political opponents used this disobedience to drive them from Geneva, whence they were, in fact, banished for several years. Later Calvin returned triumphantly at the demand of his flock. Such persecutions always become in the end the consecration of a moral power; and, in this case, Calvin's return was the beginning of his era as prophet. He then organized his religious Terror, and the executions began. On his reappearance in the city he was admitted into the ranks of the Genevese burghers; but even then, after fourteen years' residence, he was not made a member of the Council. At the time of which we write, when Catherine sent her envoy to him, this king of ideas had no other title than that of "pastor of the Church of Geneva." Moreover, Calvin never in his life received a salary of more than one hundred and fifty francs in money yearly, fifteen hundred-weight of wheat, and two barrels of wine. His brother, a tailor, kept a shop close to the place Saint-Pierre, in a street now occupied by one of the large printing establishments of Geneva. Such personal disinterestedness, which was lacking in Voltaire, Newton, and Bacon, but eminent in the lives of Rabelais, Spinosa, Loyola, Kant, and Jean-Jacques Rousseau, is indeed a magnificent frame to those ardent and sublime figures.

The career of Robespierre can alone picture to the minds of the present day that of Calvin, who, founding his power on the same bases, was as despotic and as cruel as the lawyer of Arras. It is a noticeable fact that Picardy (Arras and Noyon) furnished both these instruments of reformation! Persons who wish to study the motives of the executions ordered by Calvin will find, all relations considered, another 1793 in Geneva. Calvin cut off the head of Jacques Gruet "for having written impious letters, libertine verses, and for working to overthrow ecclesiastical ordinances." Reflect upon that sentence, and ask yourselves if the worst tyrants in their saturnalias ever gave more horribly burlesque reasons for their cruelties. Valentin Gentilis, condemned to death for "involuntary heresy," escaped execution only by making a submission far more ignominious than was ever imposed by the Catholic Church. Seven years before the conference which was now to take place in Calvin's house on the proposals of the queen-mother, Michel Servet, *a Frenchman*, travelling through Switzerland, was arrested at Geneva, tried, condemned, and burned alive, on Calvin's accusation, for having "attacked the mystery of the Trinity," in a book which was neither written nor published in Geneva. Remember the eloquent remonstrance of Jean-Jacques Rousseau, whose book, overthrowing the Catholic religion, written in France and published in Holland, was burned by the hangman, while the author, a foreigner, was merely banished from the kingdom where he had endeavored to destroy the fundamental proofs of religion and of authority. Compare the conduct of our Parliament with that of the Genevese tyrant. Again: Bolsee was brought to trial for "having other ideas than those of Calvin on predestination." Consider these things, and ask yourselves if Fourquier-Tinville did worse. The savage religious intolerance of Calvin was, morally speaking, more implacable than the savage political intolerance of Robespierre. On a larger stage than that of Geneva, Calvin would have shed more blood than did the terrible apostle of political equality as opposed to Catholic equality. Three centuries earlier a monk of Picardy drove the whole West upon the East. Peter the Hermit, Calvin, and Robespierre, each at an interval of three hundred years and all three from the same region, were, politically speaking, the Archimedean screws of their age,—at each epoch a Thought which found its fulcrum in the self-interest of mankind.

Calvin was undoubtedly the maker of that melancholy town called

Geneva, where, only ten years ago, a man said, pointing to a porte-cochere in the upper town, the first ever built there: "By that door luxury has invaded Geneva." Calvin gave birth, by the sternness of his doctrines and his executions, to that form of hypocritical sentiment called "cant."[*] According to those who practice it, good morals consist in renouncing the arts and the charms of life, in eating richly but without luxury, in silently amassing money without enjoying it otherwise than as Calvin enjoyed power—by thought. Calvin imposed on all the citizens of his adopted town the same gloomy pall which he spread over his own life. He created in the Consistory a Calvinistic inquisition, absolutely similar to the revolutionary tribunal of Robespierre. The Consistory denounced the persons to be condemned to the Council, and Calvin ruled the Council through the Consistory, just as Robespierre ruled the Convention through the Club of the Jacobins. In this way an eminent magistrate of Geneva was condemned to two months' imprisonment, the loss of all his offices, and the right of ever obtaining others "because he led a disorderly life and was intimate with Calvin's enemies." Calvin thus became a legislator. He created the austere, sober, commonplace, and hideously sad, but irreproachable manners and customs which characterize Geneva to the present day,—customs preceding those of England called Puritanism, which were due to the Cameronians, disciples of Cameron (a Frenchman deriving his doctrine from Calvin), whom Sir Walter Scott depicts so admirably. The poverty of a man, a sovereign master, who negotiated, power to power, with kings, demanding armies and subsidies, and plunging both hands into their savings laid aside for the unfortunate, proves that thought, used solely as a means of domination, gives birth to political misers,—men who enjoy by their brains only, and, like the Jesuits, want power for power's sake. Pitt, Luther, Calvin, Robespierre, all those Harpagons of power, died without a penny. The inventory taken in Calvin's house after his death, which comprised all his property, even his books, amounted in value, as history records, to two hundred and fifty francs. That of Luther came to about the same sum; his widow, the famous Catherine de Bora, was forced to petition for a pension of five hundred francs, which as granted to her by an Elector of Germany. Potemkin, Richelieu, Mazarin, those men of thought and action, all three of whom made or laid the foundation of empires, each left over three hundred millions behind them. They had hearts; they loved women and the arts; they built, they conquered; whereas with the exception of the wife of Luther, the Helen of that Iliad, all the others had no tenderness, no beating of the heart for any woman with which to reproach themselves.

[*] *Momerie.*

This brief digression was necessary in order to explain Calvin's position in Geneva.

During the first days of the month of February in the year 1561, on a soft, warm evening such as we may sometimes find at that season on Lake Leman, two horsemen arrived at the Pre-l'Eveque,—thus called because it was the former country-place of the Bishop of Geneva, driven from Switzerland about thirty years earlier. These horsemen, who no doubt knew the laws of Geneva about the closing of the gates (then a necessity and now very ridiculous) rode in the direction of the Porte de Rive; but they stopped their horses suddenly on catching sight of a man, about fifty years of age, leaning on the arm of a servant-woman, and walking slowly toward the town. This man, who was rather stout, walked with difficulty, putting one foot after the other with pain apparently, for he wore round shoes of black velvet, laced in front.

"It is he!" said Chaudieu to the other horseman, who immediately dismounted, threw the reins to his companion, and went forward, opening wide his arms to the man on foot.

The man, who was Jean Calvin, drew back to avoid the embrace, casting a stern look at his disciple. At fifty years of age Calvin looked as though he were sixty. Stout and stocky in figure, he seemed shorter still because the horrible sufferings of stone in the bladder obliged him to bend almost double as he walked. These pains were complicated by attacks of gout of the worst kind. Every one trembled before that face, almost as broad as it was long, on which, in spite of its roundness, there was as little human-kindness as on that of Henry the Eighth, whom Calvin greatly resembled. Sufferings which gave him no respite were manifest in the deep-cut lines starting from each side of the nose and following the curve of the moustache till they were lost in the thick gray beard. This face, though red and inflamed like that of a heavy drinker, showed spots where the skin was yellow. In spite of the velvet cap, which covered the huge square head, a vast forehead of noble shape could be seen and admired; beneath it shone two dark eyes, which must have flashed forth flame in moments of anger. Whether by reason of his obesity, or because of his thick, short neck, or in consequence of his vigils and his constant labors, Calvin's head was sunk between his broad shoulders, which obliged him to wear a fluted ruff of very small dimensions, on which his face seemed to lie like the head of John the Baptist on a charger. Between his moustache and his beard could be seen, like a rose, his small and fresh and eloquent little mouth, shaped in perfection. The face was divided by a square nose, remarkable for the flexibility of its entire length, the tip of which was significantly flat, seeming the more in harmony with the prodigious power expressed by the form of that imperial head. Though it might have been difficult to discover on his features any trace of the weekly headaches which tormented Calvin in the intervals of the slow fever that consumed him, suffering, ceaselessly resisted by study and by will, gave to that mask, superficially so florid, a certain something that was terrible. Perhaps this impression was explainable by the color of a sort of greasy layer on the skin, due to the sedentary habits of the toiler, showing evidence of the perpetual struggle which went on between that valetudinarian temperament and one of the strongest wills ever known in the history of the human mind. The mouth, though charming, had an expression of cruelty. Chastity, necessitated by vast designs, exacted by so many sickly conditions, was written upon that face. Regrets were there, notwithstanding the serenity of that all-powerful brow, together with pain in the glance of those eyes, the calmness of which was terrifying.

Calvin's costume brought into full relief this powerful head. He wore the well-known cassock of black cloth, fastened round his waist by a black cloth belt with a brass buckle, which became thenceforth the distinctive dress of all Calvinist ministers, and was so uninteresting to the eye that it forced the spectator's attention upon the wearer's face.

"I suffer too much, Theodore, to embrace you," said Calvin to the elegant cavalier.

Theodore de Beze, then forty-two years of age and lately admitted, at Calvin's request, as a Genevese burgher, formed a violent contrast to the terrible pastor whom he had chosen as his sovereign guide and ruler. Calvin, like all burghers raised to moral sovereignty, and all inventors of social systems, was eaten up with jealousy. He abhorred his disciples; he wanted no equals; he could not bear the slightest contradiction. Yet there was between him and this graceful cavalier so marked a difference, Theodore de Beze was gifted with so charming a personality enhanced by a politeness trained by court life, and Calvin felt him to be so unlike his other surly janissaries, that the stern reformer departed in de Beze's case from his usual habits. He never loved him, for this harsh legislator totally ignored all friendship, but, not fearing him in the light of a successor, he liked to play with Theodore as Richelieu played with his cat; he found him supple and agile. Seeing how admirably de Beze succeeded in all his missions, he took a fancy to the polished instrument of which he knew himself the mainspring and the manipulator; so true is it that the sternest of men cannot do without some semblance of affection. Theodore was Calvin's spoilt child; the harsh reformer never scolded him; he forgave him his dissipations, his amours, his fine clothes and his elegance of language. Perhaps Calvin was not unwilling to show that the

Reformation had a few men of the world to compare with the men of the court. Theodore de Beze was anxious to introduce a taste for the arts, for literature, and for poesy into Geneva, and Calvin listened to his plans without knitting his thick gray eyebrows. Thus the contrast of character and person between these two celebrated men was as complete and marked as the difference in their minds.

Calvin acknowledged Chaudieu's very humble salutation by a slight inclination of the head. Chaudieu slipped the bridles of both horses through his arms and followed the two great men of the Reformation, walking to the left, behind de Beze, who was on Calvin's right. The servant-woman hastened on in advance to prevent the closing of the Porte de Rive, by informing the captain of the guard that Calvin had been seized with sudden acute pains.

Theodore de Beze was a native of the canton of Vezelay, which was the first to enter the Confederation, the curious history of which transaction has been written by one of the Thierrys. The burgher spirit of resistance, endemic at Vezelay, no doubt, played its part in the person of this man, in the great revolt of the Reformers; for de Beze was undoubtedly one of the most singular personalities of the Heresy.

"You suffer still?" said Theodore to Calvin.

"A Catholic would say, 'like a lost soul,'" replied the Reformer, with the bitterness he gave to his slightest remarks. "Ah! I shall not be here long, my son. What will become of you without me?"

"We shall fight by the light of your books," said Chaudieu.

Calvin smiled; his red face changed to a pleased expression, and he looked favorably at Chaudieu.

"Well, have you brought me news? Have they massacred many of our people?" he said smiling, and letting a sarcastic joy shine in his brown eyes.

"No," said Chaudieu, "all is peaceful."

"So much the worse," cried Calvin; "so much the worse! All pacification is an evil, if indeed it is not a trap. Our strength lies in persecution. Where should we be if the Church accepted Reform?"

"But," said Theodore, "that is precisely what the queen-mother appears to wish."

"She is capable of it," remarked Calvin. "I study that woman—"

"What, at this distance?" cried Chaudieu.

"Is there any distance for the mind?" replied Calvin, sternly, for he thought the interruption irreverent. "Catherine seeks power, and women with that in their eye have neither honor nor faith. But what is she doing now?"

"I bring you a proposal from her to call a species of council," replied

Theodore de Beze.

"Near Paris?" asked Calvin, hastily.

"Yes."

"Ha! so much the better!" exclaimed the Reformer.

"We are to try to understand each other and draw up some public agreement which shall unite the two churches."

"Ah! if she would only have the courage to separate the French Church from the court of Rome, and create a patriarch for France as they did in the Greek Church!" cried Calvin, his eyes glistening at the idea thus presented to his mind of a possible throne. "But, my son, can the niece of a Pope be sincere? She is only trying to gain time."

"She has sent away the Queen of Scots," said Chaudieu.

"One less!" remarked Calvin, as they passed through the Porte de Rive. "Elizabeth of England will restrain that one for us. Two neighboring queens will soon be at war with each other. One is handsome, the other ugly,—a first cause for irritation; besides, there's the question of illegitimacy—"

He rubbed his hands, and the character of his joy was so evidently ferocious that de Beze shuddered: he saw the sea of blood his master was contemplating.

"The Guises have irritated the house of Bourbon," said Theodore after a pause. "They came to an open rupture at Orleans."

"Ah!" said Calvin, "you would not believe me, my son, when I told you the last time you started for Nerac that we should end by stirring up war to the death between the two branches of the house of France? I have, at least, one court, one king and royal family on my side. My doctrine is producing its effect upon the masses. The burghers, too, understand me; they regard as idolators all who go to Mass, who paint the walls of their churches, and put pictures and statues within them. Ha! it is far more easy for a people to demolish churches and palaces than to argue the question of justification by faith, or the real presence. Luther was an argufier, but I,—I am an army! He was a reasoner, I am a system. In short, my sons, he was merely a skirmisher, but I am Tarquin! Yes, *my* faithful shall destroy pictures and pull down churches; they shall make mill-stones of statues to grind the flour of the peoples. There are guilds and corporations in the States-general—I will have nothing there but individuals. Corporations resist; they see clear where the masses are blind. We must join to our doctrine political interests which will consolidate it, and keep together the *materiel* of my armies. I have satisfied the logic of cautious souls and the minds of thinkers by this bared and naked worship which carries religion into the world of ideas; I have made the peoples understand the advantages of suppressing ceremony. It is for you, Theodore, to enlist their interests; hold to that; go not beyond it. All is said in the way of doctrine; let no one add one iota. Why does Cameron, that little Gascon pastor, presume to write of it?"

Calvin, de Beze, and Chaudieu were mounting the steep steps of the upper town in the midst of a crowd, but the crowd paid not the slightest attention to the men who were unchaining the mobs of other cities and preparing them to ravage France.

After this terrible tirade, the three marched on in silence till they entered the little place Saint-Pierre and turned toward the pastor's house. On the second story of that house (never noted, and of which in these days no one is ever told in Geneva, where, it may be remarked, Calvin has no statue) his lodging consisted of three chambers with common pine floors and wainscots, at the end of which were the kitchen and the bedroom of his woman-servant. The entrance, as usually happened in most of the burgher households of Geneva, was through the kitchen, which opened into a little room with two windows, serving as parlor, salon, and dining-room. Calvin's study, where his thought had wrestled with suffering for the last fourteen years, came next, with the bedroom beyond it. Four oaken chairs covered with tapestry and placed around a square table were the sole furniture of the parlor. A stove of white porcelain, standing in one corner of the room, cast out a gentle heat. Panels and a wainscot of pine wood left in its natural state without decoration covered the walls. Thus the nakedness of the place was in keeping with the sober and simple life of the Reformer.

"Well?" said de Beze as they entered, profiting by a few moments when Chaudieu left them to put up the horse at a neighboring inn, "what am I to do? Will you agree to the colloquy?"

"Of course," replied Calvin. "And it is you, my son, who will fight for us there. Be peremptory, be arbitrary. No one, neither the queen nor the Guises nor I, wants a pacification; it would not suit us at all. I have confidence in Duplessis-Mornay; let him play the leading part. Are we alone?" he added, with a glance of distrust into the kitchen, where two shirts and a few collars were stretched on a line to dry. "Go and shut all the doors. Well," he continued when Theodore had returned, "we must drive the king of Navarre to join the Guises and the Connetable by advising him to break with Queen Catherine de' Medici. Let us all get the benefit of that poor creature's weakness. If he turns against the Italian she will, when she sees herself deprived of that support, necessarily unite with the Prince de Conde and Coligny. Perhaps this manoeuvre will so compromise her that she will be forced to remain on our side."

Theodore de Beze caught the hem of Calvin's cassock and kissed it.

"Oh! my master," he exclaimed, "how great you are!"

"Unfortunately, my dear Theodore, I am dying. If I die without seeing you again," he added, sinking his voice and speaking in the ear of his minister of foreign affairs, "remember to strike a great blow by the hand of some one of our martyrs."

"Another Minard to be killed?"

"Something better than a mere lawyer."

"A king?"

"Still better!—a man who wants to be a king."

"The Duc de Guise!" exclaimed Theodore, with an involuntary gesture.

"Well?" cried Calvin, who thought he saw disappointment or resistance in the gesture, and did not see at the same moment the entrance of Chaudieu. "Have we not the right to strike as we are struck?—yes, to strike in silence and in darkness. May we not return them wound for wound, and death for death? Would the Catholics hesitate to lay traps for us and massacre us? Assuredly not. Let us burn their churches! Forward, my children! And if you have devoted youths—"

"I have," said Chaudieu.

"Use them as engines of war! our cause justifies all means. Le Balafre, that horrible soldier, is, like me, more than a man; he is a dynasty, just as I am a system. He is able to annihilate us; therefore, I say, Death to the Guise!"

"I would rather have a peaceful victory, won by time and reason," said de Beze.

"Time!" exclaimed Calvin, dashing his chair to the ground, "reason! Are you mad? Can reason achieve conquests? You know nothing of men, you who deal with them, idiot! The thing that injures my doctrine, you triple fool! is the reason that is in it. By the lightning of Saul, by the sword of Vengeance, thou pumpkin-head, do you not see the vigor given to my Reform by the massacre at Amboise? Ideas never grow till they are watered with blood. The slaying of the Duc de Guise will lead to a horrible persecution, and I pray for it with all my might. Our reverses are preferable to success. The Reformation has an object to gain in being attacked; do you hear me, dolt? It cannot hurt us to be defeated, whereas Catholicism is at an end if we should win but a single battle. Ha! what are my lieutenants?—rags, wet rags instead of men! white-haired cravens! baptized apes! O God, grant me ten years more of life! If I die too soon the cause of true religion is lost in the hands of such boobies! You are as great a fool as Antoine de Navarre! Out of my sight! Leave me; I want a better negotiator than you! You are an ass, a popinjay, a poet! Go and make your elegies and your acrostics, you trifler! Hence!"

The pains of his body were absolutely overcome by the fire of his anger;

even the gout subsided under this horrible excitement of his mind. Calvin's face flushed purple, like the sky before a storm. His vast brow shone. His eyes flamed. He was no longer himself. He gave way utterly to the species of epileptic motion, full of passion, which was common with him. But in the very midst of it he was struck by the attitude of the two witnesses; then, as he caught the words of Chaudieu saying to de Beze, "The Burning Bush!" he sat down, was silent, and covered his face with his two hands, the knotted veins of which were throbbing in spite of their coarse texture.

Some minutes later, still shaken by this storm raised within him by the continence of his life, he said in a voice of emotion:—

"My sins, which are many, cost me less trouble to subdue, than my impatience. Oh, savage beast! shall I never vanquish you?" he cried, beating his breast.

"My dear master," said de Beze, in a tender voice, taking Calvin's hand and kissing it, "Jupiter thunders, but he knows how to smile."

Calvin looked at his disciple with a softened eye and said:—

"Understand me, my friends."

"I understand that the pastors of peoples bear great burdens," replied Theodore. "You have a world upon your shoulders."

"I have three martyrs," said Chaudieu, whom the master's outburst had rendered thoughtful, "on whom we can rely. Stuart, who killed Minard, is at liberty—"

"You are mistaken," said Calvin, gently, smiling after the manner of great men who bring fair weather into their faces as though they were ashamed of the previous storm. "I know human nature; a man may kill one president, but not two."

"Is it absolutely necessary?" asked de Beze.

"Again!" exclaimed Calvin, his nostrils swelling. "Come, leave me, you will drive me to fury. Take my decision to the queen. You, Chaudieu, go your way, and hold your flock together in Paris. God guide you! Dinah, light my friends to the door."

"Will you not permit me to embrace you?" said Theodore, much moved. "Who knows what may happen to us on the morrow? We may be seized in spite of our safe-conduct."

"And yet you want to spare them!" cried Calvin, embracing de Beze. Then he took Chaudieu's hand and said: "Above all, no Huguenots, no Reformers, but *Calvinists*! Use no term but Calvinism. Alas! this is not ambition, for I am dying,—but it is necessary to destroy the whole of Luther, even to the name of Lutheran and Lutheranism."

"Ah! man divine," cried Chaudieu, "you well deserve such honors."

"Maintain the uniformity of the doctrine; let no one henceforth change or remark it. We are lost if new sects issue from our bosom."

We will here anticipate the events on which this Study is based, and close the history of Theodore de Beze, who went to Paris with Chaudieu. It is to be remarked that Poltrot, who fired at the Duc de Guise fifteen months later, confessed under torture that he had been urged to the crime by Theodore de Beze; though he retracted that avowal during subsequent tortures; so that Bossuet, after weighing all historical considerations, felt obliged to acquit Beze of instigating the crime. Since Bossuet's time, however, an apparently futile dissertation, apropos of a celebrated song, has led a compiler of the eighteenth century to prove that the verses on the death of the Duc de Guise, sung by the Huguenots from one end of France to the other, was the work of Theodore de Beze; and it is also proved that the famous song on the burial of Marlborough was a plagiarism on it.[*]

> [*] One of the most remarkable instances of the transmission
> of songs is that of Marlborough. Written in the first
> instance by a Huguenot on the death of the Duc de Guise in
> 1563, it was preserved in the French army, and appears to
> have been sung with variations, suppressions, and additions
> at the death of all generals of importance. When the
> intestine wars were over the song followed the soldiers into
> civil life. It was never forgotten (though the habit of
> singing it may have lessened), and in 1781, sixty years
> after the death of Marlborough, the wet-nurse of the Dauphin
> was heard to sing it as she suckled her nursling. When and
> why the name of the Duke of Marlborough was substituted for
> that of the Duc de Guise has never been ascertained. See
> "Chansons Populaires," par Charles Nisard: Paris, Dentu,
> 1867.—Tr.

XIV. CATHERINE IN POWER

The day on which Theodore de Beze and Chaudieu arrived in Paris, the court returned from Rheims, where Charles IX. was crowned. This ceremony, which Catherine made magnificent with splendid fetes, enabled her to gather about her the leaders of the various parties. Having studied all interests and all factions, she found herself with two alternatives from which to choose; either to rally them all to the throne, or to pit them one against the other. The Connetable de Montmorency, supremely Catholic, whose nephew, the Prince de Conde, was leader of the Reformers, and whose sons were inclined to the new religion, blamed the alliance of the queen-mother with the Reformation. The Guises, on their side, were endeavoring to gain over Antoine de Bourbon, king of Navarre, a weak prince; a manoeuvre which his wife, Jeanne d'Albret, instructed by de Beze, allowed to succeed. The difficulties were plain to Catherine, whose dawning power needed a period of tranquillity. She therefore impatiently awaited Calvin's reply to the message which the Prince de Conde, the king of Navarre, Coligny, d'Andelot, and the Cardinal de Chatillon had sent him through de Beze and Chaudieu. Meantime, however, she was faithful to her promises as to the Prince de Conde. The chancellor put an end to the proceedings in which Christophe was involved by referring the affair to the Parliament of Paris, which at once set aside the judgment of the committee, declaring it without power to try a prince of the blood. The Parliament then reopened the trial, at the request of the Guises and the queen-mother. Lasagne's papers had already been given to Catherine, who burned them. The giving up of these papers was a first pledge, uselessly made by the Guises to the queen-mother. The Parliament, no longer able to take cognizance of those decisive proofs, reinstated the prince in all his rights, property, and honors. Christophe, released during the tumult at Orleans on the death of the king, was acquitted in the first instance, and appointed, in compensation for his sufferings, solicitor to the Parliament, at the request of his godfather Monsieur de Thou.

The Triumvirate, that coming coalition of self-interests threatened by Catherine's first acts, was now forming itself under her very eyes. Just as in chemistry antagonistic substances separate at the first shock which jars their enforced union, so in politics the alliance of opposing interests never lasts. Catherine thoroughly understood that sooner or later she should return to the Guises and combine with them and the Connetable to do battle against the Huguenots. The proposed "colloquy" which tempted the vanity of the orators of all parties, and offered an imposing spectacle to succeed that of the coronation and enliven the bloody ground of a religious war which, in point of fact, had already begun, was as futile in the eyes of the Duc de Guise as in those of Catherine. The Catholics would, in one sense be worsted; for the Huguenots, under pretext of conferring, would be able to proclaim their doctrine, with the sanction of the king and his mother, to the ears of all France. The Cardinal de Lorraine, flattered by Catherine into the idea of destroying the heresy by the eloquence of the Church, persuaded his brother to consent; and thus the queen obtained what was all-essential to her, six months of peace.

158

A slight event, occurring at this time, came near compromising the power which Catherine had so painfully built up. The following scene, preserved in history, took place, on the very day the envoys returned from Geneva, in the hotel de Coligny near the Louvre. At his coronation, Charles IX., who was greatly attached to his tutor Amyot, appointed him grand-almoner of France. This affection was shared by his brother the Duc d'Anjou, afterwards Henri III., another of Anjou's pupils. Catherine heard the news of this appointment from the two Gondis during the journey from Rheims to Paris. She had counted on that office in the gift of the Crown to gain a supporter in the Church with whom to oppose the Cardinal de Lorraine. Her choice had fallen on the Cardinal de Tournon, in whom she expected to find, as in l'Hopital, another *crutch*—the word is her own. As soon as she reached the Louvre she sent for the tutor, and her anger was such, on seeing the disaster to her policy caused by the ambition of this son of a shoemaker, that she was betrayed into using the following extraordinary language, which several memoirs of the day have handed down to us:—

"What!" she cried, "am I, who compel the Guises, the Colignys, the Connetables, the house of Navarre, the Prince de Conde, to serve my ends, am I to be opposed by a priestling like you who are not satisfied to be bishop of Auxerre?"

Amyot excused himself. He assured the queen that he had asked nothing; the king of his own will had given him the office of which he, the son of a poor tailor, felt himself quite unworthy.

"Be assured, *maitre*," replied Catherine (that being the name which the two kings, Charles IX. and Henri III., gave to the great writer) "that you will not stand on your feet twenty-four hours hence, unless you make your pupil change his mind."

Between the death thus threatened and the resignation of the highest ecclesiastical office in the gift of the crown, the son of the shoemaker, who had lately become extremely eager after honors, and may even have coveted a cardinal's hat, thought it prudent to temporize. He left the court and hid himself in the abbey of Saint-Germain. When Charles IX. did not see him at his first dinner, he asked where he was. Some Guisard doubtless told him of what had occurred between Amyot and the queen-mother.

"Has he been forced to disappear because I made him grand-almoner?" cried the king.

He thereupon rushed to his mother in the violent wrath of angry children when their caprices are opposed.

"Madame," he said on entering, "did I not kindly sign the letter you asked me to send to Parliament, by means of which you govern my kingdom? Did you not promise that if I did so my will should be yours? And here, the first favor that I wish to bestow excites your jealousy! The chancellor talks of declaring my majority at fourteen, three years from now, and you wish to treat me as a child. By God, I will be king, and a king as my father and grandfather were kings!"

The tone and manner in which these words were said gave Catherine a revelation of her son's true character; it was like a blow in the breast.

"He speaks to me thus, he whom I made a king!" she thought. "Monsieur," she said aloud, "the office of a king, in times like these, is a very difficult one; you do not yet know the shrewd men with whom you have to deal. You will never have a safer and more sincere friend than your mother, or better servants than those who have been so long attached to her person, without whose services you might perhaps not even exist to-day. The Guises want both your life and your throne, be sure of that. If they could sew me into a sack and fling me into the river," she said, pointing to the Seine, "it would be done to-night. They know that I am a lioness defending her young, and that I alone prevent their daring hands from seizing your crown. To whom—to whose party does your tutor belong? Who are his allies? What authority has he? What services can he do you? What weight do his words carry? Instead of finding a prop to sustain your power, you have cut the ground from under it. The Cardinal de Lorraine is a living threat to you; he plays the king; he keeps his hat on his head before the princes of the blood; it was urgently necessary to invest another cardinal with powers greater than his own. But what have you done? Is Amyot, that shoemaker, fit only to tie the ribbons of his shoes, is he capable of making head against the Guise ambition? However, you love Amyot, you have appointed him; your will must now be done, monsieur. But before you make such gifts again, I pray you to consult me in affectionate good faith. Listen to reasons of state; and your own good sense as a child may perhaps agree with my old experience, when you really understand the difficulties that lie before you."

"Then I can have my master back again?" cried the king, not listening to his mother's words, which he considered to be mere reproaches.

"Yes, you shall have him," she replied. "But it is not here, nor that brutal Cypierre who will teach you how to reign."

"It is for you to do so, my dear mother," said the boy, mollified by his victory and relaxing the surly and threatening look stamped by nature upon his countenance.

Catherine sent Gondi to recall the new grand-almoner. When the Italian discovered the place of Amyot's retreat, and the bishop heard that the courtier was sent by the queen, he was seized with terror and refused to leave the abbey. In this extremity Catherine was obliged to write to him herself, in such terms that he returned to Paris and received from her own lips the assurance of her protection,—on condition, however, that he would blindly promote her wishes with Charles IX.

This little domestic tempest over, the queen, now re-established in the Louvre after an absence of more than a year, held council with her closest friends as to the proper conduct to pursue with the young king whom Cypierre had complimented on his firmness.

"What is best to be done?" she said to the two Gondis, Ruggiero, Birago, and Chiverni who had lately become governor and chancellor to the Duc d'Anjou.

"Before all else," replied Birago, "get rid of Cypierre. He is not a courtier; he will never accommodate himself to your ideas, and will think he does his duty in thwarting you."

"Whom can I trust?" cried the queen.

"One of us," said Birago.

"On my honor!" exclaimed Gondi, "I'll promise you to make the king as docile as the king of Navarre."

"You allowed the late king to perish to save your other children," said Albert de Gondi. "Do, then, as the great signors of Constantinople do,—divert the anger and amuse the caprices of the present king. He loves art and poetry and hunting, also a little girl he saw at Orleans; *there's* occupation enough for him."

"Will you really be the king's governor?" said Catherine to the ablest of the Gondis.

"Yes, if you will give me the necessary authority; you may even be obliged to make me marshal of France and a duke. Cypierre is altogether too small a man to hold the office. In future, the governor of a king of France should be of some great dignity, like that of duke and marshal."

"He is right," said Birago.

"Poet and huntsman," said Catherine in a dreamy tone.

"We will hunt and make love!" cried Gondi.

"Moreover," remarked Chiverni, "you are sure of Amyot, who will always fear poison in case of disobedience; so that you and he and Gondi can hold the king in leading-strings."

"Amyot has deeply offended me," said Catherine.

"He does not know what he owes to you; if he did know, you would be in danger," replied Birago, gravely, emphasizing his words.

"Then, it is agreed," exclaimed Catherine, on whom Birago's reply made a powerful impression, "that you, Gondi, are to be the king's governor. My son must consent to do for one of my friends a favor equal to the one I have just permitted for his knave of a bishop. That fool has lost the hat;

for never, as long as I live, will I consent that the Pope shall give it to him! How strong we might have been with Cardinal de Tournon! What a trio with Tournon for grand-almoner, and l'Hopital, and de Thou! As for the burghers of Paris, I intend to make my son cajole them; we will get a support there."

Accordingly, Albert de Gondi became a marshal of France and was created Duc de Retz and governor of the king a few days later.

At the moment when this little private council ended, Cardinal de Tournon announced to the queen the arrival of the emissaries sent to Calvin. Admiral Coligny accompanied the party in order that his presence might ensure them due respect at the Louvre. The queen gathered the formidable phalanx of her maids of honor about her, and passed into the reception hall, built by her husband, which no longer exists in the Louvre of to-day.

At the period of which we write the staircase of the Louvre occupied the clock tower. Catherine's apartments were in the old buildings which still exist in the court of the Musee. The present staircase of the museum was built in what was formerly the *salle des ballets*. The ballet of those days was a sort of dramatic entertainment performed by the whole court.

Revolutionary passions gave rise to a most laughable error about Charles IX., in connection with the Louvre. During the Revolution hostile opinions as to this king, whose real character was masked, made a monster of him. Joseph Cheniers tragedy was written under the influence of certain words scratched on the window of the projecting wing of the Louvre, looking toward the quay. The words were as follows: "It was from this window that Charles IX., of execrable memory, fired upon French citizens." It is well to inform future historians and all sensible persons that this portion of the Louvre—called to-day the old Louvre—which projects upon the quay and is connected with the Louvre by the room called the Apollo gallery (while the great halls of the Museum connect the Louvre with the Tuileries) did not exist in the time of Charles IX. The greater part of the space where the frontage on the quay now stands, and where the Garden of the Infanta is laid out, was then occupied by the hotel de Bourbon, which belonged to and was the residence of the house of Navarre. It was absolutely impossible, therefore, for Charles IX. to fire from the Louvre of Henri II. upon a boat full of Huguenots crossing the river, although *at the present time* the Seine can be seen from its windows. Even if learned men and libraries did not possess maps of the Louvre made in the time of Charles IX., on which its then position is clearly indicated, the building itself refutes the error. All the kings who co-operated in the work of erecting this enormous mass of buildings never failed to put their initials or some special monogram on the parts they had severally built. Now the part we speak of, the venerable and now blackened wing of the Louvre, projecting on the quay and overlooking the garden of the Infanta, bears the monograms of Henri III. and Henri IV., which are totally different from that of Henri II., who invariably joined his H to the two C's of Catherine, forming a D,—which, by the bye, has constantly deceived superficial persons into fancying that the king put the initial of his mistress, Diane, on great public buildings. Henri IV. united the Louvre with his own hotel de Bourbon, its garden and dependencies. He was the first to think of connecting Catherine de' Medici's palace of the Tuileries with the Louvre by his unfinished galleries, the precious sculptures of which have been so cruelly neglected. Even if the map of Paris, and the monograms of Henri III. and Henri IV. did not exist, the difference of architecture is refutation enough to the calumny. The vermiculated stone copings of the hotel de la Force mark the transition between what is called the architecture of the Renaissance and that of Henri III., Henri IV., and Louis XIII. This archaeological digression (continuing the sketches of old Paris with which we began this history) enables us to picture to our minds the then appearance of this other corner of the old city, of which nothing now remains but Henri IV.'s addition to the Louvre, with its admirable bas-reliefs, now being rapidly annihilated.

When the court heard that the queen was about to give an audience to Theodore de Beze and Chaudieu, presented by Admiral Coligny, all the courtiers who had the right of entrance to the reception hall, hastened thither to witness the interview. It was about six o'clock in the evening; Coligny had just supped, and was using a toothpick as he came up the staircase of the Louvre between the two Reformers. The practice of using a toothpick was so inveterate a habit with the admiral that he was seen to do it on the battle-field while planning a retreat. "Distrust the admiral's toothpick, the *No* of the Connetable, and Catherine's *Yes*," was a court proverb of that day. After the Saint-Bartholomew the populace made a horrible jest on the body of Coligny, which hung for three days at Montfaucon, by putting a grotesque toothpick into his mouth. History has recorded this atrocious levity. So petty an act done in the midst of that great catastrophe pictures the Parisian populace, which deserves the sarcastic jibe of Boileau: "Frenchmen, born *malin*, created the guillotine." The Parisian of all time cracks jokes and makes lampoons before, during, and after the most horrible revolutions.

Theodore de Beze wore the dress of a courtier, black silk stockings, low shoes with straps across the instep, tight breeches, a black silk doublet with slashed sleeves, and a small black velvet mantle, over which lay an elegant white fluted ruff. His beard was trimmed to a moustache and *virgule* (now called imperial) and he carried a sword at his side and a cane in his hand. Whosoever knows the galleries of Versailles or the collections of Odieuvre, knows also his round, almost jovial face and lively eyes, surmounted by the broad forehead which characterized the writers and poets of that day. De Beze had, what served him admirably, an agreeable air and manner. In this he was a great contrast to Coligny, of austere countenance, and to the sour, bilious Chaudieu, who chose to wear on this occasion the robe and bands of a Calvinist minister.

The scenes that happen in our day in the Chamber of Deputies, and which, no doubt, happened in the Convention, will give an idea of how, at this court, at this epoch, these men, who six months later were to fight to the death in a war without quarter, could meet and talk to each other with courtesy and even laughter. Birago, who was coldly to advise the Saint-Bartholomew, and Cardinal de Lorraine, who charged his servant Besme "not to miss the admiral," now advanced to meet Coligny; Birago saying, with a smile:—

"Well, my dear admiral, so you have really taken upon yourself to present these gentlemen from Geneva?"

"Perhaps you will call it a crime in *me*," replied the admiral, jesting, "whereas if you had done it yourself you would make a merit of it."

"They say that the Sieur Calvin is very ill," remarked the Cardinal de Lorraine to Theodore de Beze. "I hope no one suspects us of giving him his broth."

"Ah! monseigneur; it would be too great a risk," replied de Beze, maliciously.

The Duc de Guise, who was watching Chaudieu, looked fixedly at his brother and at Birago, who were both taken aback by de Beze's answer.

"Good God!" remarked the cardinal, "heretics are not diplomatic!"

To avoid embarrassment, the queen, who was announced at this moment, had arranged to remain standing during the audience. She began by speaking to the Connetable, who had previously remonstrated with her vehemently on the scandal of receiving messengers from Calvin.

"You see, my dear Connetable," she said, "that I receive them without ceremony."

"Madame," said the admiral, approaching the queen, "these are two teachers of the new religion, who have come to an understanding with Calvin, and who have his instructions as to a conference in which the churches of France may be able to settle their differences."

"This is Monsieur de Beze, to whom my wife is much attached," said the king of Navarre, coming forward and taking de Beze by the hand.

"And this is Chaudieu," said the Prince de Conde. "*My friend* the Duc de Guise knows the soldier," he added, looking at Le Balafre, "perhaps he will now like to know the minister."

This gasconade made the whole court laugh, even Catherine.

"Faith!" replied the Duc de Guise, "I am enchanted to see a *gars* who knows so well how to choose his men and to employ them in their right sphere. One of your agents," he said to Chaudieu, "actually endured the extraordinary question without dying and without confessing a single thing. I call myself brave; but I don't know that I could have endured it as he did."

"Hum!" muttered Ambroise, "you did not say a word when I pulled the javelin out of your face at Calais."

Catherine, standing at the centre of a semicircle of the courtiers and maids of honor, kept silence. She was observing the two Reformers, trying to penetrate their minds as, with the shrewd, intelligent glance of her black eyes, she studied them.

"One seems to be the scabbard, the other the blade," whispered Albert de Gondi in her ear.

"Well, gentlemen," said Catherine at last, unable to restrain a smile, "has your master given you permission to unite in a public conference, at which you will be converted by the arguments of the Fathers of the Church who are the glory of our State?"

"We have no master but the Lord," said Chaudieu.

"But surely you will allow some little authority to the king of France?" said Catherine, smiling.

"And much to the queen," said de Beze, bowing low.

"You will find," continued the queen, "that our most submissive subjects are heretics."

"Ah, madame!" cried Coligny, "we will indeed endeavor to make you a noble and peaceful kingdom! Europe has profited, alas! by our internal divisions. For the last fifty years she has had the advantage of one-half of the French people being against the other half."

"Are we here to sing anthems to the glory of heretics," said the Connetable, brutally.

"No, but to bring them to repentance," whispered the Cardinal de Lorraine in his ear; "we want to coax them by a little sugar."

"Do you know what I should have done under the late king?" said the Connetable, angrily. "I'd have called in the provost and hung those two knaves, then and there, on the gallows of the Louvre."

"Well, gentlemen, who are the learned men whom you have selected as our opponents?" inquired the queen, imposing silence on the Connetable by a look.

"Duplessis-Mornay and Theodore de Beze will speak on our side," replied Chaudieu.

"The court will doubtless go to Saint-Germain, and as it would be improper that this *colloquy* should take place in a royal residence, we will have it in the little town of Poissy," said Catherine.

"Shall we be safe there, madame?" asked Chaudieu.

"Ah!" replied the queen, with a sort of naivete, "you will surely know how to take precautions. The Admiral will arrange all that with my cousins the Guises and de Montmorency."

"The devil take them!" cried the Connetable, "I'll have nothing to do with it."

"How do you contrive to give such strength of character to your converts?" said the queen, leading Chaudieu apart. "The son of my furrier was actually sublime."

"We have faith," replied Chaudieu.

At this moment the hall presented a scene of animated groups, all discussing the question of the proposed assembly, to which the few words said by the queen had already given the name of the "Colloquy of Poissy." Catherine glanced at Chaudieu and was able to say to him unheard:—

"Yes, a new faith!"

"Ah, madame, if you were not blinded by your alliance with the court of Rome, you would see that we are returning to the true doctrines of Jesus Christ, who, recognizing the equality of souls, bestows upon all men equal rights on earth."

"Do you think yourself the equal of Calvin?" asked the queen, shrewdly.

"No, no; we are equals only in church. What! would you unbind the tie of the people to the throne?" she cried. "Then you are not only heretics, you are revolutionists,—rebels against obedience to the king as you are against that to the Pope!" So saying, she left Chaudieu abruptly and returned to Theodore de Beze. "I count on you, monsieur," she said, "to conduct this colloquy in good faith. Take all the time you need."

"I had supposed," said Chaudieu to the Prince de Conde, the King of Navarre, and Admiral Coligny, as they left the hall, "that a great State matter would be treated more seriously."

"Oh! we know very well what you want," exclaimed the Prince de Conde, exchanging a sly look with Theodore de Beze.

The prince now left his adherents to attend a rendezvous. This great leader of a party was also one of the most favored gallants of the court. The two choice beauties of that day were even then striving with such desperate eagerness for his affections that one of them, the Marechale de Saint-Andre, the wife of the future triumvir, gave him her beautiful estate of Saint-Valery, hoping to win him away from the Duchesse de Guise, the wife of the man who had tried to take his head on the scaffold.

The duchess, not being able to detach the Duc de Nemours from Mademoiselle de Rohan, fell in love, *en attendant*, with the leader of the Reformers.

"What a contrast to Geneva!" said Chaudieu to Theodore de Beze, as they crossed the little bridge of the Louvre.

"The people here are certainly gayer than the Genevese. I don't see why they should be so treacherous," replied de Beze.

"To treachery oppose treachery," replied Chaudieu, whispering the words in his companion's ear. "I have *saints* in Paris on whom I can rely, and I intend to make Calvin a prophet. Christophe Lecamus shall deliver us from our most dangerous enemy."

"The queen-mother, for whom the poor devil endured his torture, has already, with a high hand, caused him to be appointed solicitor to the Parliament; and solicitors make better prosecutors than murderers. Don't you remember how Avenelles betrayed the secrets of our first uprising?"

"I know Christophe," said Chaudieu, in a positive tone, as he turned to leave the envoy from Geneva.

XV. COMPENSATION

A few days after the reception of Calvin's emissaries by the queen, that is to say, toward the close of the year (for the year then began at Easter and the present calendar was not adopted until later in the reign of Charles IX.), Christophe reclined in an easy chair beside the fire in the large brown hall, dedicated to family life, that overlooked the river in his father's house, where the present drama was begun. His feet rested on a stool; his mother and Babette Lallier had just renewed the compresses, saturated with a solution brought by Ambroise Pare, who was charged by Catherine de' Medici to take care of the young man. Once restored to his family, Christophe became the object of the most devoted care. Babette, authorized by her father, came very morning and only left the Lecamus household at night. Christophe, the admiration of the apprentices, gave rise throughout the quarter to various tales, which invested him with mysterious poesy. He had borne the worst torture; the celebrated Ambroise Pare was employing all his skill to cure him. What great deed had he done to be thus treated? Neither Christophe nor his father said a word on the subject. Catherine, then all-powerful, was concerned in their silence as well as the Prince de Conde. The constant visits of Pare, now chief surgeon of both the king and the house of Guise, whom the queen-mother and the Lorrains allowed to treat a youth accused of heresy, strangely complicated an affair through which no one saw clearly. Moreover, the rector of Saint-Pierre-aux-Boeufs came several times to visit the son of his church-warden, and these visits made the causes of Christophe's present condition still more unintelligible to his neighbors.

The old syndic, who had his plan, gave evasive answers to his brother-furriers, the merchants of the neighborhood, and to all friends who spoke to him of his son: "Yes, I am very thankful to have saved him."—"Well, you know, it won't do to put your finger between the bark and the tree."—"My son touched fire and came near burning up my house."—"They took advantage of his youth; we burghers get nothing but shame and evil by frequenting the grandees."—"This affair decides me to make a lawyer of Christophe; the practice of law will teach him to weigh his words and his acts."—"The young queen, who is now in Scotland, had a great deal to do with it; but then, to be sure, my son may have been imprudent."—"I have had cruel anxieties."—"All this may decide me to give up my business; I do not wish ever to go to court again."—"My son has had enough of the Reformation; it has cracked all his joints. If it had not been for Ambroise, I don't know what would have become of me."

Thanks to these ambiguous remarks and to the great discretion of such conduct, it was generally averred in the neighborhood that Christophe had seen the error of his ways; everybody thought it natural that the old syndic should wish to get his son appointed to the Parliament, and the rector's visits no longer seemed extraordinary. As the neighbors reflected on the old man's anxieties they no longer thought, as they would otherwise have done, that his ambition was inordinate. The young lawyer, who had lain helpless for months on the bed which his family made up for him in the old hall, was now, for the last week, able to rise and move about by the aid of crutches. Babette's love and his mother's tenderness had deeply touched his heart; and they, while they had him helpless in their hands, lectured him severely on religion. President de Thou paid his godson a visit during which he showed himself most fatherly. Christophe, being now a solicitor of the Parliament, must of course, he said, be Catholic; his oath would bind him to that; and the president, who assumed not to doubt of his godson's orthodoxy, ended his remarks by saying with great earnestness:

"My son, you have been cruelly tried. I am myself ignorant of the reasons which made the Messieurs de Guise treat you thus; but I advise you in future to live peacefully, without entering into the troubles of the times; for the favor of the king and queen will not be shown to the makers of revolt. You are not important enough to play fast and loose with the king as the Guises do. If you wish to be some day counsellor to the Parliament remember that you cannot obtain that noble office unless by a real and serious attachment to the royal cause."

Nevertheless, neither President de Thou's visit, nor the seductions of Babette, nor the urgency of his mother, were sufficient to shake the constancy of the martyr of the Reformation. Christophe held to his religion all the more because he had suffered for it.

"My father will never let me marry a heretic," whispered Babette in his ear.

Christophe answered only by tears, which made the young girl silent and thoughtful.

Old Lecamus maintained his paternal and magisterial dignity; he observed his son and said little. The stern old man, after recovering his dear Christophe, was dissatisfied with himself; he repented the tenderness he had shown for this only son; but he admired him secretly. At no period of his life did the syndic pull more wires to reach his ends, for he saw the field ripe for the harvest so painfully sown, and he wanted to gather the whole of it. Some days before the morning of which we write, he had had, being alone with Christophe, a long conversation with him in which he endeavored to discover the secret reason of the young man's resistance. Christophe, who was not without ambition, betrayed his faith in the Prince de Conde. The generous promise of the prince, who, of course, was only exercising his profession of prince, remained graven on his heart; little did he think that Conde had sent him, mentally, to the devil in Orleans, muttering, "A Gascon would have understood me better," when Christophe called out a touching farewell as the prince passed the window of his dungeon.

But besides this sentiment of admiration for the prince, Christophe had also conceived a profound reverence for the great queen, who had explained to him by a single look the necessity which compelled her to sacrifice him; and who during his agony had given him an illimitable promise in a single tear. During the silent months of his weakness, as he lay there waiting for recovery, he thought over each event at Blois and at Orleans. He weighed, one might almost say in spite of himself, the relative worth of these two protections. He floated between the queen and the prince. He had certainly served Catherine more than he had served the Reformation, and in a young man both heart and mind would naturally incline toward the queen; less because she was a queen than because she was a woman. Under such circumstances a man will always hope more from a woman than from a man.

"I sacrificed myself for her; what will she do for me?"

This question Christophe put to himself almost involuntarily as he remembered the tone in which she had said the words, *Povero mio*! It is difficult to believe how egotistical a man can become when he lies on a bed of sickness. Everything, even the exclusive devotion of which he is the object, drives him to think only of himself. By exaggerating in his own mind the obligation which the Prince de Conde was under to him he had come to expect that some office would be given to him at the court of Navarre. Still new to the world of political life, he forgot its contending interests and the rapid march of events which control and force the hand of all leaders of parties; he forgot it the more because he was practically a prisoner in solitary confinement on his bed in that old brown room. Each party is, necessarily, ungrateful while the struggle lasts; when it triumphs it has too many persons to reward not to be ungrateful still. Soldiers submit to this ingratitude; but their leaders turn against the new master at whose side they have acted and suffered like equals for so long. Christophe, who alone remembered his sufferings, felt himself already among the leaders of the Reformation by the fact of his martyrdom. His father, that old fox of commerce, so shrewd, so perspicacious, ended by divining the secret thought of his son; consequently, all his manoeuvres were now based on the natural expectancy to which Christophe had yielded himself.

"Wouldn't it be a fine thing," he had said to Babette, in presence of the family a few days before his interview with his son, "to be the wife of a counsellor of the Parliament? You would be called *madame*!"

"You are crazy, *compere*," said Lallier. "Where would you get ten thousand crowns' income from landed property, which a counsellor must have, according to law; and from whom could you buy the office? No one but the queen-mother and regent could help your son into Parliament, and I'm afraid he's too tainted with the new opinions for that."

"What would you pay to see your daughter the wife of a counsellor?"

"Ah! you want to look into my purse, shrewd-head!" said Lallier.

Counsellor to the Parliament! The words worked powerfully in Christophe's brain.

Sometime after this conversation, one morning when Christophe was gazing at the river and thinking of the scene which began this history, of the Prince de Conde, Chaudieu, La Renaudie, of his journey to Blois,—in short, the whole story of his hopes,—his father came and sat down beside him, scarcely concealing a joyful thought beneath a serious manner.

"My son," he said, "after what passed between you and the leaders of the Tumult of Amboise, they owe you enough to make the care of your future incumbent on the house of Navarre."

"Yes," replied Christophe.

"Well," continued his father, "I have asked their permission to buy a legal practice for you in the province of Bearn. Our good friend Pare undertook to present the letters which I wrote on your behalf to the Prince de Conde and the queen of Navarre. Here, read the answer of Monsieur de Pibrac, vice-chancellor of Navarre:—

To the Sieur Lecamus, syndic of the guild of furriers:

Monseigneur le Prince de Conde desires me to express his regret that he cannot do what you ask for his late companion in the tower of Saint-Aignan, whom he perfectly remembers, and to whom, meanwhile, he offers the place of gendarme in his company; which will put your son in the way of making his mark as a man of courage, which he is.

The queen of Navarre awaits an opportunity to reward the Sieur Christophe, and will not fail to take advantage of it.

Upon which, Monsieur le syndic, we pray God to have you in His keeping.

Pibrac,

At Nerac.
Chancellor of Navarre."

"Nerac, Pibrac, crack!" cried Babette. "There's no confidence to be placed in Gascons; they think only of themselves."

Old Lecamus looked at his son, smiling scornfully.

"They propose to put on horseback a poor boy whose knees and ankles were shattered for their sakes!" cried the mother. "What a wicked jest!"

"I shall never see you a counsellor of Navarre," said his father.

"I wish I knew what Queen Catherine would do for me, if I made a claim upon her," said Christophe, cast down by the prince's answer.

"She made you no promise," said the old man, "but I am certain that *she* will never mock you like these others; she will remember your sufferings. Still, how can the queen make a counsellor of the Parliament out of a protestant burgher?"

"But Christophe has not abjured!" cried Babette. "He can very well keep his private opinions secret."

"The Prince de Conde would be less disdainful of a counsellor of the Parliament," said Lallier.

"Well, what say you, Christophe?" urged Babette.

"You are counting without the queen," replied the young lawyer.

A few days after this rather bitter disillusion, an apprentice brought

Christophe the following laconic little missive:—
Chaudieu wishes to see his son.

"Let him come in!" cried Christophe.

"Oh! my sacred martyr!" said the minister, embracing him; "have you recovered from your sufferings?"

"Yes, thanks to Pare."

"Thanks rather to God, who gave you the strength to endure the torture. But what is this I hear? Have you allowed them to make you a solicitor? Have you taken the oath of fidelity? Surely you will not recognize that prostitute, the Roman, Catholic, and apostolic Church?"

"My father wished it."

"But ought we not to leave fathers and mothers and wives and children, all, all, for the sacred cause of Calvinism; nay, must we not suffer all things? Ah! Christophe, Calvin, the great Calvin, the whole party, the whole world, the Future counts upon your courage and the grandeur of your soul. We want your life."

It is a remarkable fact in the mind of man that the most devoted spirits, even while devoting themselves, build romantic hopes upon their perilous enterprises. When the prince, the soldier, and the minister had asked Christophe, under the bridge, to convey to Catherine the treaty which, if discovered, would in all probability cost him his life, the lad had relied on his nerve, upon chance, upon the powers of his mind, and confident in such hopes he bravely, nay, audaciously put himself between those terrible adversaries, the Guises and Catherine. During the torture he still kept saying to himself: "I shall come out of it! it is only pain!" But when this second and brutal demand, "Die, we want your life," was made upon a boy who was still almost helpless, scarcely recovered from his late torture, and clinging all the more to life because he had just seen death so near, it was impossible for him to launch into further illusions.

Christophe answered quietly:—

"What is it now?"

"To fire a pistol courageously, as Stuart did on Minard."

"On whom?"

"The Duc de Guise."

"A murder?"

"A vengeance. Have you forgotten the hundred gentlemen massacred on the scaffold at Amboise? A child who saw that butchery, the little d'Aubigne cried out, 'They have slaughtered France!'"

"You should receive the blows of others and give none; that is the religion of the gospel," said Christophe. "If you imitate the Catholics in

172

their cruelty, of what good is it to reform the Church?"

"Oh! Christophe, they have made you a lawyer, and now you argue!" said Chaudieu.

"No, my friend," replied the young man, "but parties are ungrateful; and you will be, both you and yours, nothing more than puppets of the Bourbons."

"Christophe, if you could hear Calvin, you would know how we wear them like gloves! The Bourbons are the gloves, we are the hand."

"Read that," said Christophe, giving Chaudieu Pibrac's letter containing the answer of the Prince de Conde.

"Oh! my son; you are ambitious, you can no longer make the sacrifice of yourself!—I pity you!"

With those fine words Chaudieu turned and left him.

Some days after that scene, the Lallier family and the Lecamus family were gathered together in honor of the formal betrothal of Christophe and Babette, in the old brown hall, from which Christophe's bed had been removed; for he was now able to drag himself about and even mount the stairs without his crutches. It was nine o'clock in the evening and the company were awaiting Ambroise Pare. The family notary sat before a table on which lay various contracts. The furrier was selling his house and business to his head-clerk, who was to pay down forty thousand francs for the house and then mortgage it as security for the payment of the goods, for which, however, he paid twenty thousand francs on account.

Lecamus was also buying for his son a magnificent stone house, built by Philibert de l'Orme in the rue Saint-Pierre-aux-Boeufs, which he gave to Christophe as a marriage portion. He also took two hundred thousand francs from his own fortune, and Lallier gave as much more, for the purchase of a fine seignorial manor in Picardy, the price of which was five hundred thousand francs. As this manor was a tenure from the Crown it was necessary to obtain letters-patent (called *rescriptions*) granted by the king, and also to make payment to the Crown of considerable feudal dues. The marriage had been postponed until this royal favor was obtained. Though the burghers of Paris had lately acquired the right to purchase manors, the wisdom of the privy council had been exercised in putting certain restrictions on the sale of those estates which were dependencies of the Crown; and the one which old Lecamus had had in his eye for the last dozen years was among them. Ambroise was pledged to bring the royal ordinance that evening; and the old furrier went and came from the hall to the door in a state of impatience which showed how great his long-repressed ambition had been. Ambroise at last appeared.

"My old friend!" cried the surgeon, in an agitated manner, with a glance at the supper table, "let me see your linen. Good. Oh! you must have wax candles. Quick, quick! get out your best things!"

"Why? what is it all about?" asked the rector of Saint-Pierre-aux-Boeufs.

"The queen-mother and the young king are coming to sup with you," replied the surgeon. "They are only waiting for an old counsellor who agreed to sell his place to Christophe, and with whom Monsieur de Thou has concluded a bargain. Don't appear to know anything; I have escaped from the Louvre to warn you."

In a second the whole family were astir; Christophe's mother and Babette's aunt bustled about with the celerity of housekeepers suddenly surprised. But in spite of the apparent confusion into which the news had thrown the entire family, the precautions were promptly made, with an activity that was nothing short of marvellous. Christophe, amazed and confounded by such a favor, was speechless, gazing mechanically at what went on.

"The queen and king here in our house!" said the old mother.

"The queen!" repeated Babette. "What must we say and do?"

In less than an hour all was changed; the hall was decorated; the supper-table sparkled. Presently the noise of horses sounded in the street. The light of torches carried by the horsemen of the escort brought all the burghers of the neighborhood to their windows. The noise soon subsided and the escort rode away, leaving the queen-mother and her son, King Charles IX., Charles de Gondi, now Grand-master of the wardrobe and governor of the king, Monsieur de Thou, Pinard, secretary of State, the old counsellor, and two pages, under the arcade before the door.

"My worthy people," said the queen as she entered, "the king, my son, and I have come to sign the marriage-contract of the son of my furrier,— but only on condition that he remains a Catholic. A man must be a Catholic to enter Parliament; he must be a Catholic to own land which derives from the Crown; he must be a Catholic if he would sit at the king's table. That is so, is it not, Pinard?"

The secretary of State entered and showed the letters-patent.

"If we are not all Catholics," said the little king, "Pinard will throw those papers into the fire. But we are all Catholics here, I think," he continued, casting his somewhat haughty eyes over the company.

"Yes, sire," replied Christophe, bending his injured knees with difficulty, and kissing the hand which the king held out to him.

Queen Catherine stretched out her hand to Christophe and, raising him hastily, drew him aside into a corner, saying in a low voice:—

"Ah ca! my lad, no evasions here. Are you playing above-board now?"

"Yes, madame," he answered, won by the dazzling reward and the honor done him by the grateful queen.

"Very good. Monsieur Lecamus, the king, my son, and I permit you to purchase the office of the goodman Groslay, counsellor of the Parliament, here present. Young man, you will follow, I hope, in the steps of your predecessor."

De Thou advanced and said: "I will answer for him, madame."

"Very well; draw up the deed, notary," said Pinard.

"Inasmuch as the king our master does us the favor to sign my daughter's marriage contract," cried Lallier, "I will pay the whole price of the manor."

"The ladies may sit down," said the young king, graciously: "As a wedding present to the bride I remit, with my mother's consent, all my dues and rights in the manor."

Old Lecamus and Lallier fell on their knees and kissed the king's hand.

"*Mordieu*! sire, what quantities of money these burghers have!" whispered de Gondi in his ear.

The young king laughed.

"As their Highnesses are so kind," said old Lecamus, "will they permit me to present to them my successor, and ask them to continue to him the royal patent of furrier to their Majesties?"

"Let us see him," said the king.

Lecamus led forward his successor, who was livid with fear.

"If my mother consents, we will now sit down to table," said the little king.

Old Lecamus had bethought himself of presenting to the king a silver goblet which he had bought of Benvenuto Cellini when the latter stayed in Paris at the hotel de Nesle. This treasure of art had cost the furrier no less than two thousand crowns.

"Oh! my dear mother, see this beautiful work!" cried the young king, lifting the goblet by its stem.

"It was made in Florence," replied Catherine.

"Pardon me, madame," said Lecamus, "it was made in Paris by a Florentine. All that is made in Florence would belong to your Majesty; that which is made in France is the king's."

"I accept it, my good man," cried Charles IX.; "and it shall henceforth be my particular drinking cup."

"It is beautiful enough," said the queen, examining the masterpiece, "to be included among the crown-jewels. Well, Maitre Ambroise," she whispered in the surgeon's ear, with a glance at Christophe, "have you taken good care of him? Will he walk again?"

"He will run," replied the surgeon, smiling. "Ah! you have cleverly made him a renegade."

"Ha!" said the queen, with the levity for which she has been blamed, though it was only on the surface, "the Church won't stand still for want of one monk!"

The supper was gay; the queen thought Babette pretty, and, in the regal manner which was natural to her, she slipped upon the girl's finger a diamond ring which compensated in value for the goblet bestowed upon the king. Charles IX., who afterwards became rather too fond of these invasions of burgher homes, supped with a good appetite. Then, at a word from his new governor (who, it is said, was instructed to make him forget the virtuous teachings of Cypierre), he obliged all the men present to drink so deeply that the queen, observing that the gaiety was about to become too noisy, rose to leave the room. As she rose, Christophe, his father, and the two women took torches and accompanied her to the shop-door. There Christophe ventured to touch the queen's wide sleeve and to make her a sign that he had something to say. Catherine stopped, made a gesture to the father and the two women to leave her, and said, turning to Christophe:

"What is it?"

"It may serve you to know, madame," replied Christophe, whispering in her ear, "that the Duc de Guise is being followed by assassins."

"You are a loyal subject," said Catherine, smiling, "and I shall never forget you."

She held out to him her hand, so celebrated for its beauty, first ungloving it, which was indeed a mark of favor,—so much so that Christophe, then and there, became altogether royalist as he kissed that adorable hand.

"So they mean to rid me of that bully without my having a finger in it," thought she as she replaced her glove.

Then she mounted her mule and returned to the Louvre, attended by her two pages.

Christophe went back to the supper-table, but was thoughtful and gloomy even while he drank; the fine, austere face of Ambroise Pare seemed to reproach him for his apostasy. But subsequent events justified the manoeuvres of the old syndic. Christophe would certainly not have escaped the massacre of Saint-Bartholomew; his wealth and his landed estates would have made him a mark for the murderers. History has recorded the cruel fate of the wife of Lallier's successor, a beautiful woman, whose naked body hung by the hair for three days from one of the buttresses of the Pont au Change. Babette trembled as she thought that she, too, might have endured the same treatment if Christophe had continued a Calvinist,—for such became the name of the Reformers. Calvin's personal ambition was thus gratified, though not until after his death.

Such was the origin of the celebrated parliamentary house of Lecamus. Tallemant des Reaux is in error when he states that they came originally from Picardy. It is only true that the Lecamus family found it for their interest in after days to date from the time the old furrier bought their principal estate, which, as we have said, was situated in Picardy. Christophe's son, who succeeded him under Louis XIII., was the father of the rich president Lecamus who built, in the reign of Louis XIV., that magnificent mansion which shares with the hotel Lambert the admiration of Parisians and foreigners, and was assuredly one of the finest buildings in Paris. It may still be seen in the rue Thorigny, though at the beginning of the Revolution it was pillaged as having belonged to Monsieur de Juigne, the archbishop of Paris. All the decorations were then destroyed; and the tenants who lodge there have greatly damaged it; nevertheless this palace, which is reached through the old house in the rue de la Pelleterie, still shows the noble results obtained in former days by the spirit of family. It may be doubted whether modern individualism, brought about by the equal division of inheritances, will ever raise such noble buildings.

PART II. THE SECRETS OF THE RUGGIERI

I. THE COURT UNDER CHARLES IX.

Between eleven o'clock and midnight toward the end of October, 1573, two Italians, Florentines and brothers, Albert de Gondi, Duc de Retz and marshal of France, and Charles de Gondi la Tour, Grand-master of the robes of Charles IX., were sitting on the roof of a house in the rue Saint-Honore, at the edge of a gutter. This gutter was one of those stone channels which in former days were constructed below the roofs of houses to receive the rain-water, discharging it at regular intervals through those long gargoyles carved in the shape of fantastic animals with gaping mouths. In spite of the zeal with which our present general pulls down and demolishes venerable buildings, there still existed many of these projecting gutters until, quite recently, an ordinance of the police as to water-conduits compelled them to disappear. But even so, a few of these carved gargoyles still remain, chiefly in the *quartier* Saint-Antoine, where low rents and values hinder the building of new storeys

177

under the eaves of the roofs.

It certainly seems strange that two personages invested with such important offices should be playing the part of cats. But whosoever will burrow into the historic treasures of those days, when personal interests jostled and thwarted each other around the throne till the whole political centre of France was like a skein of tangled thread, will readily understand that the two Florentines were cats indeed, and very much in their places in a gutter. Their devotion to the person of the queen-mother, Catherine de' Medici—who had brought them to the court of France and foisted them into their high offices—compelled them not to recoil before any of the consequences of their intrusion. But to explain how and why these courtiers were thus perched, it is necessary to relate a scene which had taken place an hour earlier not far from this very gutter, in that beautiful brown room of the Louvre, all that now remains to us of the apartments of Henri II., in which after supper the courtiers had been paying court to the two queens, Catherine de' Medici and Elizabeth of Austria, and to their son and husband King Charles IX.

In those days the majority of the burghers and great lords supped at six, or at seven o'clock, but the more refined and elegant supped at eight or even nine. This repast was the dinner of to-day. Many persons erroneously believe that etiquette was invented by Louis XIV.; on the contrary it was introduced into France by Catherine de' Medici, who made it so severe that the Connetable de Montmorency had more difficulty in obtaining permission to enter the court of the Louvre on horseback than in winning his sword; moreover, that unheard-of distinction was granted to him only on account of his great age. Etiquette, which was, it is true, slightly relaxed under the first two Bourbon kings, took an Oriental form under the Great Monarch, for it was introduced from the Eastern Empire, which derived it from Persia. In 1573 few persons had the right to enter the courtyard of the Louvre with their servants and torches (under Louis XIV. the coaches of none but dukes and peers were allowed to pass under the peristyle); moreover, the cost of obtaining entrance after supper to the royal apartments was very heavy. The Marechal de Retz, whom we have just seen, perched on a gutter, offered on one occasion a thousand crowns of that day, six thousand francs of our present money, to the usher of the king's cabinet to be allowed to speak to Henri III. on a day when he was not on duty. To an historian who knows the truth, it is laughable to see the well-known picture of the courtyard at Blois, in which the artist has introduced a courtier on horseback!

On the present occasion, therefore, none but the most eminent personages in the kingdom were in the royal apartments. The queen,

Elizabeth of Austria, and her mother-in-law, Catherine de' Medici, were seated together on the left of the fireplace. On the other side sat the king, buried in an arm-chair, affecting a lethargy consequent on digestion,— for he had just supped like a prince returned from hunting; possibly he was seeking to avoid conversation in presence of so many persons who were spies upon his thoughts. The courtiers stood erect and uncovered at the end of the room. Some talked in a low voice; others watched the king, awaiting the bestowal of a look or a word. Occasionally one was called up by the queen-mother, who talked with him for a few moments; another risked saying a word to the king, who replied with either a nod or a brief sentence. A German nobleman, the Comte de Solern, stood at the corner of the fireplace behind the young queen, the granddaughter of Charles V., whom he had accompanied into France. Near to her on a stool sat her lady of honor, the Comtesse de Fiesque, a Strozzi, and a relation of Catherine de' Medici. The beautiful Madame de Sauves, a descendant of Jacques Coeur, mistress of the king of Navarre, then of the king of Poland, and lastly of the Duc d'Alencon, had been invited to supper; but she stood like the rest of the court, her husband's rank (that of secretary of State) giving her no right to be seated. Behind these two ladies stood the two Gondis, talking to them. They alone of this dismal assembly were smiling. Albert Gondi, now Duc de Retz, marshal of France, and gentleman of the bed-chamber, had been deputed to marry the queen by proxy at Spire. In the first line of courtiers nearest to the king stood the Marechal de Tavannes, who was present on court business; Neufville de Villeroy, one of the ablest bankers of the period, who laid the foundation of the great house of that name; Birago and Chiverni, gentlemen of the queen-mother, who, knowing her preference for her son Henri (the brother whom Charles IX. regarded as an enemy), attached themselves especially to him; then Strozzi, Catherine's cousin; and finally, a number of great lords, among them the old Cardinal de Lorraine and his nephew, the young Duc de Guise, who were held at a distance by the king and his mother. These two leaders of the Holy Alliance, and later of the League (founded in conjunction with Spain a few years earlier), affected the submission of servants who are only waiting an opportunity to make themselves masters. Catherine and Charles IX. watched each other with close attention.

At this gloomy court, as gloomy as the room in which it was held, each individual had his or her own reasons for being sad or thoughtful. The young queen, Elizabeth, was a prey to the tortures of jealousy, and could ill-disguise them, though she smiled upon her husband, whom she passionately adored, good and pious woman that she was! Marie Touchet, the only mistress Charles IX. ever had and to whom he was loyally faithful, had lately returned from the chateau de Fayet in Dauphine, whither she had gone to give birth to a child. She brought back to Charles IX. a son, his only son, Charles de Valois, first Comte d'Auvergne, and afterward Duc d'Angouleme. The poor queen, in addition to the mortification of her abandonment, now endured the pang of knowing that her rival had borne a son to her husband while she had brought him only a daughter. And these were not her only troubles and disillusions, for Catherine de' Medici, who had seemed her friend in the first instance, now, out of policy, favored her betrayal, preferring to serve the mistress rather than the wife of the king,—for the following reason.

When Charles IX. openly avowed his passion for Marie Touchet, Catherine showed favor to the girl in the interests of her own desire for domination. Marie Touchet, who was very young when brought to court, came at an age when all the noblest sentiments are predominant. She loved the king for himself alone. Frightened at the fate to which ambition had led the Duchesse de Valentinois (better known as Diane de Poitiers), she dreaded the queen-mother, and greatly preferred her simple happiness to grandeur. Perhaps she thought that lovers as young as the king and herself could never struggle successfully against the queen-mother. As the daughter of Jean Touchet, Sieur de Beauvais and Quillard, she was born between the burgher class and the lower nobility; she had none of the inborn ambitions of the Pisseleus and Saint-Valliers, girls of rank, who battled for their families with the hidden weapons of love. Marie Touchet, without family or friends, spared Catherine de' Medici all antagonism with her son's mistress; the daughter of a great house would have been her rival. Jean Touchet, the father, one of the finest wits of the time, a man to whom poets dedicated their works, wanted nothing at court. Marie, a young girl without connections, intelligent and well-educated, and also simple and artless, whose desires would probably never be aggressive to the royal power, suited the queen-mother admirably. In short, she made the parliament recognize the son to whom Marie Touchet had just given birth in the month of April, and she allowed him to take the title of Comte d'Auvergne, assuring Charles IX. that she would leave the boy her personal property, the counties of Auvergne and Laraguais. At a later period, Marguerite de Valois, queen of Navarre, contested this legacy after she was queen of France, and the parliament annulled it. But later still, Louis XIII., out of respect for the Valois blood, indemnified the Comte d'Auvergne by the gift of the duchy of Angouleme.

Catherine had already given Marie Touchet, who asked nothing, the manor of Belleville, an estate close to Vincennes which carried no title;

and thither she went whenever the king hunted and spent the night at the castle. It was in this gloomy fortress that Charles IX. passed the greater part of his last years, ending his life there, according to some historians, as Louis XII. had ended his.

The queen-mother kept close watch upon her son. All the occupations of his personal life, outside of politics, were reported to her. The king had begun to look upon his mother as an enemy, but the kind intentions she expressed toward his son diverted his suspicions for a time. Catherine's motives in this matter were never understood by Queen Elizabeth, who, according to Brantome, was one of the gentlest queens that ever reigned, who never did harm or even gave pain to any one, "and was careful to read her prayer-book secretly." But this single-minded princess began at last to see the precipices yawning around the throne,—a dreadful discovery, which might indeed have made her quail; it was some such remembrance, no doubt, that led her to say to one of her ladies, after the death of the king, in reply to a condolence that she had no son, and could not, therefore, be regent and queen-mother:

"Ah! I thank God that I have no son. I know well what would have happened. My poor son would have been despoiled and wronged like the king, my husband, and I should have been the cause of it. God had mercy on the State; he has done all for the best."

This princess, whose portrait Brantome thinks he draws by saying that her complexion was as beautiful and delicate as the ladies of her suite were charming and agreeable, and that her figure was fine though rather short, was of little account at her own court. Suffering from a double grief, her saddened attitude added another gloomy tone to a scene which most young queens, less cruelly injured, might have enlivened. The pious Elizabeth proved at this crisis that the qualities which are the shining glory of women in the ordinary ways of life can be fatal to a sovereign. A princess able to occupy herself with other things besides her prayer-book might have been a useful helper to Charles IX., who found no prop to lean on, either in his wife or in his mistress.

The queen-mother, as she sat there in that brown room, was closely observing the king, who, during supper, had exhibited a boisterous good-humor which she felt to be assumed in order to mask some intention against her. This sudden gaiety contrasted too vividly with the struggle of mind he endeavored to conceal by his eagerness in hunting, and by an almost maniacal toil at his forge, where he spent many hours in hammering iron; and Catherine was not deceived by it. Without being able even to guess which of the statesmen about the king was employed to prepare or negotiate it (for Charles IX. contrived to mislead his mother's spies), Catherine felt no doubt whatever that some scheme for her overthrow was being planned. The unlooked-for presence of Tavannes, who arrived at the same time as Strozzi, whom she herself had summoned, gave her food for thought. Strong in the strength of her political combination, Catherine was above the reach of circumstances; but she was powerless against some hidden violence. As many persons are ignorant of the actual state of public affairs then so complicated by the various parties that distracted France, the leaders of which had each their private interests to carry out, it is necessary to describe, in a few words, the perilous game in which the queen-mother was now engaged. To show Catherine de' Medici in a new light is, in fact, the root and stock of our present history.

Two words explain this woman, so curiously interesting to study, a woman whose influence has left such deep impressions upon France. Those words are: Power and Astrology. Exclusively ambitious, Catherine de' Medici had no other passion than that of power. Superstitious and fatalistic, like so many superior men, she had no sincere belief except in occult sciences. Unless this double mainspring is known, the conduct of Catherine de' Medici will remain forever misunderstood. As we picture her faith in judicial astrology, the light will fall upon two personages, who are, in fact, the philosophical subjects of this Study.

There lived a man for whom Catherine cared more than for any of her children; his name was Cosmo Ruggiero. He lived in a house belonging to her, the hotel de Soissons; she made him her supreme adviser. It was his duty to tell her whether the stars ratified the advice and judgment of her ordinary counsellors. Certain remarkable antecedents warranted the power which Cosmo Ruggiero retained over his mistress to her last hour. One of the most learned men of the sixteenth century was physician to Lorenzo de' Medici, Duc d'Urbino, Catherine's father. This physician was called Ruggiero the Elder (Vecchio Ruggier and Roger l'Ancien in the French authors who have written on alchemy), to distinguish him from his two sons, Lorenzo Ruggiero, called the Great by cabalistic writers, and Cosmo Ruggiero, Catherine's astrologer, also called Roger by several French historians. In France it was the custom to pronounce the name in general as Ruggieri. Ruggiero the elder was so highly valued by the Medici that the two dukes, Cosmo and Lorenzo, stood godfathers to his two sons. He cast, in concert with the famous mathematician, Basilio, the horoscope of Catherine's nativity, in his official capacity as mathematicion, astrologer, and physician to the house of Medici; three offices which are often confounded.

At the period of which we write the occult sciences were studied with an ardor that may surprise the incredulous minds of our own age, which is supremely analytical. Perhaps such minds may find in this historical sketch the dawn, or rather the germ, of the positive sciences which have flowered in the nineteenth century, though without the poetic grandeur given to them by the audacious Seekers of the sixteenth, who, instead of using them solely for mechanical industries, magnified Art and fertilized Thought by their means. The protection universally given to occult science by the sovereigns of those days was justified by the noble creations of many inventors, who, starting in quest of the Great Work (the so-called philosophers' stone), attained to astonishing results. At no period were the sovereigns of the world more eager for the study of these mysteries. The Fuggers of Augsburg, in whom all modern Luculluses will recognize their princes, and all bankers their masters, were gifted with powers of calculation it would be difficult to surpass. Well, those practical men, who loaned the funds of all Europe to the sovereigns of the sixteenth century (as deeply in debt as the kings of the present day), those illustrious guests of Charles V. were sleeping partners in the crucibles of Paracelsus. At the beginning of the sixteenth century, Ruggiero the elder was the head of that secret university from which issued the Cardans, the Nostradamuses, and the Agrippas (all in their turn physicians of the house of Valois); also the astronomers, astrologers, and alchemists who surrounded the princes of Christendom and were more especially welcomed and protected in France by Catherine de' Medici. In the nativity drawn by Basilio and Ruggiero the elder, the principal events of Catherine's life were foretold with a correctness which is quite disheartening for those who deny the power of occult science. This horoscope predicted the misfortunes which during the siege of Florence imperilled the beginning of her life; also her marriage with a son of the king of France, the unexpected succession of that son to his father's throne, the birth of her children, their number, and the fact that three of her sons would be kings in succession, that two of her daughters would be queens, and that all of them were destined to die without posterity. This prediction was so fully realized that many historians have assumed that it was written after the events.

It is well known that Nostradamus took to the chateau de Chaumont, whither Catherine went after the conspiracy of La Renaudie, a woman who possessed the faculty of reading the future. Now, during the reign of Francois II., while the queen had with her her four sons, all young and in good health, and before the marriage of her daughter Elizabeth with Philip II., king of Spain, or that of her daughter Marguerite with Henri de Bourbon, king of Navarre (afterward Henri IV.), Nostradamus and this woman reiterated the circumstances formerly predicted in the famous nativity. This woman, who was no doubt gifted with second sight, and who belonged to the great school of Seekers of the Great Work, though the particulars of her life and name are lost to history, stated that the last crowned child would be assassinated. Having placed the queen-mother in front of a magic mirror, in which was reflected a wheel on the several spokes of which were the faces of her children, the sorceress set the wheel revolving, and Catherine counted the number of revolutions which it made. Each revolution was for each son one year of his reign. Henri IV. was also put upon the wheel, which then made twenty-four rounds, and the woman (some historians have said it was a man) told the frightened queen that Henri de Bourbon would be king of France and reign that number of years. From that time forth Catherine de' Medici vowed a mortal hatred to the man whom she knew would succeed the last of her Valois sons, who was to die assassinated. Anxious to know what her own death would be, she was warned to beware of Saint-Germain. Supposing, therefore, that she would be either put to death or imprisoned in the chateau de Saint-Germain, she would never so much as put her foot there, although that residence was far more convenient for her political plans, owing to its proximity to Paris, than the other castles to which she retreated with the king during the troubles. When she was taken suddenly ill, a few days after the murder of the Duc de Guise at Blois, she asked the name of the bishop who came to assist her. Being told it was Saint-Germain, she cried out, "I am dead!" and did actually die on the morrow,—having, moreover, lived the exact number of years given to her by all her horoscopes.

These predictions, which were known to the Cardinal de Lorraine, who regarded them as witchcraft, were now in process of realization. Francois II. had reigned his two revolutions of the wheel, and Charles IX. was now making his last turn. If Catherine said the strange words which history has attributed to her when her son Henri started for Poland,— "You will soon return,"—they must be set down to her faith in occult science and not to the intention of poisoning Charles IX.

Many other circumstances corroborated Catherine's faith in the occult sciences. The night before the tournament at which Henri II. was killed, Catherine saw the fatal blow in a dream. Her astrological council, then composed of Nostradamus and the two Ruggieri, had already predicted to her the death of the king. History has recorded the efforts made by Catherine to persuade her husband not to enter the lists. The prognostic, and the dream produced by the prognostic, were verified. The memoirs of the day relate another fact that was no less singular. The courier who announced the victory of Moncontour arrived in the night, after riding with such speed that he killed three horses. The queen-mother was awakened to receive the news, to which she replied, "I knew it already."

In fact, as Brantome relates, she had told of her son's triumph the evening before, and narrated several circumstances of the battle. The astrologer of the house of Bourbon predicted that the youngest of all the princes descended from Saint-Louis (the son of Antoine de Bourbon) would ascend the throne of France. This prediction, related by Sully, was accomplished in the precise terms of the horoscope; which led Henri IV. to say that by dint of lying these people sometimes hit the truth. However that may be, if most of the great minds of that epoch believed in this vast science,—called Magic by the masters of judicial astrology, and Sorcery by the public,—they were justified in doing so by the fulfilment of horoscopes.

It was for the use of Cosmo Ruggiero, her mathematician, astronomer, and astrologer, that Catherine de' Medici erected the tower behind the Halle aux Bles,—all that now remains of the hotel de Soissons. Cosmo Ruggiero possessed, like confessors, a mysterious influence, the possession of which, like them again, sufficed him. He cherished an ambitious thought superior to all vulgar ambitions. This man, whom dramatists and romance-writers depict as a juggler, owned the rich abbey of Saint-Mahe in Lower Brittany, and refused many high ecclesiastical dignities; the gold which the superstitious passions of the age poured into his coffers sufficed for his secret enterprise; and the queen's hand, stretched above his head, preserved every hair of it from danger.

II. SCHEMES AGAINST SCHEMES

The thirst for power which consumed the queen-mother, her desire for dominion, was so great that in order to retain it she had, as we have seen, allied herself to the Guises, those enemies of the throne; to keep the reins of power, now obtained, within her hands, she was using every means, even to the sacrifice of her friends and that of her children. This woman, of whom one of her enemies said at her death, "It is more than a queen, it is monarchy itself that has died,"—this woman could not exist without the intrigues of government, as a gambler can live only by the emotions of play. Although she was an Italian of the voluptuous race of the Medici, the Calvinists who calumniated her never accused her of having a lover. A great admirer of the maxim, "Divide to reign," she had learned the art of perpetually pitting one force against another. No sooner had she grasped the reins of power than she was forced to keep up dissensions in order to neutralize the strength of two rival houses, and thus save the Crown. Catherine invented the game of political see-saw (since imitated

185

by all princes who find themselves in a like situation), by instigating, first the Calvinists against the Guises, and then the Guises against the Calvinists. Next, after pitting the two religions against each other in the heart of the nation, Catherine instigated the Duc d'Anjou against his brother Charles IX. After neutralizing events by opposing them to one another, she neutralized men, by holding the thread of all their interests in her hands. But so fearful a game, which needs the head of a Louis XI. to play it, draws down inevitably the hatred of all parties upon the player, who condemns himself forever to the necessity of conquering; for one lost game will turn every selfish interest into an enemy.

The greater part of the reign of Charles IX. witnessed the triumph of the domestic policy of this astonishing woman. What adroit persuasion must Catherine have employed to have obtained the command of the armies for the Duc d'Anjou under a young and brave king, thirsting for glory, capable of military achievement, generous, and in presence, too, of the Connetable de Montmorency. In the eyes of the statesmen of Europe the Duc d'Anjou had all the honors of the Saint-Bartholomew, and Charles IX. all the odium. After inspiring the king with a false and secret jealousy of his brother, she used that passion to wear out by the intrigues of fraternal jealousy the really noble qualities of Charles IX. Cypierre, the king's first governor, and Amyot, his first tutor, had made him so great a man, they had paved the way for so noble a reign, that the queen-mother began to hate her son as soon as she found reason to fear the loss of the power she had so slowly and so painfully obtained. On these general grounds most historians have believed that Catherine de' Medici felt a preference for Henri III.; but her conduct at the period of which we are now writing, proves the absolute indifference of her heart toward all her children.

When the Duc d'Anjou went to reign in Poland Catherine was deprived of the instrument by which she had worked to keep the king's passions occupied in domestic intrigues, which neutralized his energy in other directions. She then set up the conspiracy of La Mole and Coconnas, in which her youngest son, the Duc d'Alencon (afterwards Duc d'Anjou, on the accession of Henri III.) took part, lending himself very willingly to his mother's wishes, and displaying an ambition much encouraged by his sister Marguerite, then queen of Navarre. This secret conspiracy had now reached the point to which Catherine sought to bring it. Its object was to put the young duke and his brother-in-law, the king of Navarre, at the head of the Calvinists, to seize the person of Charles IX., and imprison that king without an heir,—leaving the throne to the Duc d'Alencon, whose intention it was to establish Calvinism as the religion of France. Calvin, as we have already said, had obtained, a few days before his death, the reward he had so deeply coveted,—the Reformation was now called Calvinism in his honor.

If Le Laboureur and other sensible writers had not already proved that La Mole and Coconnas,—arrested fifty nights after the day on which our present history begins, and beheaded the following April,—even, we say, if it had not been made historically clear that these men were the victims of the queen-mother's policy, the part which Cosmo Ruggiero took in this affair would go far to show that she secretly directed their enterprise. Ruggiero, against whom the king had suspicions, and for whom he cherished a hatred the motives of which we are about to explain, was included in the prosecution. He admitted having given to La Mole a wax figure representing the king, which was pierced through the heart by two needles. This method of casting spells constituted a crime, which, in those days, was punished by death. It presents one of the most startling and infernal images of hatred that humanity could invent; it pictures admirably the magnetic and terrible working in the occult world of a constant malevolent desire surrounding the person doomed to death; the effects of which on the person are exhibited by the figure of wax. The law in those days thought, and thought justly, that a desire to which an actual form was given should be regarded as a crime of *lese majeste*. Charles IX. demanded the death of Ruggiero; Catherine, more powerful than her son, obtained from the Parliament, through the young counsellor, Lecamus, a commutation of the sentence, and Cosmo was sent to the galleys. The following year, on the death of the king, he was pardoned by a decree of Henri III., who restored his pension, and received him at court.

But, to return now to the moment of which we are writing, Catherine had, by this time, struck so many blows on the heart of her son that he was eagerly desirous of casting off her yoke. During the absence of Marie Touchet, Charles IX., deprived of his usual occupation, had taken to observing everything about him. He cleverly set traps for the persons in whom he trusted most, in order to test their fidelity. He spied on his mother's actions, concealing from her all knowledge of his own, employing for this deception the evil qualities she had fostered in him. Consumed by a desire to blot out the horror excited in France by the Saint-Bartholomew, he busied himself actively in public affairs; he presided at the Council, and tried to seize the reins of government by well-laid schemes. Though the queen-mother endeavored to check these attempts of her son by employing all the means of influence over his mind which her maternal authority and a long habit of domineering gave her, his rush into distrust was so vehement that he went too far at the first bound ever to return from it. The day on which his mother's speech to the king of Poland was reported to him, Charles IX., conscious of his failing health, conceived the most horrible suspicions, and when such thoughts take possession of the mind of a son and a king nothing can remove them. In fact, on his deathbed, at the moment when he confided his wife and daughter to Henri IV., he began to put the latter on his guard against Catherine, so that she cried out passionately, endeavoring to silence him, "Do not say that, monsieur!"

Though Charles IX. never ceased to show her the outward respect of which she was so tenacious that she would never call the kings her sons anything but "Monsieur," the queen-mother had detected in her son's manner during the last few months an ill-disguised purpose of vengeance. But clever indeed must be the man who counted on taking Catherine unawares. She held ready in her hand at this moment the conspiracy of the Duke d'Alencon and La Mole, in order to counteract, by another fraternal struggle, the efforts Charles IX. was making toward emancipation. But, before employing this means, she wanted to remove his distrust of her, which would render impossible their future reconciliation; for was he likely to restore power to the hands of a mother whom he thought capable of poisoning him? She felt herself at this moment in such serious danger that she had sent for Strozzi, her relation and a soldier noted for his promptitude of action. She took counsel in secret with Birago and the two Gondis, and never did she so frequently consult her oracle, Cosmo Ruggiero, as at the present crisis.

Though the habit of dissimulation, together with advancing age, had given the queen-mother that well-known abbess face, with its haughty and macerated mask, expressionless yet full of depth, inscrutable yet vigilant, remarked by all who have studied her portrait, the courtiers now observed some clouds on her icy countenance. No sovereign was ever so imposing as this woman from the day when she succeeded in restraining the Guises after the death of Francois II. Her black velvet cap, made with a point upon the forehead (for she never relinquished her widow's mourning) seemed a species of feminine cowl around the cold, imperious face, to which, however, she knew how to give, at the right moment, a seductive Italian charm. Catherine de' Medici was so well made that she was accused of inventing side-saddles to show the shape of her legs, which were absolutely perfect. Women followed her example in this respect throughout Europe, which even then took its fashions from France. Those who desire to bring this grand figure before their minds will find that the scene now taking place in the brown hall of the Louvre presents it in a striking aspect.

The two queens, different in spirit, in beauty, in dress, and now estranged,—one naive and thoughtful, the other thoughtful and gravely abstracted,—were far too preoccupied to think of giving the order awaited by the courtiers for the amusements of the evening. The carefully concealed drama, played for the last six months by the mother and son was more than suspected by many of the courtiers; but the Italians were watching it with special anxiety, for Catherine's failure involved their ruin.

During this evening Charles IX., weary with the day's hunting, looked to be forty years old. He had reached the last stages of the malady of which he died, the symptoms of which were such that many reflecting persons were justified in thinking that he was poisoned. According to de Thou (the Tacitus of the Valois) the surgeons found suspicious spots—*ex causa incognita reperti livores*—on his body. Moreover, his funeral was even more neglected than that of Francois II. The body was conducted from Saint-Lazare to Saint-Denis by Brantome and a few archers of the guard under command of the Comte de Solern. This circumstances, coupled with the supposed hatred of the mother to the son, may or may not give color to de Thou's supposition, but it proves how little affection Catherine felt for any of her children,—a want of feeling which may be explained by her implicit faith in the predictions of judicial astrology. This woman was unable to feel affection for the instruments which were destined to fail her. Henri III. was the last king under whom her reign of power was to last; that was the sole consideration of her heart and mind.

In these days, however, we can readily believe that Charles IX. died a natural death. His excesses, his manner of life, the sudden development of his faculties, his last spasmodic attempt to recover the reins of power, his desire to live, the abuse of his vital strength, his final sufferings and last pleasures, all prove to an impartial mind that he died of consumption, a disease scarcely studied at that time, and very little understood, the symptoms of which might, not unnaturally, lead Charles IX. to believe himself poisoned. The real poison which his mother gave him was in the fatal counsels of the courtiers whom she placed about him,—men who led him to waste his intellectual as well as his physical vigor, thus bringing on a malady which was purely fortuitous and not constitutional. Under these harrowing circumstances, Charles IX. displayed a gloomy majesty of demeanor which was not unbecoming to a king. The solemnity of his secret thoughts was reflected on his face, the olive tones of which he inherited from his mother. This ivory pallor, so fine by candlelight, so suited to the expression of melancholy thought, brought out vigorously the fire of the blue-black eyes, which gazed from their thick and heavy lids with the keen perception our fancy lends to kings, their color being a cloak for dissimulation. Those eyes were terrible,— especially from the movement of their brows, which he could raise or lower at will on his bald, high forehead. His nose was broad and long, thick at the end,—the nose of a lion; his ears were large, his hair sandy, his lips blood-red, like those of all consumptives, the upper lip thin and sarcastic, the lower one firm, and full enough to give an impression of the noblest qualities of the heart. The wrinkles of his brow, the youth of which was killed by dreadful cares, inspired the strongest interest; remorse, caused by the uselessness of the Saint-Bartholomew, accounted for some, but there were two others on that face which would have been eloquent indeed to any student whose premature genius had led him to divine the principles of modern physiology. These wrinkles made a deeply indented furrow going from each cheek-bone to each corner of the mouth, revealing the inward efforts of an organization wearied by the toil of thought and the violent excitements of the body. Charles IX. was worn-out. If policy did not stifle remorse in the breasts of those who sit beneath the purple, the queen-mother, looking at her own work, would surely have felt it. Had Catherine foreseen the effect of her intrigues upon her son, would she have recoiled from them? What a fearful spectacle was this! A king born vigorous, and now so feeble; a mind powerfully tempered, shaken by distrust; a man clothed with authority, conscious of no support; a firm mind brought to the pass of having lost all confidence in itself! His warlike valor had changed by degrees to ferocity; his discretion to deceit; the refined and delicate love of a Valois was now a mere quenchless thirst for pleasure. This perverted and misjudged great man, with all the many facets of a noble soul worn-out,—a king without power, a generous heart without a friend, dragged hither and thither by a thousand conflicting intrigues,—presented the melancholy spectacle of a youth, only twenty-four years old, disillusioned of life, distrusting everybody and everything, now resolving to risk all, even his life, on a last effort. For some time past he had fully understood his royal mission, his power, his resources, and the obstacles which his mother opposed to the pacification of the kingdom; but alas! this light now burned in a shattered lantern.

Two men, whom Charles IX. loved sufficiently to protect under circumstances of great danger,—Jean Chapelain, his physician, whom he saved from the Saint-Bartholomew, and Ambroise Pare, with whom he went to dine when Pare's enemies were accusing him of intending to poison the king,—had arrived this evening in haste from the provinces, recalled by the queen-mother. Both were watching their master anxiously. A few courtiers spoke to them in a low voice; but the men of science made guarded answers, carefully concealing the fatal verdict which was in their minds. Every now and then the king would raise his heavy eyelids and give his mother a furtive look which he tried to

190

conceal from those about him. Suddenly he sprang up and stood before the fireplace.

"Monsieur de Chiverni," he said abruptly, "why do you keep the title of chancellor of Anjou and Poland? Are you in our service, or in that of our brother?"

"I am all yours, sire," replied Chiverni, bowing low.

"Then come to me to-morrow; I intend to send you to Spain. Very strange things are happening at the court of Madrid, gentlemen."

The king looked at his wife and flung himself back into his chair.

"Strange things are happening everywhere," said the Marechal de Tavannes, one of the friends of the king's youth, in a low voice.

The king rose again and led this companion of his youthful pleasures apart into the embrasure of the window at the corner of the room, saying, when they were out of hearing:—

"I want you. Remain here when the others go. I shall know to-night whether you are for me or against me. Don't look astonished. I am about to burst my bonds. My mother is the cause of all the evil about me. Three months hence I shall be king indeed, or dead. Silence, if you value your life! You will have my secret, you and Solern and Villeroy only. If it is betrayed, it will be by one of you three. Don't keep near me; go and pay your court to my mother. Tell her I am dying, and that you don't regret it, for I am only a poor creature."

The king was leaning on the shoulder of his old favorite, and pretending to tell him of his ailments, in order to mislead the inquisitive eyes about him; then, not wishing to make his aversion too visible, he went up to his wife and mother and talked with them, calling Birago to their side.

Just then Pinard, one of the secretaries of State, glided like an eel through the door and along the wall until he reached the queen-mother, in whose ear he said a few words, to which she replied by an affirmative sign. The king did not ask his mother the meaning of this conference, but he returned to his seat and kept silence, darting terrible looks of anger and suspicion all about him.

This little circumstance seemed of enormous consequence in the eyes of the courtiers; and, in truth, so marked an exercise of power by the queen-mother, without reference to the king, was like a drop of water overflowing the cup. Queen Elizabeth and the Comtesse de Fiesque now retired, but the king paid no attention to their movements, though the queen-mother rose and attended her daughter-in-law to the door; after which the courtiers, understanding that their presence was unwelcome, took their leave. By ten o'clock no one remained in the hall but a few intimates,—the two Gondis, Tavannes, Solern, Birago, the king, and the queen-mother.

The king sat plunged in the blackest melancholy. The silence was oppressive. Catherine seemed embarrassed. She wished to leave the room, and waited for the king to escort her to the door; but he still continued obstinately lost in thought. At last she rose to bid him good-night, and Charles IX. was forced to do likewise. As she took his arm and made a few steps toward the door, she bent to his ear and whispered:—

"Monsieur, I have important things to say to you."

Passing a mirror on her way, she glanced into it and made a sign with her eyes to the two Gondis, which escaped the king's notice, for he was at the moment exchanging looks of intelligence with the Comte de Solern and Villeroy. Tavannes was thoughtful.

"Sire," said the latter, coming out of his reverie, "I think you are royally ennuyed; don't you ever amuse yourself now? *Vive Dieu!* have you forgotten the times when we used to vagabondize about the streets at night?"

"Ah! those were the good old times!" said the king, with a sigh.

"Why not bring them back?" said Birago, glancing significantly at the Gondis as he took his leave.

"Yes, I always think of those days with pleasure," said Albert de Gondi, Duc de Retz.

"I'd like to see you on the roofs once more, monsieur le duc," remarked Tavannes. "Damned Italian cat! I wish he might break his neck!" he added in a whisper to the king.

"I don't know which of us two could climb the quickest in these days," replied de Gondi; "but one thing I do know, that neither of us fears to die."

"Well, sire, will you start upon a frolic in the streets to-night, as you did in the days of your youth?" said the other Gondi, master of the Wardrobe. The days of his youth! so at twenty-four years of age the wretched king seemed no longer young to any one, not even to his flatterers!

Tavannes and his master now reminded each other, like two school-boys, of certain pranks they had played in Paris, and the evening's amusement was soon arranged. The two Italians, challenged to climb roofs, and jump from one to another across alleys and streets, wagered that they would follow the king wherever he went. They and Tavannes went off to change their clothes. The Comte de Solern, left alone with the king, looked at him in amazement. Though the worthy German, filled with compassion for the hapless position of the king of France, was honor and fidelity itself, he was certainly not quick of perception. Charles IX., surrounded by hostile persons, unable to trust any one, not even his wife (who had been guilty of some indiscretions, unaware as she was that his

192

mother and his servants were his enemies), had been fortunate enough to find in Monsieur de Solern a faithful friend in whom he could place entire confidence. Tavannes and Villeroy were trusted with only a part of the king's secrets. The Comte de Solern alone knew the whole of the plan which he was now about to carry out. This devoted friend was also useful to his master, in possessing a body of discreet and affectionate followers, who blindly obeyed his orders. He commanded a detachment of the archers of the guards, and for the last few days he had been sifting out the men who were faithfully attached to the king, in order to make a company of tried men when the need came. The king took thought of everything.

"Why are you surprised, Solern?" he said. "You know very well I need a pretext to be out to-night. It is true, I have Madame de Belleville, but this is better; for who knows whether my mother does not hear of all that goes on at Marie's?"

Monsieur de Solern, who was to follow the king, asked if he might not take a few of his Germans to patrol the streets, and Charles consented. About eleven o'clock the king, who was now very gay, set forth with his three courtiers,—namely, Tavannes and the two Gondis.

"I'll go and take my little Marie by surprise," said Charles IX. to Tavannes, "as we pass through the rue de l'Autruche." That street being on the way to the rue Saint-Honore, it would have been strange indeed for the king to pass the house of his love without stopping.

Looking out for a chance of mischief,—a belated burgher to frighten, or a watchman to thrash—the king went along with his nose in the air, watching all the lighted windows to see what was happening, and striving to hear the conversations. But alas! he found his good city of Paris in a state of deplorable tranquillity. Suddenly, as he passed the house of a perfumer named Rene, who supplied the court, the king, noticing a strong light from a window in the roof, was seized by one of those apparently hasty inspirations which, to some minds, suggest a previous intention.

This perfumer was strongly suspected of curing rich uncles who thought themselves ill. The court laid at his door the famous "Elixir of Inheritance," and even accused him of poisoning Jeanne d'Albret, mother of Henri of Navarre, who was buried (in spite of Charles IX.'s positive order) without her head being opened. For the last two months the king had sought some way of sending a spy into Rene's laboratory, where, as he was well aware, Cosmo Ruggiero spent much time. The king intended, if anything suspicious were discovered, to proceed in the matter alone, without the assistance of the police or law, with whom, as he well knew, his mother would counteract him by means of either corruption or fear.

It is certain that during the sixteenth century, and the years that preceded and followed it, poisoning was brought to a perfection unknown to modern chemistry, as history itself will prove. Italy, the cradle of modern science, was, at this period, the inventor and mistress of these secrets, many of which are now lost. Hence the reputation for that crime which weighed for the two following centuries on Italy. Romance-writers have so greatly abused it that wherever they have introduced Italians into their tales they have almost always made them play the part of assassins and poisoners.[*] If Italy then had the traffic in subtle poisons which some historians attribute to her, we should remember her supremacy in the art of toxicology, as we do her pre-eminence in all other human knowledge and art in which she took the lead in Europe. The crimes of that period were not her crimes specially. She served the passions of the age, just as she built magnificent edifices, commanded armies, painted noble frescos, sang romances, loved queens, delighted kings, devised ballets and fetes, and ruled all policies. The horrible art of poisoning reached to such a pitch in Florence that a woman, dividing a peach with a duke, using a golden fruit-knife with one side of its blade poisoned, ate one half of the peach herself and killed the duke with the other half. A pair of perfumed gloves were known to have infiltrated mortal illness through the pores of the skin. Poison was instilled into bunches of natural roses, and the fragrance, when inhaled, gave death. Don John of Austria was poisoned, it was said, by a pair of boots.

    [*] Written sixty-six years ago.—Tr.

Charles IX. had good reason to be curious in the matter; we know already the dark suspicions and beliefs which now prompted him to surprise the perfumer Rene at his work.

The old fountain at the corner of the rue de l'Arbre-See, which has since been rebuilt, offered every facility for the royal vagabonds to climb upon the roof of a house not far from that of Rene, which the king wished to visit. Charles, followed by his companions, began to ramble over the roofs, to the great terror of the burghers awakened by the tramp of these false thieves, who called to them in saucy language, listened to their talk, and even pretended to force an entrance. When the Italians saw the king and Tavannes threading their way among the roofs of the house next to that of Rene, Albert de Gondi sat down, declaring that he was tired, and his brother followed his example.

"So much the better," thought the king, glad to leave his spies behind him.

Tavannes began to laugh at the two Florentines, left sitting alone in the midst of deep silence, in a place where they had nought but the skies above them, and the cats for auditors. But the brothers made use of their position to exchange thoughts they would not dare to utter on any other spot in the world,—thoughts inspired by the events of the evening.

"Albert," said the Grand-master to the marechal, "the king will get the better of the queen-mother; we are doing a foolish thing for our own interests to stay by those of Catherine. If we go over to the king now, when he is searching everywhere for support against her and for able men to serve him, we shall not be driven away like wild beasts when the queen-mother is banished, imprisoned, or killed."

"You wouldn't get far with such ideas, Charles," replied the marechal, gravely. "You'd follow the king into the grave, and he won't live long; he is ruined by excesses. Cosmo Ruggiero predicts his death within a year."

"The dying boar has often killed the huntsman," said Charles de Gondi. "This conspiracy of the Duc d'Alencon, the king of Navarre, and the Prince de Conde, with whom La Mole and Coconnas are negotiating, is more dangerous than useful. In the first place, the king of Navarre, whom the queen-mother hoped to catch in the very act, distrusts her, and declines to run his head into the noose. He means to profit by the conspiracy without taking any of its risks. Besides, the notion now is to put the crown on the head of the Duc d'Alencon, who has turned Calvinist."

"*Budelone*! but don't you see that this conspiracy enables the queen-mother to find out what the Huguenots can do with the Duc d'Alencon, and what the king can do with the Huguenots?—for the king is even now negotiating with them; but he'll be finely pilloried to-morrow, when Catherine reveals to him the counter-conspiracy which will neutralize all his projects."

"Ah!" exclaimed Charles de Gondi, "by dint of profiting by our advice she's clever and stronger than we! Well, that's all right."

"All right for the Duc d'Anjou, who prefers to be king of France rather than king of Poland; I am going now to explain the matter to him."

"When do you start, Albert?"

"To-morrow. I am ordered to accompany the king of Poland; and I expect to join him in Venice, where the patricians have taken upon themselves to amuse and delay him."

"You are prudence itself!"

"*Che bestia*! I swear to you there is not the slightest danger for either of us in remaining at court. If there were, do you think I would go away? I should stay by the side of our kind mistress."

"Kind!" exclaimed the Grand-master; "she is a woman to drop all her instruments the moment she finds them heavy."

"*O coglione*! you pretend to be a soldier, and you fear death! Every business has its duties, and we have ours in making our fortune. By attaching ourselves to kings, the source of all temporal power which protects, elevates, and enriches families, we are forced to give them as devoted a love as that which burns in the hearts of martyrs toward heaven. We must suffer in their cause; when they sacrifice us to the interests of their throne we may perish, for we die as much for ourselves as for them, but our name and our families perish not. *Ecco!*"

"You are right as to yourself, Albert; for they have given you the ancient title and duchy of de Retz."

"Now listen to me," replied his brother. "The queen hopes much from the cleverness of the Ruggieri; she expects them to bring the king once more under her control. When Charles refused to use Rene's perfumes any longer the wary woman knew at once on whom his suspicions really rested. But who can tell the schemes that are in his mind? Perhaps he is only hesitating as to what fate he shall give his mother; he hates her, you know. He said a few words about it to his wife; she repeated them to Madame de Fiesque, and Madame de Fiesque told the queen-mother. Since then the king has kept away from his wife."

"The time has come," said Charles de Gondi.

"To do what?" asked the marechal.

"To lay hold of the king's mind," replied the Grand-master, who, if he was not so much in the queen's confidence as his brother, was by no means less clear-sighted.

"Charles, I have opened a great career to you," said his brother gravely. "If you wish to be a duke also, be, as I am, the accomplice and cat's-paw of our mistress; she is the strongest here, and she will continue in power. Madame de Sauves is on her side, and the king of Navarre and the Duc d'Alencon are still for Madame de Sauves. Catherine holds the pair in a leash under Charles IX., and she will hold them in future under Henri III. God grant that Henri may not prove ungrateful."

"How so?"

"His mother is doing too much for him."

"Hush! what noise is that I hear in the rue Saint-Honore?" cried the Grand-master. "Listen! there is some one at Rene's door! Don't you hear the footsteps of many men. Can they have arrested the Ruggieri?"

"Ah, *diavolo*! this is prudence indeed. The king has not shown his usual impetuosity. But where will they imprison them? Let us go down into the street and see."

The two brothers reached the corner of the rue de l'Autruche just as the king was entering the house of his mistress, Marie Touchet. By the light of the torches which the concierge carried, they distinguished Tavannes and the two Ruggieri.

196

"Hey, Tavannes!" cried the grand-master, running after the king's companion, who had turned and was making his way back to the Louvre, "What happened to you?"

"We fell into a nest of sorcerers and arrested two, compatriots of yours, who may perhaps be able to explain to the minds of French gentlemen how you, who are not Frenchmen, have managed to lay hands on two of the chief offices of the Crown," replied Tavannes, half jesting, half in earnest.

"But the king?" inquired the Grand-master, who cared little for Tavanne's enmity.

"He stays with his mistress."

"We reached our present distinction through an absolute devotion to our masters,—a noble course, my dear Tavannes, which I see that you also have adopted," replied Albert de Gondi.

The three courtiers walked on in silence. At the moment when they parted, on meeting their servants who then escorted them, two men glided swiftly along the walls of the rue de l'Autruche. These men were the king and the Comte de Solern, who soon reached the banks of the Seine, at a point where a boat and two rowers, carefully selected by de Solern, awaited them. In a very few moments they reached the other shore.

"My mother has not gone to bed," cried the king. "She will see us; we chose a bad place for the interview."

"She will think it a duel," replied Solern; "and she cannot possibly distinguish who we are at this distance."

"Well, let her see me!" exclaimed Charles IX. "I am resolved now!"

The king and his confidant sprang ashore and walked quickly in the direction of the Pre-aux-Clercs. When they reached it the Comte de Solern, preceding the king, met a man who was evidently on the watch, and with whom he exchanged a few words; the man then retired to a distance. Presently two other men, who seemed to be princes by the marks of respect which the first man paid to them, left the place where they were evidently hiding behind the broken fence of a field, and approached the king, to whom they bent the knee. But Charles IX. raised them before they touched the ground, saying:—

"No ceremony, we are all gentlemen here."

A venerable old man, who might have been taken for the Chancelier de l'Hopital, had the latter not died in the preceding year, now joined the three gentlemen, all four walking rapidly so as to reach a spot where their conference could not be overheard by their attendants. The Comte de Solern followed at a slight distance to keep watch over the king. That faithful servant was filled with a distrust not shared by Charles IX., a man to whom life was now a burden. He was the only person on the king's side who witnessed this mysterious conference, which presently became animated.

"Sire," said one of the new-comers, "the Connetable de Montmorency, the closest friend of the king your father, agreed with the Marechal de Saint-Andre in declaring that Madame Catherine ought to be sewn up in a sack and flung into the river. If that had been done then, many worthy persons would still be alive."

"I have enough executions on my conscience, monsieur," replied the king.

"But, sire," said the youngest of the four personages, "if you merely banish her, from the depths of her exile Queen Catherine will continue to stir up strife, and to find auxiliaries. We have everything to fear from the Guises, who, for the last nine years, have schemed for a vast Catholic alliance, in the secret of which your Majesty is not included; and it threatens your throne. This alliance was invented by Spain, which will never renounce its project of destroying the boundary of the Pyrenees. Sire, Calvinism will save France by setting up a moral barrier between her and a nation which covets the empire of the world. If the queen-mother is exiled, she will turn for help to Spain and to the Guises."

"Gentlemen," said the king, "know this, if by your help peace without distrust is once established, I will take upon myself the duty of making all subjects tremble. *Tete-Dieu*! it is time indeed for royalty to assert itself. My mother is right in that, at any rate. You ought to know that it is to your interest was well as mine, for your hands, your fortunes depend upon our throne. If religion is overthrown, the hands you allow to do it will be laid next upon the throne and then upon you. I no longer care to fight ideas with weapons that cannot touch them. Let us see now if Protestantism will make progress when left to itself; above all, I would like to see with whom and what the spirit of that faction will wrestle. The admiral, God rest his soul! was not my enemy; he swore to me to restrain the revolt within spiritual limits, and to leave the ruling of the kingdom to the monarch, his master, with submissive subjects. Gentlemen, if the matter be still within your power, set that example now; help your sovereign to put down a spirit of rebellion which takes tranquillity from each and all of us. War is depriving us of revenue; it is ruining the kingdom. I am weary of these constant troubles; so weary, that if it is absolutely necessary I will sacrifice my mother. Nay, I will go farther; I will keep an equal number of Protestants and Catholics about me, and I will hold the axe of Louis XI. above their heads to force them to be on good terms. If the Messieurs de Guise plot a Holy Alliance to attack our crown, the executioner shall begin with their heads. I see the miseries of my people, and I will make short work of the great lords who care little for consciences,—let them hold what opinions they like; what I want in future is submissive subjects, who will work, according to my will, for the prosperity of the State. Gentlemen, I give you ten days to negotiate with your friends, to break off your plots, and to return to me who will be your father. If you refuse you will see great changes. I shall use the mass of the people, who will rise at my voice against the lords. I will make myself a king who pacificates his kingdom by striking down those who are more powerful even than you, and who dare defy him. If the troops fail me, I have my brother of Spain, on whom I shall call to defend our menaced thrones, and if I lack a minister to carry out my will, he can lend me the Duke of Alba."

"But in that case, sire, we should have Germans to oppose to your Spaniards," said one of his hearers.

"Cousin," replied Charles IX., coldly, "my wife's name is Elizabeth of Austria; support might fail you on the German side. But, for Heaven's sake, let us fight, if fight we must, alone, without the help of foreigners. You are the object of my mother's hatred, and you stand near enough to me to be my second in the duel I am about to fight with her; well then, listen to what I now say. You seem to me so worthy of confidence that I offer you the post of *connetable*; *you* will not betray me like the other."

The prince to whom Charles IX. had addressed himself, struck his hand into that of the king, exclaiming:

"*Ventre-saint-gris*! brother; this is enough to make me forget many wrongs. But, sire, the head cannot march without the tail, and ours is a long tail to drag. Give me more than ten days; we want at least a month to make our friends hear reason. At the end of that time we shall be masters."

"A month, so be it! My only negotiator will be Villeroy; trust no one else, no matter what is said to you."

"One month," echoed the other seigneurs, "that is sufficient."

"Gentlemen, we are five," said the king,—"five men of honor. If any betrayal takes place, we shall know on whom to avenge it."

The three strangers kissed the hand of Charles IX. and took leave of him with every mark of the utmost respect. As the king recrossed the Seine, four o'clock was ringing from the clock-tower of the Louvre. Lights were on in the queen-mother's room; she had not yet gone to bed.

"My mother is still on the watch," said Charles to the Comte de Solern.

"She has her forge as you have yours," remarked the German.

"Dear count, what do you think of a king who is reduced to become a conspirator?" said Charles IX., bitterly, after a pause.

"I think, sire, that if you would allow me to fling that woman into the river, as your young cousin said, France would soon be at peace."

"What! a parricide in addition to the Saint-Bartholomew, count?" cried the king. "No, no! I will exile her. Once fallen, my mother will no longer have either servants or partisans."

"Well, then, sire," replied the Comte de Solern, "give me the order to arrest her at once and take her out of the kingdom; for to-morrow she will have forced you to change your mind."

"Come to my forge," said the king, "no one can overhear us there; besides, I don't want my mother to suspect the capture of the Ruggieri. If she knows I am in my work-shop she'll suppose nothing, and we can consult about the proper measures for her arrest."

As the king entered a lower room of the palace, which he used for a workshop, he called his companion's attention to the forge and his implements with a laugh.

"I don't believe," he said, "among all the kings that France will ever have, there'll be another to take pleasure in such work as that. But when I am really king, I'll forge no swords; they shall all go back into their scabbards."

"Sire," said the Comte de Solern, "the fatigues of tennis and hunting, your toil at this forge, and—if I may say it—love, are chariots which the devil is offering you to get the faster to Saint-Denis."

"Solern," said the king, in a piteous tone, "if you knew the fire they have put into my soul and body! nothing can quench it. Are you sure of the men who are guarding the Ruggieri?"

"As sure as of myself."

"Very good; then, during this coming day I shall take my own course. Think of the proper means of making the arrest, and I will give you my final orders by five o'clock at Madame de Belleville's."

As the first rays of dawn were struggling with the lights of the workshop, Charles IX., left alone by the departure of the Comte de Solern, heard the door of the apartment turn on its hinges, and saw his mother standing within it in the dim light like a phantom. Though very nervous and impressible, the king did not quiver, albeit, under the circumstances in which he then stood, this apparition had a certain air of mystery and horror.

"Monsieur," she said, "you are killing yourself."

"I am fulfilling my horoscope," he replied with a bitter smile. "But you, madame, you appear to be as early as I."

"We have both been up all night, monsieur; but with very different intentions. While you have been conferring with your worst enemies in the open fields, concealing your acts from your mother, assisted by Tavannes and the Gondis, with whom you have been scouring the town,

I have been reading despatches which contained the proofs of a terrible conspiracy in which your brother, the Duc d'Alencon, your brother-in-law, the king of Navarre, the Prince de Conde, and half the nobles of your kingdom are taking part. Their purpose is nothing less than to take the crown from your head and seize your person. Those gentlemen have already fifty thousand good troops behind them."

"Bah!" exclaimed the king, incredulously.

"Your brother has turned Huguenot," she continued.

"My brother! gone over to the Huguenots!" cried Charles, brandishing the piece of iron which he held in his hand.

"Yes; the Duc d'Alencon, Huguenot at heart, will soon be one before the eyes of the world. Your sister, the queen of Navarre, has almost ceased to love you; she cares more for the Duc d'Alencon; she cares of Bussy; and she loves that little La Mole."

"What a heart!" exclaimed the king.

"That little La Mole," went on the queen, "wishes to make himself a great man by giving France a king of his own stripe. He is promised, they say, the place of connetable."

"Curse that Margot!" cried the king. "This is what comes of her marriage with a heretic."

"Heretic or not is of no consequence; the trouble is that, in spite of my advice, you have brought the head of the younger branch too near the throne by that marriage, and Henri's purpose is now to embroil you with the rest and make you kill one another. The house of Bourbon is the enemy of the house of Valois; remember that, monsieur. All younger branches should be kept in a state of poverty, for they are born conspirators. It is sheer folly to give them arms when they have none, or to leave them in possession of arms when they seize them. Let every younger son be made incapable of doing harm; that is the law of Crowns; the Sultans of Asia follow it. The proofs of this conspiracy are in my room upstairs, where I asked you to follow me last evening, when you bade me good-night; but instead of doing so, it seems you had other plans. I therefore waited for you. If we do not take the proper measures immediately you will meet the fate of Charles the Simple within a month."

"A month!" exclaimed the king, thunderstruck at the coincidence of that period with the delay asked for by the princes themselves. "'In a month we shall be masters,'" he added to himself, quoting their words. "Madame," he said aloud, "what are your proofs?"

"They are unanswerable, monsieur; they come from my daughter Marguerite. Alarmed herself at the possibilities of such a combination, her love for the throne of the Valois has proved stronger, this time, than all her other loves. She asks, as the price of her revelations that nothing shall be done to La Mole; but the scoundrel seems to me a dangerous villain whom we had better be rid of, as well as the Comte de Coconnas, your brother d'Alencon's right hand. As for the Prince de Conde, he consents to everything, provided I am thrown into the sea; perhaps that is the wedding present he gives me in return for the pretty wife I gave him! All this is a serious matter, monsieur. You talk of horoscopes! I know of the prediction which gives the throne of the Valois to the Bourbons, and if we do not take care it will be fulfilled. Do not be angry with your sister; she has behaved well in this affair. My son," continued the queen, after a pause, giving a tone of tenderness to her words, "evil persons on the side of the Guises are trying to sow dissensions between you and me; and yet we are the only ones in the kingdom whose interests are absolutely identical. You blame me, I know, for the Saint-Bartholomew; you accuse me of having forced you into it. Catholicism, monsieur, must be the bond between France, Spain, and Italy, three countries which can, by skilful management, secretly planned, be united in course of time, under the house of Valois. Do not deprive yourself of such chances by loosing the cord which binds the three kingdoms in the bonds of a common faith. Why should not the Valois and the Medici carry out for their own glory the scheme of Charles the Fifth, whose head failed him? Let us fling off that race of Jeanne la Folle. The Medici, masters of Florence and of Rome, will force Italy to support your interests; they will guarantee you advantages by treaties of commerce and alliance which shall recognize your fiefs in Piedmont, the Milanais, and Naples, where you have rights. These, monsieur, are the reasons of the war to the death which we make against the Huguenots. Why do you force me to repeat these things? Charlemagne was wrong in advancing toward the north. France is a body whose heart is on the Gulf of Lyons, and its two arms over Spain and Italy. Therefore, she must rule the Mediterranean, that basket into which are poured all the riches of the Orient, now turned to the profit of those seigneurs of Venice, in the very teeth of Philip II. If the friendship of the Medici and your rights justify you in hoping for Italy, force, alliances, or a possible inheritance may give you Spain. Warn the house of Austria as to this,—that ambitious house to which the Guelphs sold Italy, and which is even now hankering after Spain. Though your wife is of that house, humble it! Clasp it so closely that you will smother it! *There* are the enemies of your kingdom; thence comes help to the Reformers. Do not listen to those who find their profit in causing us to disagree, and who torment your life by making you believe I am your secret enemy. Have *I* prevented you from having heirs? Why has your mistress given you a son, and your wife a daughter? Why have you not to-day three legitimate heirs to root out the hopes of these seditious persons? Is it I, monsieur, who am responsible for such failures? If you had an heir, would the Duc d'Alencon be now conspiring?"

As she ended these words, Catherine fixed upon her son the magnetic glance of a bird of prey upon its victim. The daughter of the Medici became magnificent; her real self shone upon her face, which, like that of a gambler over the green table, glittered with vast cupidities. Charles IX. saw no longer the mother of one man, but (as was said of her) the mother of armies and of empires,—*mater castrorum*. Catherine had now spread wide the wings of her genius, and boldly flown to the heights of the Medici and Valois policy, tracing once more the mighty plans which terrified in earlier days her husband Henri II., and which, transmitted by the genius of the Medici to Richelieu, remain in writing among the papers of the house of Bourbon. But Charles IX., hearing the unusual persuasions his mother was using, thought that there must be some necessity for them, and he began to ask himself what could be her motive. He dropped his eyes; he hesitated; his distrust was not lessened by her studied phrases. Catherine was amazed at the depths of suspicion she now beheld in her son's heart.

"Well, monsieur," she said, "do you not understand me? What are we, you and I, in comparison with the eternity of royal crowns? Do you suppose me to have other designs than those that ought to actuate all royal persons who inhabit the sphere where empires are ruled?"

"Madame, I will follow you to your cabinet; we must act—"

"Act!" cried Catherine; "let our enemies alone; let *them* act; take them red-handed, and law and justice will deliver you from their assaults. For God's sake, monsieur, show them good-will."

The queen withdrew; the king remained alone for a few moments, for he was utterly overwhelmed.

"On which side is the trap?" thought he. "Which of the two—she or they—deceive me? What is my best policy? *Deus, discerne causam meam*!" he muttered with tears in his eyes. "Life is a burden to me! I prefer death, natural or violent, to these perpetual torments!" he cried presently, bringing down his hammer upon the anvil with such force that the vaults of the palace trembled.

"My God!" he said, as he went outside and looked up at the sky, "thou for whose holy religion I struggle, give me the light of thy countenance that I may penetrate the secrets of my mother's heart while I question the Ruggieri."

III. MARIE TOUCHET

The little house of Madame de Belleville, where Charles IX. had deposited his prisoners, was the last but one in the rue de l'Autruche on the side of the rue Saint-Honore. The street gate, flanked by two little brick pavilions, seemed very simple in those days, when gates and their accessories were so elaborately treated. It had two pilasters of stone cut in facets, and the coping represented a reclining woman holding a cornucopia. The gate itself, closed by enormous locks, had a wicket through which to examine those who asked admittance. In each pavilion lived a porter; for the king's extremely capricious pleasure required a porter by day and by night. The house had a little courtyard, paved like those of Venice. At this period, before carriages were invented, ladies went about on horseback, or in litters, so that courtyards could be made magnificent without fear of injury from horses or carriages. This fact is always to be remembered as an explanation of the narrowness of streets, the small size of courtyards, and certain other details of the private dwellings of the fifteenth and sixteenth centuries.

The house, of one story only above the ground-floor, was capped by a sculptured frieze, above which rose a roof with four sides, the peak being flattened to form a platform. Dormer windows were cut in this roof, with casings and pediments which the chisel of some great artist had covered with arabesques and dentils; each of the three windows on the main floor were equally beautiful in stone embroidery, which the brick of the walls showed off to great advantage. On the ground-floor, a double portico, very delicately decorated, led to the entrance door, which was covered with bosses cut with facets in the Venetian manner,—a style of decoration which was further carried on round the windows placed to right and left of the door.

A garden, carefully laid out in the fashion of the times and filled with choice flowers, occupied a space behind the house equal to that of the courtyard in front. A grape-vine draped its walls. In the centre of a grass plot rose a silver fir-tree. The flower-borders were separated from the grass by meandering paths which led to an arbor of clipped yews at the farther end of the little garden. The walls were covered with a mosaic of variously colored pebbles, coarse in design, it is true, but pleasing to the eye from the harmony of its tints with those of the flower-beds. The house had a carved balcony on the garden side, above the door, and also on the front toward the courtyard, and around the middle windows. On both sides of the house the ornamentation of the principal window, which projected some feet from the wall, rose to the frieze; so that it formed a little pavilion, hung there like a lantern. The casings of the other windows were inlaid on the stone with precious marbles.

In spite of the exquisite taste displayed in the little house, there was an air of melancholy about it. It was darkened by the buildings that surrounded it and by the roofs of the hotel d'Alencon which threw a heavy shadow over both court and garden; moreover, a deep silence reigned there. But this silence, these half-lights, this solitude, soothed a royal soul, which could there surrender itself to a single emotion, as in a cloister where men pray, or in some sheltered home wherein they love.

It is easy now to imagine the interior charm and choiceness of this haven, the sole spot in his kingdom where this dying Valois could pour out his soul, reveal his sufferings, exercise his taste for art, and give himself up to the poesy he loved,—pleasures denied him by the cares of a cruel royalty. Here, alone, were his great soul and his high intrinsic worth appreciated; here he could give himself up, for a few brief months, the last of his life, to the joys of fatherhood,—pleasures into which he flung himself with the frenzy that a sense of his coming and dreadful death impressed on all his actions.

In the afternoon of the day succeeding the night-scene we have just described, Marie Touchet was finishing her toilet in the oratory, which was the boudoir of those days. She was arranging the long curls of her beautiful black hair, blending them with the velvet of a new coif, and gazing intently into her mirror.

"It is nearly four o'clock; that interminable council must surely be over," she thought to herself. "Jacob has returned from the Louvre; he says that everybody he saw was excited about the number of the councillors summoned and the length of the session. What can have happened? Is it some misfortune? Good God! surely *he* knows how suspense wears out the soul! Perhaps he has gone a-hunting? If he is happy and amused, it is all right. When I see him gay, I forget all I have suffered."

She drew her hands round her slender waist as if to smooth some trifling wrinkle in her gown, turning sideways to see if its folds fell properly, and as she did so, she caught sight of the king on the couch behind her. The carpet had so muffled the sound of his steps that he had slipped in softly without being heard.

"You frightened me!" she said, with a cry of surprise, which was quickly repressed.

"Were you thinking of me?" said the king.

"When do I not think of you?" she answered, sitting down beside him.

She took off his cap and cloak, passing her hands through his hair as though she combed it with her fingers. Charles let her do as she pleased, but made no answer. Surprised at this, Marie knelt down to study the pale face of her royal master, and then saw the signs of a dreadful weariness and a more consummate melancholy than any she had yet consoled. She repressed her tears and kept silence, that she might not irritate by mistaken words the sorrow which, as yet, she did not understand. In this she did as tender women do under like circumstances. She kissed that forehead, seamed with untimely wrinkles, and those livid cheeks, trying to convey to the worn-out soul the freshness of hers,— pouring her spirit into the sweet caresses which met with no response. Presently she raised her head to the level of the king's, clasping him softly in her arms; then she lay still, her face hidden on that suffering breast, watching for the opportune moment to question his dejected mind. "My Charlot," she said at last, "will you not tell your poor, distressed Marie the troubles that cloud that precious brow, and whiten those beautiful red lips?"

"Except Charlemagne," he said in a hollow voice, "all the kings of France named Charles have ended miserably."

"Pooh!" she said, "look at Charles VIII."

"That poor prince!" exclaimed the king. "In the flower of his age he struck his head against a low door at the chateau of Amboise, which he was having decorated, and died in horrible agony. It was his death which gave the crown to our family."

"Charles VII. reconquered his kingdom."

"Darling, he died" (the king lowered his voice) "of hunger; for he feared being poisoned by the dauphin, who had already caused the death of his beautiful Agnes. The father feared his son; to-day the son dreads his mother!"

"Why drag up the past?" she said hastily, remembering the dreadful life of Charles VI.

"Ah! sweetest, kings have no need to go to sorcerers to discover their coming fate; they need only turn to history. I am at this moment endeavoring to escape the fate of Charles the Simple, who was robbed of his crown, and died in prison after seven years' captivity."

"Charles V. conquered the English," she cried triumphantly.

"No, not he, but du Guesclin. He himself, poisoned by Charles de Navarre, dragged out a wretched existence."

"Well, Charles IV., then?"

"He married three times to obtain an heir, in spite of the masculine beauty of the children of Philippe le Bel. The first house of Valois ended with him, and the second is about to end in the same way. The queen has given me only a daughter, and I shall die without leaving her pregnant; for a long minority would be the greatest curse I could bequeath to the kingdom. Besides, if I had a son, would he live? The name of Charles is fatal; Charlemagne exhausted the luck of it. If I left a son I would tremble at the thought that he would be Charles X."

"Who is it that wants to seize your crown?"

"My brother d'Alencon conspires against it. Enemies are all about me."

"Monsieur," said Marie, with a charming little pout, "do tell me something gayer."

"Ah! my little jewel, my treasure, don't call me 'monsieur,' even in jest; you remind me of my mother, who stabs me incessantly with that title, by which she seems to snatch away my crown. She says 'my son' to the Duc d'Anjou—I mean the king of Poland."

"Sire," exclaimed Marie, clasping her hands as though she were praying, "there is a kingdom where you are worshipped. Your Majesty fills it with his glory, his power; and there the word 'monsieur,' means 'my beloved lord.'"

She unclasped her hands, and with a pretty gesture pointed to her heart. The words were so *musiques* (to use a word of the times which depicted the melodies of love) that Charles IX. caught her round the waist with the nervous force that characterized him, and seated her on his knee, rubbing his forehead gently against the pretty curls so coquettishly arranged. Marie thought the moment favorable; she ventured a few kisses, which Charles allowed rather than accepted, then she said softly:—

"If my servants were not mistaken you were out all night in the streets, as in the days when you played the pranks of a younger son."

"Yes," replied the king, still lost in his own thoughts.

"Did you fight the watchman and frighten some of the burghers? Who are the men you brought here and locked up? They must be very criminal, as you won't allow any communication with them. No girl was ever locked in as carefully, and they have not had a mouthful to eat since they came. The Germans whom Solern left to guard them won't let any one go near the room. Is it a joke you are playing; or is it something serious?"

"Yes, you are right," said the king, coming out of his reverie, "last night I did scour the roofs with Tavannes and the Gondis. I wanted to try my old follies with the old companions; but my legs were not what they once were; I did not dare leap the streets; though we did jump two alleys from one roof to the next. At the second, however, Tavannes and I, holding on to a chimney, agreed that we couldn't do it again. If either of us had been alone we couldn't have done it then."

"I'll wager that you sprang first." The king smiled. "I know why you risk your life in that way."

"And why, you little witch?"

"You are tired of life."

"Ah, sorceress! But I am being hunted down by sorcery," said the king, resuming his anxious look.

"My sorcery is love," she replied, smiling. "Since the happy day when you first loved me, have I not always divined your thoughts? And—if you will let me speak the truth—the thoughts which torture you to-day are not worthy of a king."

"Am I a king?" he said bitterly.

"Cannot you be one? What did Charles VII. do? He listened to his mistress, monseigneur, and he reconquered his kingdom, invaded by the English as yours is now by the enemies of our religion. Your last *coup d'Etat* showed you the course you have to follow. Exterminate heresy."

"You blamed the Saint-Bartholomew," said Charles, "and now you—"

"That is over," she said; "besides, I agree with Madame Catherine that it was better to do it yourselves than let the Guises do it."

"Charles VII. had only men to fight; I am face to face with ideas," resumed the king. "We can kill men, but we can't kill words! The Emperor Charles V. gave up the attempt; his son Philip has spent his strength upon it; we shall all perish, we kings, in that struggle. On whom can I rely? To right, among the Catholics, I find the Guises, who are my enemies; to left, the Calvinists, who will never forgive me the death of my poor old Coligny, nor that bloody day in August; besides, they want to suppress the throne; and in front of me what have I?—my mother!"

"Arrest her; reign alone," said Marie in a low voice, whispering in his ear.

"I meant to do so yesterday; to-day I no longer intend it. You speak of it rather coolly."

"Between the daughter of an apothecary and that of a doctor there is no great difference," replied Touchet, always ready to laugh at the false origin attributed to her.

The king frowned.

"Marie, don't take such liberties. Catherine de' Medici is my mother, and you ought to tremble lest—"

"What is it you fear?"

"Poison!" cried the king, beside himself.

"Poor child!" cried Marie, restraining her tears; for the sight of such strength united to such weakness touched her deeply. "Ah!" she continued, "you make me hate Madame Catherine, who has been so good to me; her kindness now seems perfidy. Why is she so kind to me, and bad to you? During my stay in Dauphine I heard many things about the beginning of your reign which you concealed from me; it seems to me that the queen, your mother, is the real cause of all your troubles."

"In what way?" cried the king, deeply interested.

"Women whose souls and whose intentions are pure use virtue wherewith to rule the men they love; but women who do not seek good rule men through their evil instincts. Now, the queen made vices out of certain of your noblest qualities, and she taught you to believe that your worst inclinations were virtues. Was that the part of a mother? Be a tyrant like Louis XI.; inspire terror; imitate Philip II.; banish the Italians; drive out the Guises; confiscate the lands of the Calvinists. Out of this solitude you will rise a king; you will save the throne. The moment is propitious; your brother is in Poland."

"We are two children at statecraft," said Charles, bitterly; "we know nothing except how to love. Alas! my treasure, yesterday I, too, thought all these things; I dreamed of accomplishing great deeds—bah! my mother blew down my house of cards! From a distance we see great questions outlined like the summits of mountains, and it is easy to say: 'I'll make an end of Calvinism; I'll bring those Guises to task; I'll separate from the Court of Rome; I'll rely upon my people, upon the burghers—' ah! yes, from afar it all seems simple enough! but try to climb those mountains and the higher you go the more the difficulties appear. Calvinism, in itself, is the last thing the leaders of that party care for; and the Guises, those rabid Catholics, would be sorry indeed to see the Calvinists put down. Each side considers its own interests exclusively, and religious opinions are but a cloak for insatiable ambition. The party of Charles IX. is the feeblest of all. That of the king of Navarre, that of the king of Poland, that of the Duc d'Alencon, that of the Condes, that of the Guises, that of my mother, are all intriguing one against another, but they take no account of me, not even in my own council. My mother, in the midst of so many contending elements, is, nevertheless, the strongest among them; she has just proved to me the inanity of my plans. We are surrounded by rebellious subjects who defy the law. The axe of Louis XI. of which you speak, is lacking to us. Parliament would not condemn the Guises, nor the king of Navarre, nor the Condes, nor my brother. No! the courage to assassinate is needed; the throne will be forced to strike down those insolent men who suppress both law and justice; but where can we find the faithful arm? The council I held this morning has disgusted me with everything; treason everywhere; contending interests all about me. I am tired with the burden of my crown. I only want to die in peace."

He dropped into a sort of gloomy somnolence.

"Disgusted with everything!" repeated Marie Touchet, sadly; but she did not disturb the black torpor of her lover.

Charles was the victim of a complete prostration of mind and body, produced by three things,—the exhaustion of all his faculties, aggravated by the disheartenment of realizing the extent of an evil; the recognized impossibility of surmounting his weakness; and the aspect of difficulties so great that genius itself would dread them. The king's depression was in proportion to the courage and the loftiness of ideas to which he had risen during the last few months. In addition to this, an attack of nervous melancholy, caused by his malady, had seized him as he left the protracted council which had taken place in his private cabinet. Marie saw that he was in one of those crises when the least word, even of love, would be importunate and painful; so she remained kneeling quietly beside him, her head on his knee, the king's hand buried in her hair, and he himself motionless, without a word, without a sigh, as still as Marie herself,—Charles IX. in the lethargy of impotence, Marie in the stupor of despair which comes to a loving woman when she perceives the boundaries at which love ends.

The lovers thus remained, in the deepest silence, during one of those terrible hours when all reflection wounds, when the clouds of an inward tempest veil even the memory of happiness. Marie believed that she herself was partly the cause of this frightful dejection. She asked herself, not without horror, if the excessive joys and the violent love which she had never yet found strength to resist, did not contribute to weaken the mind and body of the king. As she raised her eyes, bathed in tears, toward her lover, she saw the slow tears rolling down his pallid cheeks. This mark of the sympathy that united them so moved the king that he rushed from his depression like a spurred horse. He took Marie in his arms and placed her on the sofa.

"I will no longer be a king," he cried. "I will be your lover, your lover only, wholly given up to that happiness. I will die happy, and not consumed by the cares and miseries of a throne."

The tone of these words, the fire that shone in the half-extinct eyes of the king, gave Marie a terrible shock instead of happiness; she blamed her love as an accomplice in the malady of which the king was dying.

"Meanwhile you forget your prisoners," she said, rising abruptly.

"Hey! what care I for them? I give them leave to kill me."

"What! are they murderers?"

"Oh, don't be frightened, little one; we hold them fast. Don't think of them, but of me. Do you love me?"

"Sire!" she cried.

"Sire!" he repeated, sparks darting from his eyes, so violent was the rush of his anger at the untimely respect of his mistress. "You are in league with my mother."

"O God!" cried Marie, looking at the picture above her *prie-dieu* and turning toward it to say her prayer, "grant that he comprehend me!"

"Ah!" said the king suspiciously, "you have some wrong to me upon your conscience!" Then looking at her from between his arms, he plunged his eyes into hers. "I have heard some talk of the mad passion of a certain Entragues," he went on wildly. "Ever since their grandfather, the soldier Balzac, married a viscontessa at Milan that family hold their heads too high."

Marie looked at the king with so proud an air that he was ashamed. At that instant the cries of little Charles de Valois, who had just awakened, were heard in the next room. Marie ran to the door.

"Come in, Bourguignonne!" she said, taking the child from its nurse and carrying it to the king. "You are more of a child than he," she cried, half angry, half appeased.

"He is beautiful!" said Charles IX., taking his son in his arms.

"I alone know how like he is to you," said Marie; "already he has your smile and your gestures."

"So tiny as that!" said the king, laughing at her.

"Oh, I know men don't believe such things; but watch him, my Charlot, play with him. Look there! See! Am I not right?"

"True!" exclaimed the king, astonished by a motion of the child which seemed the very miniature of a gesture of his own.

"Ah, the pretty flower!" cried the mother. "Never shall he leave us! *He* will never cause me grief."

The king frolicked with his son; he tossed him in his arms, and kissed him passionately, talking the foolish, unmeaning talk, the pretty, baby language invented by nurses and mothers. His voice grew child-like. At last his forehead cleared, joy returned to his saddened face, and then, as Marie saw that he had forgotten his troubles, she laid her head upon his shoulder and whispered in his ear:—

"Won't you tell me, Charlot, why you have made me keep murderers in my house? Who are these men, and what do you mean to do with them? In short, I want to know what you were doing on the roofs. I hope there was no woman in the business?"

"Then you love me as much as ever!" cried the king, meeting the clear, interrogatory glance that women know so well how to cast upon occasion.

"You doubted *me*," she replied, as a tear shone on her beautiful eyelashes.

"There are women in my adventure," said the king; "but they are sorceresses. How far had I told you?"

"You were on the roofs near by—what street was it?"

"Rue Saint-Honore, sweetest," said the king, who seemed to have recovered himself. Collecting this thoughts, he began to explain to his mistress what had happened, as if to prepare her for a scene that was presently to take place in her presence.

"As I was passing through the street last night on a frolic," he said, "I chanced to see a bright light from the dormer window of the house occupied by Rene, my mother's glover and perfumer, and once yours. I have strong doubts about that man and what goes on in his house. If I am poisoned, the drug will come from there."

"I shall dismiss him to-morrow."

"Ah! so you kept him after I had given him up?" cried the king. "I thought my life was safe with you," he added gloomily; "but no doubt death is following me even here."

"But, my dearest, I have only just returned from Dauphine with our dauphin," she said, smiling, "and Rene has supplied me with nothing since the death of the Queen of Navarre. Go on; you climbed to the roof of Rene's house?"

IV. THE KING'S TALE

"Yes," returned the king. "In a second I was there, followed by Tavannes, and then we clambered to a spot where I could see without being seen the interior of that devil's kitchen, in which I beheld extraordinary things which inspired me to take certain measures. Did you ever notice the end of the roof of that cursed perfumer? The windows toward the street are always closed and dark, except the last, from which can be seen the hotel de Soissons and the observatory which my mother built for that astrologer, Cosmo Ruggiero. Under the roof are lodging-rooms and a gallery which have no windows except on the courtyard, so that in order to see what was going on within, it was necessary to go where no man before ever dreamed of climbing,—along the coping of a high wall which adjoins the roof of Rene's house. The men who set up in that house the furnaces by which they distil death, reckoned on the cowardice of Parisians to save them from being overlooked; but they little thought of Charles de Valois! I crept along the coping until I came to a window, against the casing of which I was able to stand up straight with my arm round a carved monkey which ornamented it."

"What did you see, dear heart?" said Marie, trembling.

"A den, where works of darkness were being done," replied the king. "The first object on which my eyes lighted was a tall old man seated in a chair, with a magnificent white beard, like that of old l'Hopital, and dressed like him in a black velvet robe. On his broad forehead furrowed deep with wrinkles, on his crown of white hair, on his calm, attentive face, pale with toil and vigils, fell the concentrated rays of a lamp from

212

which shone a vivid light. His attention was divided between an old manuscript, the parchment of which must have been centuries old, and two lighted furnaces on which heretical compounds were cooking. Neither the floor nor the ceiling of the laboratory could be seen, because of the myriads of hanging skeletons, bodies of animals, dried plants, minerals, and articles of all kinds that masked the walls; while on the floor were books, instruments for distilling, chests filled with utensils for magic and astrology; in one place I saw horoscopes and nativities, phials, wax-figures under spells, and possibly poisons. Tavannes and I were fascinated, I do assure you, by the sight of this devil's-arsenal. Only to see it puts one under a spell, and if I had not been King of France, I might have been awed by it. 'You can tremble for both of us,' I whispered to Tavannes. But Tavannes' eyes were already caught by the most mysterious feature of the scene. On a couch, near the old man, lay a girl of strangest beauty,—slender and long like a snake, white as ermine, livid as death, motionless as a statue. Perhaps it was a woman just taken from her grave, on whom they were trying experiments, for she seemed to wear a shroud; her eyes were fixed, and I could not see that she breathed. The old fellow paid no attention to her. I looked at him so intently that, after a while, his soul seemed to pass into mine. By dint of studying him, I ended by admiring the glance of his eye,—so keen, so profound, so bold, in spite of the chilling power of age. I admired his mouth, mobile with thoughts emanating from a desire which seemed to be the solitary desire of his soul, and was stamped upon every line of the face. All things in that man expressed a hope which nothing discouraged, and nothing could check. His attitude,—a quivering immovability,— those outlines so free, carved by a single passion as by the chisel of a sculptor, that IDEA concentrated on some experiment criminal or scientific, that seeking Mind in quest of Nature, thwarted by her, bending but never broken under the weight of its own audacity, which it would not renounce, threatening creation with the fire it derived from it,—ah! all that held me in a spell for the time being. I saw before me an old man who was more of a king than I, for his glance embraced the world and mastered it. I will forge swords no longer; I will soar above the abysses of existence, like that man; for his science, methinks, is true royalty! Yes, I believe in occult science."

"You, the eldest son, the defender of the Holy Catholic, Apostolic, and Roman Church?" said Marie.

"**I.**"

"What happened to you? Go on, go on; I will fear for you, and you will have courage for me."

"Looking at a clock, the old man rose," continued the king. "He went out,

213

I don't know where; but I heard the window on the side toward the rue Saint-Honore open. Soon a brilliant light gleamed out upon the darkness; then I saw in the observatory of the hotel de Soissons another light replying to that of the old man, and by it I beheld the figure of Cosmo Ruggiero on the tower. 'See, they communicate!' I said to Tavannes, who from that moment thought the matter frightfully suspicious, and agreed with me that we ought to seize the two men and search, incontinently, their accursed workshop. But before proceeding to do so, we wanted to see what was going to happen. After about fifteen minutes the door opened, and Cosmo Ruggiero, my mother's counsellor,—the bottomless pit which holds the secrets of the court, he from whom all women ask help against their husbands and lovers, and all the men ask help against their unfaithful wives and mistresses, he who traffics on the future as on the past, receiving pay with both hands, who sells horoscopes and is supposed to know all things,—that semi-devil came in, saying to the old man, 'Good-day to you, brother.' With him he brought a hideous old woman,—toothless, humpbacked, twisted, bent, like a Chinese image, only worse. She was wrinkled as a withered apple; her skin was saffron-colored; her chin bit her nose; her mouth was a mere line scarcely visible; her eyes were like the black spots on a dice; her forehead emitted bitterness; her hair escaped in straggling gray locks from a dirty coif; she walked with a crutch; she smelt of heresy and witchcraft. The sight of her actually frightened us, Tavannes and me! We didn't think her a natural woman. God never made a woman so fearful as that. She sat down on a stool near the pretty snake with whom Tavannes was in love. The two brothers paid no attention to the old woman nor to the young woman, who together made a horrible couple,—on the one side life in death, on the other death in life—"

"Ah! my sweet poet!" cried Marie, kissing the king.

"'Good-day, Cosmo,' replied the old alchemist. And they both looked into the furnace. 'What strength has the moon to-day?' asked the elder. 'But, *caro Lorenzo*,' replied my mother's astrologer, 'the September tides are not yet over; we can learn nothing while that disorder lasts.' 'What says the East to-night?' 'It discloses in the air a creative force which returns to earth all that earth takes from it. The conclusion is that all things here below are the product of a slow transformation, but that all diversities are the forms of one and the same substance.' 'That is what my predecessor thought,' replied Lorenzo. 'This morning Bernard Palissy told me that metals were the result of compression, and that fire, which divides all, also unites all; fire has the power to compress as well as to separate. That man has genius.' Though I was placed where it was impossible for them to see me, Cosmo said, lifting the hand of the dead girl: 'Some one is near us! Who is it' 'The king,' she answered. I at once showed myself and rapped on the window. Ruggiero opened it, and I sprang into that hellish kitchen, followed by Tavannes. 'Yes, the king,' I said to the two Florentines, who seemed terrified. 'In spite of your furnaces and your books, your sciences and your sorceries, you did not foresee my visit. I am very glad to meet the famous Lorenzo Ruggiero, of whom my mother speaks mysteriously,' I said, addressing the old man, who rose and bowed. 'You are in this kingdom without my consent, my good man. For whom are you working here, you whose ancestors from father to son have been devoted in heart to the house of Medici? Listen to me! You dive into so many purses that by this time, if you are grasping men, you have piled up gold. You are too shrewd and cautious to cast yourselves imprudently into criminal actions; but, nevertheless, you are not here in this kitchen without a purpose. Yes, you have some secret scheme, you who are satisfied neither by gold nor power. Whom do you serve,—God or the devil? What are you concocting here? I choose to know the whole truth; I am a man who can hear it and keep silence about your enterprise, however blamable it maybe. Therefore you will tell me all, without reserve. If you deceive me you will be treated severely. Pagans or Christians, Calvinists or Mohammedans, you have my royal word that you shall leave the kingdom in safety if you have any misdemeanors to relate. I shall leave you for the rest of the night and the forenoon of to-morrow to examine your thoughts; for you are now my prisoners, and you will at once follow me to a place where you will be guarded carefully.' Before obeying me the two Italians consulted each other by a subtle glance; then Lorenzo Ruggiero said I might be assured that no torture could wring their secrets from them; that in spite of their apparent feebleness neither pain nor human feelings had any power of them; confidence alone could make their mouth say what their mind contained. I must not, he said, be surprised if they treated as equals with a king who recognized God only as above him, for their thoughts came from God alone. They therefore claimed from me as much confidence and trust as they should give to me. But before engaging themselves to answer me without reserve they must request me to put my left hand into that of the young girl lying there, and my right into that of the old woman. Not wishing them to think I was afraid of their sorcery, I held out my hands; Lorenzo took the right, Cosmo the left, and each placed a hand in that of each woman, so that I was like Jesus Christ between the two thieves. During the time that the two witches were examining my hands Cosmo held a mirror before me and asked me to look into it; his brother, meanwhile, was talking with the two women in a language unknown to me. Neither Tavannes nor I could catch the meaning of a

215

single sentence. Before bringing the men here we put seals on all the outlets of the laboratory, which Tavannes undertook to guard until such time as, by my express orders, Bernard Palissy, and Chapelain, my physician, could be brought there to examine thoroughly the drugs the place contained and which were evidently made there. In order to keep the Ruggieri ignorant of this search, and to prevent them from communicating with a single soul outside, I put the two devils in your lower rooms in charge of Solern's Germans, who are better than the walls of a jail. Rene, the perfumer, is kept under guard in his own house by Solern's equerry, and so are the two witches. Now, my sweetest, inasmuch as I hold the keys of the whole cabal,—the kings of Thune, the chiefs of sorcery, the gypsy fortune-tellers, the masters of the future, the heirs of all past soothsayers,—I intend by their means to read *you*, to know your heart; and, together, we will find out what is to happen to us."

"I shall be glad if they can lay my heart bare before you," said Marie, without the slightest fear.

"I know why sorcerers don't frighten you,—because you are a witch yourself."

"Will you have a peach?" she said, offering him some delicious fruit on a gold plate. "See these grapes, these pears; I went to Vincennes myself and gathered them for you."

"Yes, I'll eat them; there is no poison there except a philter from your hands."

"You ought to eat a great deal of fruit, Charles; it would cool your blood, which you heat by such excitements."

"Must I love you less?"

"Perhaps so," she said. "If the things you love injure you—and I have feared it—I shall find strength in my heart to refuse them. I adore Charles more than I love the king; I want the man to live, released from the tortures that make him grieve."

"Royalty has ruined me."

"Yes," she replied. "If you were only a poor prince, like your brother-in-law of Navarre, without a penny, possessing only a miserable little kingdom in Spain where he never sets his foot, and Bearn in France which doesn't give him revenue enough to feed him, I should be happy, much happier than if I were really Queen of France."

"But you are more than the Queen of France. She has King Charles for the sake of the kingdom only; royal marriages are only politics."

Marie smiled and made a pretty little grimace as she said: "Yes, yes, I know that, sire. And my sonnet, have you written it?"

"Dearest, verses are as difficult to write as treaties of peace; but you shall have them soon. Ah, me! life is so easy here, I wish I might never leave you. However, we must send for those Italians and question them. *Tete-Dieu*! I thought one Ruggiero in the kingdom was one too many, but it seems there are two. Now listen, my precious; you don't lack sense, you would make an excellent lieutenant of police, for you can penetrate things—"

"But, sire, we women suppose all we fear, and we turn what is probable into truths; that is the whole of our art in a nutshell."

"Well, help me to sound these men. Just now all my plans depend on the result of their examination. Are they innocent? Are they guilty? My mother is behind them."

"I hear Jacob's voice in the next room," said Marie.

Jacob was the favorite valet of the king, and the one who accompanied him on all his private excursions. He now came to ask if it was the king's good pleasure to speak to the two prisoners. The king made a sign in the affirmative, and the mistress of the house gave her orders.

"Jacob," she said, "clear the house of everybody, except the nurse and Monsieur le Dauphin d'Auvergne, who may remain. As for you, stay in the lower hall; but first, close the windows, draw the curtains of the salon, and light the candles."

The king's impatience was so great that while these preparations were being made he sat down upon a raised seat at the corner of a lofty fireplace of white marble in which a bright fire was blazing, placing his pretty mistress by his side. His portrait, framed in velvet, was over the mantle in place of a mirror. Charles IX. rested his elbow on the arm of the seat as if to watch the two Florentines the better under cover of his hand.

The shutters closed, and the curtains drawn, Jacob lighted the wax tapers in a tall candelabrum of chiselled silver, which he placed on the table where the Florentines were to stand,—an object, by the bye, which they would readily recognize as the work of their compatriot, Benvenuto Cellini. The richness of the room, decorated in the taste of Charles IX., now shone forth. The red-brown of the tapestries showed to better advantage than by daylight. The various articles of furniture, delicately made or carved, reflected in their ebony panels the glow of the fire and the sparkle of the lights. Gilding, soberly applied, shone here and there like eyes, brightening the brown color which prevailed in this nest of love.

Jacob presently gave two knocks, and, receiving permission, ushered in the Italians. Marie Touchet was instantly affected by the grandeur of Lorenzo's presence, which struck all those who met him, great and small alike. The silvery whiteness of the old man's beard was heightened by a robe of black velvet; his brow was like a marble dome. His austere face,

217

illumined by two black eyes which cast a pointed flame, conveyed an impression of genius issuing from solitude, and all the more effective because its power had not been dulled by contact with men. It was like the steel of a blade that had never been fleshed.

As for Cosmo Ruggiero, he wore the dress of a courtier of the time. Marie made a sign to the king to assure him that he had not exaggerated his description, and to thank him for having shown her these extraordinary men.

"I would like to have seen the sorceresses, too," she whispered in his ear.

V. THE ALCHEMISTS

Again absorbed in thought, Charles IX. made her no answer; he was idly flicking crumbs of bread from his doublet and breeches.

"Your science cannot change the heavens or make the sun to shine, messieurs," he said at last, pointing to the curtains which the gray atmosphere of Paris darkened.

"Our science can make the skies what we like, sire," replied Lorenzo Ruggiero. "The weather is always fine for those who work in a laboratory by the light of a furnace."

"That is true," said the king. "Well, father," he added, using an expression familiar to him when addressing old men, "explain to us clearly the object of your studies."

"What will guarantee our safety?"

"The word of a king," replied Charles IX., whose curiosity was keenly excited by the question.

Lorenzo Ruggiero seemed to hesitate, and Charles IX. cried out: "What hinders you? We are here alone."

"But is the King of France here?" asked Lorenzo.

Charles reflected an instant, and then answered, "No."

The imposing old man then took a chair, and seated himself. Cosmo, astonished at this boldness, dared not imitate it.

Charles IX. remarked, with cutting sarcasm: "The king is not here, monsieur, but a lady is, whose permission it was your duty to await."

"He whom you see before you, madame," said the old man, "is as far above kings as kings are above their subjects; you will think me courteous when you know my powers."

Hearing these audacious words, with Italian emphasis, Charles and Marie looked at each other, and also at Cosmo, who, with his eyes fixed on his brother, seemed to be asking himself: "How does he intend to get

218

us out of the danger in which we are?"

In fact, there was but one person present who could understand the boldness and the art of Lorenzo Ruggiero's first step; and that person was neither the king nor his young mistress, on whom that great seer had already flung the spell of his audacity,—it was Cosmo Ruggiero, his wily brother. Though superior himself to the ablest men at court, perhaps even to Catherine de' Medici herself, the astrologer always recognized his brother Lorenzo as his master.

Buried in studious solitude, the old savant weighed and estimated sovereigns, most of whom were worn out by the perpetual turmoil of politics, the crises of which at this period came so suddenly and were so keen, so intense, so unexpected. He knew their ennui, their lassitude, their disgust with things about them; he knew the ardor with which they sought what seemed to them new or strange or fantastic; above all, how they loved to enter some unknown intellectual region to escape their endless struggle with men and events. To those who have exhausted statecraft, nothing remains but the realm of pure thought. Charles the Fifth proved this by his abdication. Charles IX., who wrote sonnets and forged blades to escape the exhausting cares of an age in which both throne and king were threatened, to whom royalty had brought only cares and never pleasures, was likely to be roused to a high pitch of interest by the bold denial of his power thus uttered by Lorenzo. Religious doubt was not surprising in an age when Catholicism was so violently arraigned; but the upsetting of all religion, given as the basis of a strange, mysterious art, would surely strike the king's mind, and drag it from its present preoccupations. The essential thing for the two brothers was to make the king forget his suspicions by turning his mind to new ideas.

The Ruggieri were well aware that their stake in this game was their own life, and the glances, so humble, and yet so proud, which they exchanged with the searching, suspicious eyes of Marie and the king, were a scene in themselves.

"Sire," said Lorenzo Ruggiero, "you have asked me for the truth; but, to show the truth in all her nakedness, I must also show you and make you sound the depths of the well from which she comes. I appeal to the gentleman and the poet to pardon words which the eldest son of the Church might take for blasphemy,—I believe that God does not concern himself with human affairs."

Though determined to maintain a kingly composure, Charles IX. could not repress a motion of surprise.

"Without that conviction I should have no faith whatever in the miraculous work to which my life is devoted. To do that work I must have this belief; and if the finger of God guides all things, then—I am a madman. Therefore, let the king understand, once for all, that this work means a victory to be won over the present course of Nature. I am an alchemist, sire. But do not think, as the common-minded do, that I seek to make gold. The making of gold is not the object but an incident of our researches; otherwise our toil could not be called the GREAT WORK. The Great Work is something far loftier than that. If, therefore, I were forced to admit the presence of God in matter, my voice must logically command the extinction of furnaces kept burning throughout the ages. But to deny the direct action of God in the world is not to deny God; do not make that mistake. We place the Creator of all things far higher than the sphere to which religions have degraded Him. Do not accuse of atheism those who look for immortality. Like Lucifer, we are jealous of our God; and jealousy means love. Though the doctrine of which I speak is the basis of our work, all our disciples are not imbued with it. Cosmo," said the old man, pointing to his brother, "Cosmo is devout; he pays for masses for the repose of our father's soul, and he goes to hear them. Your mother's astrologer believes in the divinity of Christ, in the Immaculate Conception, in Transubstantiation; he believes also in the Pope's indulgences and in hell, and in a multitude of such things. His hour has not yet come. I have drawn his horoscope; he will live to be almost a centenarian; he will live through two more reigns, and he will see two kings of France assassinated."

"Who are they?" asked the king.

"The last of the Valois and the first of the Bourbons," replied Lorenzo. "But Cosmo shares my opinion. It is impossible to be an alchemist and a Catholic, to have faith in the despotism of man over matter, and also in the sovereignty of the divine."

"Cosmo to die a centenarian!" exclaimed the king, with his terrible frown of the eyebrows.

"Yes, sire," replied Lorenzo, with authority; "and he will die peaceably in his bed."

"If you have power to foresee the moment of your death, why are you ignorant of the outcome of your researches?" asked the king.

Charles IX. smiled as he said this, looking triumphantly at Marie Touchet. The brothers exchanged a rapid glance of satisfaction.

"He begins to be interested," thought they. "We are saved!"

"Our prognostics depend on the immediate relations which exist at the time between man and Nature; but our purpose itself is to change those relations entirely," replied Lorenzo.

The king was thoughtful.

"But, if you are certain of dying you are certain of defeat," he said, at last.

220

"Like our predecessors," replied Lorenzo, raising his hand and letting it fall again with an emphatic and solemn gesture, which presented visibly the grandeur of his thought. "But your mind has bounded to the confines of the matter, sire; we must return upon our steps. If you do not know the ground on which our edifice is built, you may well think it doomed to crumble with our lives, and so judge the Science cultivated from century to century by the greatest among men, as the common herd judge of it."
The king made a sign of assent.

"I think," continued Lorenzo, "that this earth belongs to man; he is the master of it, and he can appropriate to his use all forces and all substances. Man is not a creation issuing directly from the hand of God; but the development of a principle sown broadcast into the infinite of ether, from which millions of creatures are produced,—differing beings in different worlds, because the conditions surrounding life are varied. Yes, sire, the subtle element which we call *life* takes its rise beyond the visible worlds; creation divides that principle according to the centres into which it flows; and all beings, even the lowest, share it, taking so much as they can take of it at their own risk and peril. It is for them to protect themselves from death,—the whole purpose of alchemy lies there, sire. If man, the most perfect animal on this globe, bore within himself a portion of the divine, he would not die; but he does die. To solve this difficulty, Socrates and his school invented the Soul. I, the successor of so many great and unknown kings, the rulers of this science, I stand for the ancient theories, not the new. I believe in the transformations of matter which I see, and not in the possible eternity of a soul which I do not see. I do not recognize that world of the soul. If such a world existed, the substances whose magnificent conjunction produced your body, and are so dazzling in that of Madame, would not resolve themselves after your death each into its own element, water to water, fire to fire, metal to metal, just as the elements of my coal, when burned, return to their primitive molecules. If you believe that a certain part of us survives, *we* do not survive; for all that makes our actual being perishes. Now, it is this actual being that I am striving to continue beyond the limit assigned to life; it is our present transformation to which I wish to give a greater duration. Why! the trees live for centuries, but man lives only years, though the former are passive, the others active; the first motionless and speechless, the others gifted with language and motion. No created thing should be superior in this world to man, either in power or in duration. Already we are widening our perceptions, for we look into the stars; therefore we ought to be able to lengthen the duration of our lives. I place life before power. What good is power if life escapes us? A wise man should have no other purpose than to seek, not whether he has some other life within him, but the secret springs of his actual form, in order that he may prolong its existence at his will. That is the desire which has whitened my hair; but I walk boldly in the darkness, marshalling to the search all those great intellects that share my faith. Life will some day be ours,—ours to control."

"Ah! but how?" cried the king, rising hastily.

"The first condition of our faith being that the earth belongs to man, you must grant me that point," said Lorenzo.

"So be it!" said Charles de Valois, already under the spell.

"Then, sire, if we take God out of this world, what remains? Man. Let us therefore examine our domain. The material world is composed of elements; these elements are themselves principles; these principles resolve themselves into an ultimate principle, endowed with motion. The number THREE is the formula of creation: Matter, Motion, Product."

"Stop!" cried the king, "what proof is there of this?"

"Do you not see the effects?" replied Lorenzo. "We have tried in our crucibles the acorn which produces the oak, and the embryo from which grows a man; from this tiny substance results a single principle, to which some force, some movement must be given. Since there is no overruling creator, this principle must give to itself the outward forms which constitute our world—for this phenomenon of life is the same everywhere. Yes, for metals as for human beings, for plants as for men, life begins in an imperceptible embryo which develops itself. A primitive principle exists; let us seize it at the point where it begins to act upon itself, where it is a unit, where it is a principle before taking definite form, a cause before being an effect; we must see it single, without form, susceptible of clothing itself with all the outward forms we shall see it take. When we are face to face with this atomic particle, when we shall have caught its movement at the very instant of motion, *then* we shall know the law; thenceforth we are the masters of life, masters who can impose upon that principle the form we choose,—with gold to win the world, and the power to make for ourselves centuries of life in which to enjoy it! That is what my people and I are seeking. All our strength, all our thoughts are strained in that direction; nothing distracts us from it. One hour wasted on any other passion is a theft committed against our true grandeur. Just as you have never found your hounds relinquishing the hunted animal or failing to be in at the death, so I have never seen one of my patient disciples diverted from this great quest by the love of woman or a selfish thought. If an adept seeks power and wealth, the desire is instigated by our needs; he grasps treasure as a thirsty dog laps water while he swims a stream, because his crucibles are in need of a diamond to melt or an ingot of gold to reduce to powder. To each his own work. One seeks the secret of vegetable nature; he watches the slow life of plants; he notes the parity of motion among all the species, and the parity of their nutrition; he finds everywhere the need of sun and air and water, to fecundate and nourish them. Another scrutinizes the blood of animals. A third studies the laws of universal motion and its connection with celestial revolutions. Nearly all are eager to struggle with the intractable nature of metal, for while we find many principles in other things, we find all metals like unto themselves in every particular. Hence a common error as to our work. Behold these patient, indefatigable athletes, ever vanquished, yet ever returning to the combat! Humanity, sire, is behind us, as the huntsman is behind your hounds. She cries to us: 'Make haste! neglect nothing! sacrifice all, even a man, ye who sacrifice yourselves! Hasten! hasten! Beat down the arms of DEATH, mine enemy!' Yes, sire, we are inspired by a hope which involves the happiness of all coming generations. We have buried many men—and what men!—dying of this Search. Setting foot in this career we cannot work for ourselves; we may die without discovering the Secret; and our death is that of those who do not believe in another life; it is this life that we have sought, and failed to perpetuate. We are glorious martyrs; we have the welfare of the race at heart; we have failed but we live again in our successors. As we go through this existence we discover secrets with which we endow the liberal and the mechanical arts. From our furnaces gleam lights which illumine industrial enterprises, and perfect them. Gunpowder issued from our alembics; nay, we have mastered the lightning. In our persistent vigils lie political revolutions."

"Can this be true?" cried the king, springing once more from his chair.

"Why not?" said the grand-master of the new Templars. "*Tradidit mundum disputationibus!* God has given us the earth. Hear this once more: man is master here below; matter is his; all forces, all means are at his disposal. Who created us? Motion. What power maintains life in us? Motion. Why cannot science seize the secret of that motion? Nothing is lost here below; nothing escapes from our planet to go elsewhere,— otherwise the stars would stumble over each other; the waters of the deluge are still with us in their principle, and not a drop is lost. Around us, above us, beneath us, are to be found the elements from which have come innumerable hosts of men who have crowded the earth before and since the deluge. What is the secret of our struggle? To discover the force that disunites, and then, *then* we shall discover that which binds. We are the product of a visible manufacture. When the waters covered the globe men issued from them who found the elements of their life in the crust of the earth, in the air, and in the nourishment derived from them. Earth and air possess, therefore, the principle of human transformations; those transformations take place under our eyes, by means of that which is also under our eyes. We are able, therefore, to discover that secret,—not limiting the effort of the search to one man or to one age, but devoting humanity in its duration to it. We are engaged, hand to hand, in a struggle with Matter, into whose secret, I, the grand-master of our order, seek to penetrate. Christophe Columbus gave a world to the King of Spain; I seek an ever-living people for the King of France. Standing on the confines which separate us from a knowledge of material things, a patient observer of atoms, I destroy forms, I dissolve the bonds of combinations; I imitate death that I may learn how to imitate life. I strike incessantly at the door of creation, and I shall continue so to strike until the day of my death. When I am dead the knocker will pass into other hands equally persistent with those of the mighty men who handed it to me. Fabulous and uncomprehended beings, like Prometheus, Ixion, Adonis, Pan, and others, who have entered into the religious beliefs of all countries and all ages, prove to the world that the hopes we now embody were born with the human races. Chaldea, India, Persia, Egypt, Greece, the Moors, have transmitted from one to another Magic, the highest of all the occult sciences, which holds within it, as a precious deposit the fruits of the studies of each generation. In it lay the tie that bound the grand and majestic institution of the Templars. Sire, when one of your predecessors burned the Templars, he burned men only,—their Secret lived. The reconstruction of the Temple is a vow of an unknown nation, a race of daring seekers, whose faces are turned to the Orient of *life*,—all brothers, all inseparable, all united by one idea, and stamped with the mark of toil. I am the sovereign leader of that people, sovereign by election, not by birth. I guide them onward to a knowledge of the essence of life. Grand-master, Red-Cross-bearers, companions, adepts, we forever follow the imperceptible molecule which still escapes our eyes. But soon we shall make ourselves eyes more powerful than those which Nature has given us; we shall attain to a sight of the primitive atom, the corpuscular element so persistently sought by the wise and learned of all ages who have preceded us in the glorious search. Sire, when a man is astride of that abyss, when he commands bold divers like my disciples, all other human interests are as nothing. Therefore we are not dangerous. Religious disputes and political struggles are far away from us; we have passed beyond and above them. No man takes others by the throat when his whole strength is given to a struggle with Nature. Besides, in our science results are perceivable; we can measure effects and predict them; whereas all things are uncertain and vacillating in the struggles of men and their selfish interests. We decompose the diamond in our crucibles, and we shall make diamonds, we shall make gold! We shall impel vessels (as they have at Barcelona) with fire and a little water! We test the wind, and we shall make wind; we shall make light; we shall renew the face of empires with new industries! But we shall never debase ourselves to mount a throne to be crucified by the peoples!"

In spite of his strong determination not to be taken in by Italian wiles, the king, together with his gentle mistress, was already caught and snared by the ambiguous phrases and doublings of this pompous and humbugging loquacity. The eyes of the two lovers showed how their minds were dazzled by the mysterious riches of power thus displayed; they saw, as it were, a series of subterranean caverns filled with gnomes at their toil. The impatience of their curiosity put to flight all suspicion.

"But," cried the king, "if this be so, you are great statesmen who can enlighten us."

"No, sire," said Lorenzo, naively.

"Why not?" asked the king.

"Sire, it is not given to any man to foresee what will happen when thousands of men are gathered together. We can tell what one man will do, how long he will live, whether he will be happy or unhappy; but we cannot tell what a collection of wills may do; and to calculate the oscillations of their selfish interests is more difficult still, for interests are men *plus* things. We can, in solitude, see the future as a whole, and that is all. The Protestantism that now torments you will be destroyed in turn by its material consequences, which will turn to theories in due time. Europe is at the present moment getting the better of religion; to-morrow it will attack royalty."

"Then the Saint-Bartholomew was a great conception?"

"Yes, sire; for if the people triumph it will have a Saint-Bartholomew of its own. When religion and royalty are destroyed the people will attack the nobles; after the nobles, the rich. When Europe has become a mere troop of men without consistence or stability, because without leaders, it will fall a prey to brutal conquerors. Twenty times already has the world seen that sight, and Europe is now preparing to renew it. Ideas consume the ages as passions consume men. When man is cured, humanity may possibly cure itself. Science is the essence of humanity, and we are its pontiffs; whoso concerns himself about the essence cares little about the individual life."

"To what have you attained, so far?" asked the king.

"We advance slowly; but we lose nothing that we have won."

"Then you are the king of sorcerers?" retorted the king, piqued at being of no account in the presence of this man.

The majestic grand-master of the Rosicrucians cast a look on Charles IX. which withered him.

"You are the king of men," he said; "I am the king of ideas. If we were sorcerers, you would already have burned us. We have had our martyrs."

"But by what means are you able to cast nativities?" persisted the king. "How did you know that the man who came to your window last night was King of France? What power authorized one of you to tell my mother the fate of her three sons? Can you, grand-master of an art which claims to mould the world, can you tell me what my mother is planning at this moment?"

"Yes, sire."

This answer was given before Cosmo could pull his brother's robe to enjoin silence.

"Do you know why my brother, the King of Poland, has returned?"

"Yes, sire."

"Why?"

"To take your place."

"Our most cruel enemies are our nearest in blood!" exclaimed the king, violently, rising and walking about the room with hasty steps. "Kings have neither brothers, nor sons, nor mothers. Coligny was right; my murderers are not among the Huguenots, but in the Louvre. You are either imposters or regicides!—Jacob, call Solern."

"Sire," said Marie Touchet, "the Ruggieri have your word as a gentleman. You wanted to taste of the fruit of the tree of knowledge; do not complain of its bitterness."

The king smiled, with an expression of bitter self-contempt; he thought his material royalty petty in presence of the august intellectual royalty of Lorenzo Ruggiero. Charles IX. knew that he could scarcely govern France, but this grand-master of Rosicrucians ruled a submissive and intelligent world.

"Answer me truthfully; I pledge my word as a gentleman that your answer, in case it confesses dreadful crimes, shall be as if it were never uttered," resumed the king. "Do you deal with poisons?"

"To discover that which gives life, we must also have full knowledge of that which kills."

"Do you possess the secret of many poisons?"

"Yes, sire,—in theory, but not in practice. We understand all poisons, but do not use them."

"Has my mother asked you for any?" said the king, breathlessly.

"Sire," replied Lorenzo, "Queen Catherine is too able a woman to employ such means. She knows that the sovereign who poisons dies by poison. The Borgias, also Bianca Capello, Grand Duchess of Tuscany,

226

are noted examples of the dangers of that miserable resource. All things are known at courts; there can be no concealment. It may be possible to kill a poor devil—and what is the good of that?—but to aim at great men cannot be done secretly. Who shot Coligny? It could only be you, or the queen-mother, or the Guises. Not a soul is doubtful of that. Believe me, poison cannot be twice used with impunity in statecraft. Princes have successors. As for other men, if, like Luther, they are sovereigns through the power of ideas, their doctrines are not killed by killing them. The queen is from Florence; she knows that poison should never be used except as a weapon of personal revenge. My brother, who has not been parted from her since her arrival in France, knows the grief that Madame Diane caused your mother. But she never thought of poisoning her, though she might easily have done so. What could your father have said? Never had a woman a better right to do it; and she could have done it with impunity; but Madame de Valentinois still lives."

"But what of those waxen images?" asked the king.

"Sire," said Cosmo, "these things are so absolutely harmless that we lend ourselves to the practice to satisfy blind passions, just as physicians give bread pills to imaginary invalids. A disappointed woman fancies that by stabbing the heart of a wax-figure she has brought misfortunes upon the head of the man who has been unfaithful to her. What harm in that? Besides, it is our revenue."

"The Pope sells indulgences," said Lorenzo Ruggiero, smiling.

"Has my mother practised these spells with waxen images?"

"What good would such harmless means be to one who has the actual power to do all things?"

"Has Queen Catherine the power to save you at this moment?" inquired the king, in a threatening manner.

"Sire, we are not in any danger," replied Lorenzo, tranquilly. "I knew before I came into this house that I should leave it safely, just as I know that the king will be evilly disposed to my brother Cosmo a few weeks hence. My brother may run some danger then, but he will escape it. If the king reigns by the sword, he also reigns by justice," added the old man, alluding to the famous motto on a medal struck for Charles IX.

"You know all, and you know that I shall die soon, which is very well," said the king, hiding his anger under nervous impatience; "but how will my brother die,—he whom you say is to be Henri III.?"

"By a violent death."

"And the Duc d'Alencon?"

"He will not reign."

"Then Henri de Bourbon will be king of France?"

"Yes, sire."

227

"How will he die?"

"By a violent death."

"When I am dead what will become of madame?" asked the king, motioning to Marie Touchet.

"Madame de Belleville will marry, sire."

"You are imposters!" cried Marie Touchet. "Send them away, sire."

"Dearest, the Ruggieri have my word as a gentleman," replied the king, smiling. "Will madame have children?" he continued.

"Yes, sire; and madame will live to be more than eighty years old."

"Shall I order them to be hanged?" said the king to his mistress. "But about my son, the Comte d'Auvergne?" he continued, going into the next room to fetch the child.

"Why did you tell him I should marry?" said Marie to the two brothers, the moment they were alone.

"Madame," replied Lorenzo, with dignity, "the king bound us to tell the truth, and we have told it."

"*Is* that true?" she exclaimed.

"As true as it is that the governor of the city of Orleans is madly in love with you."

"But I do not love him," she cried.

"That is true, madame," replied Lorenzo; "but your horoscope declares that you will marry the man who is in love with you at the present time."

"Can you not lie a little for my sake?" she said smiling; "for if the king believes your predictions—"

"Is it not also necessary that he should believe our innocence?" interrupted Cosmo, with a wily glance at the young favorite. "The precautions taken against us by the king have made us think during the time we have spent in your charming jail that the occult sciences have been traduced to him."

"Do not feel uneasy," replied Marie. "I know him; his suspicions are at an end."

"We are innocent," said the grand-master of the Rosicrucians, proudly.

"So much the better for you," said Marie, "for your laboratory, and your retorts and phials are now being searched by order of the king."

The brothers looked at each other smiling. Marie Touchet took that smile for one of innocence, though it really signified: "Poor fools! can they suppose that if we brew poisons, we do not hide them?"

"Where are the king's searchers?"

"In Rene's laboratory," replied Marie.

Again the brothers glanced at each other with a look which said: "The hotel de Soissons is inviolable."

The king had so completely forgotten his suspicions that when, as he took his boy in his arms, Jacob gave him a note from Chapelain, he opened it with the certainty of finding in his physician's report that nothing had been discovered in the laboratory but what related exclusively to alchemy.

"Will he live a happy man?" asked the king, presenting his son to the two alchemists.

"That is a question which concerns Cosmo," replied Lorenzo, signing his brother.

Cosmo took the tiny hand of the child, and examined it carefully.

"Monsieur," said Charles IX. to the old man, "if you find it necessary to deny the existence of the soul in order to believe in the possibility of your enterprise, will you explain to my why you should doubt what your power does? Thought, which you seek to nullify, is the certainty, the torch which lights your researches. Ha! ha! is not that the motion of a spirit within you, while you deny such motion?" cried the king, pleased with his argument, and looking triumphantly at his mistress.

"Thought," replied Lorenzo Ruggiero, "is the exercise of an inward sense; just as the faculty of seeing several objects and noticing their size and color is an effect of sight. It has no connection with what people choose to call another life. Thought is a faculty which ceases, with the forces which produced it, when we cease to breathe."

"You are logical," said the king, surprised. "But alchemy must therefore be an atheistical science.'

"A materialist science, sire, which is a very different thing. Materialism is the outcome of Indian doctrines, transmitted through the mysteries of Isis to Chaldea and Egypt, and brought to Greece by Pythagoras, one of the demigods of humanity. His doctrine of re-incarnation is the mathematics of materialism, the vital law of its phases. To each of the different creations which form the terrestrial creation belongs the power of retarding the movement which sweeps on the rest."

"Alchemy is the science of sciences!" cried Charles IX., enthusiastically. "I want to see you at work."

"Whenever it pleases you, sire; you cannot be more interested than Madame the Queen-mother."

"Ah! so this is why she cares for you?" exclaimed the king.

"The house of Medici has secretly protected our Search for more than a century."

"Sire," said Cosmo, "this child will live nearly a hundred years; he will have trials; nevertheless, he will be happy and honored, because he has in his veins the blood of the Valois."

"I will go and see you in your laboratory, messieurs," said the king, his good-humor quite restored. "You may now go."

The brothers bowed to Marie and to the king and then withdrew. They went down the steps of the portico gravely, without looking or speaking to each other; neither did they turn their faces to the windows as they crossed the courtyard, feeling sure that the king's eye watched them. But as they passed sideways out of the gate into the street they looked back and saw Charles IX. gazing after them from a window. When the alchemist and the astrologer were safely in the rue de l'Autruche, they cast their eyes before and behind them, to see if they were followed or overheard; then they continued their way to the moat of the Louvre without uttering a word. Once there, however, feeling themselves securely alone, Lorenzo said to Cosmo, in the Tuscan Italian of that day:—

"Affe d'Iddio! how we have fooled him!"

"Much good may it do him; let him make what he can of it!" said Cosmo. "We have given him a helping hand,—whether the queen pays it back to us or not."

Some days after this scene, which struck the king's mistress as forcibly as it did the king, Marie suddenly exclaimed, in one of those moments when the soul seems, as it were, disengaged from the body in the plenitude of happiness:—

"Charles, I understand Lorenzo Ruggiero; but did you observe that Cosmo said nothing?"

"True," said the king, struck by that sudden light. "After all, there was as much falsehood as truth in what they said. Those Italians are as supple as the silk they weave."

This suspicion explains the rancor which the king showed against Cosmo when the trial of La Mole and Coconnas took place a few weeks later. Finding him one of the agents of that conspiracy, he thought the Italians had tricked him; for it was proved that his mother's astrologer was not exclusively concerned with stars, the powder of projection, and the primitive atom. Lorenzo had by that time left the kingdom.

In spite of the incredulity which most persons show in these matters, the events which followed the scene we have narrated confirmed the predictions of the Ruggieri.

The king died within three months.

Charles de Gondi followed Charles IX. to the grave, as had been foretold to him jestingly by his brother the Marechal de Retz, a friend of the Ruggieri, who believed in their predictions.

Marie Touchet married Charles de Balzac, Marquis d'Entragues, the governor of Orleans, by whom she had two daughters. The most celebrated of these daughters, the half-sister of the Comte d'Auvergne, was the mistress of Henri IV., and it was she who endeavored, at the time of Biron's conspiracy, to put her brother on the throne of France by driving out the Bourbons.

The Comte d'Auvergne, who became the Duc d'Angouleme, lived into the reign of Louis XIV. He coined money on his estates and altered the inscriptions; but Louis XIV. let him do as he pleased, out of respect for the blood of the Valois.

Cosmo Ruggiero lived till the middle of the reign of Louis XIII.; he witnessed the fall of the house of the Medici in France, also that of the Concini. History has taken pains to record that he died an atheist, that is, a materialist.

The Marquise d'Entragues was over eighty when she died.

The famous Comte de Saint-Germain, who made so much noise under Louis XIV., was a pupil of Lorenzo and Cosmo Ruggiero. This celebrated alchemist lived to be one hundred and thirty years old,—an age which some biographers give to Marion de Lorme. He must have heard from the Ruggieri the various incidents of the Saint-Bartholomew and of the reigns of the Valois kings, which he afterwards recounted in the first person singular, as though he had played a part in them. The Comte de Saint-Germain was the last of the alchemists who knew how to clearly explain their science; but he left no writings. The cabalistic doctrine presented in this Study is that taught by this mysterious personage.

And here, behold a strange thing! Three lives, that of the old man from whom I have obtained these facts, that of the Comte de Saint-Germain, and that of Cosmo Ruggiero, suffice to cover the whole of European history from Francois I. to Napoleon! Only fifty such lives are needed to reach back to the first known period of the world. "What are fifty generations for the study of the mysteries of life?" said the Comte de Saint-Germain.

PART III

I. TWO DREAMS

In 1786 Bodard de Saint-James, treasurer of the navy, excited more attention and gossip as to his luxury than any other financier in Paris. At this period he was building his famous "Folie" at Neuilly, and his wife had just bought a set of feathers to crown the tester of her bed, the price of which had been too great for even the queen to pay.

Bodard owned the magnificent mansion in the place Vendome, which the *fermier-general*, Dange, had lately been forced to leave. That celebrated epicurean was now dead, and on the day of his interment his intimate friend, Monsieur de Bievre, raised a laugh by saying that he "could now pass through the place Vendome without *danger*." This allusion to the hellish gambling which went on in the dead man's house, was his only funeral oration. The house is opposite to the Chancellerie.

To end in a few words the history of Bodard,—he became a poor man, having failed for fourteen millions after the bankruptcy of the Prince de Guemenee. The stupidity he showed in not anticipating that "serenissime disaster," to use the expression of Lebrun Pindare, was the reason why no notice was taken of his misfortunes. He died, like Bourvalais, Bouret, and so many others, in a garret.

Madame Bodard de Saint-James was ambitious, and professed to receive none but persons of quality at her house,—an old absurdity which is ever new. To her thinking, even the parliamentary judges were of small account; she wished for titled persons in her salons, or at all events, those who had the right of entrance at court. To say that many*cordons bleus* were seen at her house would be false; but it is quite certain that she managed to obtain the good-will and civilities of several members of the house of Rohan, as was proved later in the affair of the too celebrated diamond necklace.

One evening—it was, I think, in August, 1786—I was much surprised to meet in the salons of this lady, so exacting in the matter of gentility, two new faces which struck me as belonging to men of inferior social position. She came to me presently in the embrasure of a window where I had ensconced myself.

"Tell me," I said to her, with a glance toward one of the new-comers, "who and what is that queer species? Why do you have that kind of thing here?"

"He is charming."

"Do you see him through a prism of love, or am I blind?"

"You are not blind," she said, laughing. "The man is as ugly as a caterpillar; but he has done me the most immense service a woman can receive from a man."

As I looked at her rather maliciously she hastened to add: "He's a physician, and he has completely cured me of those odious red blotches which spoiled my complexion and made me look like a peasant woman."

I shrugged my shoulders with disgust.

"He is a charlatan."

"No," she said, "he is the surgeon of the court pages. He has a fine intellect, I assure you; in fact, he is a writer, and a very learned man."

"Heavens! if his style resembles his face!" I said scoffingly. "But who is the other?"

"What other?"

"That spruce, affected little popinjay over there, who looks as if he had been drinking verjuice."

"He is a rather well-born man," she replied; "just arrived from some province, I forget which—oh! from Artois. He is sent here to conclude an affair in which the Cardinal de Rohan is interested, and his Eminence in person had just presented him to Monsieur de Saint-James. It seems they have both chosen my husband as arbitrator. The provincial didn't show his wisdom in that; but fancy what simpletons the people who sent him here must be to trust a case to a man of his sort! He is as meek as a sheep and as timid as a girl. His Eminence is very kind to him."

"What is the nature of the affair?"

"Oh! a question of three hundred thousand francs."

"Then the man is a lawyer?" I said, with a slight shrug.

"Yes," she replied.

Somewhat confused by this humiliating avowal, Madame Bodard returned to her place at a faro-table.

All the tables were full. I had nothing to do, no one to speak to, and I had just lost two thousand crowns to Monsieur de Laval. I flung myself on a sofa near the fireplace. Presently, if there was ever a man on earth most utterly astonished it was I, when, on looking up, I saw, seated on another sofa on the opposite side of the fireplace, Monsieur de Calonne, the comptroller-general. He seemed to be dozing, or else he was buried in one of those deep meditations which overtake statesmen. When I pointed out the famous minister to Beaumarchais, who happened to come near me at that moment, the father of Figaro explained the mystery of his presence in that house without uttering a word. He pointed first at my head, then at Bodard's with a malicious gesture which consisted in turning to each of us two fingers of his hand while he kept the others doubled up. My first impulse was to rise and say something rousing to Calonne; then I paused, first, because I thought of a trick I could play the statesman, and secondly, because Beaumarchais caught me familiarly by the hand.

"Why do you do that, monsieur?" I said.

He winked at the comptroller.

"Don't wake him," he said in a low voice. "A man is happy when asleep."

"Pray, is sleep a financial scheme?" I whispered.

"Indeed, yes!" said Calonne, who had guessed our words from the mere motion of our lips. "Would to God we could sleep long, and then the awakening you are about to see would never happen."

"Monseigneur," said the dramatist, "I must thank you—"

"For what?"

"Monsieur de Mirabeau has started for Berlin. I don't know whether we might not both have drowned ourselves in that affair of 'les Eaux.'"

"You have too much memory, and too little gratitude," replied the minister, annoyed at having one of his secrets divulged in my presence.

"Possibly," said Beaumarchais, cut to the quick; "but I have millions that can balance many a score."

Calonne pretended not to hear.

It was long past midnight when the play ceased. Supper was announced. There were ten of us at table: Bodard and his wife, Calonne, Beaumarchais, the two strange men, two pretty women, whose names I will not give here, a *fermier-general*, Lavoisier, and myself. Out of thirty guests who were in the salon when I entered it, only these ten remained. The two *queer species* did not consent to stay until they were urged to do so by Madame Bodard, who probably thought she was paying her obligations to the surgeon by giving him something to eat, and pleasing her husband (with whom she appeared, I don't precisely know why, to be coquetting) by inviting the lawyer.

The supper began by being frightfully dull. The two strangers and the *fermier-general* oppressed us. I made a sign to Beaumarchais to intoxicate the son of Esculapius, who sat on his right, giving him to understand that I would do the same by the lawyer, who was next to me. As there seemed no other way to amuse ourselves, and it offered a chance to draw out the two men, who were already sufficiently singular, Monsieur de Calonne smiled at our project. The ladies present also shared in the bacchanal conspiracy, and the wine of Sillery crowned our glasses again and again with its silvery foam. The surgeon was easily managed; but at the second glass which I offered to my neighbor the lawyer, he told me with the frigid politeness of a usurer that he should drink no more.

At this instant Madame de Saint-James chanced to introduce, I scarcely know how, the topic of the marvellous suppers to the Comte de Cagliostro, given by the Cardinal de Rohan. My mind was not very attentive to what the mistress of the house was saying, because I was watching with extreme curiosity the pinched and livid face of my little neighbor, whose principal feature was a turned-up and at the same time pointed nose, which made him, at times, look very like a weasel. Suddenly his cheeks flushed as he caught the words of a dispute between

Madame de Saint-James and Monsieur de Calonne.

"But I assure you, monsieur," she was saying, with an imperious air, "that I *saw* Cleopatra, the queen."

"I can believe it, madame," said my neighbor, "for I myself have spoken to Catherine de' Medici."

"Oh! oh!" exclaimed Monsieur de Calonne.

The words uttered by the little provincial were said in a voice of strange sonorousness, if I may be permitted to borrow that expression from the science of physics. This sudden clearness of intonation, coming from a man who had hitherto scarcely spoken, and then in a low and modulated tone, surprised all present exceedingly.

"Why, he is talking!" said the surgeon, who was now in a satisfactory state of drunkenness, addressing Beaumarchais.

"His neighbor must have pulled his wires," replied the satirist.

My man flushed again as he overheard the words, though they were said in a low voice.

"And pray, how was the late queen?" asked Calonne, jestingly.

"I will not swear that the person with whom I supped last night at the house of the Cardinal de Rohan was Catherine de' Medici in person. That miracle would justly seem impossible to Christians as well as to philosophers," said the little lawyer, resting the tips of his fingers on the table, and leaning back in his chair as if preparing to make a speech. "Nevertheless, I do assert that the woman I saw resembled Catherine de' Medici as closely as though they were twin-sisters. She was dressed in a black velvet gown, precisely like that of the queen in the well-known portrait which belongs to the king; on her head was the pointed velvet coif, which is characteristic of her; and she had the wan complexion, and the features we all know well. I could not help betraying my surprise to his Eminence. The suddenness of the evocation seemed to me all the more amazing because Monsieur de Cagliostro had been unable to divine the name of the person with whom I wished to communicate. I was confounded. The magical spectacle of a supper, where one of the illustrious women of past times presented herself, took from me my presence of mind. I listened without daring to question. When I roused myself about midnight from the spell of that magic, I was inclined to doubt my senses. But even this great marvel seemed natural in comparison with the singular hallucination to which I was presently subjected. I don't know in what words I can describe to you the state of my senses. But I declare, in the sincerity of my heart, I no longer wonder that souls have been found weak enough, or strong enough, to believe in the mysteries of magic and in the power of demons. For myself, until I am better informed, I regard as possible the apparitions which Cardan and other thaumaturgists describe."

These words, said with indescribable eloquence of tone, were of a nature to rouse the curiosity of all present. We looked at the speaker and kept silence; our eyes alone betrayed our interest, their pupils reflecting the light of the wax-candles in the sconces. By dint of observing this unknown little man, I fancied I could see the pores of his skin, especially those of his forehead, emitting an inward sentiment with which he was saturated. This man, apparently so cold and formal, seemed to contain within him a burning altar, the flames of which beat down upon us.

"I do not know," he continued, "if the Figure evoked followed me invisibly, but no sooner had my head touched the pillow in my own chamber than I saw once more that grand Shade of Catherine rise before me. I felt myself, instinctively, in a luminous sphere, and my eyes, fastened upon the queen with intolerable fixity, saw naught but her. Suddenly, she bent toward me."

At these words the ladies present made a unanimous movement of curiosity.

"But," continued the lawyer, "I am not sure that I ought to relate what happened, for though I am inclined to believe it was all a dream, it concerns grave matters.

"Of religion?" asked Beaumarchais.

"If there is any impropriety," remarked Calonne, "these ladies will excuse it."

"It relates to the government," replied the lawyer.

"Go on, then," said the minister; "Voltaire, Diderot, and their fellows have already begun to tutor us on that subject."

Calonne became very attentive, and his neighbor, Madame de Genlis, rather anxious. The little provincial still hesitated, and Beaumarchais said to him somewhat roughly:—

"Go on, *maitre*, go on! Don't you know that when the laws allow but little liberty the people seek their freedom in their morals?"

Thus adjured, the small man told his tale:—

"Whether it was that certain ideas were fermenting in my brain, or that some strange power impelled me, I said to her: 'Ah! madame, you committed a very great crime.' 'What crime?' she asked in a grave voice. 'The crime for which the signal was given from the clock of the palace on the 24th of August,' I answered. She smiled disdainfully, and a few deep wrinkles appeared on her pallid cheeks. 'You call that a crime which was only a misfortune,' she said. 'The enterprise, being ill-managed, failed; the benefit we expected for France, for Europe, for the Catholic Church was lost. Impossible to foresee that. Our orders were ill executed; we did not find as many Montlucs as we needed. Posterity will

236

not hold us responsible for the failure of communications, which deprived our work of the unity of movement which is essential to all great strokes of policy; that was our misfortune! If on the 25th of August not the shadow of a Huguenot had been left in France, I should go down to the uttermost posterity as a noble image of Providence. How many, many times have the clear-sighted souls of Sixtus the Fifth, Richelieu, Bossuet, reproached me secretly for having failed in that enterprise after having the boldness to conceive it! How many and deep regrets for that failure attended my deathbed! Thirty years after the Saint-Bartholomew the evil it might have cured was still in existence. That failure caused ten times more blood to flow in France than if the massacre of August 24th had been completed on the 26th. The revocation of the Edict of Nantes, in honor of which you have struck medals, has cost more tears, more blood, more money, and killed the prosperity of France far more than three Saint-Bartholomews. Letellier with his pen gave effect to a decree which the throne had secretly promulgated since my time; but, though the vast execution was necessary of the 25th of August, 1572, on the 25th of August, 1685, it was useless. Under the second son of Henri de Valois heresy had scarcely conceived an offspring; under the second son of Henri de Bourbon that teeming mother had cast her spawn over the whole universe. You accuse me of a crime, and you put up statues to the son of Anne of Austria! Nevertheless, he and I attempted the same thing; he succeeded, I failed; but Louis XIV. found the Protestants without arms, whereas in my reign they had powerful armies, statesmen, warriors, and all Germany on their side.' At these words, slowly uttered, I felt an inward shudder pass through me. I fancied I breathed the fumes of blood from I know not what great mass of victims. Catherine was magnified. She stood before me like an evil genius; she sought, it seemed to me, to enter my consciousness and abide there."

"He dreamed all that," whispered Beaumarchais; "he certainly never invented it."

"'My reason is bewildered,' I said to the queen. 'You praise yourself for an act which three generations of men have condemned, stigmatized, and—' 'Add,' she rejoined, 'that historians have been more unjust toward me than my contemporaries. None have defended me. I, rich and all-powerful, am accused of ambition! I am taxed with cruelty,—I who have but two deaths upon my conscience. Even to impartial minds I am still a problem. Do you believe that I was actuated by hatred, that vengeance and fury were the breath of my nostrils?' She smiled with pity. 'No,' she continued, 'I was cold and calm as reason itself. I condemned the Huguenots without pity, but without passion; they were the rotten fruit in my basket and I cast them out. Had I been Queen of England, I should have treated seditious Catholics in the same way. The life of our power in those days depended on their being but one God, one Faith, one Master in the State. Happily for me, I uttered my justification in one sentence which history is transmitting. When Birago falsely announced to me the loss of the battle of Dreux, I answered: "Well then; we will go to the Protestant churches." Did I hate the reformers? No, I esteemed them much, and I knew them little. If I felt any aversion to the politicians of my time, it was to that base Cardinal de Lorraine, and to his brother the shrewd and brutal soldier who spied upon my every act. They were the real enemies of my children; they sought to snatch the crown; I saw them daily at work and they wore me out. If *we* had not ordered the Saint-Bartholomew, the Guises would have done the same thing by the help of Rome and the monks. The League, which was powerful only in consequence of my old age, would have begun in 1573.' 'But, madame, instead of ordering that horrible murder (pardon my plainness) why not have employed the vast resources of your political power in giving to the Reformers those wise institutions which made the reign of Henri IV. so glorious and so peaceful?' She smiled again and shrugged her shoulders, the hollow wrinkles of her pallid face giving her an expression of the bitterest sarcasm. 'The peoples,' she said, 'need periods of rest after savage feuds; there lies the secret of that reign. But Henri IV. committed two irreparable blunders. He ought neither to have abjured Protestantism, nor, after becoming a Catholic himself, should he have left France Catholic. He, alone, was in a position to have changed the whole of France without a jar. Either not a stole, or not a conventicle—that should have been his motto. To leave two bitter enemies, two antagonistic principles in a government with nothing to balance them, that is the crime of kings; it is thus that they sow revolutions. To God alone belongs the right to keep good and evil perpetually together in his work. But it may be,' she said reflectively, 'that that sentence was inscribed on the foundation of Henri IV.'s policy, and it may have caused his death. It is impossible that Sully did not cast covetous eyes on the vast wealth of the clergy,—which the clergy did not possess in peace, for the nobles robbed them of at least two-thirds of their revenue. Sully, the Reformer, himself owned abbeys.' She paused, and appeared to reflect. 'But,' she resumed, 'remember you are asking the niece of a Pope to justify her Catholicism.' She stopped again. 'And yet, after all,' she added with a gesture of some levity, 'I should have made a good Calvinist! Do the wise men of your century still think that religion had anything to do with that struggle, the greatest which Europe has ever seen?—a vast revolution, retarded by little causes which, however, will not be prevented from overwhelming the world because I failed to smother it; a revolution,' she said, giving me a solemn look, 'which is still advancing, and which you might consummate. Yes, *you*, who hear me!' I shuddered. 'What! has no one yet understood that the old interests and the new interests seized Rome and Luther as mere banners? What! do they not know Louis IX., to escape just such a struggle, dragged a population a hundredfold more in number than I destroyed from their homes and left their bones on the sands of Egypt, for which he was made a saint? while I—But I,' she added, '*failed.*' She bowed her head and was silent for some moments. I no longer beheld a queen, but rather one of those ancient druidesses to whom human lives are sacrificed; who unroll the pages of the future and exhume the teachings of the past. But soon she uplifted her regal and majestic form. 'Luther and Calvin,' she said, 'by calling the attention of the burghers to the abuses of the Roman Church, gave birth in Europe to a spirit of investigation which was certain to lead the peoples to examine all things. Examination leads to doubt. Instead of faith, which is necessary to all societies, those two men drew after them, in the far distance, a strange philosophy, armed with hammers, hungry for destruction. Science sprang, sparkling with her specious lights, from the bosom of heresy. It was far less a question of reforming a Church than of winning indefinite liberty for man—which is the death of power. I saw that. The consequence of the successes won by the religionists in their struggle against the priesthood (already better armed and more formidable than the Crown) was the destruction of the monarchical power raised by Louis IX. at such vast cost upon the ruins of feudality. It involved, in fact, nothing less than the annihilation of religion and royalty, on the ruins of which the whole burgher class of Europe meant to stand. The struggle was therefore war without quarter between the new ideas and the law,—that is, the old beliefs. The Catholics were the emblem of the material interests of royalty, of the great lords, and of the clergy. It was a duel to the death between two giants; unfortunately, the Saint-Bartholomew proved to be only a wound. Remember this: because a few drops of blood were spared at that opportune moment, torrents were compelled to flow at a later period. The intellect which soars above a nation cannot escape a great misfortune; I mean the misfortune of finding no equals capable of judging it when it succumbs beneath the weight of untoward events. My equals are few; fools are in the majority: that statement explains it all. If my name is execrated in France, the fault lies with the commonplace minds who form the mass of all generations. In the great crises through which I passed, the duty of reigning was not the mere giving of audiences, reviewing of troops, signing of decrees. I may have committed mistakes, for I was but a woman. But why was there then no man who rose above his age? The Duke of Alba had a soul of iron; Philip II. was stupefied by Catholic belief; Henri IV. was a gambling soldier and a libertine; the Admiral, a stubborn mule. Louis XI. lived too soon, Richelieu too late. Virtuous or criminal, guilty or not in the Saint-Bartholomew, I accept the onus of it; I stand between those two great men,—the visible link of an unseen chain. The day will come when some paradoxical writer will ask if the peoples have not bestowed the title of executioner among their victims. It will not be the first time that humanity has preferred to immolate a god rather than admit its own guilt. You are shedding upon two hundred clowns, sacrificed for a purpose, the tears you refuse to a generation, a century, a world! You forget that political liberty, the tranquillity of a nation, nay, knowledge itself, are gifts on which destiny has laid a tax of blood!' 'But,' I exclaimed, with tears in my eyes, 'will the nations never be happy at less cost?' 'Truth never leaves her well but to bathe in the blood which refreshes her,' she replied. 'Christianity, itself the essence of all truth, since it comes from God, was fed by the blood of martyrs, which flowed in torrents; and shall it not ever flow? You will learn this, you who are destined to be one of the builders of the social edifice founded by the Apostles. So long as you level heads you will be applauded, but take your trowel in hand, begin to reconstruct, and your fellows will kill you.' Blood! blood! the word sounded in my ears like a knell. 'According to you,' I cried, 'Protestantism has the right to reason as you do!' But Catherine had disappeared, as if some puff of air had suddenly extinguished the supernatural light which enabled my mind to see that Figure whose proportions had gradually become gigantic. And then, without warning, I found within me a portion of myself which adopted the monstrous doctrine delivered by the Italian. I woke, weeping, bathed in sweat, at the moment when my reason told me firmly, in a gentle voice, that neither kings nor nations had the right to apply such principles, fit only for a world of atheists."

"How would you save a falling monarchy?" asked Beaumarchais.

"God is present," replied the little lawyer.

"Therefore," remarked Monsieur de Calonne, with the inconceivable levity which characterized him, "we have the agreeable resource of believing ourselves the instruments of God, according to the Gospel of Bossuet."

As soon as the ladies discovered that the tale related only to a conversation between the queen and the lawyer, they had begun to whisper and to show signs of impatience,—interjecting, now and then, little phrases through his speech. "How wearisome he is!" "My dear, when will he finish?" were among those which reached my ear.

When the strange little man had ceased speaking the ladies too were silent; Monsieur Bodard was sound asleep; the surgeon, half drunk; Monsieur de Calonne was smiling at the lady next him. Lavoisier, Beaumarchais, and I alone had listened to the lawyer's dream. The silence at this moment had something solemn about it. The gleam of the candles seemed to me magical. A sentiment bound all three of us by some mysterious tie to that singular little man, who made me, strange to say, conceive, suddenly, the inexplicable influences of fanaticism. Nothing less than the hollow, cavernous voice of Beaumarchais's neighbor, the surgeon, could, I think, have roused me.

"I, too, have dreamed," he said.

I looked at him more attentively, and a feeling of some strange horror came over me. His livid skin, his features, huge and yet ignoble, gave an exact idea of what you must allow me to call the *scum* of the earth. A few bluish-black spots were scattered over his face, like bits of mud, and his eyes shot forth an evil gleam. The face seemed, perhaps, darker, more lowering than it was, because of the white hair piled like hoarfrost on his head.

"That man must have buried many a patient," I whispered to my neighbor the lawyer.

"I wouldn't trust him with my dog," he answered.

"I hate him involuntarily."

"For my part, I despise him."

"Perhaps we are unjust," I remarked.

"Ha! to-morrow he may be as famous as Volange the actor."

Monsieur de Calonne here motioned us to look at the surgeon, with a gesture that seemed to say: "I think he'll be very amusing."

"Did you dream of a queen?" asked Beaumarchais.

"No, I dreamed of a People," replied the surgeon, with an emphasis which made us laugh. "I was then in charge of a patient whose leg I was to amputate the next day—"

"Did you find the People in the leg of your patient?" asked Monsieur de Calonne.

"Precisely," replied the surgeon.

"How amusing!" cried Madame de Genlis.

"I was somewhat surprised," went on the speaker, without noticing the interruption, and sticking his hands into the gussets of his breeches, "to hear something talking to me within that leg. I then found I had the singular faculty of entering the being of my patient. Once within his skin I saw a marvellous number of little creatures which moved, and thought, and reasoned. Some of them lived in the body of the man, others lived in his mind. His ideas were things which were born, and grew, and died; they were sick and well, and gay, and sad; they all had special countenances; they fought with each other, or they embraced each other. Some ideas sprang forth and went to live in the world of intellect. I began to see that there were two worlds, two universes,—the visible universe, and the invisible universe; that the earth had, like man, a body and a soul. Nature illumined herself for me; I felt her immensity when I saw the oceans of beings who, in masses and in species, spread everywhere, making one sole and uniform animated Matter, from the stone of the earth to God. Magnificent vision! In short, I found a universe within my patient. When I inserted my knife into his gangrened leg I cut into a million of those little beings. Oh! you laugh, madame; let me tell you that you are eaten up by such creatures—"

"No personalities!" interposed Monsieur de Calonne. "Speak for yourself and for your patient."

"My patient, frightened by the cries of his animalcules, wanted to stop the operation; but I went on regardless of his remonstrances; telling him that those evil animals were already gnawing at his bones. He made a sudden movement of resistance, not understanding that what I did was for his good, and my knife slipped aside, entered my own body, and—"

"He is stupid," said Lavoisier.

"No, he is drunk," replied Beaumarchais.

"But, gentlemen, my dream has a meaning," cried the surgeon.

"Oh! oh!" exclaimed Bodard, waking up; "my leg is asleep!"

"Your animalcules must be dead," said his wife.

"That man has a vocation," announced my little neighbor, who had stared imperturbably at the surgeon while he was speaking.

"It is to yours," said the ugly man, "what the action is to the word, the body to the soul."

But his tongue grew thick, his words were indistinct, and he said no more. Fortunately for us the conversation took another turn. At the end of half an hour we had forgotten the surgeon of the king's pages, who was fast asleep. Rain was falling in torrents as we left the supper-table.

"The lawyer is no fool," I said to Beaumarchais.

"True, but he is cold and dull. You see, however, that the provinces are still sending us worthy men who take a serious view of political theories and the history of France. It is a leaven which will rise."

"Is your carriage here?" asked Madame de Saint-James, addressing me.

"No," I replied, "I did not think that I should need it to-night."

Madame de Saint-James then rang the bell, ordered her own carriage to be brought round, and said to the little lawyer in a low voice:—

"Monsieur de Robespierre, will you do me the kindness to drop Monsieur Marat at his own door?—for he is not in a state to go alone."

"With pleasure, madame," replied Monsieur de Robespierre, with his finical gallantry. "I only wish you had requested me to do something more difficult."

THE END

Freeriver is a community project working to create a place for people to visit and potentially live, long-term, in peace, free from the normal stresses of modern life.

We aim to provide a place where people can spend time discovering themselves and discovering nature. We aim to focus on creativity, health and wellbeing. We plan to provide events and classes for people in the local area and enhance the community.

Please visit our website for more details

www.freerivercommunity.com
freerivercommunity@hotmail.com

www.freerivercommunity.com

244

Made in the USA
Middletown, DE
07 December 2023

44903725R00139